"What on ear
in the

"I'm sleeping on the ____. Remember?" Jake didn't get up.

Even if Marla Jean's brain was foggy with sleep, everything primitive and female inside her was busy waking up.

Jake found an unruly curl and brushed it from her cheek. Jake's face was only a dim shadow, but his voice drifted past her ear, amused and warm and intimate.

This wasn't the way she'd imagined it.

And she had imagined it. More than once. Years ago in her adolescent fantasies—back when she barely knew what a fantasy was, and again lately. He'd been starring in much more grown up versions these days.

By some trick of light, some shifting of the clouds and moon peeking in her bedroom window, the shadows lifted and she could see his face. He wasn't laughing now. His dark eyes drilled clean through to her core. His stark cheekbones looked like carved granite. His mouth moved closer.

It looked like he was about to kiss her...

"Sweet, sassy, and oh, my yes—sexy! Molly Cannon's debut AIN'T MISBEHAVING is delicious fun! If you like Susan Elizabeth Phillips and Kristan Higgins, you'll love Molly Cannon."

—Mariah Stewart, *New York Times* bestselling author of *Hometown Girl*

Ain't Misbehaving

MOLLY CANNON

FOREVER

NEW YORK   BOSTON

Forever
Hachette Book Group
237 Park Avenue
New York, NY 10017
www.HachetteBookGroup.com

Printed in the United States of America

First Edition: June 2012
10 9 8 7 6 5 4 3 2 1

Forever is an imprint of Grand Central Publishing.
The Forever name and logo are trademarks of Hachette Book Group, Inc.

The Hachette Speakers Bureau provides a wide range of authors for speaking events. To find out more, go to www.hachettespeakersbureau .com or call (866) 376-6591.

The publisher is not responsible for websites (or their content) that are not owned by the publisher.

To my husband Bill. The best man I know.

And if the answer isn't "War" or "Black Keys"
you're asking the wrong question.

Acknowledgments

I am blessed to be surrounded by so many wonderful people who've helped me while writing this book. The list is long and my gratitude is never-ending.

This book exists, first and foremost, because of Danna Middleton. One day, oh so many years ago, she looked at me and said, let's write a book. She started me on this journey, and I'm forever in her debt. I love you, Danna. And I have to mention Nancy Haddock and Lynne Smith who helped make those days so much fun.

My family for their constant support—hey Moo!—and particularly my sisters Sherrionne Brown and Patricia Gregory, my niece Maddie Nance, and my daughter Emily Williams for volunteering when I needed extra eyes.

Everyone at NTRWA—we laughed together, cried together, and cheered each other on. Good times!

For critiques, retreats and kicks in the backside I have to thank Misa Ramirez, Beatriz Terrazas, Kym Roberts, Mary Malcolm, Jessica Davidson, Tracy Ward, Jill Wilson,

Kim Quinton, Angi Platt, Jen FitzGerald, Gina Nelson, Regina Richards, Elizabeth Klein, and Janet Carter.

To Cecilia Danaher, Judi Sampson, and Debra Dennis for always having my back.

And special thanks to Chris Keniston who was always there to critique, support, and celebrate with frozen drinks and Bill's cookies.

Wendy Lynn Watson who told me this book was the one. I'm glad I listened to you, Wendy.

My agent Kim Lionetti, who loved Marla Jean as much as I did. Thank you, Kim.

From the Grand Central Publishing family I must mention Amy Pierpont who was supportive from the start; Kallie Shimek and Oliver Baranczyk for copy edits; Diane Luger and Chris Cocozza for the beautiful cover art and design. And to my editor, Michele Bidelspach, who held my hand through this process, pushed me to be better, and then gave me a dog. Thank you, Michele.

Ain't Misbehaving

Chapter One

Stop it, Donny Joe."

"Come on, Marla Jean. I thought you wanted to."

An hour earlier she would have agreed with him. An hour earlier she wiggled into her tight red dress, tugged on her favorite cowboy boots, and headed out to the local watering hole sure of exactly what she wanted. An hour earlier she'd left her house with every intention of finding a willing man and having her way with him.

Lately she'd felt dried up, dustier than a ghost town in an old Western movie. The swinging saloon doors of her nether portal were rusted shut from lack of use. In other words, Miss Kitty hadn't seen any action in a long, long time.

And now, because she'd decided to rectify the situation, she, Marla Jean Bandy, found herself sitting in the front seat of a Ford pick-up truck with Donny Joe Ledbetter's hand stuck halfway up her skirt.

But it didn't feel right somehow, and that really pissed her off.

Sex had always been something she'd embraced enthusiastically right up until the moment her husband dumped her for another woman. If he'd dumped her for some young bimbo, it would have been embarrassing and humiliating. She would have been mad, outraged even, but no—Bradley left her for Libby Comstock, the fifty-four-year-old, never-been-married librarian who drove the Bookmobile. She'd started to wonder why he ran out the door like a kid who'd just heard the ice cream truck whenever it turned the corner onto their street. But she'd always told him he should read more, and this was the one time in their six-year marriage he decided to listen to her.

Libby seduced him with the Russian classics, challenging him to stretch his mind and feed his soul. He tackled Dostoevsky, Tolstoy, Brodsky, Pushkin, and eventually he tackled Ms. Comstock, too. The fact that he'd left her for someone twenty years older, frumpier, smarter, and fluent in five languages was something she'd never forgive him for.

But back to Donny Joe. He was a stud. A big fish in a small pond. A lover of all things female, and his ability to make the earth move was heralded far and wide by most every woman in and around Everson, Texas.

So when she decided it was time to get back on the horse, he was the natural choice for her to throw a rope around. He would have no problem with a quickie in the front seat of his truck. A quickie, and then they'd never speak of it again. No complications, no angst, no wounded emotional fallout. So why was she getting cold feet? This was the ideal setup, the perfect no-attachment sex she'd been looking for.

She sighed, a petulant, frustrated sigh. "I'm sorry, Donny Joe, but I think I've changed my mind."

"You're just a little skittish, sugar. We'll take it slow. Why don't we go back inside and slide around the dance floor a few times while I coax you back into the right mood?"

He was placing little nibbles on her neck while he whispered his encouragement. His hand took up a neutral position at the edge of her dress, not moving up, but not giving up all the territory he'd gained, either. She tried closing her eyes, tried to let herself be coaxed, but it wasn't working. She was about to agree to a few dances just to ease her way out of an uncomfortable situation when the door on her side of the truck flew open so abruptly that if Donny Joe hadn't had a good grip on her she would've fallen out on her head.

A dark silhouette loomed at her side, and a deep voice commanded, "Take your hands off her, Donny Joe."

If her life followed any kind of normal, predictable pattern, she would have turned to confront her ex-husband, maybe, or her overprotective big brother, but that was not the case. Abel Jacobson—known by everyone around town as Jake—stood just inside the open door, filling up the space with his broad shoulders, glowering like some avenging angel in a cowboy hat. He reached inside and grabbed her arm. "Come on, Marla Jean, get out of the truck."

Donny Joe tightened his grip around her waist. "Get your own woman, Jake."

"That's what I'm doing, Donny Joe."

They were pulling her in two different directions, fighting over her like a prize piece of salt water taffy. She managed to squirm away from Donny Joe, and then shoved at the hard, stubborn wall of muscle that made up

Jake's chest until she could slide past him and get out of the truck. "I'm not anyone's woman. What's wrong with you two?"

Her too-tight skirt had ridden halfway up her ass, and she struggled to pull it back down to a level that wouldn't get her arrested for indecent exposure. She was fuming while they watched. Donny Joe had a cocky grin on his face, and Jake stood with his arms crossed over his chest, glaring like he wanted to put her over his knee and spank her.

That thought sprang into her head from out of nowhere, accompanied by a vivid image of Jake's big, wide hand on her bare bottom. The restless itch that had driven her out of her house dressed like a hoochie mama—only to desert her before she could find the nerve to scratch it—was suddenly back, stronger than ever. She gave her skirt another tug and glared back at him. If anyone could scratch her itch, it was Jake. But she wanted simple and uncomplicated, and there was nothing simple or uncomplicated about Abel Jacobson.

Donny Joe climbed out of his truck and ambled her way. "I'll be inside Lu Lu's if you change your mind, sugar."

"She won't," Jake called after him pleasantly as he watched Donny Joe head back inside the bar. And then before she could blast him for his caveman act, he rounded on her. "Donny Joe? What the hell were you thinking, Marla Jean?"

"I was thinking I might get lucky, not that it's any of your business, Abel Jacobson." She stuck her nose in the air, and stomped off toward the bar.

"You've never had the sense God gave a goose when it comes to men," he muttered as he followed her across the parking lot.

"Excuse me?" She rounded on him this time, not believing the nerve of the man. "When's the last time you dated a woman who had an IQ higher than her bra size?"

"Why, Marla, I didn't think you cared."

"I don't give two figs about your love life, but I'd love to know what brought on this sudden interest in mine."

She was still scowling at him, but she was also more than a little curious about his answer. Growing up, Jake had been her older brother Lincoln's best friend, but as adults she rarely spoke to him. Of course they exchanged greetings whenever they ran across each other in town, but asking "Hey, how are you?" just to be polite was a long way from dragging her out of another man's truck as if he had every right to do it.

He kicked at a piece of gravel with the toe of his boot. "I got a call from Linc before he left town. He said you hadn't sounded like yourself lately, and he was worried. I said I'd keep an eye on you."

"I don't need watching. And Linc can keep his opinions and his concern to himself."

"Aw, give him a break, Marla. He's been worried since Bradley..." His words trailed off like he wanted to spare her from the awful truth.

"You mean since Bradley dumped me? We've been separated for a year, and the divorce has been final for six months. I'm not going to fall apart at the mention of his name."

"Bradley's an idiot."

"Finally, something we can agree on, but I'm a big girl, and I don't need a keeper." She started walking away, feeling put out all over again.

"Where are you going, Marla Jean?"

"I'm going back inside. I'm going to dance with any man who asks me, and I'm going to have a good time. If that's not okay with you and my big brother, then y'all can both kiss my rosy, pink butt."

The smell of stale beer and the sound of country music poured out of the bar as she jerked the door open and stalked inside. She pushed her way through the crowd, but Jake stayed right on her heels. Stopping abruptly, she turned around to face him. "For the love of Pete, what is it now?"

He tipped up the brim of his hat and asked with a lazy smile, "How 'bout a dance, Marla Jean?"

Chapter Two

Jake kept his smile in place as he watched Marla's eyes first widen, and then narrow at his invitation. Without warning, she grabbed his arm and hauled him out onto the dance floor—not exactly the reaction he'd expected.

"Okay Jake, let's dance. I'll talk. You just move your feet and listen."

"Yes, ma'am." She wouldn't get an argument from him. He pulled her into his arms, and they started two-stepping around the floor. She smiled at everyone like she was having the grandest of times, but Jake wasn't fooled. The tight set of her jaw and the scary vein throbbing in her forehead gave her away.

It certainly wasn't any of his business if Marla Jean Bandy wanted to make out with every cowboy in the place. While they were growing up, she'd been a pesky pain in the backside, always trying to tag along with him and her older brother. Since Linc had been his best friend, Jake had become an honorary big brother by default, teasing her, tolerating her when she was underfoot, and now and then, helping her out of the occasional scrape.

But that was a long time ago. They'd both grown up—gone their separate ways. She'd even gotten married. If it hadn't been for Linc's call he certainly wouldn't have been sticking his nose into her affairs now.

But still, Donny Joe Ledbetter? Maybe Lincoln had good reason to worry.

And Marla Jean. If he was any judge of riled-up women, and he'd seen a few in his time, Marla Jean was mad. Mad enough to spit. But that was okay. She could be mad all she wanted. He wasn't going to let Lincoln down.

"First of all, Jake—"

"Wait a minute, Marla Jean—let me talk first. I want to apologize."

She looked a lot surprised and a tad mollified. "I should think so." They made a half circle around the floor before she tilted her head back and said, "Well, I'm waiting."

"For what?" he asked while leading her into an under-arm turn.

"Your apology?" she reminded him as she followed him in a walk-around step.

"Oh, right. I shouldn't have said you were dumber than a goose." He winked and executed a little spin.

"That's what you're sorry for?"

"Yeah, that was out of line."

"And that's it? If you think—"

"Hold your horses, Marla Jean, I'm not done."

"By all means, continue."

He grew serious. "I apologize for mentioning Bradley."

She ducked her head and studied the feet of the nearby dancers. "I told you not to worry about that."

"I know, but since he left you for my Aunt Libby, I feel somehow responsible." Jake never cared for Bradley Bandy. He certainly didn't deserve a woman like Marla Jean, and now this thing with his aunt had everyone in an uproar. His Aunt Libby, on the other hand, was acting like a cat who'd just discovered heavy cream. It was kind of sweet, in a creepy sort of way. But Marla Jean didn't deserve the pain those two had caused her.

"Jake, whatever went wrong for me and Bradley started a long time before he took up story hour with your aunt."

"Humph," he grunted. "My mother's ready to disown her—says she's disgraced the family."

"Can we not talk about Bradley? I came out to have a good time tonight. I've had it up to here with sitting at home feeling sorry for myself, so I'm turning over a new leaf."

"I noticed."

"And if folks around here don't like it they can—"

"I know. They can kiss your rosy, pink butt."

"Exactly."

"But Donny Joe?"

"Don't start, Jake."

"Donny Joe is exactly the kind of thing Linc was worried about." He twirled her around and dipped her as the song came to an end. When he pulled her back upright, she stumbled against his chest. His arms tightened momentarily, and he stared down into her flashing brown eyes.

Pushing him away, she said, "Look, Jake. Leave it alone. I'll talk to Linc and put his mind at ease. You're off the hook. Okay?"

He knew when it was time to beat a tactical retreat.

"All right, I've done my duty for the night." He held up both hands and took a step back.

"Thank you. And when I talk to Linc, I'll tell him you went above and beyond."

"Well, thanks for the dance." He moved back another step, somehow reluctant to walk away, but Harry Beal marched over and inserted himself between the two of them. Back in school, Harry had been in the same grade with Marla Jean and had grown up to be the high school football coach.

"Hey, Jake. How's it going?" Without waiting for an answer, he turned to Marla. "Can I have the next dance, Marla Jean?"

Marla smiled at Harry like he'd invented butter. "Sure thing, Harry. Later, Jake."

Before he could say "alligator," the two of them waltzed away, leaving him alone in the middle of the dance floor. Jake wandered over to the nearest barstool and sat down. He ordered a beer and swiveled around until he faced the crowd of dancing couples. Marla was laughing at something Harry said—her head thrown back—her dark, curly hair cascading down her back.

Christ A'mighty. That dress.

It was short and tight and nothing but trouble.

In the best of circumstances Marla Jean Bandy, being newly divorced and out on the town, was enough to make most red-blooded men sit up and take notice. Especially in a small town like Everson where available women were few and far between. But Marla Jean Bandy poured into that skimpy getup was like waving a red flag in front of every horny bastard in the joint. No wonder Linc was worried. Telling himself he owed it to Linc to keep an eye on her, he took a long draw on his beer and settled his elbows on the bar behind him. It promised to be a real long night.

Marla tried to pay attention to Harry and ignore the disturbing fact that Abel Jacobson, of all people, was parked on a bar stool across the way watching her. Harry wasn't much of a dancer, mainly shuffling his feet from side to side, but she made an effort to listen as he rambled on about the football team. "I hate to admit it," she said, "but I haven't been to a game this year, Coach."

"You oughta come this Friday, Marla Jean. If we beat Crossville, we'll make it to play-offs."

That was no secret. The whole town was buzzing about the upcoming game. In Everson, like almost every other town in Texas, Friday night during the fall was football night. While they were married, she and Bradley had never missed a game. But that was then. These days she spent Friday nights alone at home watching her mom's old *JAG* DVDs and painting her toenails. But tonight was supposed to be about taking control of her life back, so she smiled and said, "You're absolutely right, Harry. I'll be there with bells on."

"Great! Maybe after the game we could grab some pizza?"

She wasn't really ready to start dating. At least not nice guys like Harry Beal. She'd known him since junior high. They'd been in the same homeroom from seventh grade on, and he had always been sweet and shy until you got him on the football field. Then he turned into a monster. Harry had gone on to play college ball and even had one season in the NFL before a knee injury ended his pro career. After that he moved back to town and no one was surprised when he'd been hired as Everson High's head coach as soon as there was an opening.

But the idea of getting involved with someone she could come to care for scared the blue dickens out of her. Everyone in town would be at the pizza place after the game though, so it wouldn't really count as a date. "Sounds like fun. We can celebrate your victory with pepperoni and extra cheese."

He grinned like he'd landed a three-foot bass. When the music stopped, she thanked him for the dance, but before she could make it back to her table Greg Tucker asked if he could have the honor.

After that she danced with Johnny Dean, Fergus Barnes, and Tommy Lee Stewart. They flirted, and she flirted back. No big deal. A bunch of small town wannabe Romeos checking out the lay of the land. She was smart enough to know her sudden popularity was born of a burning curiosity about her divorce. They all asked basically the same thing, "How ya holding up, darlin'?" and let her know with a wink and a sashay around the dance floor, they'd be more than happy to help her out if she needed anything at all.

She smiled, said "thanks," and kept on dancing.

That is until she saw Donny Joe headed her way, and she made a beeline for the ladies' room. She wasn't ready to go another round with him, or for that matter, to be reminded of her miserable attempt at playing the loose woman.

She splashed cool water on her flushed face and used her fingers to fluff up her hair. Smiling at her reflection, she realized that despite everything, she was having fun—even if she hadn't managed to get laid.

Even before Jake's interference she'd known she couldn't go through with her plan. Damn it all. It had sounded so simple in theory, but in practice she'd run smack dab into reality. For her, sex was tied up with love, and love wasn't something she was likely to find at Lu Lu's on a Saturday night. Not that she was looking. "Love" was a dirty word as far as she was concerned. So while on one hand, she was right back where she'd started—all alone and frustrated—on the other hand, she'd had a blast dancing her fanny off with every man in the joint, and now she had plans that included football and pizza next Friday night. All in all, it hadn't been a complete waste of time.

Wandering back out into the bar, she decided she was ready to call it a night. Jake still lounged on his barstool, but now Wanda Lee Mabry sat by him on one side and Rhoda Foster sat on the other. Both women seemed to be vying for his attention, making it much easier for her to slip out unnoticed.

Walking over to the corner table she'd claimed earlier in the evening, she searched the area for her purse. It wasn't on the table, and it wasn't on the floor, and if somebody was dumb enough to steal it they wouldn't have gotten anything but her driver's license, a twenty-dollar bill, a tube of Ripe Cherry Red lipstick, a just-in-case condom, and her car keys. At the moment, all she cared about were her car keys.

Then it dawned on her. She remembered touching up her lipstick right before she'd gone outside with Donny Joe and having her purse when she got in his truck. Dagnab-it, she'd bet all the beans in Boston she'd left it on the floorboard of his pick-up. Jake's high-handed meddling had ticked her off so much she hadn't given her purse a second thought when she'd scrambled out of that truck. She looked around the room for Donny Joe but didn't see him. The dance floor was still packed with people, so she stood on her tiptoes to see if she could see his head above the crowd.

Lana and Warren Sanders danced by. "Hey, Marla Jean," they said in unison.

"Hey guys. Have y'all seen Donny Joe?"

"Donny Joe Ledbetter?" Lana asked, not hiding her surprise. "Not lately. Sorry."

"That's okay. Thanks, anyway." She moved on around the room asking if anybody had seen him, but she finally gave up and walked over to the far end of the bar, the end farthest away from where Jake still sat surrounded by women. The bartender spotted her and moved down to her end.

"What'll it be, Marla Jean?" An older man with gray hair pulled back in a ponytail and an eye patch over one eye, Mike Benson was as much a part of Lu Lu's as the gravel parking lot and the odor of stale beer.

"Mike, have you seen Donny Joe? I know he was here a minute ago."

He picked up a bar towel and started polishing glasses. "Yeah, he was dancing with Irene Cornwell, and I saw them leave together."

"How long ago was that?"

"Oh, I don't know. A few minutes, maybe."

"Damn it, I've got to catch him." Hitching up her skirt she took off toward the front door. She burst outside, skidding to a stop on the gravel, and scanned the parking lot for his truck. If she was lucky Donny Joe and Irene would just be going at it like squirrels in his front seat.

It wouldn't even bother her to catch them *in flagrante delicto*. She'd ask them to forgive the intrusion, grab her purse, and tell them to carry on. They probably wouldn't even notice.

She hurried toward the place where he'd been parked earlier, but she could see before she got there the spot was empty. Son of a bitch. She couldn't believe this. The sound of a racing engine caught her attention, and she spotted his truck at the far exit getting ready to pull out onto the highway.

"Wait, Donny Joe, come back," she yelled, waving her arms about wildly. Hitching her skirt even higher, she took off at a sprint. If she could just get his attention it would save her a world of trouble in the long run. "Donny Joe, hey, Donny Joe, don't leave yet," she hollered at the top of her lungs, but it was no use. She stumbled to a stop and watched his red taillights recede into the dark night. "Crap, horse feathers, and double doo-doo." Cursing her luck and panting, she stood bent over with her hands braced on her knees, trying to catch her breath.

"For God's sake, Marla Jean, don't chase after the guy. Have some pride."

She whirled around at the sound of Jake's voice. He'd followed her out of the bar, obviously, and now he thought she'd lost her mind.

"You!" She pointed a finger and started marching toward him. A smart man would have shown some concern, but he stood his ground until her finger was poking him in the chest. "This is all your fault, mister."

"My fault?" The idea seemed to amuse him.

"Entirely, altogether, and completely your fault." She crossed her arms and stomped her foot like a bratty kid.

He moved closer and leaned down until they were nose to nose. "You should be down on your knees thanking me, missy. I kept you from making a God-awful mistake with Donny Joe earlier this evening. And now this? You go racing across the parking lot screaming like a banshee when he's got another woman in the truck with him? Come on, Marla Jean. You're obviously not yourself."

For the second time that night she marched across the parking lot with Jake hot on her heels. "At the risk of repeating myself, I'll make all the God-awful mistakes I want. And what I am, you big dolt, is stuck."

"Hold up, Marla Jean—"

"I was chasing after Donny Joe, because thanks to you," she turned to glare at him for emphasis, "I left my purse and my car keys in his truck. If I don't seem properly grateful, you can bite me."

"Does that offer involve your rosy, pink butt?"

She marched on, trying for the umpteenth time that evening to yank her skirt back down where it belonged. "Go to hell."

"Before or after I offer you a ride home?" He stopped by his little yellow Porsche Boxster. "Hop in."

"Yeah, right. I'll go ask Harry Beal for a ride."

"That should make his night. He'll think he's hit the jackpot."

She hesitated. She didn't want to give Harry the wrong impression. "I'll call a cab."

"That'd be a waste of good money, if you had any on you. Just get in the car."

She stopped and let out a strangled groan. "Maybe I'll walk. It's not that far."

"Were you always this stubborn? Let me explain something to you, Marla Jean. I don't care if you call a cab, hitchhike, or crawl on your hands and knees—but I'll be driving right behind you, no matter what."

"Now who's being stubborn?"

He shrugged. "I'm not about to tell Linc that because of me, you walked home from Lu Lu's at eleven-thirty at night."

"Linc's got you on a pretty short leash, doesn't he?"

"I owe Linc a lot, and he never asks for much, so for everyone's sake, please get in the car."

She sighed for what seemed like the millionth time that evening, a world-weary, put-upon sigh, and then stalked over to the car. He opened the door for her and didn't even try to pretend that he wasn't looking at her legs when her skirt rode back up to mid-thigh. She was going to go home and burn the stupid dress in the fireplace. After closing her door, Jake loped around the car, and she watched while he managed to fold his big frame into the compact driver's seat. "Wouldn't you be more comfortable in a bigger car?"

"This isn't a car. She's a beloved member of the family, and she handles like a woman in love." He started the engine and turned to face her. "Marla Jean, meet Lucinda."

"You name your cars?"

"Don't you?" He backed out of the space and headed for the nearest exit.

"Of course not. Well, I did have that clunker in high school we called 'Buck'—for bucket of bolts—but these days I try not to get personally involved with my vehicles."

"Hmm." He looked at her as if her answer gave him some important insight into her character before returning his attention to the road.

After the divorce she'd moved into her parents' old

house on Sunnyvale Street. They'd retired a few years back and moved to Padre Island. After that, her brother Lincoln lived there until his recent marriage, and then he moved into his bride's place since it was newer and bigger.

The last thing Marla wanted to do was stay in the house she'd shared with Bradley, and her folks' house was empty, so it seemed like the perfect solution until she could find a place of her own. Sometimes, though, moving back to the house she'd grown up in made her feel like she'd failed her first attempt at being an adult.

It was a short drive home, and since Jake grew up on the same street, he knew the way without being told. She closed her eyes and tried not to think about the man sitting by her side. Even when they were kids, he'd always been able to throw her off balance with a look or a word. Apparently, that hadn't changed.

He pulled into her driveway, and she let him walk her to the door. She figured he'd insist anyway, and she was too tired to argue. On the way up the walkway, she remembered her keys, and the fact that they were spending the night in the floorboard of Donny Joe's truck. Jake seemed to realize the problem at the same time. Without missing a beat, he reached into the third hanging basket from the left and pulled out the spare key—the same place the spare key had been hidden the entire time they'd been growing up.

"It's nice to know some things never change." He unlocked the front door and pushed it open. "If you need any help picking up your car tomorrow, let me know."

"Thanks, but I'll manage." It suddenly felt so familiar to be standing in the dark talking with him on the front porch. He was bigger and taller now, but he was still Jake. "Good night, Jake."

"Good night, Marla Jean." He reached for her hand and pressed the spare key into her palm. "Try to stay out of trouble."

She pulled her hand out of his and resisted the urge to stick out her tongue. "Try to mind your own business."

He laughed and brushed his thumb across her cheek. "You haven't changed, either, Marla Jean."

Before she could ask what that was supposed to mean, he bounded off the porch and was gone.

Chapter Three

Thank heavens it was Sunday morning, and she didn't have to get up and go to work for two whole days. Marla Jean drew the covers up to her chin and nestled deeper into her goose down pillow. MJ's Barber Shop still observed the traditional Sunday/Monday weekend, so she could sleep all day if she felt like it.

That was one nice thing about being single. No one could bug her about getting up and doing something productive. Bradley used to have their Sundays planned to the minute. He'd bribe her with doughnuts and fancy coffee to get her out of bed, and then they'd tackle some project around the house until it was time to watch football.

There was a certain comfort in the routine, but now she could be as lazy as she wanted and not have to answer to anybody. She turned over and spread out, taking up the whole bed. Another advantage to being single—the bed was never crowded, and after last night, that wasn't likely to change any time soon. A downright depressing thought if there ever was one.

She pulled the sheet over her head and shut her eyes. Maybe she'd stitch up a sampler. The ABCs of single-hood. Alone time, bored time, crying time...

She could admit she missed her ex-husband Bradley, or at least she missed the idea of him. They'd been high school sweethearts, and when they got married after college it seemed like the next logical step. They'd made a nice life together. Nothing earthshaking, but nice. At least she'd thought so. It turned out Bradley wanted more than nice.

But even if he had a change of heart and begged her to let him come back—a fantasy she tried not to indulge in more than once a week—she knew down deep in her heart the marriage was over.

The sound of someone pounding loudly on her front door interrupted her woe-is-me ruminations. She threw off the covers, shoved her feet into furry kitty-cat slippers, and made sure the Dallas Stars hockey jersey she'd slept in was pulled down far enough to cover all her important parts. Then she stumbled out of her bedroom, ready to kill whoever was disturbing her peaceful morning. She peeped out the peephole and groaned. She must have conjured him up, because Bradley stood on her front porch holding a big box of doughnuts.

As soon as she opened the door he barreled his way inside. Shoving the box at her like a battering ram, he demanded, "What the hell's going on, Marla Jean?"

"Excuse me?" She shoved the box back at him and tried pushing him back out the open door. "I don't remember inviting you over, Bradley, so if you don't mind—"

"I'm not leaving until you explain why Donny Joe Ledbetter answered your cell phone this morning." His chin did that jutting out thing it did whenever he decided to dig his heels in about something.

"Why do you care who answers my cell phone?"

"I was worried—"

"It's not your job to worry about me anymore, in case you've forgotten." A few months ago she would have been touched by his concern—a signal that he still cared. Now it seemed more like an unwelcome intrusion.

"I realize that, Marla Jean, but I was on my way over to the Hole-In-The-Dough to get doughnuts for Libby this morning when I saw your car sitting there big as life in Lu Lu's parking lot."

"You mean these aren't even for me?" She slapped at the box in his hands. He had a lot of nerve. "Isn't Libby going to wonder what's taking you so long?"

"Now don't go trying to change the subject. I was worried half to death, and then, when Donny Joe answered your phone, I didn't know what to think."

"Think whatever you like. I don't owe you or anyone else in this town an explanation. Sheesh." She gave him a harder push and this time managed to get him back out onto the front porch.

He sighed, and his shoulders sagged. "You know I still care about you, Marly Jay."

Marly Jay had always been his pet name for her, and she couldn't believe he had the nerve to invoke it now. Dull pain washed through her insides, leaving a raw ache where her heart used to be. She wanted to scream, or maybe kick him in the balls. Neither seemed like a good option, so she counted to ten and studied the man she'd loved off and on since high school. He'd always been nice looking in that friendly, puppy-dog kind of way, and the years hadn't changed that. His blond hair ruffled in the breeze, his cheeks were slightly pink from the cool autumn morning, and his blue eyes fairly dripped with sincere concern. She'd always felt secure with Bradley, and his devotion was the one thing she'd thought she could depend on. That had been a big mistake. One she wouldn't make again.

She knew he still cared about her, but right now his concern felt more like pity, and she wanted to take his Hole-In-The-Dough doughnuts and cram them down his two-timing gullet.

"Go home, Bradley." Before she could shut the door, the object of their conversation roared up the street and parked in front of her house.

"What's Donny Joe doing here, Marla Jean?" Bradley's face and neck had taken on the color of a medium rare T-bone steak.

She ignored his question and walked outside, waiting on the porch while Donny Joe climbed out of his truck holding her purse. Even carrying her red-sequined clutch, he still looked like God's gift to women as he strutted up the walkway toward the house. He wore a tan cowboy hat at a cocky angle, tight jeans, and a red plaid flannel shirt open over a white T-shirt. Dark shades covered his spring-green eyes, but his entire face broke out into a dazzling grin when he caught sight of them on the porch. Marla Jean heaved a sigh and wondered again what was wrong with her. Everything about the man said, "Use me and abuse me," but she just hadn't been able to do it.

Donny took off his sunglasses, bouncing up the steps two at a time. "Hey, Brad, old buddy! Read any good books lately?" He slapped Bradley on the back and winked at Marla Jean. Then in a voice that probably peeled the clothes right off most women, he said, "Mornin', sugar. I thought you might need this."

He held out her purse, and she snatched it away. It was downright silly, but her cheeks flamed like he'd just handed her a pair of crotchless panties.

"Thanks, Donny Joe. I'm awfully sorry you had to drive all the way over here for this." After all, nothing that happened at Lu Lu's had been his fault.

"Anything for you, Marla Jean. Last night things got kind of wild, and I figured your purse was the last thing on your mind." He spotted the Hole-In-The-Dough box Brad was holding, and his eyes lit up. "Hey, you wouldn't happen to have a spare cruller in there, would ya, buddy? I worked up quite an appetite last night."

Bradley snarled, crushing the doughnut box against his chest. Little pieces of glazed sugar escaped from the box and drifted down to settle on his navy blue running shoes. His nostrils pinched together like he'd suddenly caught a whiff of the foul odor inside a goalie's glove, and when he spoke his voice sounded like it was being forced through a tea strainer. "Could I speak to you for a moment, Marla Jean? Alone?"

"Now's not a good time, Bradley." She realized her ex-husband believed some kind of hanky-panky was going on between her and Donny Joe. Part of her wanted to set him straight, but most of her wanted to rub his face in the fact that just because he didn't want her anymore, didn't mean plenty of other men weren't lined up to take his place.

Of course, Donny Joe might not be the best example of the other men who wanted her, since he pretty much wanted anything that qualified as female.

Acting like he owned the joint, Donny Joe threw his arm around Marla's shoulder and pulled her close to his side. "Yeah Brad, now's not a good time."

Bradley threw the mangled box of doughnuts down onto the porch and snarled, "Take your hands off her, Donny Joe."

Jake pulled into his parents' old driveway and studied the place. Ever since he'd moved his mother into one of the new condos on the lake, he'd considered selling the house but always ended up renting it out instead. For some reason he just couldn't let it go. It sat empty now, and he had a list of fix-it jobs he'd been putting off for way too long.

That was the reason he dragged himself out of bed on a Sunday morning and loaded his toolbox into the back of his work truck. It had nothing to do with the fact that Marla Jean Bandy was back living across the street, two doors down.

A man with any brains would avoid her like a second helping of prune pit pie. She was a handful—always had been. Good-looking, smart-mouthed, clever, and now, fresh from a divorce, she was vulnerable as well. Man. That was a dangerous combination.

She probably hadn't had time to pick her car up yet, and he'd thought about renewing his offer to give her a hand with that, but decided on the drive over he was probably the last person she wanted to see. He got out of the truck and glanced across the street at her house. A big white Chevy Suburban was sitting in her driveway. It wasn't hers, but he knew who it belonged to. It belonged to her ex. Bradley.

The asshole.

Jake knew Marla and Bradley most likely had some unfinished business, and it was probably normal for them to spend time in each other's company, but whenever he thought about how that man had treated her, he wanted to pound something. Never mind that his Aunt Libby was waltzing around like a giddy teenager. He hadn't come to terms with how he felt about Bradley Bandy being responsible for that, either.

He had work to do, and it wasn't going to get done if he stood around thinking about Marla Jean and her problems. He put purpose into his stride as he found the keys to his old house and unlocked the front door. Then he stole another glance across the street. He couldn't help himself. Now he could see Bradley standing out on the porch talking to someone inside the house. Most likely, Marla Jean. Good. That meant he was leaving. The sooner, the better. Not that it was any of his concern.

As he walked back out to his truck and grabbed his toolbox, a silver pick-up came flying down the street and screeched to a stop at Marla Jean's curb. Son of a bitch. It was Donny Joe Ledbetter. Jake watched him climb out of the truck and head toward her house. Marla Jean came outside and stood on the porch by Bradley as Donny Joe approached. Jake couldn't hear what anyone was saying, but he didn't need to be a lip reader to see the steam coming out of Bradley's ears. He told himself to mind his own business.

Turning his back on the scene unfolding across the street, he walked back up the driveway toward his parents' house. Not his problem, he thought. Live and let live. That was his motto, and last night reminded him of why it had always been a good one. Marla Jean was all grown up, and she could handle herself just fine.

He reached the front steps before allowing himself one final peek. From across the way he could see Donny Joe standing on one side of Marla Jean and Bradley standing on the other. Things looked to be getting heated. Bradley shoved Donny Joe and Marla Jean scrambled to keep the men separated. Neither of them seemed to pay a bit of attention to her.

Shee-it.

Jake set his toolbox down on the porch, scrubbed a hand over his face, and let out a frustrated growl. He hurried across the yard, stopping long enough to grab a ball-peen hammer from the bed of his truck, and then took off at a run toward her house. He wasn't sure exactly what he was going to do with the hammer. Maybe threaten to bash in a couple of windshields just to get their attention. As he got closer he could hear the squabbling.

"Let her go, Donny Joe."

"Why don't you go on home to your little librarian, Brad?"

Marla aimed a fuzzy slipper at Donny Joe's kneecap and then turned to stomp on Bradley's foot with the other. "Cut it out, both of you." Neither man seemed to think she got a vote in the matter.

"Hey!" Jake yelled as he crossed the street, waving the hammer above his head like a crazy man.

They all looked up at the interruption, and Marla took the opportunity to extricate herself from the situation. Lunging off the porch, she ran down the sidewalk and grabbed Jake's arm.

"Oh good, Jake, you're here," she babbled brightly, "and

you brought your hammer. I was beginning to think you'd forgotten about promising to look at that sink in the guest bathroom."

She looked at him with wide eyes begging him to play along, so he said, "I didn't forget, Marla Jean. I just figured you might like to sleep late." He took in her wild bed-head of curly hair and gave her Dallas Stars jersey and kitty-cat slippers the once over. "But here I am. At your service."

She hooked her arm through his, dragging him up the front steps past the other two men.

Brad eyed Jake suspiciously. "Jake isn't a plumber, Marla Jean. If you've got a plumbing problem, call the Rooter Doctor. I don't mind if you charge it to our old account."

Donny Joe lounged against the porch railing with a shit-eating grin on his face. "He's gonna fix your sink with a hammer?"

"You'd be surprised what I can fix with a hammer," Jake advised him casually.

Marla Jean piped up, "It's not plumbing. It's remodeling. He's going to knock out the whole thing and start over. So, you boys should run along now." Without waiting for a good-bye or see-you-later, she pushed Jake inside the house and slammed the door in their faces.

She slumped against the closed door. "Thank God you showed up when you did, Jake. What in the world is wrong with men? Twice now in two days I've been subjected to men acting like Neanderthals. Oh wait, I forgot. You're as guilty as they are."

Jake shrugged. "Most men are animals."

"Does that include you?"

"It doesn't take much to bring out our beastly nature," he confessed.

"Well, I have to say, as a woman who's just getting back into the dating scene, it's very unattractive." She pushed off the door and walked toward the living room.

"I'll try to remember that," he said as he followed her.

"You might as well sit down." She waved him into the olive green recliner that had always been designated as her dad's chair and plopped down onto the rust and olive plaid sofa that had graced the living room since before they'd been teenagers. "I'd like to give Bradley and Donny Joe time to clear out before you leave. That is, if you're not in any hurry."

"I can spare a minute or two."

He laid the hammer on the old wooden coffee table and settled down into the chair. Not much in the room had changed. The same framed prints hung on the paneled walls, the same floor lamp with the rust-colored shade stood in the corner. The place even smelled the same—like the vanilla candles Linc and Marla's mother had favored for as long as he could remember.

Growing up, he'd spent almost as much time in this house as he had his own. His home life hadn't been the best, and Linc had been a good friend, allowing him to escape his father's bullying whenever he could. Linc's parents treated him like one of their own, and Marla Jean treated him like another brother. He didn't feel much like a brother anymore.

As a matter of fact, he sincerely wished Marla Jean would go put on some more clothes. His beastly side was being aroused by her fresh unmade-up face and all that long, dark, curly hair waving around it. The hockey jersey she had on didn't hide the fact that she wasn't wearing a bra, and the damn thing kept sliding up her long bare legs, threatening to show what lay just beyond. And those kitty-cat house shoes. They weren't doing a damn thing to make her less sexy, either. All in all, she looked a little too appealing for his peace of mind.

"I'm really grateful for the rescue this morning, Jake. You were coming to my rescue, right?"

"Nah, just being neighborly. I was working on my mom's old house, and all that noise was making it hard to concentrate."

"I'm sorry. I'm not even sure what happened. Donny Joe dropped by to return my purse, and one minute we were having a civilized conversation, and the next they were both acting like idiots."

"Well, no offense, but we are talking about Bradley and Donny Joe."

"None taken. I guess I should choose my male companions more carefully from now on."

"Any likely prospects on the horizon?" He didn't know why he asked, but the question popped out before he could stop it.

"I don't know about prospects, but I'm having pizza with Harry Beal after the football game Friday night."

"Is that a good idea?" He frowned. That wasn't exactly the best news he'd heard lately.

She shrugged. "He asked, and it seemed innocent enough."

"I guess. If you're not worried about the fact that he's been in love with you since he sat beside you in Miss Fatheree's math class back in junior high."

She looked at him like she thought he was high on wacky weed. "He has not. Why would you say that?"

He held up both hands. "Forget it. I'm probably wrong." But he wasn't. Anybody with two eyes could see that Harry Beal turned into a mush melon whenever he came within ten feet of Marla Jean. Jake always thought women were born knowing when a man was interested. Maybe not.

"I'm not looking for anything serious right now. I just want to go out, have some fun, get used to being on my own again, you know?" She looked like she was hoping to find an understanding ear.

If she expected him to give the thumbs-up on guys like Donny Joe she could forget it. He went for a neutral response instead. "I think that's a smart idea. Take things slow. Rebound relationships can be a bitch."

Her eyes gleamed with curiosity. "You sound like you're talking from experience."

"It's been a long time, now, but there was a woman I met in college." He was never comfortable talking about himself.

She tucked her legs underneath her and leaned forward. "Oh, this is fascinating. What was her name?"

He tried to keep his eyes off her legs. "You always were a nosy kid."

"Is it too painful to talk about? Poor Jake." She reached over and patted his knee.

The leather recliner creaked as he shifted in the chair. "I told you it was years ago, and her name was Sarah."

"Sarah." She repeated the name wistfully like she could feel every bit of heartbreak he'd suffered at the hands of the woman. "What happened to her?"

"After college she went to law school, married a judge, and had three kids." He hadn't given Sarah a second thought in years.

"So, was she the rebound, or was the rebound the woman that came after her?"

He pointed a finger and said, "You ask too many questions."

"Sorry. Sitting here talking to you in my parents' living room feels so much like old times. It makes me wonder why we lost touch."

"We both went off to college. You got married. Life happens." He stood up, resisting the temptation to join her on a walk down memory lane. "I better get going. I've still got a lot of work to do."

"Oh right." Marla Jean jumped off the couch and followed him to the front door. "Thanks again for your help."

He reached out and tucked an unruly strand of hair behind her ear. It was softer than he expected, and she smelled like lemons. "Don't mention it. I figure I owed you after last night."

"That's true. You did, but today almost made up for it."

"Almost?" he asked with a raised eyebrow.

"I'm not ready to let you off the hook just yet. It might come in handy if I need to be rescued again. Will you be at the game Friday night?"

He walked out onto the porch stepping over the scattered doughnuts and looking around to make sure Bradley and Donny Joe were both gone. "Where else would a body be on a Friday night in Everson?"

She tugged the hem of her hockey jersey down to a barely decent length and smiled. Probably the first real smile she'd bestowed on him since he'd pulled her out of Donny Joe's truck Saturday night. "Great. Maybe I'll see you then." With a wave she went back inside.

He'd made it halfway across the yard when she called his name.

"Jake?"

He turned around. "Yeah?"

"You forgot your hammer." She held it out in his direction.

He stuck his fingers in his back pockets and rocked back on his heels. "Keep it, Marla Jean. Next time some bozo tries to manhandle you, use it to bean him upside the head."

She seemed to perk up at the idea. "Even if that bozo is you?"

He winked and said, "Especially if it's me, darlin'."

She rolled her eyes, hugged the hammer to her chest, and disappeared inside the house.

Chapter Four

~

I didn't believe it for one minute, Marla Jean."

"I appreciate that, Mr. Begley." Marla Jean used the electric trimmers to clean up the back of Chuck Begley's neck. He was one of her regulars, but she'd just given him a haircut the week before. Today he'd come in for the gossip and not for the grooming.

He gave her a knowing look in the mirror. "I've decided Bertie only runs that diner so she can spread rumors. And she was serving 'em up thick this morning, right alongside the scrambled eggs and hash browns."

Bertie Harcourt owned the Rise-N-Shine Diner, and a lot of folks stopped by on their way to work to grab coffee and catch up on the latest juicy rumor. Apparently, Marla had made it onto this morning's menu.

"Well, what are you gonna do, Mr. Begley? People in this town like to talk. But I appreciate the heads-up." Marla hoped that would end the conversation, but it seemed he was just getting started.

"I mean who's gonna believe that Abel Jacobson and

Donny Joe Ledbetter were fighting over you in Lu Lu's parking lot?" He shook his head and clicked his false teeth.

"I know, right? It's crazy." She brushed away the little sprinkles of loose hairs and unfastened the Velcro holding the cape in place around his neck. "I think you're done. How does it look?"

He craned his neck this way and that, admiring himself in the mirror. "You do good work, Marla Jean. If your dad was alive, he'd be real proud."

"Dad is alive, remember, Mr. Begley? He just retired and moved to South Padre."

He looked momentarily confused and then stood up from the chair. "Well, that's fine then. Tell him to send me a postcard sometime." He handed her a twenty-dollar bill and told her to keep the change. As he walked out the door, he added, "And don't let me hear about you getting into any more bar fights, young lady."

"I promise, Mr. Begley."

Grabbing the broom from the back room, she started sweeping up the hair from the floor. For a Tuesday the shop had been unusually busy, and it wasn't because she'd been voted barber of the year, either. Tongues had been wagging, and the tales of her exploits at Lu Lu's Saturday night would soon be the stuff of legends. Chuck Begley wasn't the first customer who'd come in, more than happy to share what he'd heard.

Most of the stories had Jake and Donny Joe coming to blows with each other over her in the parking lot. That was bad enough, but now another version was circulating that had her getting into a catfight with Irene Cornwell, of all people.

The worst part, the part that really pissed her off? According to Melvin Krebbs, when he'd stopped by to have his sideburns trimmed earlier, Irene Cornwell had kicked her butt up one side and down the other.

As if.

She could whip Irene Cornwell's skinny little ass with one hand tied behind her back any day of the week.

"Parcheesi!" Hooter Ferguson let out a rousing yell, announcing his victory in the board game that went on almost nonstop every day at the front of her shop.

Dooley Parker slapped the board, knocking the pawns over and scattering them onto the floor. "Hell's bells, I can't concentrate today with all these fools comin' and goin'. I could go for some pie, though. How 'bout it, Hoot?"

"Pie'd be good. We'll be across the street if you need us, Marla Jean." The two older men stood up and stretched before heading for the front door of the shop.

"Okay, guys. Don't forget my iced tea, please."

Hoot pointed a finger at her on his way out the door. "With extra lemon. Will do."

Marla walked over and picked up the game pieces from the floor and then put them back on the board. The two old men had been a fixture in the shop long before she'd taken over from her dad, and if she ever sold the place they'd be included in the inventory.

When the brewery out on the highway threatened a big layoff back in the eighties, Hoot and Dooley opted for early retirement. Their wives didn't like having them underfoot, so they'd adopted her father's barber shop as a home away from home. Rain or shine, they'd show up every morning at eight and stay until five, playing Parcheesi, chewing the fat, and for no extra charge, dispensing their own brand of wisdom. She couldn't imagine the place without them. Every day around this time they'd go for pie, and every day they'd bring her back an iced tea with extra lemon.

She sat down in one of the barber chairs and spun around. When she was little, she loved to come to the shop with her dad. She'd hop up in an empty chair, and he'd spin her around and 'round. Then he'd stop the chair, and she'd climb down. Dizzy and giggling, she'd stumble around until she collapsed in a heap. "Pick a direction, Marla Jean," he'd say with a smile. "It's important to know where you're going in life."

From her vantage point on the floor she'd look up at her father, so tall, so sure of himself, so dependable. Everyone in Everson liked Milton Jones. He was hardworking, clean-living, and loved his wife and kids. Folks thought highly of her mother, Bitsy, as well. She taught music at Thornton Elementary School to several generations of Everson children, and they all still sang her praises. It made Marla proud. It made Marla feel rooted and secure.

She'd worked at the barber shop off and on as she got older, but never planned to make it her career. She always imagined herself doing something artsy, like jewelry design or illustrating children's books. But after graduating with an art degree from the University of North Texas, she moved back home to Everson, fell into helping her father again, and before she knew it she was married to Bradley and working at the barber shop full-time.

Her course in life had seemed set, and if she hadn't found genuine fulfillment, she'd at least found comfort in that. But now, since the divorce, the very things that brought her comfort before made her feel like she might suffocate. She'd lie awake some nights and fight the urge to pick up and move away to somewhere where nobody knew her or cared about her business.

It was tempting. But it was also the coward's way out. Sure, she'd been blindsided by Bradley's betrayal. Completely unprepared, and in the blink of an eye, everything changed. Libby Comstock batted her trifocal-covered eyes at Bradley, and Marla Jean had yet to recover from the repercussions.

The end of a marriage was bound to make a person question herself. When did Bradley stop loving her? And what could she have done differently? Maybe nothing, but when your husband leaves you for an older woman it's not exactly a boost to your ego.

The split with Bradley smashed up all the ideas she'd had of who she was and what her life would be—smashed them all to smithereens. The idea of selling the barber shop and taking off for parts unknown still held a certain appeal, but so far she'd resisted. As Jake put it, life happens, and all she could do was steer her way on down the road a day at a time.

Jake. His name burst inside her head like a familiar flavor, like the scent of something distant and from long ago. After he left her house on Sunday, she'd tried not to think about him at all, because thinking about Jake was like taking off on a road that led absolutely nowhere. The drive might be pretty, but it wouldn't get you anywhere.

She'd spent her entire adolescence pining after Abel Jacobson. Not the serious kind of pining, but the he's-so-dreamy kind of pining that young girls engage in. He'd been safe, older, and unattainable, the perfect guy to practice her budding feminine wiles on. He'd tolerated her, never made fun of her, and never pushed back when she'd tried to push him too far. With any other teenaged boy she would have been playing with fire. Jake always made sure she didn't get burned—unless you counted that last weekend before he'd gone off to college.

But that was years ago, and she'd had nothing but casual encounters with him for most of her married life. From all accounts he'd grown into a fine upstanding citizen—one of those sturdy, steady, calm-in-the-storm kind of men. Marla knew he'd been a loyal, true friend to Lincoln since they were kids. He took good care of his widowed mother, and his home remodeling business was a success.

But he'd managed to stay unattached all these years. Oh, there were women. In that respect he could give Donny Joe a run for his money. He might be a little more discreet than Donny Joe, but it was touted as gospel by those in the know that the woman that could rope Jake into matrimony hadn't been born. No siree, Bob. She always figured his wariness was because of his sorry excuse for a father. Talk about a terrible role model. But that was just conjecture on her part.

And now, thanks to Lincoln, the poor man had been dragged back into this mess she called her life. Her brother was going to get an earful the minute he got back into town.

"Hey, no daydreaming allowed on the job."

She jumped when a deep male voice interrupted her runaway thoughts. The bell on the door must have jingled, because when she looked up, Jake, Mr. Dreamy himself, stood just inside the entrance with his hands on his hips. The afternoon sun poured through the plate glass window, lighting him up like the angels above were smiling at the sight of him. He was wearing work clothes, but even in blue jeans and a gray flannel shirt, Abel Jacobson was guaranteed to turn a few heads just by walking down the street.

She found the way he kept turning up lately a bit unnerving, but she manufactured an unruffled smile and plastered it on her face. "Hey, Jake. Sorry, I didn't hear you come in."

"It's okay, but you looked like you were a million miles away."

"Maybe not a million, but close enough. So what's going on? I know you're not here for a haircut. You haven't been in since Dad retired."

He took a look around the place before his eyes settled back on her. "I was just passing by and thought I'd see how you were holding up."

"Holding up?" she asked, taking a second to stick the broom back in the storage room. "What do you mean?"

"Well, I don't know about you, but everywhere I go today we seem to be the main topic of conversation."

"So, you thought you'd drop by and give them something else to talk about?" She occupied herself by straightening the counter in front of her station, finally looking up to meet his gaze in the mirror.

He winked. "I'm not above stirring the pot. I waved at old lady Smithfield right before I came in the door. The old girl couldn't make it over to the diner fast enough to spread the word."

She turned to face him. "You better watch it. I bet she could still send you to detention hall if she really wanted to." When they'd been in high school, Fran Smithfield had taught world history, and right behind discussing the glories of the Roman Empire, sending Jake to detention had been her second greatest joy. "But seriously, I'm holding up just fine. All the talk has actually helped my business. It's amazing how many people suddenly need a haircut."

Jake laughed. "Well, there's a silver lining."

She patted the barber chair. "So, how 'bout it? Are you ready to let me have my way with you?" She'd itched to get her hands on his silky head of black hair for years and years, but he'd always wiggled out of it.

He raked his fingers through his hair and took a step backward. "Thanks, but I'll pass."

She moved closer. "What's the matter, Jake? Don't you trust me with your manly locks?"

"It's nothing personal, Marla Jean, but after your dad left, I started going to Floyd Cramer over in Derbyville."

"Derbyville? Isn't that a long way to go for a haircut?"

"Nah, I'm over that way once or twice a month picking up supplies."

"Likely story."

He stuck his hands in the front pocket of his jeans and shrugged. "I have a tricky cowlick. A man can't be too careful."

She laughed at his newest excuse. "Okay, be that way. I can take a hint, but if you change your mind, the first haircut's on the house."

"I'll keep that in mind." He stood there not making any attempt to leave.

"Anything else?"

"That about covers it, I guess." He started out the door and then stopped. "I'll be working on my folks' house this week, so I'm camping out there until the job's done. If you need anything, just holler."

"Thanks, but I'll try to stay out of your hair. No pun intended." She wouldn't be surprised if the offer wasn't another part of Linc's plan for Jake to keep an eye on her. She still needed to set Linc straight on a few things, but that was her problem, not Jake's.

"Okay, I'll see you around, then." He gave a small nod and started to leave again.

"Hey Jake?" She stopped him before he made it out the door.

"Yeah?"

"All these rumors you've been hearing today—did you happen to hear the one about me and Irene Cornwell having a knock-down-drag-out?"

His face split into a wide-open grin. "Sure did. That was probably my favorite."

"Just out of curiosity, in the account you heard? Who won?"

"Hmm. Let's see. I was buying lumber over at Binyon's this morning, and Larry Prindle was helping me load up. After he finished describing all the scratching, and the biting, and the clothes being pulled off, he might've mentioned that Irene came out victorious."

Her irritation mounted. "Good grief. He actually said we pulled each other's clothes off?"

"Hell yeah. What good's a catfight if clothes don't come off?" His eyes got all twinkly, like he'd just been plugged into an outlet.

"But you told him it never happened, right?"

His grin got wider, if that was possible. She could see he was having a high old time at her expense. He shook his head. "I didn't have the heart."

"Jake." She slugged him in the shoulder.

"Ow." He rubbed his arm. "But I did tell him I had fifty dollars riding on you to win, and that I doubled my money when you laid out poor old Irene with a right hook."

"Aw, Jake." Oddly touched by his effort on her behalf, she grabbed him by the arm. "You said that?"

His big hand covered hers. "Sure, slugger, I figured a little damage control was in order. And besides, I'd take you in a fight over almost any woman I know."

She beamed. "Stop with the sweet talk. You're embarrassing me."

The bell over the door tinkled as Hoot and Dooley came walking back into the barber shop. Dooley held out a paper to-go cup. "Here's your tea, Marla Jean."

She jerked her hand away from Jake's arm, feeling like they'd been caught at something.

"Abel Jacobson, as I live and breathe," Hoot declared as soon as he spotted him inside the door. "Son, I haven't seen you in here in a month of Sundays."

Jake shook hands with both men. "Hey, Hoot. How's it going, Dooley?"

Dooley held back and didn't say anything, but Hoot asked, "How about sitting in on a game of Parcheesi, for old time's sake?"

Jake looked over at the old table in the front window. For a minute he looked tempted, but then he said, "Thanks for asking, but I've got a lot of paperwork waiting for me over at the office. Maybe I'll stop by next week if the offer's still open."

Hoot clapped him on the shoulder. "Anytime, Jake. Don't be a stranger, ya hear?"

"I won't." He nodded at the two men and then turned to Marla. "Later, Marla Jean."

"Later, Jake."

He walked out, and the door barely closed before Dooley turned a stern eye in her direction. "All right, girlie. What's going on?"

"Nothing's going on, Dooley. I don't know what you're talking about."

"Do tell? We come in and find you making goo-goo eyes at Abel Jacobson, pretty as you please, but nothing's going on."

"I don't make goo-goo eyes. But if I wanted to make goo-goo eyes, I would. Why does everyone in this town have a sudden interest in my social life?"

"Leave the girl alone, Dooley." Hoot put a hand on his arm, but Dooley ignored him.

"Me and Hoot, we aren't everyone."

She sighed. "Oh Dooley, of course you're not. It's just all the gossip flying around town has me feeling out of sorts."

Dooley harrumphed, stalked over to the game table, and sat down. "I'll go back to minding my own business now, but there's one thing I'd like to know first. What in tarnation are you thinking, getting sweet on that boy again?"

Chapter Five

⁓

"This is great, Ma." Jake shoveled a forkful of macaroni and cheese into his mouth.

"Heavens, when's the last time you had a decent meal?" Ellie Jacobson sat across from her son, wide-eyed, watching him eat.

"Let's see. When's the last time you had me over for dinner?" Jake sat at his mother's dining room table helping himself to thirds.

She cut another piece of cornbread and put it on his plate, then scooted the butter dish in his direction. "You know very well that I fed you beef stew and biscuits while you were here fixing the loose rail on the front porch last Thursday."

"Well, then that's the last time I had a decent meal. Everyone else's cooking pales next to yours, especially my own."

Left to his own devices, he made an effort to eat healthy, avoided fried foods, and made sure he got the occasional fresh fruit or vegetable into his diet, but his mother was old school. She showed her love by seeing how much cream and butter she could add to a recipe.

Tonight she'd made baked ham smothered in some kind of sugary glaze, macaroni and cheese so thick he could use it to plaster walls, canned green beans boiled with bacon fat until the very life had been cooked right out of them, and jalapeño cornbread with creamed corn mixed into the batter. He was in hog heaven, and he certainly wasn't going to hurt his mother's feelings by telling her he was trying to eat light.

She was always trying to fatten him up, but this particular meal was his favorite, and was usually saved for birthdays and other special occasions. If she was bringing out the heavy artillery in the middle of the week, whatever she wanted to talk to him about must be important.

After he speared the last two green beans and washed them down with iced tea, he leaned back in his chair and rubbed his stomach. "Okay, spill it, Ma. What's this all about?"

"Your Aunt Libby, what else?" She blurted it out, not beating around the bush like she usually did. "This thing with Bradley Bandy seems to be getting very serious."

"Seems to be? He left his wife for her. I think it's been serious for a while." Jake didn't want to talk about Aunt Libby and Bradley Bandy, but he knew his mother wouldn't rest until they did.

"I realize that, but I was positive Libby was just some kind of phase for him, a novelty, and once the newness wore off, he'd dump her like he dumped Marla Jean."

"But you don't believe that anymore?"

"Well, he's been divorced for six months now, separated for awhile before that. Libby just told me she's thinking of selling her house on Crawford Street so she can move in with him."

"Are you really surprised? She spends all her time at his place as it is."

His mother made a face like the idea gave her indigestion. "I just hate to see her give up her house. She's worked so hard to fix that place up the way she wanted it. If this thing blows up in her face, she'll have a broken heart and no place to call her own." His mother stood and started gathering dishes.

His mother was an expert on broken hearts, thanks to his old man. Jake picked up the ham and the green beans and followed her into the kitchen. He rooted around in the cabinet until he found containers for the leftovers. "I'll talk to her if you want. See if I can at least convince her to hold on to the house for a while."

Ellie stacked the plates on the counter and began running a sink full of hot water. She had a perfectly good dishwasher, but most of the time she preferred washing them by hand. Said it gave her time to meditate.

If washing dishes and looking out the kitchen window at the flowerpots on the patio made her happy, he wasn't going to try to convince her otherwise. After years of watching her put up with his overbearing, son-of-a-bitch father, a man who'd micromanaged her every move, he rather enjoyed her newfound stubborn streak.

"Jake, I really don't think anything we say at this point will make a bit of difference."

He was getting whiplash trying to figure out what she wanted. "Okay then, I won't say a word."

After he put the food in the refrigerator, he stood by, prepared to dry while she washed. He waited for her to continue. If she didn't want him to talk to his aunt about her house, she obviously had something else on her mind. He knew from experience that she wouldn't say more until she was ready. He'd dried and put away the glasses and the dinner plates and was drying the ham platter when she finally spoke.

"They want to have us over on Saturday night." She rinsed the macaroni pan and set it in the dish drain.

"Who wants to have us over?" Jake stuck the platter up in the cabinet.

His mother paused with her hands still in the soapy water and gave him a look. "Libby and Bradley. Who else have we been talking about?"

That stopped him in his tracks. "Aw, jeez. I don't have to go, do I?" He'd rather stick his foot in a bear trap.

"Stop whining, Jake. It's unbecoming in a man your age."

"Bradley Bandy is a-a pinhead," he declared, cleaning up his language for his mother's benefit. And the idea of making small talk with the guy over guacamole dip while he and his aunt sat around making moon eyes at each other made him want to build a bridge just so he could throw himself off of it.

"Young man, this means a lot to your aunt." She shook a just-washed serving spoon under his nose while she scolded him. "And we are the only family she has, so we're going. I'd appreciate your support in this."

He threw the dish towel on the counter and fumed. "Well, you've certainly changed your tune. Last I heard, you were ready to disown Aunt Libby altogether. I say we go back to that plan."

She pooh-poohed his suggestion. "I was upset when I said that. I thought Libby was making a fool of herself."

He put his hands on his hips. "And now?"

She set the last bowl in the dish rack to drain and dried her hands. "Libby came by yesterday, and we had a long heart-to-heart. She's happy, Jake. In fact, she's happier than I've ever seen her. And like it or not, Bradley Bandy has a lot to do with that."

He grunted, not wanting to acknowledge the truth in what she was saying.

With her mixed feelings clearly painted on her face his mother admitted, "To be honest, I'm still afraid she's lost her everlovin' mind—"

He cut in. "A ringing endorsement if I ever heard one."

She swatted him with a dish towel. "But on the off chance that I'm wrong, my sister deserves to have a life that includes love and companionship and something besides books to keep her warm at night."

"I guess," he grumbled. The vision of Bradley keeping his aunt warm at night made him feel queasy—like he'd swallowed a spoonful of warm grease. But he loved his Aunt Libby. She'd been like a second mother to him, and he wanted her to be happy, too.

His mother took him by the arm and said gently, "If it's a mistake, it's hers to make. And she needs to know that we're in her corner, no matter what."

He exhaled noisily. "What time do you want me to pick you up?"

She kissed him on the cheek. "That's my boy. Six-thirty will be early enough. And don't bring the Porsche. I don't want to arrive with my clothes all wrinkled and my hair all windblown."

"Yes, ma'am."

"How 'bout some coffee?"

"Thanks, but it's a work night, and tomorrow comes early. I better take off."

"All right, son." She walked him to the front door. "By the way, while I was buying potting soil at the garden center today I heard a rumor that disturbed me."

Jake steeled himself. "You probably heard the same ones I've been hearing."

"These concerned Marla Jean Bandy. According to Thurman Nelson she was running wild this past weekend, kicking up her heels at Lu Lu's."

Jake snorted. "Last I heard having fun on a Saturday night was still legal in this country."

She leaned close, and in a this-is-just-between-you-and-me voice filled him in. "I know, but he said she was carrying on with a whole passel of men, and even got into a fight with that Cornwell girl."

"Ma, you taught me not believe everything I hear."

"And I didn't bring it up just to spread more gossip." He could tell her dander was up. "I'm simply worried about that girl. What with this business with Libby, and all, I can't help but feel some responsibility."

"Marla Jean was out dancing—that's it."

"And how do you know so much about it, Mister Smarty Pants?"

"If you must know, I was one of the passel she danced with. And I took her home at the end of the evening, too. The rest is just folks running their mouths." Jake folded his arms over his chest as if that settled the matter. But he should have known better.

"You took her home?" His mom's face lit up like a bug zapper in a mosquito-infested swamp. "You always did have a soft spot for that girl, didn't you?"

The calculating eyeball she cast his direction made him squirm. "I don't have a soft spot for her, Ma. She's Linc's little sister, and like you said, Aunt Libby is partly to blame for the situation she's in. So, maybe I was watching out for her. I just think she should be able to go out and have some fun without the whole town having a party to discuss it."

His mother laid her hand on his cheek. "You're a good man, Abel Gene Jacobson."

"It's no big deal."

"If you say so." Her smile said she thought otherwise.

"I say so, and now I've gotta go." He kissed her on the cheek. "Thanks for dinner."

"Anytime." She switched on the porch light and walked outside with him.

He made a mopey face and added reluctantly, "And I'll pick you up at six-thirty on Saturday for this thing with Aunt Libby."

"It won't be so bad, Jake. You'll see."

That was what she used to tell him when he had to get a shot at the doctor's. He hadn't bought it when he was a kid, and he didn't buy it now.

Chapter Six

Marla stood in the middle of her childhood bedroom studying the canvas on the easel. The painting resembled a piece of lasagna that had been flung out onto the sidewalk and trampled by a herd of livestock. A psychiatrist could have a field day with what it had to say about the state of her psyche. She was more worried about what it said about her ability to paint.

In the years since college her interest in art had taken a back seat to other things. Between the barber shop and devoting herself to Bradley, it hadn't seemed all that important. But in the months since her separation and divorce she'd taken it up again, even signing up for a couple of continuing ed art classes offered by the community college over in Derbyville. Needing a place to paint, she'd turned her old bedroom in her parents' house into an art studio.

At first she used painting as an emotional release. Heaving colors onto the canvas with savage brushstrokes, slathering veins of blood red, bottomless black, and bilious greens and yellows onto the surface with slashes of her palette knife. She tried to wring all of her emotions out—the pain, the loneliness, the self-pity. Dredging it all up and spitting it out until there was nothing left.

It helped for a while, but as she looked at the stacks of butt-ugly canvases lining the bedroom walls, she knew they'd outlived their usefulness. It was time to start fresh and get back some of the joy she used to feel when she painted—a long time ago, before her life had turned into a stinking soap opera. Painting had always been the one thing that felt like hers alone. The place where she could truly be herself. Not Milton and Bitsy's daughter. Not Bradley's wife.

Marla Jean cast one more critical look at the latest attempt resting on the easel, and reached for the tube of burnt umber. Without any plan or purpose, she started blocking out a face, painting right on top of the chaos underneath. Portraits had always been her thing, her true passion.

After Bradley left, her focus had been too scattered to express anything that wasn't purely abstract. She didn't count the stick figures of Bradley she regularly drew and dismembered those first few months. But people had always fascinated her, especially their faces.

As she worked she thought about the football game on Friday night. Harry Beal had called to remind her of her promise to join him at Romeo's pizza place after the game. She almost backed out when she thought about what Jake said about him having a crush on her all these years. But Harry sounded so normal, so pleasant, and it was nice to have plans, so instead she assured him she was looking forward to the game. And that was true. Getting out more was just what she needed.

Since Saturday night at Lu Lu's something deep inside her, the part that had hardened and calcified since Bradley's betrayal was softening, coming back to life. Maybe only part way. Maybe just a little around the edges. And maybe she'd never be able to trust with her arms wide open again the way she used to, but at least it was a beginning. The idea of actually dating anyone scared her spitless. She could be honest about that. And a big part of her still felt like a married woman.

Dooley's warning about Jake had darted in and out of her head all afternoon. Lord knows, she certainly wasn't sweet on him, but if she could have her choice of any man in this town to start some kind of no-strings something-something with, it would be Jake. Alone in the privacy of her own home she couldn't deny the idea got her juices flowing.

It seemed like a lifetime ago, but she still remembered the week before he'd gone off to college. She'd gone to the bowling alley with her girlfriends, and Jake had been sitting on the tailgate of his truck in the parking lot. Waving at her friends to go on inside without her, she'd gone over to say hello.

The August night had been summertime hot, and she'd left the house wearing a wispy yellow sundress with spaghetti straps that refused to stay on her shoulders. As soon as she'd spotted him, she felt something inside her stir, something womanly, powerful, and brazen.

That night Jake seemed different, darker, and more dangerous somehow, and he woke up everything female inside her adolescent body. All these years later, she could recall everything she'd felt and exactly the way he'd looked. The tight, worn blue jeans, the plain white T-shirt.

He wore his hair longer back then, and those unruly black curls made him look like a fallen angel.

"Hey, if it isn't Marla Jean." He'd patted the tailgate beside him, beckoning her with a lopsided smile and brooding brown eyes that took in every inch of her. "Why don't you sit down and keep me company."

"What's going on, Jake?" She climbed up beside him, smelling the beer on his breath.

"I'm waiting for Lincoln to get off work, so we can celebrate." He took a swig from the bottle in his hand.

"It looks like you've already been celebrating."

"Don't be such a goody-two-shoes. I'm finally getting out of here. After next weekend, I'll be long gone."

She sighed. Her brother and Jake were both leaving, and she was miserable about it. "Don't remind me. You're going to have so much fun at college you'll forget you ever knew me." For the longest time, she'd held onto the fantasy that someday he'd stop thinking of her as a kid and instead see her as a captivating woman. Fat chance, especially now that he was leaving town.

He threw an arm around her shoulders and pulled her close. "I'll never forget about you, brat. You are the standard by which I'll judge all the multitude of women I meet when I'm gone."

She stared at her lap. "Now you're making fun of me."

He didn't answer as he turned her body to face him. His fingers traced the thin yellow straps of her dress where they had fallen down her arms before slipping them back up to her shoulders where they belonged. Her skin tingled at his touch, and breathless, she raised her eyes to look at him.

Maybe it was the liquor that had made him less guarded

than normal. Marla Jean didn't care. All she knew was that his eyes glinted with a fire that made her want to move closer, to risk being burned by the pleasure they promised. In all the times she'd teased him, he'd never looked at her with such bold, brash intention. He leaned toward her, his face close enough to touch, his whispered words gliding across her cheek. "I'll remember you, Marla Jean."

His mouth grazed her lips once, twice before becoming hungry and demanding. She threw her arms around him, kissing him back with willing innocence. He pulled back, untangling her arms from his neck, looking at her once more, carefully, intently, as if he were committing her to memory. Then he stood up. "You better get inside with your friends, little girl, before I do something we'll both regret."

"Jake?" She reached for him, not understanding his abrupt change in mood.

His voice was harsh when he picked her up by the waist and set her on the ground. "Go on. Get out of here."

Before she could protest her brother pulled into the parking lot, honking his horn and squealing his tires. Turning away as if she didn't exist, Jake walked over to greet Linc. Marla Jean ran into the bowling alley, not sure if she should thank her brother or blast him for his lousy timing.

Much to Dooley's dismay, and Hoot's amusement, she'd mooned around about Jake for the first month or so after he was gone, convinced he harbored serious feelings for her, and as soon as he got a chance he'd come home and sweep her into his arms and declare himself. But being a senior in high school soon took up all her time and attention, and if she even saw Jake when he came home on visits she couldn't remember. That had been years ago, but it hadn't taken long last Saturday night to realize he still had the complete power to unnerve her.

She used a wide brush and roughed in the hollows for a pair of eyes. Her phone rang, and she was tempted to ignore it. Hiding from the outside world had become a habit. One she needed to break, so instead she grabbed the phone on the fourth ring.

"Hello." She continued to paint, using quick brush-strokes to work in some eyebrows.

"I was beginning to think you weren't home." Her brother's deep voice came through the receiver.

She barely let him finish before launching into a tirade. "Lincoln Samuel Patrick Randolph Jones, you are in big, big trouble." Her mother had gotten a little carried away when naming her firstborn.

"Hey," he protested. "I just got home. How can I be in trouble?"

"Why don't you ask your friend Jake?" She swirled her brush into the paint on the palette and formed a nose on the canvas in front of her.

"I don't know what you're talking about."

"Sure you do. You told him to keep an eye on me."

"Now, Marla Jean—"

"Don't you 'now, Marla Jean' me. I'm a grown woman, and I don't need you to sic Jake on me like a guard dog."

"I'm not going to apologize for worrying, so don't even try to make me feel guilty. You have to admit you haven't been yourself lately." He resorted to the haughty tone he took when he felt defensive.

"I may not ever be myself again, big brother, so get used to it. And it's not fair to put Abel Jacobson between me and whatever I decide to go after." She played with the shading around the cheekbones.

"What are you talking about?" He sounded uneasy.

"Men, Lincoln. I've decided to start dating again, and I'll probably go through a few before it's all over. I'm telling you to stay out of my way." She reshaped the chin, making it stronger.

"See, this is what I mean. You've gone off the deep end."

"And I love it. Let's see. Donny Joe Ledbetter was this last weekend, I'm going out with Harry Beal after the game on Friday night, and then I may see if Jackson Connor is free for Sunday dinner." She didn't mind exaggerating the truth if it would get under Lincoln's skin.

"Old Mr. Connor, the funeral director? He's sixty-five years old, if he's a day."

"I don't want to leave any leaf unturned. What do you think about Ted Grimes? He winked at me when I got gas the other day." Ted Grimes, owner of the local gas station, had been married four times and rumor had it, he was in the market for wife number five.

"Very funny." Lincoln didn't sound amused.

"And I haven't even started exploring the twenty-something population. I don't have a problem with being the older woman. If I learned nothing else from Bradley and Libby I learned not to limit my options."

"All right, cut it out, Marla Jean."

"I'll cut it out when you cut it out. You're my brother, and I love you. But I'm all grown up, and you have to stop treating me like a child."

"Even if you're acting like one?"

"You're not winning any points, buddy boy, but the answer is yes. Even if I'm acting like one."

"So, were you this rude to poor Jake?"

"Poor Jake can handle himself." She picked up some brown on her brush and touched it to the eyes.

"I'll take that as a yes."

"Listen, Lincoln, I'm glad you're home, but I need to go. Give Dinah a hug for me, and I'll talk to you soon."

"Marla Jean, wait."

"Good night, big brother."

He huffed. "Good night, sis. But we're not through discussing this."

Hanging up the phone, she stood back to study the painting. It was just the rough beginnings of a man's face, and she hadn't had anyone particular in mind when she started. But there was no mistaking who it resembled. The dark hair, the forceful eyes, the mouth that could tempt Mother Superior. *Son of a biscuit with cream gravy on top.* Jake's face stared back at her from the canvas.

She turned the painting over to face the wall and stalked out of the room. No matter what Dooley thought, she wasn't the same dumb little girl who'd been sweet on Jake all those years ago. Sadder but wiser, that was the old saying, and these days it described her perfectly when it came to men, especially men like Abel Jacobson.

Jake sat in a chair on his folks' old front porch with his boots propped up on the railing. It was a cool, cloudy night, dark and moonless, but he hadn't bothered turning on the porch light. It just attracted bugs, and besides, he liked sitting in the shadows. When he left his mother's house he'd thought he might finish painting the back bedroom, but he was too restless to work. Instead, he grabbed a beer from the old fridge he'd hooked up in the kitchen, and settled down on the porch. Every five seconds he found himself checking out the house across the street, two doors down.

The lights were on in Marla Jean's old bedroom window, and he could see her silhouette behind the curtains. There was no mistaking the shape of her body, or the riot of wavy hair dancing around her head. She stood in one place, barely moving.

The fact that he was curious about what she was up to right now bothered him. The fact that he was thinking about her at all bothered him even more.

For years she'd been consigned to the place in his head of Lincoln's very married kid sister. Nothing more, nothing less. Then his aunt had to go break up Marla Jean's marriage, and his danged sense of duty and responsibility kicked in all over again. When Linc asked him to keep an eye on her how could he say no?

And something else bothered him—the look on his mother's face when she'd mentioned Marla Jean. The last thing he needed was for her to stick her matchmaking, scheming, busybody nose into his love life. Not that he actually had much of a love life these days, and that was fine with him. Keeping the remodeling business going took up most of his time. He dated when he felt like it. There was never a shortage of women that liked to have a good time. And if sex was what he needed, there was no shortage of women happy to oblige in that area, either. Women who knew how the cookie crumbled.

It wasn't that he objected to meaningful relationships for other people, but in his experience the man-woman thing was a lot of work without much reward. His parents had been the perfect example. His mother had struggled until the day his dad died to make him happy, and she'd never succeeded.

And look at Marla Jean. She'd said "I do until death" and all that crap. But what had it gotten her? She'd given her heart to Bradley Bandy, and he'd stomped on it and handed it back to her six years later.

He'd meant what he said about men being dogs. Most wouldn't hesitate to take advantage of a newly divorced woman. She'd be ripe for the taking, susceptible to their smooth talk and flattery. She might even convince herself that she was the one doing the seducing.

Shit, he should just steer clear and let her make her own mistakes, but old habits die hard.

Jake took another pull on his beer and watched Marla Jean move away from the window. And he kept right on watching until the room went dark. He ignored the tug in his gut that urged him to get up and take a quick stroll across the street. He tamped down the temptation to go knock on her door and ask how the rest of her day had been. When it came to Marla Jean, it was time to get a grip.

His feet hit the wooden planks of the porch floor with a thump. Standing up, he pulled his cell phone from his jeans pocket and dialed a number. "Hey, Genna. It's Jake. You got any plans for Friday night?"

Chapter Seven

~~~

The moon floated, pearl white in the night sky, smiling down on the Everson football field. Purple and gold streamers of crepe paper were wrapped around every available pole and railing, giving the old stadium a festive feel. Excitement for the big game built as the marching band warmed up at one end of the stands, the erratic sound of bleating horns and beating drums punctuating the air. A brisk autumn breeze whipped through the stands, carrying the smell of popcorn, nacho cheese, and hot dogs along with it. Down on the asphalt track that ran around the field, the Everson cheerleading squad tumbled and jumped around, trying to get the crowd revved up to root the Cougars on to victory.

Marla Jean tried to get into the spirit of things, too. It had been over a year since she'd been to a game, and it seemed so much like part of her old life that now she didn't know how to act. For the first time ever, getting ready for the game had become a production. Normally, she would throw on jeans and a long-sleeved T-shirt, pull on her old Everson High School sweatshirt, and add as many layers on top of that as she could to keep warm. But tonight wasn't that simple. Should she try to look good for Harry? It seemed only right to make a bit of an effort, but she didn't want to send the wrong signal, so she'd tried on half of her closet to find just the right look. A look that said, "I'm looking mighty fine" without going overboard to impress anyone. Being single was way too complicated.

She settled for nice jeans and a white lacy blouse. She covered the blouse with a purple sweater to show team spirit. A little lace peeked out at the collar and sleeves, enough to make her feel feminine and a little bit saucy. And the finishing touch—her favorite cowboy boots, the beige ones covered in a winding green vine and fuchsia flower design.

As she climbed the bleachers looking for a place to sit she wrapped her jacket around herself tighter to ward off the wind. Since Harry would be coaching the team, she'd have to go it alone until after the game. She tried not to feel awkward about that.

"Go, Cougars," she responded to the enthusiastic greetings of people she knew, and that was almost everyone. "Go, team," she agreed cheerily.

She noticed Bradley almost right away. He occupied his usual place up near the top of the bleachers. Libby was by his side, and the two of them were surrounded by the same group of friends Marla Jean and Bradley had socialized with during their married years. Libby Comstock looked right at home, damn her. In fact, the older woman looked positively vibrant. She was laughing, her cheeks pink from the night air, and as she leaned into Bradley to say something her eyes seemed to adore him. Marla tried to remember if she'd ever looked at Bradley with that kind of adoration.

This was the first time she'd seen the two of them out together in a public place, and she couldn't ignore the pang she felt at being displaced. She tried to take a deep breath but it felt as if a giant boulder had lodged in her throat, choking off all the oxygen. Her cheeks blazed, and she stumbled going up the next step. Some mix of embarrassment and humiliation flooded her whole body. But there was a healthy dose of righteous indignation in the mix, too. Marla Jean grabbed onto that feeling and didn't let go. When Julie Bingham, one of the women from the group, caught her eye and waved, Marla manufactured a smile and waved back. Julie had always been a good friend, but her husband worked with Bradley, so that made things uncomfortable now. The rest of the women acted like they didn't see her. She straightened to her full height and thought with renewed conviction, *Who the hell needs them?*

She turned away, scanning the crowd, anxiously looking for a place to settle. When her brother stood up and gestured to get her attention she could have cried. She'd never been so thankful to see anyone in her life.

"Hey, Marla Jean, over here," he shouted.

Even if she was still a little put out with him, spotting Lincoln was like spotting land after being shipwrecked at sea. With a heavy sigh of relief she readily returned his wave and climbed the bleachers to reach his side. Dinah, Lincoln's bride of six months, jumped up and pulled her into a hug. "Hey, Marla Jean. I was so happy when Linc said you'd be here tonight."

The warm welcome was just what she needed. "Hey Dinah, how was the cruise? I want to hear all about it."

Lincoln and Dinah hadn't had time for a honeymoon when they first got married, so they made up for it by taking a Caribbean cruise on their six-month anniversary. Dinah was the picture of blissed-out contentment. "Come by Sunday, and I'll bore you to death with all the pictures."

Marla laughed. "You make it sound so tempting."

"I'll throw in dinner and Yellow Birds."

"Yellow Birds?"

"Yeah, it's a new drink we had on the cruise, and Linc bribed the bartender for the recipe. They'll knock you on your keister."

"Now you're talking."

"Come on, sis. Give me a hug." Lincoln Jones towered over his sister at six-foot-three. He held out his arms, beckoning with both hands until she relented and moved into his embrace.

As much as his protective nature drove her nuts sometimes, she knew he only wanted what was best for her. He was just going to have to get used to the idea that from now on, they might disagree about exactly what that was. "Welcome home, Lincoln."

He smiled and gave her another squeeze. "That's more like it. We saved you a seat." They scooted down a bit, and she sat by Dinah.

"So," Dinah said conspiratorially, "I hear you're meeting Coach Beal after the game."

Marla Jean shrugged. "He asked, and I thought it was time for me to start getting out some."

"I couldn't agree more." A burst of loud laughter traveled down from the section where Bradley and Libby and all of her old friends were seated. Dinah glanced up behind her and then turned back to Marla Jean. Placing a comforting hand on her arm she asked, "Are you okay with that?"

"I'll admit I freaked out a little when I first saw them. But I'm fine now. Really." Marla smiled and patted her sister-in-law's hand. "And I'm here to have fun."

The teams ran out onto the field and everyone stood up, clapping and cheering for the home team. The band broke into the school fight song, and Marla got caught up singing loudly to the familiar battle cry.

Everyone had just settled back into their seats when Jake came climbing up the aisle toward them. He had his hand on the waist of the buxom blonde walking just ahead of him. Genna Stanley. Just the sight of her made Marla Jean flash back to high school days when she'd been a lowly sophomore band nerd and Genna had been a popular senior. Head cheerleader, homecoming queen, and voted most likely to go to Hollywood and make it big.

These days Genna's hair was blonder, her boobs were bigger, and the closest she'd been to Hollywood was a tour of Universal Studios. Still, to be fair, Genna was an attractive woman, and from what Marla had heard, lots of "fun." Okay. That was catty. But she could understand why a man like Jake might go out with her. She also figured if Genna crawled into Donny Joe Ledbetter's truck, Jake wouldn't bother pulling her out. Everyone knew that Genna could handle herself.

The two of them squeezed into the row just ahead them. Jake sat down in front of Marla, turning to greet Lincoln and Dinah as he did. "From the looks of you two, I'm guessing the cruise was a hit."

Dinah grabbed Lincoln's arm and beamed at her husband. "It was wonderful. Lincoln has a real talent for relaxing when you get him away from the job." They shared an intimate little look that seemed to shut out the rest of the world.

Marla's brother was a workaholic—a CPA with his own accounting firm. Dinah had been hired to organize the place and ended up staying. Then she decided organizing Lincoln would be a full time job and married him. Unfortunately, the wedding had fallen in the middle of tax season, so the honeymoon had to wait. But Marla had never seen Linc happier. He'd waited a long time to get married, and she thought Dinah was perfect for him.

Jake turned to her next. "So, how's it going, Marla Jean? Are you staying out of trouble?"

"The night's young, so I'm not promising anything." Marla Jean flashed him a breezy smile. He studied her for a minute like he wanted to say something else, but he didn't.

Genna's greeting barely made it to lukewarm on the friendly scale. "Hey, Marla Jean."

Marla returned her "hey" with one of her own. Genna didn't look too happy to see her, though Marla couldn't imagine why. She saw the woman maybe once a month when she stopped by the water department to pay her bill. Genna was head clerk. Other than that, they didn't really run in the same circles.

Jake and Genna turned back to face the football field, but Lincoln kept asking him questions and every time he turned to answer, Jake's arm would brush against her knees. It was an innocent touch—the barest hint of his jacket sleeve grazing her jeans, but every time she felt like an unruly heifer being poked with a cattle prod. She scooted away the best she could, trying to avoid making contact, but there was no escaping the man. He occupied the space in front of her in the same way he'd been occupying the space in her head lately. Whenever he was anywhere in the vicinity, he tended to intrude on her state of mind. But having palpitations over a casual encounter with his leather jacket showed how long she'd been without any masculine attention. It was pathetic, really. And it wasn't as if Jake was trying to cop a feel or anything. More's the pity. She looked up when she heard someone yell her name.

"Hey, Marla Jean."

Harry Beal came running up the stadium steps, and she was alarmed to see that he carried a big, decked-out triple mum with all the ribbons and gee-gaws attached—the kind all the kids wore at homecoming. The problem was it wasn't homecoming, and she wasn't a kid.

"Harry," she greeted him with a guarded expression. Hoping against hope it wasn't for her, she tried ignoring the mum. "I didn't expect to see you until after the game."

The football team milled around on the sidelines, and it was only about three minutes until kickoff. She really thought he should be down there with the players.

"I just wanted to give you this first. I thought it might bring us luck." He hovered at the edge of the aisle awkwardly.

Folks sitting around them watched with piqued curiosity, and she understood why. The football coach didn't usually run up into the stands right before a game carrying a corsage the size of a funeral spray. And once they realized his intended target was Marla Jean Bandy, given the gossip already swirling around her, jaws would be flapping about this for weeks to come.

Marla finally took pity on the poor guy and stood up.

"Oh Harry, you shouldn't have. It's really . . ." she searched for the right word, "impressive."

"Do you think so? Mrs. Meany at the Posey Pot helped me pick out all of this stuff." The purple and gold ribbons whipped around in the breeze, and as he tried to figure out how to go about attaching it to her front side without getting too personal, it jingled and clanged like a bell choir hopped up on uppers. After several fumbling attempts he ended up stabbing his own finger with the long pin. "Ouch. Son of a—" He pulled his hand back and sucked his finger. "Sorry, Marla Jean. I seem to be all thumbs."

"Let me help, Harry." She took one of the pearl-tipped pins and together they finished affixing the thing. It was so heavy, it drooped halfway down her chest, and the ribbons dragged the ground. He looked at her helplessly, so she assured him that it was fine. "Hey, you better get back down to the team, or they'll have to start without you. Oh, and good luck, Coach. We'll be up here cheering for you." She squeezed his arm and smiled.

"Thanks, Marla Jean. I'll see you later." He grinned and bolted back down the stands. The people in the crowd started clapping. Someone yelled, "Way to go, Coach."

He turned and gave the crowd a thumbs-up and vaulted over the railing down onto the field. Then she lost sight of him as the team huddled around him for his last-minute instructions.

She sat down to find Jake watching her. Okay, he'd warned her that Harry had a thing for her. But she figured anybody asking her out must find her reasonably attractive, or they wouldn't bother. But giving her this big-assed mum felt like some kind of bold declaration of intentions on his part. She'd have to nip it in the bud if that was the case. Like she'd told Jake, she wasn't looking for anything serious. Harry was a nice man, but if serious was what he had in mind, he was going to be disappointed.

Maybe she was reading too much into it. Maybe he was just caught up in the excitement of a chance to make the play-offs, and the football mum was just a by-product of all the hoopla surrounding the game. Accompanied by the rustle of ribbons and bells, she sat down.

Dinah immediately started sifting through the array of ribbons on her chest. "Oh look, this ribbon has Harry's name written in glitter and this one has yours. That's so cute."

"Cut it out." Marla very much wanted to act as if the mum didn't exist, but Dinah was more excited than a dog in a fire hydrant factory.

"Oh, and you have a little megaphone, and an itty-bitty football, and a teeny-weeny purple helmet, and aw, this ribbon has cougar paw prints all up and down it." Marla batted her hand away, but Dinah would not be restrained.

"There's even a cowbell buried in here." Dinah clanged the bell and with a laugh sat back in her seat. "Wow, Marla Jean. I think Coach Beal must be smitten."

Jake turned and gave her a wide-eyed "told ya" look. She gave him a "shove off" look and said, "I think he's just excited because the team might make the play-offs. Don't make too big a deal out of it."

Lincoln leaned forward to get a better look and smirked. "Hey sis, now I know what a blooming idiot looks like."

Dinah swatted him playfully on the arm. "Stop it, Lincoln. I think it's sweet."

Genna turned around and remarked, "I think that's bigger than the one I wore when I won Homecoming queen."

Marla ignored them all. "Oh look," she pointed out,

"we're about to kick off." Thank goodness that turned everyone's attention from her to the game. Marla clinked and clattered while she tried to arrange the conglomeration hanging on her jacket. She kept stepping on the long streamers and noticed that she was sprinkling glitter onto the back of Jake's jacket and into his hair.

The Cougars took the opening kickoff and ran it back for forty yards. They had good field position at the visiting team's thirty-yard line. It was a terrific start and everyone jumped to their feet whooping and hollering. Forgetting her resolve to avoid touching him, Marla reached out and brushed the glitter from Jake's shoulder. He turned his head to look at her questioningly.

"You're sparkly," she said lamely as she finished cleaning him up. She made a final sweep through his dark hair, and her whole hand tingled this time. She rubbed her palm to erase the sensation.

His dark eyes seemed to turn intense and moody. "I think everyone within a five-mile radius of you is gonna be sparkly before the night's over."

Genna grabbed his arm and whispered something in his ear. He turned back to his date. She tried to concentrate on football and forget about Jake, which turned out to be pretty easy, after all. It was a very exciting game, and by halftime the Cougars led by two touchdowns.

Lincoln and Jake announced they were making a run to the concession stand and took orders from everyone. Genna and Dinah decided to brave the restroom. The line at halftime for the ladies was usually halfway around the stadium so Marla decided not to risk it. She'd probably get tripped up on her ribbons and fall and break her neck going down the bleachers.

The marching band filed out onto the playing field in formation. She laughed when they broke into a neutered rendition of "Sexy Back." The old high school bandleader, Mr. Griffin, would be spinning in his grave.

People kept stopping to chat with her on their way to the concession stand. She figured most folks wanted a close-up look at the mum. The way this town liked to gossip, she wouldn't be surprised to hear by morning that Harry Beal hadn't just given her the mum to beat all mums, but had asked her to marry him and bear his children, to boot.

"Evening, Marla Jean." She recognized Bradley's voice even before she turned to look at him.

He was wearing his tan corduroy pants and the ragged Everson Cougar sweatshirt he wore to every game since she'd known him. Instead of his usual baseball cap, a jaunty black beret sat atop his blond hair and instead of his usual friendly demeanor, the expression in his blue eyes simmered somewhere between sad and stormy.

She remembered the way he'd come home on Friday afternoons and start the frantic search for his lucky purple sweatshirt even though it was always folded up neatly in his dresser drawer. She used to find his zeal endearing. Now she just wondered if he did his own laundry these days, or if he'd conned Libby into doing it for him. "Evening, Bradley. Are you enjoying the game?"

He eyed the profusion of blossoms on her chest and gave a noncommittal shrug. "Sure, if they keep the running game going we should be able to put this one in the win column." He always sounded like he was doing an interview for sports radio when he talked about Everson football. He nudged her over so he could sit beside her on the bleachers. In a pained voice that said he was only doing this for her own good, he warned her, "You seem to be making quite a spectacle of yourself lately, Marla Jean."

She scooted away from him. "You're one to talk. What's that thing on your head?"

He touched the beret self-consciously. "At present I'm exploring 19th century French literature—you know, Flaubert, Dumas, Hugo—but enough about me."

"I didn't know reading required costumes," she quipped.

He wouldn't allow himself to be distracted. "Don't change the subject. I want to talk about you. First Donny Joe and now this. Look at that ridiculous thing you're wearing. Not to mention Coach Beal running through the stands before the game, waving it behind him like he was flying a dad-gummed kite."

Resentment strong and powerful flooded her body. The gall of the man. She suddenly decided her big-assed mum was the prettiest thing on the face of the earth. Harry had gone out of his way to do something special just for her, and okay, so he'd gone a little overboard, but she'd be damned if she'd let Bradley dismiss it as ridiculous. Damn him, anyway.

She unclenched her jaw and smiled sweetly. "Wasn't that just the dearest thing you've ever seen?" She picked up a ribbon and held it out for his perusal. "Look, Bradley, this ribbon has Harry's name on it, and this one has mine in glitter. It's been years since a man gave me flowers." A nice shower of iridescent glitter settled on his pants leg.

He seemed affronted by her statement. "I used to give you flowers."

"Yeah, as I recall, the day you told me you were leaving me for Libby you brought me a big bunch of daisies. And I threw them in your face. That doesn't count."

"Being bitter doesn't become you." He tried brushing the sparkles from his pants, but they clung stubbornly to the grooves in the corduroy.

"I'm not bitter, Bradley. I'm moving on, just like you did. I would think that would make you happy."

"So, this thing with you and Harry Beal is serious?"

"I hope not." She winked and gave him her best saucy smile. "I'm not in the market for serious."

He looked like he'd swallowed a June bug. "You're certainly not the woman I married, Marla Jean."

It was all she could do not to pull out one of the long pearl-tipped pins holding the mum in place and jab him smack dab in the cornea, but she managed to hold onto her dignity by the skinniest of threads. "No, but I'm the woman you divorced. You better get on back to Libby, now."

He didn't move, but sat watching her like she'd sprouted feathers. She stared straight ahead. If she ignored him long enough, he was bound to go away.

Another voice got her attention. "Hey, Marla Jean, are you two-timing me with Harry Beal?" Donny Joe Ledbetter stood at the end of the aisle smiling like the very idea tickled him pink. "By the way, that's some hood ornament you're wearing there."

Marla was delighted to see him. "Hey, Donny Joe." Finally, a man who didn't take everything so seriously. "You know me. I like to keep a spare man handy for emergencies."

Donny Joe thumbed the brim of his cowboy hat up and winked. "I hear ya, sugar."

Jake came trotting back to the seats loaded down with

a full drink carrier in one hand and nachos and popcorn in the other. Fighting with the ribbons, she stood up to help him before he spilled it all. He took one look at the other men surrounding Marla Jean and said, "Why don't you get lost, Donny Joe. You too, Bradley."

"Well, well," Donny Joe declared. "If it ain't Jake, the bodyguard."

Bradley threw up his hands and scooted out of the aisle glowering at Donny Joe on his way past. "I can see I'm wasting my time here. I'll see you tomorrow night, Jake."

Marla looked from Bradley to Jake and back again.

"Yeah, sure," Jake said, looking out of sorts.

Bradley nodded curtly and started the climb back up to his perch at the top of the stadium.

Before Marla could sit back down Donny Joe grabbed her hand. "Any chance you're gonna be at Lu Lu's tomorrow night?"

She hesitated. "My plans for tomorrow night aren't exactly nailed down yet." She should probably stay home and give the good folks of Everson a chance to gossip about somebody else.

He leaned into her space smelling like spice and good times. "Well, if you happen to end up at Lu Lu's, save a dance for me. Okay?"

"Sure thing, Donny Joe." And maybe some wild, uninhibited woman would invade her body tonight while she was sleeping so she could take him up on what he was offering, but she wasn't holding her breath.

He kissed her hand, winked at Jake, and whistled as he sauntered down the stadium steps.

Jake watched him go and then shook his head at her in disbelief. Before he could start up about Donny Joe and her choices in men she asked, "What did Bradley mean when he said he'd see you tomorrow night?"

He looked embarrassed. "Bradley and Libby invited my mother and me to have dinner at his house tomorrow night."

"Oh." She didn't know why it bothered her. It wasn't as if she expected him to cut off all contact with his aunt. She raised her chin and faked a pleasant expression. "That should be nice."

Jake sat down and swiveled around to face her. "Nice? It won't be nice. It'll be a colossal pain in the backside, but I promised my mother I'd go and be polite, so I will."

"Oh, how bad can it be?" She laughed at his long-suffering expression. "But seriously, Jake, if your aunt is trying to make things work with Bradley, you won't be able to avoid them forever."

"Are you gonna give me advice on how to handle him? It seems kind of strange to be getting counsel from his ex-wife."

She shook her head. "No, I'm not giving you advice. I'm just saying I think he might really love her, so of course he wants a chance to prove himself to her family. Bradley's big on needing approval."

He tilted his head to the side and studied her. "It seems to me that love is an easy promise to make, but not such an easy promise to keep."

"When did you get so cynical?" This was a side of Jake she didn't know.

"I'm not cynical. I'm realistic. How many happily-ever-afters do you see when you look around? Your marriage couldn't even make it to the seven-year itch, and my parents' marriage was no walk in the park, that's for sure."

"What about my parents—"

He held up his hand, cutting her off. "And your parents don't count. Their relationship is some kind of freak of nature."

"Okay. Well, there's Lincoln and Dinah."

He shrugged. "They show potential. Check back with me in ten years."

"Wow. I'm the one that's been burned, and you're the one that wants love to come with some kind of ironclad guarantee." She understood caution. After all, a serious relationship was the last thing she wanted right now, but that didn't mean somewhere far, far down the road she wouldn't be ready to try again.

"I just believe in playing the odds. That's all, kiddo." He handed her one of the drinks from the carrier beside him.

Her fingers brushed his, and this time she felt the jolt in places she was too polite to think about in public. She hid her reaction and managed to take the drink without dumping it in his lap.

After finding her composure, she said, "If you ask me, Jake, I'd say you're afraid to play at all."

It was meant as a lighthearted taunt, but he fired back as if she'd struck a nerve. "And I'd say you're ready to play with anyone who asks, Marla Jean."

Marla looked up to see Jake's date standing at the end of the aisle listening to their conversation. Genna was wearing an expression that would curdle cream cheese when she asked, "And what exactly are you two playing?"

Chapter Eight

～

Jake pushed open the door to Romeo's pizza place, allowing Genna to walk in ahead of him.

"Thank you, Jake." She looked back at him, gracing him with one of her full-blown man-killer smiles, a smile she normally wouldn't bother wasting on him.

God help him.

He smiled his I'm-gonna-pretend-you're-not-acting-weird smile. "Sure thing, Genna."

He'd half expected her to ask him to take her straight home after the game. She'd been in a snit the whole second half, but now she'd decided to go the flirty, territorial route. Her long red nails sank into the leather of his jacket as she grabbed his arm. He didn't like women who were territorial, especially not when it was Genna—queen of having a good time and playing the field. That's why they normally got along so well. Over the years they'd agreed on three things—no strings, no baggage, and no expectations.

But damn if Genna didn't seem to be expecting something from him tonight. Ever since they sat down at the game with Linc and Dinah, and by default, Marla Jean, she'd been acting downright jealous. Maybe it was all the attention Marla Jean was getting lately. Genna didn't like playing second fiddle to anyone, and what with Marla's divorce and being newly single, Genna would naturally view her as competition. Which probably explained her sudden clinginess. He was sure she'd heard about his tussle with Donny Joe. Everyone else in town had. And she'd probably heard that Marla Jean was the reason, too.

But he didn't owe Genna any kind of explanation. Period. End of subject, as far as he was concerned. Accountability had never been a part of their relationship. Despite their understanding, he didn't think she was seeing it that way tonight.

The pizza place vibrated with loud conversation and hoots of laughter as the town folks got busy celebrating the team's victory. Jake spotted Linc and Dinah already at a table in the corner and herded Genna in that direction.

Linc waved at the chairs across from them. "Sit down, guys. I ordered a pitcher of beer. If you want anything else to drink, you're on your own."

Genna actually simpered when she said, "I'll take a diet soda, please Jake."

Jake held out Genna's chair while she sat and said, "You got it. I'll be right back."

Jake made his way through the tables full of people to the counter and ordered Genna's drink. Marla Jean and Harry Beal weren't there yet. Not that he was keeping track. He saw Bradley and Aunt Libby in the next room sitting at a big table with their friends. He'd avoided speaking to his aunt at the game, but he knew he should at least say hello. He was going to put that off for a while longer if he could.

Shouts of congratulations greeted members of the football team as they came straggling in, their hair still wet from showers, their faces flushed with the thrill of winning the big game.

"Way to go, boys."

"Great game, fellas."

Coach Beal came in next with Marla Jean on his arm. Jake thought he looked like he'd won more than a football game. She came in weighed down by that stupid mum, smiling at Harry like he was some kind of conquering hero. Something in Jake's gut tightened. She looked ridiculous. She looked beautiful. She looked happy.

From across the room she caught his eye and lifted her hand in a brief greeting. He raised an eyebrow in acknowledgment before she was swept off into the crowd of football players.

Determined not to give Marla Jean Bandy another thought, Jake grabbed Genna's diet soda and headed back to the table. It was Linc's fault he'd gotten dragged back into Marla Jean's life in the first place, but that wouldn't stop him from trying to kick his butt if he knew the kinds of thoughts he'd been having about his baby sister the last couple of days.

Genna sat quietly, not joining in the conversation—not at all her usual life-of-the-party self. And he felt guilty about that, because if nothing else, he and Genna had been friends for a long time. Besides, he'd been raised to dance with the one who "brung" him. Whatever the hell was going on in his mixed-up, sideways brain, he needed to get his act together, pronto.

• • •

Marla Jean sat beside Harry as he relived every play of the game in exacting detail, and found with surprise she was enjoying herself. Harry's pride in the team, and his excitement about the win, was contagious. When they arrived he'd insisted that they sit at a table away from the players since they were supposed to be on a date. A date. At first she cringed at the implication, but what the heck, she might as well give in and call it what it was. A duck by any other name would quack as loud and all that. She sighed. It was definitely a date.

That's what her new, big life plan was all about, wasn't it? Getting back out there. Stepping up to life again and Harry was attentive and entertaining. He told her how he'd anguished about whether to call a screen pass or a run on the crucial third-down play in the fourth quarter, and it was actually kind of touching to watch him talk about something that meant so much to him. He gave everything to his job and the boys on the team. That was clear. Who knew quiet, steady Harry Beal had such passion inside him?

Her brother's distinctive laughter drifted in occasionally from the other room, and she tried not to wonder if Jake was laughing, too. She also did her best to ignore Bradley and Libby across the way. Her ex-husband's face had turned into a thundercloud when she came walking in with Harry, and she'd made a point of not looking in their direction since then. If Bradley was going to act like a jerk every time she looked at another man, it was going to get old fast.

Harry nodded toward the extra chair that held her jacket and the giant corsage. She'd made an excuse about being warm and taken it off the minute they'd gotten inside. "So, I guess the mum was good luck," he said.

She wanted to discourage that kind of thinking. "I really don't think it was the mum, Harry. I think it was your coaching."

"Well, just to be safe, I plan to get you an even bigger one for the next game."

Marla tried to keep a neutral expression on her face. The next game. And a bigger mum. Good gravy. She hadn't really planned on a repeat performance. Not that seeing Harry again was out of the question. Maybe a dinner date or a movie, but she didn't really want the job as the high school football team's good luck charm. That was way too much pressure. Her stomach made a loud growling sound.

Harry looked embarrassed. "You must be hungry, and here I am yammering on about the game. It's not like you weren't right there watching it the whole time. But I get carried away. What kind of pizza do you want?"

"Pepperoni's my favorite, but I'll eat anything except onions. I'd rather not have onions."

"Pepperoni it is, then." He waved at a waiter and leaned toward her and said in a low voice, "I'm with you. No onions unless we're both eating them, right?" Then he winked.

It was so unexpected, so un-Harry like it took her a moment to realize what he was implying. "No, actually, I'm allergic. Onions make me break out in big welts, and I get violently ill."

"Oh." He straightened in his chair, looking a bit flustered. "No onions then. Absolutely."

Damn it, he'd thought she'd been flirting. She wasn't

sure she remembered how. She needed to regroup. "Harry, would you excuse me for a minute? I'd like to freshen up."

He stood and helped pull out her chair. "Of course, Marla Jean, and I'll order the pizza while you're gone."

"Thanks, I'll be right back." Smiling, she hurried off toward the ladies room.

She pulled the door open and rushed inside. Closeting herself in a stall, she closed the lid and sat down to think. She was lousy at picking up on the games men and women played. It had been too long since she'd had to bother. Like that thing with the onions. Obviously Harry was counting on some extracurricular activity after the pizza. At the very least, a good-night kiss. And it was a reasonable expectation.

It was just too weird, though—the idea that for the rest of her life she'd be kissing other men. Men other than Bradley. She'd kissed Donny Joe Saturday night, but part of the problem had been her brain wouldn't stop analyzing the kiss long enough for her to enjoy it.

Bradley's lips were the only lips she'd kissed for years and years. Okay, so maybe some of the old passion had faded, but it had been comfortable, like slipping into her favorite pair of house shoes. The ratty ones with holes that had been worn so much they molded to fit her feet. If that was her idea of romance, it was no wonder Bradley found another woman.

He'd moved on, and it was time she did the same. If she needed to kiss a bunch of men until she got the hang of it again, she'd just have to persevere. She was going to kiss Harry Beal tonight, and damn it, she was going to enjoy it. Filled with new resolve, she opened the stall door.

Just her luck. Genna Stanley stood in front of the

mirrors touching up her lipstick. After blotting her bright pink lips on a tissue she faced Marla Jean with a glacial smile. "Marla Jean." All semblance of friendliness was gone now that they were alone.

"Genna." Marla acknowledged the other woman before sticking her hands under the automatic water faucet. She pumped out extra blue soap, working up a mound of lather, while hoping Genna would leave, but the woman evidently had a few things to say.

"It won't do you any good, you know." Genna's tone was condescending.

"Sorry?" Marla Jean had a feeling she'd regret asking for an explanation.

"Chasing after Jake the way you have been. It won't do you any good. He feels sorry for you, but that's all."

Marla Jean's scalp prickled with outrage, but she took a deep breath and managed to ask calmly, "And why exactly should he feel sorry for me?"

Genna looked at her like she was thickheaded. "Well, it's not just Jake. It's the whole town. If my husband dumped me for a woman old enough to be my grandma, I wouldn't want to show my face. But look at you, out and about. I actually admire that, Marla Jean."

She decided to ignore the whole town part and focus on the Jake part since she had no doubt he was the bone of Genna's contention. "Jake and I have been friends since we were kids, Genna. I don't need your two cents on what he's feeling."

With a flip of her blonde hair Genna informed her pointedly, "As long as you realize a friend is all you'll ever be, sweetie, then we're cool."

Marla pulled some towels from the metal dispenser

hanging on the wall and dried her hands while struggling to keep a lid on her temper. "Your concern is real touching, Genna, but if you want to know a secret, sweetie, I'm not the one who's been doing the chasing."

So what if it was just so he could play the big brother. Genna didn't need to know that. Pleased at having had the last word, she threw the paper towels into the trash can, turned on her heels and marched toward the bathroom door, pushing it open with greater force than necessary.

"Ow!" A yowl of pain came from the other side of the door as she felt it smack into something solid.

Opening the door, Marla Jean came face to face with the woman who'd caused the whole town to feel sorry for her. Libby Comstock staggered and fell into her arms.

Chapter Nine

◦

Oh, Miss Comstock, I'm so sorry." Marla Jean stepped forward to catch her. This part was just plain awkward. Marla Jean had called the woman "Miss Comstock" since she was a little girl. Just because Bradley was boffing her now didn't mean she suddenly felt comfortable addressing her by her first name.

Miss Comstock swayed a bit, holding one hand over her nose. Her eyes were red and watering. Terrific. Marla Jean had managed to avoid a direct confrontation with the woman for months, and now she'd bashed her face in with half the town as witnesses.

Right behind her, Genna came barreling out of the bathroom all in a tizzy. She pushed Marla Jean out of the way and put an arm around the older woman. "Oh Lordy, Miss Comstock, let me help you."

"Libby? *Mon amour*, are you all right?" Bradley came rushing over, his face filled with alarm, his beret slipping down over one eye. He took one look at her and wheeled around. "What did you do, Marla Jean? Did you hit her?"

"Don't be an idiot, Bradley. Of course I didn't hit her. I mean, I hit her with the door, but—"

The room had gotten quiet as people close by stopped eating to watch the drama unfolding.

"You hit her with the door?" Bradley's voice was loud and filled with accusation.

"Simmer down, Bradley," Libby croaked. "I wasn't watching where I was going."

Genna surrendered Libby into Bradley's care, and in a voice that projected, a voice she probably hadn't used since her cheerleader days, she declared scornfully, "Really, Marla Jean, you ought to be ashamed." Shaking her head, she walked away.

Marla Jean thought Genna ought to be ashamed of that chicken fried excuse of a blonde hairdo she wore on her head, but right now she had more pressing matters on her hands.

"I feel just awful." Marla Jean reached out her hand in a feeble gesture of apology.

"You should feel awful." Bradley batted her hand away and wrapped his arm around Libby's waist, while glaring daggers at Marla Jean.

Libby still had her hand over her nose and her voice quavered. "Nonsense, it wasn't Marla Jean's fault, Brad. Can we just go sit down, please? I'm still a little wobbly."

"Of course, *ma chérie*." He led Libby away murmuring French sweet nothings, but not before he glowered at Marla Jean once more for good measure.

"I really am sorry," she offered again as they walked away. Whispered conversation picked up again around her, and she saw the not-so-discreet glimpses in her direction. She didn't know whether to laugh or cry. Over at the table she could see Harry deep in conversation with the father of one of his players. Thankfully, he seemed to have missed the entire incident. How, she didn't know, but he was busy talking football, so he probably wouldn't miss her if she slipped outside for a few minutes, either.

It occurred to her as she scurried to the front door of the restaurant and stepped outside that she'd been spending a lot of time during her evenings out walking around in parking lots.

Pacing up and down the first line of cars and trucks, she tried to control the flush of anger and mortification rushing through her. Where did Bradley get off acting so indignant? And why did she feel like some kind of bully? If Libby hadn't been so much older than her, she wouldn't be feeling bad at all. It would have felt like some kind of cosmic justice that placed Libby on the other side of the door at the exact moment she was marching out of it. The woman had stolen her husband for Pete's sake, and smacking her in the face seemed like a piddly-assed punishment compared to what she really deserved.

And it wasn't as if Marla Jean had done it on purpose, but of course, she would be painted as the bad guy in all this. Just because the woman was old. That had to be some kind of reverse ageism.

She wanted to lash out at something, and the tire on the pick-up truck in front of her was handy. She hauled off and gave it a swift kick, and nearly doubled over in pain.

"Shit, mother friggin' son of a bitch," she yelled, getting a disapproving look from some late-arriving parents. Sinking to the ground, she cradled her foot. Under her breath she muttered, "Damn, damn, damn, damn, damn." It felt like she'd broken all five toes.

"What the hell are you doing, Marla Jean."

Jake's deep voice seeped through the fog of her misery. Great. Jake acting all high and mighty was all she needed. She continued to rock back and forth. "I just broke your aunt's nose, and now I'm looking for some more old ladies to beat up. What does it look like I'm doing?"

"I heard what happened with Aunt Libby. Are you all right?" He squatted down on his haunches beside her.

"Just peachy." She struggled to her feet, wincing when she tried to put weight on her foot.

He offered his hand to help but she ignored it. "What's wrong with your foot?" he demanded.

She nodded at the pick-up parked in front of them. "I kicked that tire, and it kicked back."

He looked at the Dodge Ram truck and then looked back at her. "You kicked my truck tire? Are you nuts? I swear you can find more ways to get into trouble than any ten women I've ever known."

"So, who asked for your two cents? And a thousand apologies. I didn't realize it was your truck. Geez, you seem more worried about your precious truck than you do your aunt." Figuring she should go try to salvage what was left of her date, she limped back toward the pizza place. Her toes were swelling up inside her boot with every step.

Before she realized what he was doing Jake scooped her up into his arms. "Aunt Libby is fine. And I don't give a rat's ass about my truck, but you can barely walk. I'm taking you to the emergency room." He opened the truck door and started to set her inside.

"You can't do that. Harry will be wondering what happened to me by now, and Genna isn't going to like it if you disappear."

"Harry should have been paying closer attention, but you're right." He nudged the truck door closed and still holding her in his arms started marching toward Romeo's front door.

For a moment she bounced along with her arms wrapped around his neck, forgetting to be incensed by his overbearing manner. His stubborn chin was right at eye level and he smelled like leather and a hint of aftershave. Then she came to her senses and tried to wriggle out of his hold. "What are you doing, Jake? Let go of me this instant."

He ignored her, pulled open the restaurant door, and walked inside. If she'd thought people were staring at her before, it was nothing compared to the wide-eyed ogling she was subjected to now.

Linc stood up as soon as they walked in the door. "What's going on, Jake?"

"Marla Jean hurt her foot. She needs to go to the emergency room."

"You okay, sis?" Linc and Dinah both hurried over.

"I'm fine, Linc. Just call off your guard dog." She shoved at the unyielding wall of Jake's chest, but he ignored her.

Harry charged into the front room. "What in the world? What happened, Marla Jean?"

"It's nothing, Harry. It was stupid, really. I hurt my foot. Put me down, Jake." She said the last part under her breath, a little more adamantly this time.

"She needs to go to the emergency room, and I'm not going to stand around discussing it, so ya'll can follow or not. That's where we'll be." Jake made the announcement and then turned to leave.

"Hold on, I'm coming, too," Harry announced. He ran back to their table and grabbed her jacket and purse.

Marla Jean felt awful. This was a big night for the football team. "Harry, you should stay here with the team and celebrate. Lincoln will make sure I get home okay."

He glanced at the team and back at her, looking torn. "Are you sure?"

The muscles in Jake's arms bunched beneath her as he shifted her in his arms impatiently.

"I'm positive," Marla Jean insisted. "But I'll make it up to you. What if I cook dinner one night next week?"

Harry smiled and handed the purse and mum-laden jacket to Dinah, who was hovering nearby. "That would be super. I'll call tomorrow, and see how you're doing."

"Great. I'll look forward to it." Marla Jean was glad he was taking it so well.

"Yeah, great," Jake said. "If you two are through filling in your social calendars, we better get going."

"In a minute, but first, put me down. I mean it, Jake."

He didn't look happy, but he stood her on her feet. She hobbled two steps over to Harry who met her halfway. "I had a great time tonight, Harry." She leaned up and kissed him on the mouth. It was short and chaste, but it got the crowd murmuring. Harry stood stock still, looking all but bowled over when the kiss ended. Jake snorted and swept her back up into his arms before Harry had a chance to kiss her back.

Marla waved at Harry over Jake's shoulder as he turned and headed out the door. "Bye, Harry. I'm really sorry."

That seemed to break Harry out of his stupor. His face bloomed into a grin as broad as a side of beef. "Bye, Marla Jean. I'll call first thing tomorrow."

Marla caught a glimpse of Bradley and Libby staring from their table. Bradley was looking at her with a creased brow, like she'd disappointed him somehow, again, and she had the urge to flip him the bird. She resisted because she was a mature woman, and because her toes hurt like somebody had taken a croquet mallet to them.

Looking around for Jake's date, Marla Jean asked, "What about Genna?"

Jake's expression revealed nothing when he said, "Genna took off a few minutes ago. She implied that I wasn't much fun tonight."

"Oh." After her encounter with Genna in the bathroom, Marla Jean didn't know what to think about that.

Jake was already halfway to his truck, and since she didn't seem to have much choice in the matter, she held on tighter and gritted her teeth against the pain.

"We're right behind you, sis," Linc yelled. Marla could see all the purple and gold ribbons from her mum streaming behind Dinah as they hurried to their car.

Jake didn't even slow down. This time when he set her inside his truck he scooted her to the middle and turned her so her foot was straight out on the bench seat. "Is that all right?"

"I'll live. And thanks, Jake." She decided she might as well give in to the inevitable and quit fighting him every inch of the way. He was an obstinate man, and it seemed come hell, high water, or a plague of locusts he was taking her to the emergency room.

He scrutinized her for half a beat, like he didn't quite trust her sudden change in demeanor, but then closed her door and walked around to the driver's side. Once he was behind the wheel he reached around her, fastening the seatbelt. "Lean against me, if you need to. I'll try not to hit too many pot holes on the way."

"What? No Lucinda tonight?" She grimaced and stretched out her leg, happy not to be stuffed into his beloved sports car.

"Genna doesn't like Lucinda. Says she cramps her style, but I think she's jealous."

"I bet." She didn't really give a hoot what Genna did or didn't like, but talking kept her mind off the pain. "So, what kind of rough, tough name might a pick-up truck of yours be blessed with? Rambo? Elvis? Rooster Cogburn?"

He patted the dashboard of the Dodge like it was his prizewinning hound dog. "Don't be silly. Marla Jean, meet Gertrude. If you ask real nice you can call her Miss Gertie for short."

He put Gertie in reverse and backed up. Lincoln pulled in behind him and tooted his horn. Jake gave a wave in the rearview mirror and took off like it was a matter of life and death.

Marla Jean closed her eyes, leaned against Jake's shoulder, and tried to ignore her throbbing toes. "Nice to make your acquaintance, Miss Gertie."

Jake paced around the waiting room, trying not to feel like ten kinds of foolish. He'd practically kidnapped Marla Jean from her date with Harry Beal. Harry could have taken her to the emergency room. Lincoln and Dinah could have driven her, for that matter. But he hadn't allowed himself to stop and think. He'd just reacted.

It was fortunate that Genna had gotten fed up with him and left with Scott Barley. She told him that she and Scott were going to go play pool at Clicks, and he could tell she wanted him to object.

He hadn't been able to dredge up the energy. He kissed her on the cheek, and said he'd talk to her later. She'd told him not to bother. Maybe he'd send her some flowers tomorrow, try to make amends. It wasn't her fault he'd been in such a lousy mood, and knowing Genna, she was probably having a high old time with Scott Barley at this very moment. Out of sight, out of mind. That was the way she always played the game. But none of that excused his lack of attention.

Right after Genna left, he'd seen Marla Jean rush out of Romeo's and without asking himself why, he'd gotten up to follow her. It should have been her date or her big brother looking after her, but Linc was occupied with his new wife. He glanced into the other room and saw Harry talking to a group of parents and players. Obviously, he wasn't concerned about her, either. And then he noticed his Aunt Libby and Bradley Bandy. Her hand was covering her face and the slime ball was patting her back soothingly. His instinct was to go after Marla Jean, but familial duty and genuine concern for his aunt won out.

"Are you okay, Aunt Libby?" He approached their table in time to hear Bradley ask if she wanted to leave.

"Oh, Jake." She looked happy to see him. They hadn't talked much since she'd taken up with Marla Jean's husband.

Ex-husband.

"What happened?" he demanded glaring at Bradley like it must be his fault.

His aunt answered, "It was so silly. I walked into the bathroom door just as someone was coming out."

Bradley got all huffy. In a strident voice he announced. "Not just someone. It was Marla Jean."

The man could be such a dipshit. No wonder she'd hurried outside like hunting dogs were nipping at her heels.

"Now, Bradley, it was an accident. My nose is a little sore, but I'm going to be fine. Please stop making such a fuss over it."

Jake laid a hand on his aunt's shoulder. "Well, if you're okay, I'm going to go check on Marla Jean. I'm sure she's upset about what happened."

His aunt reached up and patted his hand. "Thanks, Jake. And tell her not to worry about it, for goodness sakes." She hesitated and then asked, "We'll see you tomorrow night, won't we?" She sounded so uncertain it broke his heart.

"Ma and I are both looking forward to it." She squeezed his hand, and before he said anything to Bradley he'd regret, he left to find Marla Jean.

And now here he was, prowling around the emergency room waiting to hear how she was doing. Lincoln and Dinah had gone with her once the nurse called her to the back, and he'd been left in the waiting room feeling about as necessary as a ninth leg on an octopus.

The woman wasn't his concern. That was the same argument he'd been having with himself for the past week. He wasn't her brother, either, but damn it, somebody needed to take care of her. She'd hate that. She'd told him as much last Saturday night at Lu Lu's. But she'd been sitting out in the parking lot all alone kicking tires, for God's sake, and that wasn't right.

Linc came out of the gray swinging doors and waved him over. "She wants to see you."

Jake was past Linc and through the doors in a flash. "Is she okay?"

"The doctor said she'll be on crutches for a while. She really did a number on her foot. She has a sprained ankle, two broken toes, and she cracked two others."

Linc pointed him to the examination room. Dinah smiled as he came in and moved to stand by Lincoln. Marla was sitting on the table with her foot wrapped in an ACE bandage.

"Hey Jake! Did you know they had to cut off my boot?" She had a loopy smile on her face.

"I'm sorry." Jake saw a pair of cowboy boots on the floor. Girly beige boots decorated with green vines and pink flowers. One had been irreparably sliced open. "I hear you broke some toes."

"Yep. Broke 'em in two. Just like that." She giggled and tried unsuccessfully to snap her fingers.

Linc shook his head. "You never could handle pain pills, sis." To Jake he said, "They make her downright goofy."

"I can see that." He watched Dinah grab Linc's hand and pull him out of the room. Linc gave his wife a questioning look, but followed without arguing.

"I wanna get out of here, Jake," Marla said, waving him closer. "Take me home, would ja?" She lay down on the table and stretched. "I'll even let you tuck me in, if you want."

"Is that right?" Jake ignored her seductive tone. "Let me go find the nurse then."

She grabbed his arm before he could leave. "Oh, and I didn't eat any onions, if you know what I mean." She gave him an exaggerated wink and waggled her eyebrows. Her stomach made a loud growling noise, causing her to frown. "Come to think of it, I haven't eaten anything since lunch."

Before he could figure out what the heck she was talking about the nurse came waltzing into the room pushing a wheelchair and holding a clipboard. "Here you go. Sign these forms, and you're free to go." Linc and Dinah returned to hover in the doorway.

Marla Jean struggled to a sitting position. "It's about time. Give me that pen, Nurse Bloomfield."

"Mind your manners, missy." The nurse scolded Marla Jean before handing her the clipboard. They'd all known Nurse Bloomfield since they were kids. She worked as the school nurse at the junior high during the week, and took shifts at the hospital emergency room on weekends. Even though she was getting up in years she never seemed to slow down.

"Will we need to rent crutches?" Linc asked.

"I've got a pair she can use," Dinah said. "They're up in the attic, Linc. You'll have to crawl up and get them down."

"That's fine," Nurse Bloomfield interjected, "but for the next few days she needs to stay off her foot as much as possible. Make an appointment with Doc Baker for Monday, Marla Jean. He'll tell you when you can go from crutches to a walking boot. And here's a prescription for pain medication the doctor ordered."

Lincoln took the prescription while Jake picked up Marla Jean from the exam table and turned toward the wheelchair.

"Why don't you just carry me some more, Jake?" She made cow eyes at him.

"And get in trouble with Nurse Bloomfield? Not a

chance," He tried to put her in the chair, but Marla Jean held on stubbornly until he pried her arms off of his neck.

"Hospital policy says you'll ride out of here in the wheelchair, young lady." Nurse Bloomfield gave her a stern look over the top of her glasses. "And you mind your family. Relax and let them take care of you."

"I'll push," Jake ordered. "You sit."

"You're not the boss of me, Jake Jacobson." Marla Jean shook her finger in his face.

Linc was laughing as he ran ahead to hold the doors open. "Did you hear that, sis? You have to mind us. This might not be so bad, after all."

"I've got your purse," Dinah said helpfully and trotted along beside while Jake wheeled her outside. "Do you want us to stay with you tonight?"

"Oh no, don't be silly, Dinah. I'll be fine and dandy."

"Lincoln, tell her she shouldn't be alone. She's supposed to stay off her foot."

Marla Jean waved a hand in Dinah's direction. "Don't be such a worry wart. I plan to go to bed and stay there, and it's not going to kill me to limp back and forth to the bathroom when the need arises. If y'all want to stop by and bring me breakfast tomorrow morning, I won't say no, but otherwise, go home and sleep in your own bed."

"I don't know," Lincoln hesitated.

Jake knew he'd regret it, but he opened his big mouth and volunteered. "I'll sleep on the living room couch and keep an eye on her."

"Jake, you don't have to do that," Lincoln protested. "We've imposed on you enough lately."

"Hey, I'm working across the street at the old house right now, anyway, and Marla Jean's couch is probably more comfortable than the creaky twin bed I've been sacking out on every night."

Dinah looked amused, and Lincoln looked uncertain.

Marla Jean smiled serenely before listing sideways in the wheelchair. "Oh goodie, Jake will take me home. It's all settled then."

Jake, on the other hand, had never felt more unsettled in his life.

Chapter Ten

~~

Marla Jean rocked along on the bench seat of Jake's truck all drowsy and contented. Her cheek was nestled against his shoulder. Solid, warm, covered in leather. He smelled divine. And if that wasn't enough to make the world a lovely place, her toes didn't hurt. In fact, nothing hurt. The pain medication had taken care of that and gone to her head like a downed slug of whiskey. Singing suddenly seemed like an absolutely grand idea.

She opened her mouth and warbled, "I'm forever blowing bubbles..."

Jake cut his eyes in her direction, but kept his opinion of her vocal talent to himself. She knew she couldn't carry a tune in a bucket and seldom remembered the right words, but she always tried to make up for it in volume.

"Soapy bubbles I declare. They drift along while I sing my song, and like my dreams they just burst in midair."

The last line of the song put a damper on her sunny mood. She scrunched up her face in a grumpy frown. "Life is like a bubble, don't you think, Jake?"

"If you say so." He kept his eyes on the road.

"I mean you're floating along pretty as you please, over hill and dale, and then pop! Life as you know it is over. Done. Finished. And you're nothing but a soapy spot in somebody's front yard, all alone and forgotten."

"That's very philosophical."

"I know," she nodded twisting to face him. "I'm a very deep thinker these days."

"All that thinking will curdle your brain. Sounds like you have too much time on your hands."

"Exactly. You've hit the nail on the head, buddy boy. And that's why I've decided to take up kissing."

"Pardon me?"

"I owe it to myself."

"You lost me, Marla Jean."

"It's really very simple. Your aunt," she whispered as if it was a secret, "is certainly floating Bradley's boat these days. But what about mine? Huh? Nobody gives a fig about my boat."

"What happened to the bubbles?"

She had a sneaky feeling he was making fun of her, so she decided to ignore him. "That's why I had to kiss Harry."

"To float your boat?" he asked.

She sighed. "I wish it was that simple. But no, I had to kiss him cuz he wasn't Bradley."

He made a harrumphing sound. "So you're trying to make Bradley jealous?"

"Don't be silly." She reached over and tweaked his nose. "He's a soapy spot on yesterday's lawn as far as I'm concerned, but he was Dial and Donny Joe is more like Irish Spring and Harry—well I'm not sure about Harry yet, maybe Lava. But you get the idea."

"I couldn't be more confused if you were speaking Chinese."

"That's all right. Don't worry your pretty little head about it, Jake, old boy. I just came up with the plan tonight, so I haven't worked out all the kinks. The kissing kinks. Or the kinks in the kissing. Well, you get the idea."

They pulled up in front of the house, and Jake shut off the engine. He got out and walked around to the passenger side. Marla Jean patted Gertie on the dashboard. "Thanks for the lift, old girl. It's been a slice. I like Gertie, Jake," she told him when he opened her door.

"That's good to know," Jake said. Picking her up from the seat of the truck, he carried her up the front steps.

She tucked her head against his shoulder, enjoying the ride while it lasted. "You don't have to stay, you know. You should go home. I'll just give a yoo-hoo if I need something."

"Fat chance," he said without breaking stride. "I told your brother I'd watch out for you, and I will. Lincoln would tan my hide if I just dropped you off like a sack of potatoes and went home." Jake shifted her so he could unlock the front door. "You weigh a hell of a lot more than a sack of potatoes, by the way."

"That's because I have curves. Womanly curves. I'm not the scrawny kid you used to know."

He went down the hall to her old bedroom but stopped when he walked in and saw the easel set up and all the paintings lining the walls, but no bed. "Wow, you've been busy."

"I'm painting again. I even signed up for some art classes."

"That's nice, but where do you sleep?"

"Oops." Marla Jean giggled. "I forgot to tell you I'm using my parents' bedroom now." Being careful of her foot, he turned around and went the other direction and she asked, "Okay, back to this thing between you and my brother. What exactly did Lincoln do that has you in his debt?"

"That's between me and Lincoln. Your brother's one of the good guys though. But you already know that."

"Okay, I can take a hint. I'll quit prying."

"That'll be the day." He sat her down on the yellow wing chair in the corner of the bedroom and started turning down the bed. "What about pajamas?" He walked to her dresser and looked questioningly at the drawers.

"Second drawer from the top." It made her feel odd to see him in her bedroom, sorting through her personal stuff. He picked up the Dallas Stars jersey she'd worn the last time he'd been over and tossed it to her. Then he kept pawing through the drawer. "What are you looking for now?"

"Pants. You need something to cover up your womanly curves."

Using the arm of the chair for support, she stood up and started limping the few feet to the master bathroom so she could change. "Nah, that's okay. This is fine."

He stopped and shot her a look that said he didn't think so, and her stomach did a flip at the idea that he might be affected by the sight of her showing a little skin. "Okay, okay. Throw me those purple leggings."

He tossed those to her as well, and said, "Can you manage?"

"Why? Are you offering to help?"

He headed for the bedroom door. "Holler when you're

decent, and I'll help you get settled in bed." He left the room without waiting for her answer.

She hopped over to the bathroom and shut the door. Sitting on the closed toilet, she managed to get undressed and into the jersey without much trouble. But the leggings were a different story. She got one leg on without a problem, but when she tried to stretch them over her bandaged toes the pressure hurt too much. And then the room decided to spin.

To hell with modesty, she thought. Not having the energy or the inclination to take them off, she hobbled out of the bathroom, one leg in the leggings and one leg out, and collapsed onto her bed. She stuck her good leg under the covers but left her injured foot out and eased it onto the pillows Jake had thoughtfully stacked at the end of the bed for elevation.

As soon as she became horizontal, exhaustion hit her like a punch from a heavyweight boxer. On top of that, the room insisted on revolving like a runaway tilt-a-whirl. It was only fitting. Her whole evening had been filled with more ups and downs than a carnival ride. She closed her eyes. Between Harry and the mum that ate Chicago, and Bradley and his holier-than-thou attitude, she'd been under way too much stress for an evening that was supposed to be fun.

Actually, smashing Libby's nose in with a bathroom door had been therapeutic in a twisted way. From the beginning, she'd bent over backward to remain civilized about Bradley and Libby's affair. All the upbringing drummed into her head about being a nice girl, and minding her manners, made her stifle her real inclinations. Inclinations which included, but weren't limited to, setting all of Bradley's possessions on fire and slashing the tires of Miss Libby's precious Bookmobile.

But she was too polite, too refined. She hadn't done any of those things, so it was a relief to finally get a lick in. *Bam*—right in the old schnoz-ola. Even though it had been an accident. She giggled, and then sobered.

Some people said there were no such things as accidents.

Kicking Jake's truck tire hadn't been an accident. It had been stupid and pointless and dumb. She'd have been better off baying at the moon. She lay there in a heap, thinking about her mangled foot, thinking about her mangled life.

Wild nights of dancing at Lu Lu's were out for a while. Wild nights in pick-up trucks in Lu Lu's parking lot were out for damn sure. But they'd been out even before she hurt her foot. She just wasn't cut out for casual sex—at least not with guys like Donny Joe. That was the truth of it.

Why couldn't she be more like a man? *Wham*, *bam*, thank you mister. That would solve a lot of problems. She wasn't saying she had to be in love with the guy, but it would have to be someone she liked and respected. What was the term people used these days? Friends with benefits? She wondered if that's what Jake and Genna were. The idea made her restless and squirmy.

There was a knock on the bedroom door, and Jake asked, "Are you decent?"

"Who is it?" she asked in a silly sing-songy voice.

"Florence Nightingale. Who do you think?" Jake told her as he opened the door. He came in carrying a tray. "You said you hadn't eaten since lunch, and I thought you could use something besides pain medication in your stomach."

She scooted up a little in the bed. "Oh, Florence, you're a lifesaver. I could eat a horse."

"You'll have to settle for grilled cheese and tomato soup." He started to set the tray across her lap, but noticed her uncovered leg. He put the tray on the dresser, picked up a plaid throw from the chair, and spread it across her legs.

She shrugged. "I couldn't get those stupid leggings on over my foot, so you'll have to put up with my half-naked body. Try not to swoon."

"Men don't swoon."

"Oh, really? What do men do?"

He retrieved the tray from the dresser and set it across her now safely covered legs. "We throw plaid blankets over anything that looks like trouble."

She brightened. "I look like trouble?"

He leaned over her and adjusted the pillow behind her back to give her better support. His face was only inches from hers. "Marla Jean, you've been trouble since you turned sixteen." Then he winked. That same old infuriating wink that always let her know he didn't mean anything by the remark. She was still good old Marla Jean, and he was still good old Jake.

She leaned forward and kissed him. An impulsive, unbridled kiss, before she could think better of it. Just to let him know that she wasn't the same old Marla Jean he'd always known.

He didn't exactly kiss her back, but he didn't move away, either. She brushed her lips against his again. He tasted like the middle of the night and everything sinful.

A shot of whiskey and slow dancing in dark corners. A stolen touch and skinny-dipping in the moonlight. Damn. That was new. Waxing poetic while she kissed someone had never happened before. She decided to blame it on the pain pills. When she finally pulled away, he blinked. "What was that?"

"I put you on my list." Her voice sounded breathless to her own ears.

"Your list?" He frowned and straightened up.

"You know, my kissing list." Shit. After only one tiny touch of his mouth, lust and yearning roiled around inside her like macaroni in a pot of boiling water, but she strove for a matter-of-fact tone. "And it was a thank-you—for being so nice—taking care of me, and all kiss. Even if you are only doing it because of whatever the hell it is you owe Lincoln." The urge to pull him down onto the bed and lick tomato soup from his navel washed over her like a rogue wave.

"You don't have to thank me, Marla Jean. You're uh... like the little sister I never had." As if he had to keep reminding her. Then he patted her on the head. "And you'd do the same for me, right?"

"Right," she muttered. He'd patted her. On the head. Like a puppy dog who went wee-wee when he was let out in the back yard to do his business. Obviously the kiss made no impression on him whatsoever.

"Now, eat your soup before it gets cold." He walked over to the door and stopped with his hand on the doorknob. "Out of curiosity, how many men are on this kissing list?"

"I'm just getting started, but you were number three."

"Let me guess, Donny Joe, Harry, and me."

"Sorry about that. You were an impulse—ya know, due to proximity and pain pills and gratitude."

"Understood."

"I'll probably kiss millions more before I'm done." But she was beginning to wonder if any of them could compete with that little peck she'd just stolen from Jake.

"Men will be lined up in the streets, kiddo. I'm going to go make up the couch now."

"Sheets and blankets are in the hall closet. I feel like the worst hostess just lying here letting you do all the work."

"I'm not a guest. I'm kind of like family, remember? I'll be back to get your dishes in a bit." He walked out of her room, taking his miraculous kissing lips with him.

She took a big bite of her grilled cheese sandwich and chewed distractedly. To the empty doorway she hollered, "In case you haven't noticed, Abel Jacobson, I already have a brother." Under her breath she added, "And believe me, one brother's enough."

Chapter Eleven

⌒

"Christ on a bagel." Jake hurried away from Marla Jean's bedroom like he was allergic to bees and she was a buzzing hive. What the hell just happened in there?

Marla Jean kissed him.

Okay. It was no big deal. And just like she said, it was motivated by pain pills and proximity. But that kind of thing was just the first step leading down the wrong trail.

He pulled the bedding from the shelf in the linen closet. It wasn't the first time he'd made up the couch in the Jones's living room. As a teenager he'd been known to sleep over when things got ugly over at his house. Usually he slept on one of the twin beds in Lincoln's room, but there had been occasions when Linc had been sick or staying up late working on a school paper, when Jake had been installed on the couch instead. Mrs. Jones never blinked an eye when he showed up on their doorstep. She'd ask if he was hungry and then grab the sheets and an extra pillow, no questions asked.

He remembered one time in particular. His parents had

been fighting, as usual, and he'd stormed out and sought refuge at Linc's house. In the past he'd tried to intervene, tried to get his dad to leave his mother alone, but she'd begged him to stay out of it, telling him later that it only made things worse when he got involved. She apologized with tears in her eyes, while assuring him that she knew how to handle his father.

With all the yelling and accusations and threats going on, it always sounded like they were having a real knock-down-drag-out, but his father never laid a hand on his mother. His specialty was bullying and belittling. He had it down to an art. But his mom liked to say he was all hot air and bluster and once he let off steam, he calmed down like a balloon with a slow leak. She made Jake promise to stay out of their arguments. Reluctantly, he agreed, but he couldn't stay in the house and listen. That was asking too much.

He'd been tossing and turning on the Jones's couch, furious with his dad, furious with his mom, and unable to sleep when Marla Jean snuck in the front door. She'd been out on a date with Bradley. They'd gone steady on and off all through high school. But it was way past her curfew, so she was trying to be quiet. Instead she stumbled into an ottoman. Jake had pushed it out of the way when he put the sheets on the couch and forgot to move it back where it belonged.

"Shitfire and horse dookie." She muttered the unlady-like exclamation under her breath, but he heard it just the same.

He leaned up on one elbow. "You're gonna get in more trouble for cussin' than you are for coming in late, young lady."

"Geez, Jake, you scared the crap out of me. If people wouldn't put dad-gummed obstacles in my way, I wouldn't get caught doing either one." After being initially startled at finding him there, she seemed to take his presence on the family couch in stride. She plopped down on the footstool she'd just tripped over and glared at him.

He could see the hazy shape of her bathed in moonlight from the front window, but the shadows of gray and gold that danced across her face didn't hide the fact that she'd recently been crying.

He sat up all the way, his protective instincts going on full alert. "What's wrong, Marla Jean?"

She stood hastily. "It's nothing, and I better get to bed before Mom wakes up. G'night, Jake."

"If it's nothing, why the hell are you crying? Did Bradley hurt you?" Even before she answered, he felt the urge to go find the punk and see if he could make him bawl like a baby.

"Now who's gonna get in trouble for cussing? Of course he didn't hurt me, unless you count hurt feelings. But I'll live." She started down the hallway.

"Why do you put up with him, Marla Jean?" He'd had a front-row seat to her relationship with this idiot, and he still didn't understand what she saw in him.

She sighed and turned around, though he could barely see her in the dark. Her voice floated to him on the sleepy gray light of the quiet house, and it was filled with frustration and despair. "He can be really sweet sometimes."

"But I'm guessing he wasn't so sweet tonight?" Maybe by asking, he was seeking insight into women in general. Maybe he was trying to understand why a girl like Marla Jean would let a scrawny-assed kid like Bradley Bandy make her feel bad as often as he did. And maybe, while he was at it, Jake was trying to understand his mother, too.

"It's no big deal. He forgot my birthday, that's all." She was standing at the end of the sofa now and tried to sound matter of fact.

"Your birthday's not until next weekend." The fact that he knew that, and Bradley didn't, said a lot.

"Oh, I know, but he made plans to go camping with some of the guys from the baseball team. And it's my fault really. I was dumb enough to assume we'd do something together."

"See, this is what I hate." He shoved to his feet, letting the blanket fall to the couch. She looked startled and took a step back. "The Marla Jean I used to know wouldn't let some asshole treat her like that, and she certainly wouldn't lie down like a whipped dog and take the blame on top of it. What the hell's wrong with you?"

She sank down onto the sofa and stared at him. The tears that she'd managed to control earlier started running down her face again. He sat down beside her and pulled her into a clumsy hug. "Aw, Marla Jean, I'm sorry. I'm an asshole, too."

She buried her face in his collarbone and sniffled, pounding him with a weak fist. "You really are, Abel Jacobson."

He could tell she was trying not to cry. He patted her on the back, feeling her wet lashes brush his neck. Her long arms wound themselves around his waist. She held on to him tightly, exhaling shaky little puffs of air against his collarbone, and his horny teenaged body was suddenly too aware of the way her breasts were rising and falling, her upper body pressed flush against his chest. He found out just how small she felt in his arms, delicate and fragile, and he noticed she smelled sweet and clean, like some fruity shampoo.

He also knew he should take his hands off her.

He patted her again and said, "You know boys are all dicks when it comes to mushy stuff, Marla Jean. I bet Bradley feels bad about all of this, too." He didn't know why he was defending the guy, but the safest path around the swamp of feelings he'd just stumbled into was to put the focus back on her boyfriend.

She shook her head and let out a long sigh. "He sure didn't sound sorry."

"He was probably embarrassed. We hate it when we screw up and get caught."

For some reason, that seemed to put the steel back in her spine. She pushed away from him with eyes flashing. "Well, that's just ignorant. All he had to do was act like he felt bad, even a little bit, for disappointing me, you know? And I would have said, 'Go, have a good time with your buddies.' But no, he had to make me into the bad guy, and I was stupid enough to let him do it."

"You're not stupid, Marla Jean."

She stood up and used her hand to wipe the last of the tears away. "You're right about one thing, Jake. This isn't like me, and I'm sick and tired of coming in last on his list of what's important. So that's it. Bradley Bandy can go fu—"

"Jeez, watch your language, would ja? Your mom's gonna be out here any minute with a bar of soap in her hand, and I don't want to get caught in the crossfire."

She glanced in the direction of her parents' bedroom and wrinkled her nose. "He can go fly a kite. That's all I was going to say, Mr. Hall Monitor." Then she leaned down and kissed him on the cheek. "Thanks for the pep talk, Jake. It was just what I needed." With one last watery smile, she ran off down the hallway.

He watched her disappear into the darkness and lay back down on the couch. After smacking himself in the forehead with the heel of his hand, he rubbed the place on his cheek still tingling from her kiss.

Not that the kiss meant anything. It was nothing. But for the first time since he'd known her, when he thought of Marla Jean, she didn't seem so young, or so bratty. Instead she seemed like a mine buried in the middle of an innocent-looking field. One false step and *kablooey*.

And here he was, all these years later, making up the same couch, still listening to Marla Jean discuss the state of her love life and still trying not to step in something.

Some things never changed. She still thought of him as the harmless guy she could tease without consequences. But he was no saint, and she wasn't an innocent schoolgirl anymore.

He thought back to another time when he'd kissed her. That weekend before he'd left for college. He'd had one too many beers, but that was no excuse. He'd noticed her the minute she'd gotten out of the car with her friends. That yellow dress, barely covering her, half falling off of her in his heated imagination. She'd climbed up beside him on the tailgate of his truck and she'd kissed him, or he'd kissed her. He couldn't remember anymore. He just remembered she was dangerous all those years ago, and she was just as dangerous now.

He spread out the sheet and threw the pillow onto the couch. Then he started back down the hall to pick up her dishes.

He knocked on the doorframe and stuck his head around the corner. The bed tray had been set over to the side of the bed, and Marla Jean was curled on her side, sound asleep. He was happy to see she'd kept her foot propped up on the pile of pillows, and as he walked around to the far side of the bed to pick up the tray, he could see she'd eaten most of the sandwich and all of the soup.

Putting the tray on the dresser he moved around to her side of the bed, gently straightening the blankets and tucking them under her chin. Her dark hair was a riot of curls spreading over the pale yellow pillowcase. She sighed and snuggled deeper into the sheets.

Jake took a moment to study her while she couldn't talk back. She'd always been cute, and her go-screw-yourself attitude added to her appeal for some weird reason. But seeing her now, those long lashes fanned across her cheek, her pink lips parted in sleep, she looked sweet, and vulnerable, and a little lost.

He straightened and moved away from the bed before he gave into the urge to touch her. Maybe he was projecting, but being around Marla Jean this last week had made him feel a little lost himself. Unsettled, like his life was going nowhere fast. She made him want things he'd decided a long time ago he didn't need. Things like a home and family. A wife and kids. Maybe a dog. Plain old ordinary things to most folks.

But to him they were fairytale things, and he was too old to start believing in fairytales now. Especially ones involving Marla Jean Bandy. Leaving sleeping beauty undisturbed, he picked up the tray and went to spend what promised to be a restless night on the living room sofa.

• • •

"Cut it out, Pooky. Nice doggy."

"Grrrr, Grrr-rr, Grrrr."

Marla Jean tried without success to shake the growling dog off her foot.

Pooky was Mrs. Reece's beagle, her next-door neighbor's newest puppy, her pride and joy. At the moment the little sweetheart's sharp, razor-like teeth were sunk clean up to the gums into Marla Jean's foot.

She'd never really trusted Pooky. Not for a minute. Behind those laughing puppy dog eyes and lolling, drooling tongue lurked the real Pooky, the sneaky one that took nips out of her ankles whenever Mrs. Reece wasn't looking. Marla shook her leg and dragged herself and the attached canine across the yard and up the walkway to her front door. Pooky didn't seem to care. On top of the fact that the puppy was having her foot for dinner, Marla Jean really needed to go to the bathroom in the worst way, and she really didn't want Pooky going with her.

"Come on, Pooky, give me a break. For Pete's sake, let go."

"Who's Pooky?"

Marla Jean's eyes flew open at the sound of the man's voice. She realized she'd been dreaming. She was in her bedroom, in her own bed. Pooky was gone, and even though her foot still hurt like a son of a pipefitter, she would have been relieved if it hadn't been for the shadowy shape of a large man looming over her.

She came up swinging. Her dad taught her to throw a punch the first time she came home from school crying because Tony Busby said she hit like a girl. She made Tony Busby eat those words the next day. Her mom grounded her for two weeks, but her dad snuck her extra cookies when he came to tuck her in that night.

The big shadowy guy yelled and ducked the first punch. He made a grab for her, but she rolled toward him instead of moving away and the second blow connected solidly. Right in the eye.

"Ow!" His shout was filled with pain and surprise. "What the—"

He didn't finish whatever he was going to say because she kept pummeling him, and he was busy trying to minimize the damage. He lunged, pinning her to the bed and for a minute the only noise in the room was the sound of their harsh panting. She tried not to panic, but he was stronger than her. It seemed pointless, but it wasn't in her to give up without a fight, so she kept thrashing, trying to throw him off.

"Cut it out, Marla Jean. You're gonna hurt yourself. It's me, Jake. You were having a bad dream."

"Jake?" She was still half asleep, but she stopped flailing around as soon as she recognized his voice. Her racing heart slowed to an idle. "What on earth are you doing in my bedroom in the middle of the night?"

"I'm sleeping on the couch? Remember? At least I was trying to, before you starting moaning and carrying on about somebody named Pooky." He didn't get up, but stayed with his big body slam-bam on top of hers. He did, however, prop himself up on his forearms, supporting some of his weight.

"Pooky's a dog," she explained in a slumber-rough voice, although explaining Pooky wasn't the most pressing thing on her mind at the moment. Jake's big sturdy body holding her to the bed seemed much more interesting.

Even if her brain was foggy with sleep, everything primitive and female inside her was busy waking up and saying howdy-doo-dee, mister.

Jake found an unruly curl and brushed it from her cheek. "All that ruckus over one little ole dog? I thought you must be fending off an entire pack of rabid jackals." Jake's face was only a dim shadow, but his voice drifted past her ear, amused and warm and intimate.

"Pooky's much worse than a pack of anything, and he lives right next door." This wasn't the way she'd imagined it.

Jake in her bed.

And she had imagined it. More than once. Years ago in her adolescent fantasies—back when she barely knew what a fantasy was, and again lately. He'd been starring in much more grown up versions these days.

He laughed. "Mrs. Reece's newest little fur ball? Why Marla Jean, that puppy wouldn't hurt a fly."

"If I was a fly, I'd be relieved to hear that." She shifted beneath him, relishing the contact.

By some trick of light, some shifting of the clouds and moon peeking in her bedroom window, the shadows lifted and she could see his face. He wasn't laughing now. His dark eyes drilled clean through to her core. His stark cheekbones looked like carved granite. His mouth moved closer. It didn't look like he was thinking about Pooky anymore, either.

It looked like he was about to kiss her.

Chapter Twelve

⁓

His mouth teased hers, a whisper of a touch, a mere hint of lip against lip, before he moved on to her jaw, tracing it with his tongue on his way to the sensitive spot behind her ear. Although she could barely catch her breath, she prayed she wasn't still dreaming. Her foot still felt like it had been used for a game of Whac-a-Mole, and then it all came flooding back to her.

Kicking the tire, Jake bringing her home, tucking her into bed. And she'd kissed him, too, but he'd acted unaffected by it, amused, even. He didn't seem amused now. In fact, he seemed to be on a mission.

"Jake?"

"Hmm?" He was nuzzling her neck, working his way down to her collarbone.

His whiskers scraped against her skin, pushing down the stretched out neckline of the hockey jersey she wore. His sweet, wet mouth blazed a trail across the top of her breasts.

"Jake?"

He lifted his head and asked, "What?" before heading back toward her mouth.

This time, when he kissed her all teasing was gone, and she forgot what she wanted to say. This time involved scalding heat and full body contact. His mouth crashed down, stealing any chance she had of speaking. She closed her eyes and met him more than halfway. Deep, dark pleasure rappelled down her body, swinging, sliding pleasure that made her greedy and hungry.

Like any good kiss, it robbed her of all common sense. Filled her with mad, urgent joy she wanted to capture and keep. She wrapped her arms around his broad back, her hands scraping down the cotton texture of his T-shirt until she found the bottom hem. There was nothing cautious about the way her hands pulled it up exposing bare skin. He groaned, encouraging her touch, welcoming her exploration.

And then he gentled the kiss, slowed things down even while his hand moved to cover her breast through the fabric of the hockey jersey. She arched into his touch, squirming to get closer still, as his fingers found her nipple and circled it slowly. Oh dear God, this was what she'd been looking for when she wriggled into that tight red dress last Saturday night. Mindless, glorious, thought-obliterating sex. There was no mistaking the hard erection nestled between her legs. Her hips bucked with need as he rubbed against her. She pushed her hands inside the waistband of his boxers, and froze when the overhead light in the bedroom snapped on.

"Marla Jean? Jake? What the hell?"

Lincoln stood in the doorway staring at them like he'd spotted a two-headed cow and couldn't quite believe his eyes.

Jake didn't move for a long moment and his eyes sought

hers, seeming to offer regret or apology, neither of which she wanted or needed. He leaned close and whispered, "I said you were trouble, didn't I?" But then he winked and arranged her clothes so that she was covered before easing himself off the bed. The gentleness of the gesture touched her. If he was worried about what Linc thought, she sure couldn't tell by looking at him.

Lincoln, on the other hand, she could read like a book. She watched as his confusion turned to anger. Her brother held up a small white pharmacy sack and shook it. "I thought you might need these, Marla Jean. And is this your idea of looking out for my little sister, Jake?" He emphasized the word little, as if to magnify the size of the betrayal. His face was tomato red with anger.

Marla Jean pushed herself up on the bed. "Oh, good grief. Cut it out, Lincoln."

Ignoring her, Linc threw the sack on her dresser and took a threatening step toward Jake with his fist cocked. "You've got three seconds to get out of here before I start beating the living shit out of you."

Jake stood his ground. "I know you're upset, Linc, but face it, you haven't been able to beat me up since seventh grade."

"I was never this motivated before," Lincoln snarled and took another step toward Jake.

Jake held up a hand to ward him off. "I'm not going to fight you, Linc. Besides I've already gotten one black eye tonight."

Marla Jean quickly scooted to the edge of her bed, stood up on one leg, and threw herself between the two men. Grimacing at the red swelling starting under Jake's eye, she asked, "Oh, Jake, did I do that? I'm so sorry!"

"Don't worry. I'll live. But I think it's best if I go home now. Good night, Marla Jean." He kissed her on the cheek, slipped past his scowling best friend, and walked out the bedroom door. Before leaving he added solemnly, "I'll talk to you later, Lincoln."

"Why did she hit you?" he yelled at Jake's retreating back. Turning back to Marla Jean, he demanded, "Why did you hit him?"

"Let it go, Lincoln. I think you've caused enough trouble for one night."

"Me? I've caused trouble?"

"It's never a good idea to go barging into a woman's bedroom in the middle of the night."

"You're not a woman, you're my sister."

"Do you know how ridiculous you sound?"

They heard the sound of the front door closing. A vein throbbed in Linc's forehead. "I'm asking again, and I'd like an answer. Why does Jake have a black eye?"

"I was having a bad dream, and when he tried to wake me up, I slugged him."

"That doesn't explain what was going on when I turned on the light."

Now that she was fully awake, she urgently needed to heed nature's call. "If you don't mind, Lincoln, could we continue this conversation in the kitchen? I need to go to the bathroom before I pee my pants." She wobbled on her good foot and tripped over the stupid leggings still hanging half off her leg.

Linc was there in an instant and helped her make it to the bathroom door. "I've got you, sis. I'll make some coffee, because I've got a lot more to say, and you're going to sit and listen to every word."

"Fine," she grumbled. Shaking off the hand he had on her elbow she said ungraciously, "I can take it from here."

As soon as the door closed she tried to marshal her shaky breathing and ignore the way her skin was still singing from the feel of Jake's mouth roaming across it.

Lord, preserve me, she thought. Put me in a jar and close the lid. Her body ached with arousal and need. She felt clumsy with it. Half drunk, half wanton. She sat down on the toilet and pulled the leggings off her good leg and flung them in the direction of the hamper. She sat there, wanting to postpone the confrontation with Linc, wanting to savor what had almost happened with Jake. Jake, for God's sake.

She wasn't sure what triggered the change in Jake's arm-length attitude toward her, and she could kill her big brother for his usual lousy timing. Murder him in cold blood, chop him into little pieces, and feed him to the snapping turtles down at the pond.

And Jake. He hadn't seemed the least bit embarrassed when Linc barged in on them. He just rolled off the bed and walked away as if things like that happened to him every day. Maybe they did. She was having trouble being so blasé.

But right now she had to worry about dealing with an irate brother parked at her kitchen table. She knew him well enough to know he wouldn't leave until he'd finished reading her the riot act, so she might as well get it over with.

When she came out of the bathroom, her bedroom was empty, and the only signs of her recent wrestling match with Jake were the bed covers scattered this way and that. ·

Maybe it was the draining effects of her frustrated

libido, but the pain pounding in her toes suddenly became impossible to ignore. Her entire foot felt like a tube of toothpaste being squeezed by King Kong. The pain pills had definitely worn off.

She grabbed the bag of pain medication from her dresser, and using the hallway wall as support, she hopped along toward the kitchen. Lincoln was standing at the counter with his back to her, making coffee. He turned around when she walked in but didn't say a word—just stared at her, long and hard, like he was making a critical decision. Then he turned his back to her and asked, "Do you want some coffee? It's not decaf but I've given up on getting any sleep tonight."

"Sure, I'll take a cup." She shuffled to the nearest chair. After she sat down, she dragged another chair closer and propped both feet on it.

Her toes were still screaming so she reached down, unhooked the fasteners holding the ACE bandage in place, and started unwrapping her foot. The more she unwrapped the better her toes felt. Between the tightness of the bandage and the swelling of her ankle all circulation had been cut off and now she could feel the blood rushing back into her mangled toes. She exhaled a big whoosh of air, a breath she didn't realize she'd been holding and groaned with relief. She might make it through the night, after all.

Linc placed a mug of coffee in front of her and looked at the discarded bandage. "You think that's smart?"

"I think that dang thing felt more like a sausage casing than a bandage. Why do they put these on so tight, anyway?"

"Do you need another pain pill?" Pulling the prescription bottle from the sack, he set it next to her mug. He filled a glass with tap water and gave that to her, too. Then he sat down across from her with both hands wrapped around his coffee mug like it was anchoring him in place.

She ignored the pills. "I'm not taking anything until after you're through lecturing me. I need to keep my wits about me so I can defend myself." She watched him, trying unsuccessfully to gauge his mood.

Finally he said, "I'm calling Mom first thing tomorrow morning." He crossed his arms over his chest like he was daring her to object.

She laughed. "Because I had a man in my bed? What's she gonna do, ground me?"

"Somebody ought to. First Donny Joe and now—" he paused as if he could barely bring himself to speak his name, "and now Jake. But no, I'll spare her all that." He sounded so damned puritanical, she wanted to kick him, but she couldn't risk another injured foot.

"Then please enlighten me, Saint Lincoln. Why are you calling her?"

"Dinah and I already discussed it before I came over, and she agrees with me. I'm going to tell Mom about your foot."

She held up a hand. "Whoa, whoa, whoa. Hold on there, buddy boy."

He talked right over her objections. "You're going to need some help getting around, and since they planned to come home for Thanksgiving, anyway, I'm sure they won't mind coming home a few weeks earlier, instead."

"Don't do that, Lincoln. Honestly, it's not necessary. I can manage."

"Really? What about the barber shop? You can't afford

to shut it down until you're on your feet again. And besides, Dad would probably have fun running things for a little while."

That was true. And she did have bills to pay, but the idea of her parents coming home to rescue her didn't sit right. She did miss them, though. And Lincoln was going to push until she gave in.

"Okay, call them. But if they can't change their plans, I'll figure something out."

"Wow, now I'm nervous. You gave in way too easily."

"Because I want you to do something for me, Lincoln."

"I knew it. What's the catch?"

"Go easy on Jake."

His face clouded over. "Fat chance. I'll go easy on him right after I rearrange his pretty face."

"I mean it, Lincoln."

He glared at her. "Why should I? I trusted him. He was supposed to be here taking care of you."

She raised her eyebrows. "I believe that's what he was doing when you interrupted us." She laughed at the horrified look on her brother's face.

"It's not funny. You aren't seriously thinking about getting involved with him, are you?"

"I'm not seriously thinking about getting involved with anyone. But if I was, why would that be so bad? He's a good guy, not to mention he's your best friend."

"He also goes through women like Kleenex."

"Sounds perfect."

"Marla Jean." His tone held warning and a hint of panic.

"Relax. Go home to your wife, Lincoln. You've scared him off, at least for tonight. Let me worry about my own affairs."

"I wish you'd find a different way to phrase that. And I'm not sure I should leave you here alone."

"Well, since you ran off my nursemaid, it's either that or you can sleep on the couch. But I'll be fine."

"Are you sure?"

"I'm going to take a pain pill, and then you can help me back to the bedroom and tuck me in. I'll be asleep before you know it."

He seemed to think it over. "I guess that'll be okay."

"I wouldn't mind if you stopped by with doughnuts in the morning. After tonight, you owe me big time."

Lincoln sighed. "I'll spring for the doughnuts, but I'm not making any promises about Jake."

She popped a pill in her mouth and downed it with water. "So, tell me. What is it with you and Jake, anyway? What's this big secret thing he thinks he owes you, and why don't I know about it?" She'd rarely seen Linc look so uncomfortable. He stood abruptly and turned away, putting the coffee mugs in the sink. Then he hooked his arm around her and started helping her down the hall. "Come on, spill, Lincoln. Did he kill someone, and you hid the body? Did he rob a bank, and you drove the getaway car?"

They reached her room, and he waited while she climbed back onto the bed. He busily rearranged the pillow at the end to elevate her foot. "I have no idea what you're talking about, sis. Try to get some sleep, and I'll see you in the morning."

"I want chocolate and lemon-filled," she yelled as he turned off the light. He obviously wanted to make his escape before she could pump him for any more information. But his reaction to her questions about Jake had been interesting.

Very interesting.

Chapter Thirteen

❧

It's a ten-hour drive, honey." Marla Jean listened to her mother's soothing voice over the phone line. True to his word, Lincoln called their folks at the crack of dawn, and now her mother wanted to reassure her that help was on the way. "We'll leave first thing in the morning," her mom said, "so we should be there by dinner time tomorrow night."

Marla Jean was still in bed, half asleep and groggy from the late night and pain pills, but at her mom's last announcement, she sat straight up and threw off the covers. "I can't wait, Mom. Y'all be careful."

She hung up from the conversation with her mother, her thoughts bouncing around like a pinball while she went over everything that would have to be done before they arrived.

Lincoln appeared in her bedroom doorway eating a doughnut. From the yellow goo on his chin, it appeared to be a lemon-filled. "Good morning, sis. How are you feeling?"

"I'm feeling like you better grab a mop and a bucket and get busy cleaning."

He scrunched up his face in a give-me-a-break look. "Oh, relax. The house looks fine."

"The house looks fine by our standards, but it's not fine by 'our mother is going to be here by dinner tomorrow night' standards."

Dinah stuck her head around the doorframe. "Oh, damn. I didn't think about Bitsy and her white glove. You better get to work, Lincoln. I'll help Marla Jean get dressed, and we can make a plan."

"Can I at least finish my doughnut?"

She shoved her husband toward the kitchen and said, "Run, don't walk, mister. There are a million things to do."

As soon as he was out of earshot, Dinah, her face shining and eager, plopped down on the end of the bed and rubbed her hands together. "Tell me everything. Don't leave out a single detail."

Marla Jean pushed her hair out of her face and frowned. "About what?"

"Don't play dumb with me. Lincoln came home fit to be tied last night. At first he wouldn't tell me why he was upset, but I have ways of making him talk."

Marla Jean made an "ew" face and then sighed. "So, what did he tell you?"

Dinah leaned forward and whispered, "He said he found you in bed with Jake."

"Well, there you have it. Now you know everything."

"Oh, come on. What? Why? How? I mean, we are talking about Jake, and if you think I'm going to rest until I get the particulars then you have severely underestimated me."

"It's no big deal, Dinah, and Lincoln is overreacting. Just like he has been ever since my divorce. Does he expect me to sit home and take up knitting?"

Dinah shrugged and said airily, " 'No big deal' isn't the phrase that comes to mind when I think of Abel Jacobson."

"And you a married woman. I'm shocked."

"I'm married, not blind, and Linc is only concerned that you are overcompensating for what Bradley did to you."

"This has nothing to do with Bradley. It has to do with sex."

Dinah's eyes bulged, and she bounced up and down on the bed. "Oh my goodness. So you actually did have sex with Jake?"

Marla Jean shook her head. "No, I'm beginning to think the universe and my brother have conspired to make sure I never have sex again as long as I live."

"Well, you know Jake has a reputation for avoiding serious relationships."

"For the ten millionth time I'm not ready for anything serious. Do you really think I'm emotionally prepared to trust another man right now?"

"Okay, okay." Dinah flapped her hand like that part wasn't important. "So, what did happen?"

"I had a nightmare, and he tried to wake me up. One thing led to another, and the earth was on the verge of moving when Jughead walked in on us."

Dinah giggled. "Poor Lincoln."

"Poor Lincoln? What about me? What about Jake?"

"Oh, you two can always take up where you left off if you want, but I think Lincoln is permanently scarred."

"Good. Maybe he'll quit being such a busybody, and right now we've got a ton of work to do. Why don't you go see what kind of mess Linc is making while I take a shower?"

Dinah jumped up and grabbed some crutches that were leaning against the wall. "I'll have you know your big brother climbed up in the attic this morning and found these."

Marla Jean stood and gave the crutches a trial run over to the bathroom door. "I guess I'll have to thank him, won't I?"

"Yes, he braved cobwebs and spiders just for you."

"That barely begins to balance the scales," she said before closing the bathroom door. After a quick shower, despite her newfound mobility, she was installed on the living room sofa with her foot propped up on a mountain of cushions. From that vantage point she was still capable of bossing her brother around, which suited her just fine.

"Linc, we have to get my stuff out of Mom and Dad's room and drag that old daybed out of the attic and put it back in my room, so I'll have a place to sleep."

"Attic? I already went up into one attic today." He shuddered. "Why can't you just sleep on the couch while they're here? It's not like they're moving home permanently."

"Are you going to argue with me about everything? I'm not sleeping on the couch, and your old bedroom is still full of exercise equipment."

The doorbell rang, and Dinah went to answer it. She returned with Harry on her heels.

"Hey, Harry." Marla smiled at him from the sofa.

"Good morning, Marla Jean. I wanted to stop by and

see how you were doing." He held out a big box of candy. "I thought you might want something sweet to take your mind off your foot."

"Oh Harry, that's so thoughtful." She looked at the box. "Turtles are my favorites."

"Harry, my man, you have perfect timing." Lincoln pounced on him before he had a chance to sit down. "I could use your help hauling a bed for Marla Jean down from the attic. Come with me."

Before he could protest or ask any questions, Lincoln swept him away toward the garage. Dinah started back to the kitchen to resume boiling and bleaching and scalding every surface before her mother-in-law saw them, but before she could make it out of the room, the doorbell rang again. "My, my, you're a popular woman."

When she reappeared this time Donny Joe was right behind her, carrying his cowboy hat in one hand and a big bunch of yellow daisies in the other.

"Woo-ee woman, look at you. I heard you were laid up."

"Word sure travels fast in this town." Marla Jean let out a resigned sigh as he handed her the bouquet. "Thanks for the flowers, Donny Joe. They're beautiful."

"Beautiful flowers for a beautiful woman." He winked, pouring it on thick. "Yep, you were all anybody was talking about at the Rise-N-Shine this morning." He grinned and leaned in to examine her bandaged foot. "You really did a number on yourself, didn't you? Can I do anything to help?"

Dinah didn't give Marla Jean a chance to answer. She grabbed Donny Joe by the wrist and started pulling him toward the kitchen. "I'm so glad you asked. How do you look in an apron, big boy?"

• • •

"Pigs-in-a-blanket?" Jake's Aunt Libby waved a tray under his nose. "They used to be your favorite."

Before he could respond his mother cut into the conversation, demanding, "Libby Comstock, for the last time, what happened to your face?"

His mother had asked him a similar question when he'd picked her up for dinner that evening. The blow Marla Jean had gotten in the night before had turned his eye a nice shade of purple. He'd made up some story about walking into a wall, and while it was clear she hadn't believed him, she hadn't pressed him, either. There was no way he was going to tell her that Marla Jean had taken a poke at him.

Jake remembered the way he'd cringed when his aunt opened the door to welcome them, and he'd gotten a good look at the aftermath of her run-in with Marla Jean and the bathroom door. Both of her eyes were slightly blackened and her nose was swollen and red. Marla Jean was going to get a reputation as a real brawler if word got out that she was responsible for all this carnage. But Aunt Libby acted as if nothing was out of the ordinary, so he'd played along. His mother didn't have the same reservations about being a buttinski where her sister was concerned.

Libby flapped a hand at her older sister. "It's nothing, Ellie. You know how clumsy I can be." She held out the tray of appetizers again. "Go ahead, Jake. Try one."

Jake smiled and took two. "Thanks, Aunt Libby. I haven't had these in years." He popped one in his mouth and chewed. Libby watched him with the expectant look of a kid waiting for puppies to be born.

After he swallowed he said, "Mmmmm, these are great. Just like I remember."

His aunt beamed and patted him on the head. He reached for another and his mother piped up. "Not too many. You'll ruin your appetite."

"Oh leave him alone, Ellie. He's a growing boy, and I don't get a chance to spoil him like I used to."

Jake and his mother had arrived right on time for the dreaded dinner party, and he was doing his best to be civil. His mom had been on his case all the way over about being nice to Bradley, about how much this get-together meant to his aunt, and about how she was really happy he wasn't making her go alone.

When they'd pulled up in front of Bradley's house he'd squeezed her hand and promised to behave. Now that they were there, she seemed a lot more anxious about the evening than he did. And the sight of her baby sister's battered face clearly had her worked up.

Jake sat on a big brown leather sofa, while Libby perched nervously on an ottoman. Jake didn't believe for a minute that his mother had given up on getting every detail about how her sister came to have two black eyes, but for the moment she sat at the other end of the couch engaging in innocent small talk. "This is a lovely room," she said.

Bradley walked in at that moment carrying a tray of drinks. "Yes, Marla Jean had a nice eye for decorating."

Libby's smile slipped a bit.

Jake looked around the place again with new eyes. He'd been trying to forget it had been Marla Jean's home not that long ago. In fact, he'd done his darndest not to think about Marla Jean at all today. He'd tossed and turned all night on the lumpy twin bed at his parents' old house. He should have driven home to his own bed in his own apartment, but that was way across town. And even though he knew if she needed anything she wouldn't call—Lincoln would make sure of that—he still felt better being across the street, two doors down.

All day, like gate crashers, memories of the way she'd felt last night, soft and yielding under him, her hands moving over his body like she wanted to learn every inch of him, would barge into his head at the most inappropriate times. Like right now. Holy hell, even now his body tightened remembering. And then it was almost impossible not to think about what could have happened if Linc hadn't walked in on them. About what almost certainly would have happened.

Linc. Shit. He would have to talk to him soon, straighten things out, but best friend or not, he didn't think he could bring himself to apologize. He could promise to keep his distance, though. He'd already concluded that staying away from her from now on was the best way to handle things.

After he talked to her. After he made sure she was okay.

Oh man, the look on her face when the lights came on had been like a punch in the gut. Her dark hair fanned out on the pillow, her eyes slumberous with lust as they met his, and her smart, sassy mouth, wet and bruised from his kisses.

In that moment, she had the look of a woman who knew she was desirable and sexy and gorgeous and hot, even wearing that old, faded hockey jersey and an ACE bandage on her leg. But thanks to Bradley and his aunt, he also knew she had plenty of moments when she still felt a little bruised and a lot cast aside. The last thing he wanted was to add to those feelings.

But he was probably overthinking everything. More than likely, Marla Jean would agree. Nothing like that should ever happen between the two of them again. And then she could go her merry way, and he'd go his.

He shook his head, making an effort to refocus as Bradley chattered on. The man didn't seem to realize the bucket of ice water he'd dumped over the group's mood when he mentioned Marla Jean. "But once Libby moves in, she's got a free hand to redo the whole place. I want it to feel like it's her home." He put the tray on the coffee table and gave Libby a kiss on the cheek.

Part of Jake had to admire Bradley for not pretending the specter of Marla Jean wasn't sitting in the big middle of the room like the ghost of first wives past. On the other hand the guy was never going to win any sensitivity awards.

Libby stood and turned to her sister. "Ellie, why don't you come help me in the kitchen. If you gentlemen can entertain yourselves, dinner will be ready in two shakes of a lamb's tail."

Bradley smiled and handed Jake a beer before sitting down in a big leather recliner. "Sounds good, sweetheart. Jake and I will hold down the fort."

The women hurried off to get dinner on the table, and Jake racked his brain for a neutral topic of conversation. He needn't have bothered because as soon as the women were out of earshot, Bradley leaned forward with his elbows on his knees, an expression of earnestness on his face. "Jake, I was hoping to get a minute alone so we could talk man to man. There's something I've been wanting to discuss with you."

Jake scratched his neck and shifted uncomfortably

on the leather cushion. He really hoped Bradley wasn't going to start getting all mushy about his feelings for Aunt Libby. Even though he'd promised his mother he'd be nice, he wasn't the greatest actor in the world, and if he was going to ask for his blessing or some other nonsense, he wasn't sure he could hide his real feelings about the situation.

Bradley leaned closer. "What do you know about Marla Jean and Donny Joe?"

"What?" The question caught him off guard.

"Marla Jean and Donny Joe. I'm worried that she's getting mixed up with the wrong kind of men." He whispered the statement from the side of his mouth.

Jake frowned. "That's not really any of your business anymore, is it? And why are you asking me?"

"Well, Jake, I know she always thought of you as a big brother, and I've heard the rumors about you and Donny Joe getting into that fight over her. I figured you must not think too highly of the idea of Donny Joe sniffin' around her, either."

That image of the way she'd looked last night, all mussed up and well-kissed, popped into his head again. He fidgeted around in his seat and didn't look Bradley in the eye. "I don't feel comfortable discussing this with you, and for my aunt's sake, I really wish you would drop it."

Bradley sat back, drumming his fingers on the armrest. "I wouldn't hurt Libby for the world, but I still feel some responsibility for Marla Jean's predicament."

Jake raised an eyebrow. "Predicament?"

Bradley held both hands up like it should be obvious. "You know, being single again. Out honky-tonking every weekend."

"Because you dumped her." The words were out of his mouth before he could stop them, but he wasn't sorry. The man had some nerve, Jake would give him that.

Bradley's cheeks flushed a baby pink and his nostrils flared. "That's a little harsh. We came to a mutual under-standing that we weren't right for each other anymore."

Jake could feel blood pounding in his temples. All the promises he'd made to his mother were about to fly out the window. "Was that before or after you started sleeping with my aunt?"

"Now listen here, Jake—" Bradley stood up, his fists clenched at his sides.

Jake stood up, too, trying to hold onto his temper. The little weasel was asking for it, but for his aunt's sake he counted to ten, and because his mother would tan his hide, he counted to ten again. He forced himself to take a calm-ing breath and held up his hands in a conciliatory manner. "Okay, okay, I was out of line. Let's just drop it. Besides, Harry Beal is the one I'd worry about if I were you."

Bradley took a moment but seemed to simmer down as well. "Harry. Yeah, he's had a crush on her since junior high. God, he made an ass of himself at the game last night, didn't he? With that crazy-assed flower thing?"

Jake didn't know why, but he felt the need to defend Harry. "I don't know. He's a nice guy, and he's making his move. He's single. She's single. Game on, right?"

Bradley seemed to consider it. "I guess. Do you think Marla Jean likes him?"

Jake didn't answer as a flurry of high heels clacking against the hard wood floor snagged his attention. A sec-ond later his mother rushed into the room pulling a pro-testing Libby along behind her by her elbow. "Let's go,

Jake. We aren't staying in this house a minute longer, and Libby is coming with us."

"Let go of me, Ellie. I'm not going anywhere." Libby jerked away from her sister's hold.

"What's going on?" Bradley demanded.

Ellie grabbed her purse and said in a shaky voice, "Once we were alone I asked her again what happened to her face." Her voice rose in volume, and she was glaring at Bradley with enough heat to light him up like a Tiki torch. "And do you know what she said?"

Jake walked over and put a hand on his mother's arm, trying to calm her down. "Hang on, Ma—"

Ellie was in no mood to be soothed. "She insisted that she walked into a door. A door! I mean I lived with an abusive man long enough to spot the signs a mile away, and Libby, you are not staying here another minute. Let's go." She started marching toward the door as if she expected everyone to follow.

Libby stood her ground. "I did walk into a door, Ellie, and I'm not going anywhere."

Jake's mother whirled around. "What did he say after he hit you? That he was sorry? That it would never happen again?"

During their exchange, Bradley had been standing with his mouth open, but now he jumped to his own defense. "Wait a minute. You think I hit Libby? Is that what this is about? I wouldn't hurt a single hair on her head."

Jake tried again to get his mother's attention. "Ma, listen to me. I was there when it happened."

His words seemed to sink in, and she deflated like a kid's punctured swimming floatie. "You were where?" she asked.

"At Romeo's pizza place after the game Friday night. Aunt Libby ran into the bathroom door as someone was coming out of it."

"She did? You did?" she asked turning back to her sister. "Why didn't you say so?"

"I did say so, Ellie, but you were so ready to believe the worst about Bradley that you wouldn't listen to me."

Bradley walked over and wrapped his arm around Libby's shoulder. "It's okay. Ellie was just looking out for your best interest, and I admire that."

"She owes you an apology," Libby maintained staunchly.

"Not at all, sweetheart." Bradley kissed her on the cheek. "Ellie, this isn't exactly how I planned to say this, but I love your sister. And if she'll let me, I'm going to do my best to make her happy. As her family, it's important that you and Jake know that."

Libby smiled so big Jake thought her face might crack and fall off. His mother looked ruffled as if she was having trouble making the switch from potential abuser to devoted loving man in her head that quickly.

Then Bradley got down on one knee, and Jake's eyebrows shot to the top of his forehead and stayed there. Bradley took his aunt's hand and spoke sincerely, "I was going to wait a while, but I can't think of a single reason not to do this now, Libby."

His Aunt Libby's eyes resembled bouncing beach balls and her cheeks flushed to a feverish shade of pink in anticipation. She put a hand over her heart as if she needed to hold the beating organ inside her chest, and then exhaled his name in a quavering voice, "Oh, Bradley."

"Libby, I don't want you to just move in with me. I want you to be my wife. Will you marry me?" Little beads of sweat popped out on his forehead. The man actually looked like he might be nervous.

"Wait a min—" Jake started to protest, but his mother grabbed a couple of pigs-in-a-blanket from the nearby tray and chunked them into his open mouth before he could speak. He had no choice but to chew. Apparently, all of his mother's doubts evaporated as soon as the man popped the magic question. What was it with women and marriage that made them go all gaga?

Aunt Libby screeched like a Buick with bad brakes and launched herself at him. "Of course I'll marry you, Bradley. Yes, yes, yes, yes."

Good God, thought Jake, his mouth still full of sausages. The two of them were making a spectacle of themselves down on the floor, laughing and kissing without any consideration for those having to watch. His mother had tears in her eyes and beamed like she'd orchestrated the whole thing. God help him, he'd never understand women in a million years. He finally swallowed and grabbed his beer to wash down the rest.

Bradley stood up and helped Libby to her feet. "Well, now we really have something to celebrate, don't we? What do you say we eat dinner, and we can talk about setting a date while we're at it?"

"Oh, my. I'm so excited. I'm so happy. And I love you, Bradley." Libby kissed him once more and then giggled before dancing off into the kitchen to dish up the food. Bradley was all puffed up and pleased with himself as he herded Jake and his mom into the dining room. He laughed like a little kid before kissing Ellie on both cheeks and helping her to her seat. Then he slapped Jake on the back hard enough to dislodge fillings, but he seemed so happy Jake didn't have the heart to complain.

Not until he said, "Hell, Jake, I just realized something. I'm going to be your brand new uncle. Come here and give me a hug."

Chapter Fourteen

～

As it turned out, Donny Joe looked mighty fine in an apron, and he wielded a mean broom. Harry showed off his muscles in an impressive display, by practically carrying the daybed down from the attic one-handed. Dinah ran from room to room scrubbing and dusting like a mad woman. Lincoln ate another doughnut and cheered their efforts.

Marla Jean supervised from the couch, feeling guilty that she couldn't help and feeling more and more anxious at the thought of her parents' return home. Part of her, the fragile part that was still healing from having her life so rudely rearranged by Bradley, wanted to curl up and let them take care of her like she was still their baby girl. And now with her broken toes, nobody could blame her for letting them coddle her. But the biggest part of her felt like she'd be taking a big step backward if she didn't try to maintain some degree of independence.

Earlier that morning, Hoot and Dooley stopped by with casseroles from their wives and told her they'd put a "Gone Fishing" sign on the barber shop. Then they'd called and rescheduled her appointments for the coming week. Most of the business was walk-in so there wasn't much to rearrange.

Marla Jean still hoped she'd get a walking boot and be back to work in a couple of days, but now with her father riding to the rescue, it was a relief not to worry about letting down her customers.

Her clothes had been moved back to her old bedroom, the daybed set up, and her art supplies put away in the closet. It looked scarily like her childhood bedroom, minus the stuffed animals.

Donny Joe and Harry both pitched in like they were glad to do it, but they also seemed to be trying to outdo each other in an effort to gain Marla Jean's attention.

"I thought you could use some iced tea, Marla Jean." Harry walked in with a tall glass with lemon and a sprig of mint. She wondered where the hell he found the mint.

"Thank you, Harry, but you're the one doing all the work."

"I like being useful. You just tell me what you need, and I'm ready to pitch in."

Donny Joe bounced into the room with a bag of frozen peas. "Here ya go, sugar. That bag of ice is getting all melty. In my opinion, frozen vegetables are the way to go, and I find generally that baby green peas work the best."

"You have a lot of experience with this kind of thing?" she asked.

"I've twisted my ankle playing soccer more times than I can remember, and the only reason I'm still walking today, is baby peas." He'd been a soccer star in high school and still played in an adult league.

She let him arrange the bag on her ankle without further protest. "Well, then, it sounds like you're the authority."

Harry looked miffed and decided to throw in his two cents. "Well, in football, we're no stranger to injuries. The best thing would be to plunge your foot into a bucket of ice water and leave it in as long as you can stand it."

Marla Jean smiled weakly. "Maybe I'll try that later, Harry."

Encouraged, he continued, "That's really the only way to get the cold down into the swollen joints. And your pillows for your foot should be higher than your heart." He grabbed some cushions from other chairs and started reshaping the mound supporting her foot.

Donny Joe was trying to get the peas to stay balanced on her foot at the same time. "Thanks, really guys, my foot's fine now." Since they'd been so nice she resisted the urge to swat them away like gnats, but their fussing was about to make her scream.

Dinah came into the room and collapsed on a chair. "That's it. We're done. I'm not lifting another finger."

The house sparkled by anyone's standards. Bitsy would be hard-pressed to find anything lacking. After the men made a pizza and beer run, everyone sat around the living room, tired but pleased with a job well done.

Harry scooted his chair closer to Marla Jean. "Would you like some more parmesan cheese on your pizza?"

"No thank you, Harry. I'm fine."

Donny took a swig of beer and asked, "So, where's Jake? I'm surprised he's not here helping."

The question hung in the air unanswered, like a

low-lying cloud of smelly bug spray, while Marla Jean finished chewing her pizza. After she swallowed, she said, "I believe he had plans with his mother today."

"Why are you asking about Jake, Donny Joe?" Lincoln asked casually.

"No reason. It's just lately, every time I'm around Marla Jean he seems to turn up like a bad penny."

Lincoln scowled and began tapping a finger on the end table. "Is that a fact?"

"He's like her own personal bodyguard," Donny Joe continued. "At the diner this morning, they said he scooped you up just like that *Officer and a Gentleman* movie and whisked you off to the hospital. I thought Nelda Potts and Bonnie May Thornton were gonna faint dead away, they thought it was so romantic. You should have heard them squealing and carrying on."

"Romantic?" Marla Jean tried to brush it off. "That's plain silly." She could see all this talk about Jake wasn't sitting right with Lincoln, and Harry didn't look any too pleased at Donny Joe's story, either. "He was nice enough to give me a ride to the hospital. That's all."

Donny Joe turned to Harry. "Wasn't she on a date with you, Harry? If it had been me, I sure as hell wouldn't let another man make off with my woman."

"I'm nobody's woman, and Harry was celebrating a big victory with his team. He offered to take me, but I didn't want to ruin the night for him or the kids."

Harry scooted his chair even closer to Marla Jean until he was practically sitting in her lap. "Donny Joe's right. I should have taken you. I felt bad about it all night long."

"Well, you shouldn't." She looked at her big brother and said pointedly, "I was in good hands."

Lincoln made growling noises, and Dinah jumped up from her chair. "Heavens! Look at the time. We should all get out of here, and let Marla Jean get some rest. It's been a long day, and I know I'm tired."

Even though Marla Jean had been resting all day, she was tired, too. Watching Harry and Donny Joe try to outdo each other had worn her out.

Donny Joe squatted down beside her and used his bedroom voice. "Night, Marla Jean. And if you need anything at all just call, sugar."

"Thanks for all your help, Donny Joe. I'll make it up to you when I'm back on my feet."

His eyes glinted before he leaned over and whispered, "I can think of ways you can repay me that don't require standing up."

She laughed and gave him a small push. "Good night, Donny Joe."

Harry stood by impatiently waiting for Donny Joe to clear out so he could say his good-byes. "I know you'll be busy with your parents at home, but I'd like to stop by if that's okay."

"I would like that, Harry. And don't forget, I still owe you a home-cooked dinner."

"I'll hold you to it, but there's no rush. Just worry about getting better first." He looked at the floor and then looked at her. With a quick glance at the others in the room, he leaned over and kissed her on the cheek.

Marla smiled at him sweetly. "Good night, Harry, and thanks again."

Pleased by his bravado, he smiled, too. "Good night, Marla Jean."

Lincoln herded everyone to the front door, then

stopped and asked, "Are you going to be all right by your-self, sis?"

"I'll be fine. Thanks to you, I've got my crutches to get around, remember?"

Dinah dragged her husband to the front door. "Come on, Lincoln. We're only five minutes away if she needs us."

"Okay, we'll talk to you in the morning."

"Thanks again, everybody." She watched them file out, leaving her alone on the couch.

Jake pulled into his mother's driveway. All the way to her house he listened to her bask in the pre-wedding glow of Libby's upcoming marriage.

"You think she's making a mistake, don't you?" his mother finally asked as she reached for the car door handle.

"I don't know, but you certainly did a one-eighty on this issue." Jake turned off the engine.

"He seems to really love her, Jake. Watch his face when she walks in the room. He lights up."

"That didn't keep you from being convinced he'd used her for a punching bag." His mother's logic was making his head swim.

"I jumped to the wrong conclusion. I'm sorry, but while we're on the subject, are you going to tell me how you got your black eye, mister?"

"Let's just say a lot of people were walking into doors last night."

"Okay, I learned my lesson. It's none of my business." She put a hand on his arm to stop him when he started to get out of the car. "You don't need to walk me to the door. Just wait until I get inside. Good night, sweetie." She leaned over and kissed him on the cheek.

"Good night, Ma." He watched until she was inside and backed out of the driveway, heading for his parents' old house. The lights were all on at Marla Jean's when he drove by and assorted cars lined the street. He recognized Lincoln's Toyota and Donny Joe's truck. He pulled into his driveway and shut off the headlights just as Lincoln, Dinah, Donny Joe, and Harry piled out onto the front porch. They shouted good-byes to each other, got in their cars, and drove away.

From the looks of it, there had been a party, and he hadn't been invited. He sat there wondering how long it would take Linc to cool down. He also wondered if now would be a good time to go talk to Marla Jean about the night before. For the first time in his life he wasn't sure of what he should say. Morning-after awkwardness had never been something he suffered from.

The women he slept with knew the score. There were no professions of love or promises to be broken. But where women were concerned, Marla Jean didn't fit into any normal category. She scared him, made him question the rules of the game, and that was a new feeling for him. He needed time to sort things out.

Besides, if she asked him any questions about the dinner at Bradley's he wouldn't want to lie, but he didn't want to be the one to tell her about Bradley and Aunt Libby's wedding news, either. She should probably hear that big announcement from someone else.

He got out of the car and trudged up his front steps. One thing was almost certain. If Lincoln hadn't walked in when he did, he would have made love to Marla Jean last night. And wouldn't that have complicated matters. He supposed he should consider it a narrow escape. He ignored the voice in his head that wondered if he'd missed a life-altering opportunity instead.

Right now he just wanted to take a shower and hit the sack. He'd started scraping the paint off the back of the house that morning, and if he worked all weekend, he could get most of the job done. But that meant an early start the next day.

"Hey, Jake." He'd just stepped onto the porch when a voice floated to him out of the dark.

He jumped out of his skin and turned toward the voice. Barely illuminated by the street light, he saw his half brother Theo sitting on the wooden porch glider. "Son of a bitch, Theo, you scared the bejesus out of me."

Theo laughed and got up, walking over to meet him. "It's good to see you, too, big brother."

"Aw hell, I'm sorry. I just wasn't expecting anyone to be waiting for me in the dark. Get over here."

It shouldn't have come as a total shock to find his half brother waiting for him on the porch. In the last letter he'd gotten, he'd mentioned coming to visit, but in the last few years he'd threatened to visit before and never gotten around to it.

His relationship with Theo had been nonexistent until after their father's death, and then Jake's sense of responsibility kicked in, making him take the young man under his wing. Theo had been in the Navy up until a few months ago, but his mother lived in Derbyville, and Jake knew he'd be back to see her eventually.

Theo wrapped Jake up in a bear hug. "I thought I'd see if that job offer was still open."

Jake put his hands on his hips. "I could use the help, but it involves long hours and not much pay. When did you get here?"

"I got back about a week ago. I spent some time with my mom."

"And how is she?"

"She's doing okay. Working on husband number three these days. How's your mother doing?"

"She's great. I moved her to a condo on the lake."

"I want to see her while I'm here." Over time Theo and Jake's mother had formed an odd alliance after their father died.

"She'd like that. But in the meantime I could use your help. It's high time I sold this place, but it needs a lot of work."

Theo looked at the house and said, "Just tell me what to do."

"Don't worry, I will, but not tonight. We've got some catching up to do. Do you want a beer?"

Theo grinned and followed him inside. "I thought you'd never ask. Jake, there is one more thing."

"What's that?" Jake looked back at his brother. He wasn't smiling any longer.

"This time, before I leave, you're going to tell me the truth about what happened between you and Dad even if I have to beat it out of you."

Chapter Fifteen

S-E-X. Sex. She doodled the word on the sketch pad in her lap and embellished it with curlicues, flowers, and trailing vines. That's what she wanted. To be more specific, she wanted to have sex with Jake.

Her father's recliner creaked as he shifted and grunted something in his sleep. She scratched out the word until it was nothing more than a great black blob on the page.

"We're having tuna sandwiches for lunch. Is that all right with you?" Marla Jean jumped guiltily when Bitsy bustled into the room wiping her hands on a dish towel.

She closed the sketch pad and put it on the coffee table. "Tuna sounds great, Mom. Can you put those big, chopped-up dill pickles in it?"

"I'm making it like I always do, Marla Jean, with big, chopped-up dill pickles in it. Milton, wake up. Lunch will be ready in fifteen minutes."

Her father blinked, snorted, and then grumbled something unintelligible before falling back asleep. Her mother made a *tsk*ing sound and disappeared back into the kitchen.

Thinking about having sex with Jake wasn't something she was comfortable doing while her mother chopped pickles in the kitchen and her father snored in his old recliner. But some things couldn't be helped.

Since that night with Jake, she'd felt restless and off balance. Shaky, like jumping beans lived underneath her skin. Her whole body was infused with a quivering need that wouldn't go away. Her body knew what it wanted. It wanted Jake.

But there was another reason she wanted to see Jake. In fact, as the long days of the week dragged on, it became the most pressing reason. She wanted to buy a house, a house she could call her own.

She knew she was welcome to stay here for as long as she needed to, but since her parents' return, they'd all fallen into their old patterns, like old dogs who'd forgotten their new tricks. Dad went to the barber shop in the morning, came home for lunch, took a nap in his recliner, then went back to the shop in the afternoon. Her mom cleaned house, cooked, and shopped. And she spent hours in marathon yak sessions with all of her old friends.

And Marla Jean? She stayed off her foot like a good girl, did the books for the barber shop, read, sketched, and slept. When she was awake her mother waited on her hand and foot. In just the short time they'd been home, she felt displaced and in the way. Not because of anything they said or did. Heavens no, but even before they'd come home, the ghosts of parental dictates past echoed in her brain. After she'd moved back home to their house, she couldn't put a dirty spoon on the counter without hearing her mother's scolding voice.

Sometimes she wondered if they might be home to

stay. Her father was getting such a kick out of visiting with all of his old customers. Men who hadn't been inside the shop in years were showing up to visit with good old Milton. The place was swarming with business. Hoot and Dooley pretended in their daily reports to her that they could hardly concentrate on the Parcheesi game with everyone yammering all day long, but it was plain to see that they loved having Milton back, too.

The house had been constantly full of company. Besides her folks' old friends dropping by for visits, Lincoln and Dinah ate dinner with them almost every night, happy to have some unexpected time to spend with the folks. Harry had dropped by a few times, always bringing her flowers or magazines. Donny Joe dropped by, too, and she found his unflagging attention outright surprising.

Having Harry or Donny Joe come by felt a bit unnerving, though, like she was back in high school, trying to entertain a boy on the living room sofa while her parents hovered nearby in their bedroom listening for anything untoward. Not that doing anything untoward with Harry or Donny Joe was on her list. And more than likely, her parents were sacked out and sawing logs—Bitsy with her eye mask and Milton with his white noise machine. But still, it felt awkward.

Every night she went to sleep in her old bedroom on a daybed covered in pink ruffles. She felt like a little kid again. She was finally beginning to get used to not being Bradley's wife anymore, not living in her own house. If she wanted to go forward and stand on her own two feet, something had to change, because it felt like she was moving in the wrong direction.

"Lunch is ready, you two. Milton, wake up. Do you want a tray on the couch, Marla Jean?"

Marla Jean grabbed her crutches. "No thanks, Mom, I'll sit at the table with y'all."

Milton rubbed his hands over his face and pushed down the foot rest of his recliner. "It's about time, woman. I'm so hungry my belly button is saying howdy-doo to my backbone." He patted his ample stomach and winked at Marla Jean.

She followed her father into the kitchen, hoping her mother had taken the crust off her bread and cut it into little triangles the way she liked it.

Jake spent Wednesday holed up at his office in downtown Everson catching up on paperwork. If it was up to him he'd spend every day with a hammer in his hand, knocking down a wall or putting one back up, but today he'd left Theo working on the old house by himself, making excuses about how he'd been neglecting the money making part of his business. In all honesty, it had been a flimsy attempt to avoid any in-depth conversation with his brother about their father. There wasn't much doubt Theo was old enough to hear the truth, but Jake wasn't at all certain he was ready to tell it. He tried refocusing on the bid in front of him when the door blew open and Lincoln stormed inside.

Jake watched the emotions roll across his friend's face. Lincoln's expression changed from mad to lost, from hurt to confused, all in a matter of seconds—all emotions completely out of character for Lincoln Jones. He was normally the easiest going guy on the planet. Jake almost felt sorry for him.

"Hey Lincoln, I expected you sooner." Every day since last Friday night, he figured Linc would show up wanting to tear a strip from his hide.

Linc threw himself into the chair in front of Jake's desk. "I don't even know what to say to you."

Jake put down his pencil. "Maybe because it's none of your business when you get right down to it."

Linc crossed his legs, propping a foot up on the opposite knee. "That's what Dinah said."

"She's a smart woman. Maybe you should listen to her."

Lincoln brushed aside the advice like crumbs from a table. "So, are you going to explain what was going on?"

"You know what was going on, and it didn't involve anyone but me and Marla Jean."

Lincoln set back, fuming. "Damn it, Jake, I trusted you. You crossed the line."

"What line is that? Marla Jean's not some naïve kid. She's a grown woman. For Christ's sake, she's been married and divorced."

"Exactly, divorced and ripe for some sleazy guy to take advantage. You said you'd keep an eye on her while I was out of town."

"I watched her while you were out of town. What else do you want? Let me tell you, I took my life in my hands when I pulled her out of Donny Joe's truck. But you're back now, so the way I figure it, I'm off duty." He grinned just to see his friend's jaw clinch.

"I'm glad to see you find this so funny, and it's easy for you to laugh. She's not your sister."

"Exactly, Lincoln. She's not my sister."

"So, you're not even going to say you're sorry?"

"If Marla Jean requires an apology, I'll be glad to give her one. But I'm not going to apologize to you."

"Unbelievable. I know how you are with women, and I'm not going to stand by while you dillydally with my little sister. She's still too mixed up to know what she wants."

"She's been split from Bradley for a year. Let her go, Lincoln. She's got to find her own way to whatever's next."

"Not with you she doesn't."

"I agree."

Linc looked suspicious. "You do?"

"Look, I think you need to back off and give her some space. She's might make some mistakes before it's all over, but it won't be with me. You have my word on that."

"Aren't you the noble one?" Lincoln said sarcastically.

"I'm not being noble. Marla Jean says she's not looking for anything serious right now. She wants to have fun, kick up her heels a little."

"Sounds right up your alley, Jake."

"Ordinarily that would be true. But you and your family are important to me, and I'm not a complete bastard. Marla Jean says that's what she wants right now, but we both know sooner or later she's going to start wanting love and marriage and all that baby carriage crap. She deserves a nice guy who can give it to her."

"And that's not you," Lincoln stated firmly.

"And that's not me." Jake stood up and wandered over to stare out the window that looked out onto Main Street. "As you pointed out, my record with women speaks for itself." He exhaled loudly, then turned back to face Lincoln. "Have you heard the big news?"

"Over at the Rise-N-Shine Cal Crimmins' fifty-pound pumpkin is the main topic of conversation."

"This is bigger than Cal's pumpkin. Bradley asked my Aunt Libby to marry him, and she said yes. Last I heard they were aiming for a Christmas wedding."

"No shit. I wonder if Marla Jean's heard yet."

"I just wonder if she'll consider it good news or bad news. Do you think she still loves him, Linc?"

"Who the hell knows? She makes all the right noises about being over him. But, he hurt her pretty badly. When he asked for a divorce, I honestly don't think she saw it coming. This is all she needs right now. I appreciate the heads-up, Jake."

"Sure. So, do you still need to beat me up?"

Pounding his fist on his thigh, Linc looked as if taking a poke at him would make his day complete. But he grumbled, "Nah, I'd probably just break my hand, and Dinah wouldn't speak to me for a month." He stood up and walked to the door. Pausing, he looked back at Jake like he'd just realized something significant. "You care about Marla Jean, don't you, Jake?"

One side of Jake's mouth kicked up in a half smile. "She's your sister, Lincoln. Of course, I care. Now get out of here and go do some work. Don't you have a business to run?"

"Consider me gone." He sketched a salute and walked out of the office.

Jake continued to stand at the window, watching Lincoln stride down the sidewalk toward the building that housed his accounting firm. Across the way, Bertie Harcourt swept the front steps of the Rise-N-Shine after the lunch rush, and from the corner of his eye he caught sight of the old-fashioned red-and-white striped barber pole standing guard outside of MJ's Barber Shop. Everything looked normal—just another weekday in downtown Everson, Texas.

So why did Jake's world suddenly feel so off kilter?

If he was honest with himself, he'd admit the reason had everything to do with Marla Jean. But he meant what he said to Linc. He wasn't the right man for her. Trouble was, for the first time in his life, a small part of him wished he could be.

Once lunch was over, Marla Jean returned to her spot on the sofa. Alone at last. Her dad had gone back to the barber shop for the afternoon, and her mother decided to make another completely unnecessary trip to the grocery store.

Several books were stacked on the end table beside her, and she shuffled through the pile, trying to decide if she was in the mood for a Regency romance about a duke with amnesia or a mystery about an unbalanced blonde with a thing for short men. She decided on the duke just as the doorbell rang.

The front door opened, and Bradley stuck his head inside while she was still adjusting her crutches, trying to pull herself to her feet. "Marla Jean?"

"Bradley?" She collapsed back onto the cushions. He was the last person she'd expected to see.

"Can I come in? I need to talk to you about something."

In the middle of the day? Bradley didn't leave the car dealership in the middle of the day for anything but golf. "Come on in. It sounds serious."

He shambled into the living room, hands stuffed in his pockets, not meeting her eye. "I guess you could say that." He glanced up for a fleeting moment before returning his gaze to the flowery pattern of the area rug. He cleared his throat and said, "I didn't want you to hear this from anyone else first."

"Okay, I'm listening."

"Can I sit down?"

"Please, sit."

He looked at her father's recliner but opted for the orange side chair instead. "I hear your parents are home."

"Yes, they were coming home for Thanksgiving, anyway, but they decided to come early to give me a hand." She waved at her foot.

"Oh, I'm sorry. I should have asked. How is your foot?"

"I broke some toes, but I'll live."

"That's good, I mean it's not good, but knowing you, it won't slow you down for long."

"I'm hoping to get rid of these crutches tomorrow."

"And Milton and Bitsy? I trust they're doing okay?"

"My parents are fine, Bradley. I don't think you dropped by to inquire about my parents' health."

"No, no." He laughed a little, the way he always did when he felt nervous about something—or guilty.

"Well, what is it, Bradley? I'm imagining all sorts of horrible things. Are you sick? Are you dying? Holy mackerel, just spit it out."

He did his nervous laugh thing again. "It's nothing horrible. In fact, it's good news, at least I hope you'll be happy for me."

Marla Jean suddenly knew what he was going to say, but she sat still waiting for him to speak the words out loud. Waiting for him to make it real, because once he did, their life together would officially be history. Not that it wasn't already, but this would be the final nail in the pine box holding the stinking corpse that was their dead marriage.

"I asked Libby to marry me, and she accepted. I wanted you to hear the news from me."

Even though she'd been expecting it, the crutches slipped from her grasp, clattering to the floor. Bradley was going to marry Libby. It wasn't really a surprise. Somewhere out there in that hazy, nebulous part of her brain that tried to envision the future, she'd known this would happen. How did she feel about it? How the hell should she know? Numb, depressed, pitiful for caring. On top of that, he wanted her to be happy for him.

"Great. You're getting remarried." She hated being stuck on the couch, passively sitting there while things happened around her. And Bradley's sudden try for civility made her sick. Acting so considerate, so caring. She had the sudden urge to take him by the collar and drag his butt out the door and throw him off the porch just to watch him roll. Then she'd tell him to have a nice life. It wasn't as if he'd been going out of his way to be pleasant to her lately. "I'm not sure how this concerns me."

"Now, Marla Jean, you know how Everson is. Once word gets out it'll be all over town in no time, and I wanted you to be prepared. I'd like to think we're still friends."

"Friends? I can see why you'd like to think so. Because if the good folks of Everson think we're still friends, you come out smelling like a rose in all this, don't you Bradley? See, they'd say, 'He's not a bum for cheating on his wife and leaving her for another woman. See—they're still best buds. If he was a scumbag, she wouldn't give him the time of day.' But friends don't treat friends the way you treated me the other night."

He looked exasperated. "What did you expect, Marla Jean? You whacked Libby with the bathroom door right in front of everyone."

"Fine, if that's what you want to believe, go ahead. And

since you've made your big announcement I think you should leave."

"I'm sorry, Marla Jean, but I don't think you realize how hard this has been for Libby. She's very concerned that the whole town thinks she's a home wrecker."

"Excuse me if I don't have any sympathy for what she's going through—since it was my home she wrecked." The last part was shouted, and she clamped her mouth shut, not wanting to lose control in front of him.

"You should blame me for that, not Libby."

"Okay, let's talk about you, Bradley. You say we should still be friends, but did you stop and think for one minute how hard it was for me to go to that football game? I haven't been all year because I didn't want to deal with all the gossip."

He had the nerve to smirk. "That's a good one. Try not giving everyone in town so much to gossip about."

She ignored him. "I was tired of being poor, pitiful dumped Marla Jean, tired of sitting home alone, so when Harry asked I said sure, what the heck? And when I got to the game, there you were sitting in our old seats, surrounded by all of our old friends just like it used to be. Except for one minor detail. I'd been replaced, and don't think everyone in the stands didn't have their eyes peeled, watching to make sure I wasn't going to fall apart at the sight of you and Libby together."

He held out his hands in a gesture of helplessness. "I never meant to hurt you."

"Oh shut up, Bradley. And don't flatter yourself. This isn't about you."

"What's it about then?"

"It's about what happened at the pizza parlor after

that. I was having a nice time, thinking how glad I was I'd decided to go to the game, until I happened to walk out of the bathroom at the exact same moment Libby was walking in. It was like some cosmic joke, and it might have even been funny if you hadn't decided to run across the room so you could scold me like a schoolgirl while the entire town watched."

He had the sense to look ashamed. "I might have over-reacted, but you've been running wild lately. What was I supposed to think?"

"You're supposed to think it was an accident, but you were too busy posturing, protecting poor little Libby from mean ole me."

"You hit her in the face." He sounded petulant like he still wanted to justify his outrage.

"The door hit her in the face. If I'd wanted to take a swing at her I wouldn't have hidden behind a door to do it."

"Okay, okay, you're right. You have my sincerest apologies, Marla Jean."

"That didn't sound too sincere, but I'll accept it, anyway. Besides, I'd never hit a woman who was that much older than me. I was taught to respect my elders."

He looked appalled. "That was a low blow."

"Oh, lighten up, Bradley."

"So, does this mean we have your blessing?" he persisted.

She grabbed the crutches from the floor and struggled off the couch. "Don't press your luck. It means the two of you deserve each other."

He stood there with an imploring look on his face.

Finally, she gave in. "All right. I hope you and Libby will be very happy together."

As he grabbed her up in an awkward hug, one of her crutches dug into his ribs before she could maneuver it out of the way. "Thanks, Marly Jay. That means a lot to me. By the way, I think Harry is a nice guy. You could do worse."

"Let's make a deal, Bradley. You stay out of my love life, and I won't offer Libby any advice on how to plan the wedding."

Chapter Sixteen

⁓

"Howdy, Miz Bandy. Where to?" Bo Birdwell jumped out of his taxi and opened the back door. Everson's only cab driver was tall and lanky with skinny stork legs and a smile that couldn't contain all his teeth. On duty or off, he always dressed in blue jeans, a plaid cowboy shirt, and a baseball cap featuring farm equipment covering his red hair. "Let me help you with those crutches."

"Thanks, Bo. I just need a ride to town."

"No problem. I'll have you there in a jiffy."

That was true. The ride would be over before she could settle back in her seat. It was only a few blocks to downtown, but it was too far to manage on crutches.

He got back in the driver's seat, set his meter, and took off. "Have you heard the big news?"

"I'm not sure. At lunch Dad was carrying on about Cal Crimmins and his seventy-five-pound pumpkin."

"Seventy-five pounds? That thing's gettin' bigger by the minute. But no, I was talking about the wedding. Miss Libby and Mr. Bradley are planning a big to-do…" He looked in the rearview mirror, and his words trailed off to nothing.

"That's okay, Bo. In fact, I heard all about it this afternoon."

"Me and my big mouth. I didn't mean to speak out of turn."

She waved a hand, dismissing his concern. "Not at all. I'm sure they'll be very happy together." She glued a smile on her face, but it must not have been very convincing. Bo kept giving her pitying glances in the mirror the rest of the trip and didn't say another word.

After Bradley finally left the house, Marla Jean had felt restless and penned in. All she wanted to do was get out. She wasn't supposed to drive yet, and even if she'd wanted to try, her mother had her car. Her only option had been to call Bo and his cab to take her into town.

She didn't have a clue what she was going to do once she got there, but it was better than sitting in her parents' house stewing about the things she should or shouldn't have said to Bradley.

Maybe she'd stop by the barber shop and see how they were managing without her, but she knew the answer to that. They were managing just fine. She wasn't in the mood to have it rubbed in her face. That would only make her feel more useless than she already did.

Maybe she'd go to the diner instead and eat a big piece of pie. Maybe two or three. As she was weighing her options, the taxi slowed down in front of MJ's and across the street she spotted Jake's Porsche parked in the lot by his office. Good old Lucinda. Suddenly she knew exactly where she wanted to go and why. Bo pulled the taxi to the curb and dropped her at Jake's Home Remodeling Services.

She had a proposition to make.

Letting the cool autumn breeze calm her nerves, she stood on the sidewalk, taking a moment to collect herself. The noises of everyday activity on Main Street eddied around her as she stared at the door to his business. While she'd been sitting at home on the sofa, talking to Jake had seemed simple enough, but now standing outside his office, she knew she was out of her element. She wanted to come across as casual and sophisticated, not pathetic and desperate. Taking a fortifying breath, she grabbed the metal handle with her sweaty palm, pulled open the door, and walked inside.

"Jake, how's it going?" Her voice sounded frail so she added a bright smile to bolster it.

He was sitting behind his desk, a big, old-fashioned wooden thing, his shirt sleeves rolled up to reveal strong wrists, his black hair neat and suspiciously short, and he wore eyeglasses perched on his nose as he pored over the house plans in front of him. The glasses made him look serious, studious, and good-looking in a whole new way. Like he needed more ways to look good. At the mere sight of him, a tremor rolled through her body and she came to a wobbly stop.

"Hey, Marla Jean." He sounded half friendly, half wary, but he stood up and waved her toward an uphol-stered chair. "You better sit down before you fall down." He came over to help with a hand under her elbow for support, and then took the crutches, leaning them against the wall. "What brings you to town? I saw your dad over at the barber shop."

The mere touch of his hand on her arm distracted her, made her feel addled and lightheaded, but still, when he let go, she wished for it back. Straightening in her chair she fought for composure. If she was going to get through this, she needed to stop being such a goose.

Speaking of the barber shop, she studied his head of hair as he walked around his desk and said, "I can see that. Dad gave you a haircut, didn't he?" She pointed an accusing finger at him. "What happened to that tricky cowlick of yours that only good old Floyd Cramer over in Derbyville can manage?"

Jake ran a hand over his hair, smoothing his errant curls, though one refused to cooperate and fell right back onto his forehead. "Marla Jean, your father's cut my hair since I was eight. He understands my cowlick better than anyone in the world."

"Mmm hmm. I see how it is. You're just never going to let me cut your hair, are you?"

He ignored her question and asked one of his own. "So, besides giving me a hard time, what brings you by? Lincoln said you were getting around better."

"Oh, he did? Does that mean you and Lincoln are back on speaking terms?"

"We came to an understanding." He sounded rather grim.

"I hope it didn't involve locking me away in a tower somewhere." At this point, she was only half joking.

He laughed. "No, in fact, I told him you were a grown woman, and he should back off, give you some space."

"Why thank you, Jake. Maybe by some miracle, he'll listen to you." Without warning, she changed the subject. "I guess you've heard the big news?"

"You mean Cal and his pumpkin? He's prouder than a man with a six-legged dog." He leaned back in his chair.

"No, I mean Bradley and Libby." She tried to sound breezy.

"Oh, so you've heard." He picked up a pen and clicked it a few times before putting it back down.

"I've heard." She tried a smile on for size.

Jake let out a big sigh. It could have been relief or resignation, she wasn't sure, and then he said, "I was actually a witness to the whole thing. He went down on one knee and everything."

She held up a hand. "Spare me the details."

"Sorry. It was just the last thing I expected when we went over for dinner Saturday night. I'll tell you, you could have knocked me over."

She wrinkled her nose and gestured toward his black eye. "Well, we already know you can't take a punch."

"Ha ha. How did you hear?"

"Bradley was thoughtful enough to stop by the house and tell me himself."

"Are you okay?" She could see concern in his eyes, but it wasn't the pitying kind of looks she'd gotten from Bo on the ride over, and for that, she was grateful.

"Of course. Why wouldn't I be? I was a little thrown at first, but it's not like I didn't see this coming." She'd been over Bradley for a while now. It had been the marriage she'd had trouble letting go of.

Jake nodded. "I only hope Aunt Libby knows what she's getting into."

He was sweet to worry about his aunt, but she had other fish to fry at the moment. "Enough about the happy couple. I wanted to talk to you about something else entirely."

The wariness she'd sensed when she first walked in was back. "Okay, shoot."

"I'm going to start looking for a house. To buy," she clarified. "I need a place of my own, and since you buy houses and fix them up, I thought you could steer me in the right direction."

He seemed to relax a little when he realized the topic wasn't personal. "Sure, I'll give you the name of my realtor."

That wasn't the kind of help she'd had in mind, but she didn't want to get off track. "Thanks, but that can wait. I have something else I want to talk about first." She sat there feeling the tips of her ears grow hot while she built the courage to continue.

"I'm listening," he said when she didn't elaborate.

Taking a deep breath she barreled ahead. "About the other night? Before Linc walked in on us?" Something in his expression gave her pause, but she plunged ahead. "I think we should finish what we started. Jake, would you like to have sex with me?"

Chapter Seventeen

～

He exploded from his chair, and without a word turned his back to her. She could see him fiddling with the coffee-maker on the counter behind him. Finally, without looking her direction he asked, "Do you want some coffee?"

"Coffee? No, thanks." Her stomach was already doing somersaults. It wasn't as if she'd had much practice at this sort of thing. Somehow, she couldn't picture Genna Stanley sitting down across a desk from him trying to present a logical case for why he should sleep with her. She imagined her presentation would be a bit more physical, something along the lines of a strip tease and a lap dance.

Jake finally sat back down with a mug and took a sip.

Thinking he might have misunderstood her intentions, she pressed on. The lack of enthusiasm on his part was disheartening to say the least, but she wasn't surprised that he'd have some resistance to the idea at first. He just needed to see why it was such a good idea. Trying for an air of sophistication she didn't feel, she cleared her throat and smiled. "So, as I was saying. I don't see any good reason not to finish what we started."

He removed his eyeglasses and threw them on the desk. "Look, Marla Jean—"

"Hear me out, Jake. I'm not asking you to be my steady or anything. You don't have to worry about me turning into some clinging vine that wants all your time and attention."

"Whoa, hold up there, missy. Let me get this straight. You're saying you're only interested in sex?" The intensity in his eyes made her fidget in her seat, but it was out there now.

"Exactly." A nervous laugh escaped her throat. Maybe she was better at this than she thought, and maybe this was actually the perfect way to approach him. Sitting in his office in the middle of the day. It came across as more businesslike, more woman of the world—a no strings, no hearts and flowers, no messy entanglements arrangement between two consenting adults.

"Jesus, Marla Jean."

"I know how you feel about commitment and relationships, and believe me, the last thing I need right now is anything resembling romance."

"So it would just be a service I provided." The edge to his voice was sharp enough to draw blood.

His attitude brought her up short, and she bristled at the implication that she'd be using him somehow. "You didn't seem to have a problem with the idea of 'servicing' me when you had me pinned to the bed the other night."

"Hey now. You were all riled up, and I was trying to calm you down. Things got out of hand, and okay, that was my fault."

"Is that what they're calling it these days? I believe I'm beginning to feel riled up all over again, Jake. Why don't we clear off your desk and continue that conversation right now?"

He popped out of his seat again like he'd been goosed. "Come on, Marla Jean, knock it off. You're Linc's kid sister." He turned his back on her once more, this time dumping the contents of his mug in a small sink. Whipping around to face her, he added, "And the other night you were loopy on pain medication. I shouldn't have taken advantage."

When she'd imagined this meeting, she honestly hadn't expected him to take so much convincing. And she was getting a little peeved. "I'm not loopy now. And suddenly I'm Linc's kid sister again? How convenient. As you pointed out, I'm a grown woman, for God's sake. And damn it, I should get a say in who does or doesn't take advantage of me."

"Well, it's not going to be me," he said forcefully.

"Or Donny Joe, or any other man in the neighboring counties if you and my brother have your way," she muttered.

He took a step in her direction. "So, is that what this is all about? You're still mad because I pulled you out of Donny Joe's truck?"

She threw up her hands in disgust. "Exactly, Jake. You've certainly got me all figured out."

He shook his head. "Not by a long shot."

"I'll spell it out for you then. I thought we could get busy, have a roll in the hay, fool around, get to know each other in the biblical sense, but apparently I read the signals wrong when you had your tongue down my throat Friday night."

They glared at each other for a minute without blinking. Then he drew a hand over his face and marched around the desk. Dragging an extra chair up beside hers, he sat down and said earnestly, "Marla Jean, this is a really bad idea for all kinds of reasons."

"Don't sugarcoat it, Jake. If you're not interested, just say so."

"Right now, you think this is what you want—mindless sex to get you through a few lonely nights. But you're not the kind of woman who could be happy with that kind of arrangement."

"These days you don't know me well enough to know what would make me happy, Jake, and besides, it's been good enough for you all these years, hasn't it?" She was being sarcastic, but his nearness was playing havoc with her senses. He smelled like soap and sawdust, and the faint bristle of whiskers shadowed his jaw. Her gaze fell to the purple bruise under his eye. Without weighing the cost, her hand reached out to touch him, gently tracing his cheekbone. "Does it hurt much?"

"Nah, you hit like a girl." His brown eyes flared for an instant, and she thought he might kiss her, but the moment passed and he pulled away. "Listen to me, Marla Jean, I'm flattered, and I'm tempted, and Lord knows I'm going to hate myself the minute you walk out that door. You are a fine-looking, desirable woman, but what you need to do, when you're ready, is find yourself a nice guy and make a good life with him."

"I had a nice guy and a nice life. He dumped me for your aunt, remember?"

At the mention of Bradley he seemed to get irritated all over again. He stood up. "You expect me to believe the fact that your ex-husband just told you he's getting remarried doesn't have anything to do with why you chose this particular moment to show up at my office?"

She inhaled and closed her eyes. Letting the air out in one big gust, she answered, "Maybe it does. I don't know. I'm tired of overanalyzing every move I make. I only know the other night when we were kissing I didn't once compare you to Bradley or anything else for that matter. For once I was simply feeling, and God help me, it felt amazing." She got to her feet with as much dignity as she could muster.

His face was like a closed book. "I don't know what else to say, Marla Jean."

"You don't have to say anything. Really. I just spent the better part of last year getting over a man who didn't want me, so I'm not about to spend my time convincing you of what a great bargain I'm offering. I still think we would have been good together, so I'm going to consider it your loss and move on." She grabbed her crutches and made her way to the door.

Jake got up and followed her. "Marla Jean—"

"Don't worry about it, Jake. I'm not upset. Let's file it away in the lousy idea department and move on. I've had plenty of those lately. Someday I'm sure I'll thank you for saving me from myself, but right now I'm going across the street to the diner and see how much pie I can eat before Dad closes the shop for the day."

He called after her, "Do you still want the name of my realtor?"

She didn't bother answering as she swept out of the office. She was already trying to decide between chocolate cream or lemon meringue. Neither one of those had ever let her down.

• • •

Jake watched her go. Just stood there staring at the door as it closed behind her. He felt like kicking something, and luckily there weren't any truck tires handy. The chair beside him was handy, though, and he hurled it, watching it scuttle across the floor and topple over on its side in a fetal position. He didn't feel any better for having defeated the chair.

He stomped back over to his desk and slumped into his seat. The top of his head threatened to blow off. That woman. Why should he feel like some kind of cad for not sleeping with her? He was being noble, damn it. Noble. And she had the nerve to act insulted. He was the one that should feel insulted.

He wasn't going to be a stand-in for her ex-husband. Not now, not ever. And if sex was really all she wanted from him, then she wasn't the woman he thought he knew. Marla Jean had worn her heart on her sleeve since she'd been six years old, and this kind of calculated, dry, emotionless arrangement wasn't in her nature. At least it hadn't been before Bradley and Aunt Libby taught her that caring too much was a risky proposition.

Maybe she thought they were two of a kind now. He'd demonstrated loudly and often to anyone who would listen that mushy, emotional, exposed, overwrought relationships weren't for him. He picked up a book from his desk and threw it across the office watching the spine bounce off the wall and fall, pages open, to the floor. He was the last person on God's green earth she should emulate. The very last person.

A few days later Marla Jean stepped onto the porch of her parents' house and inhaled the crisp October afternoon. She was all ready to give her new walking boot a trial run. After breakfast her mother had driven her to her doctor's appointment and—hallelujah—he'd said she could graduate from the crutches. Just in time, too. Her armpits felt like someone had scrubbed them with cactus and finished them off with a vinegar poultice. If she never saw those instruments of torture again it would be too soon. And she was sick to death of being cooped up inside the four walls of the house doing nothing.

She looked around the old neighborhood. It was the middle of the afternoon, in the middle of the week, and everything was quiet. Then the sound of an electric saw cut through the peaceful day.

She looked across the street at the old Jacobson house. Jake must be working. His truck wasn't parked in the driveway, but an old blue Jeep was there instead. How many vehicles did that man own, anyway?

She hadn't seen him since the encounter at his office. Maybe she should feel humiliated about the way he'd reacted to her blunt proposition, but she refused to let him, or any other man, make her feel bad about herself anymore. And she'd thought long and hard about his accusation that she was reacting to Bradley's announcement that he was marrying Libby.

Maybe there was some truth to it, but it certainly wasn't the whole story. Besides if a man wanted sex, for whatever reason, he went out and found it. Why should she be any different? I am woman, hear me roar. Didn't she sound bold?

But regardless of the drama, she still wanted his help finding a house. He was always buying them and fixing them up. That was what she wanted to do—find an affordable house with good bones and transform it into a place of her own. Jake was the logical person to turn to. She was just going to have to swallow her pride and ask for his help.

And maybe, if she made the first move, it would get them beyond any lingering awkwardness that might remain since she asked him to screw her brains out on top of his desk. In broad daylight. In the middle of a workday. It still sounded like a good idea.

But she wasn't going to force herself on the man, for God's sake. She had some pride, after all, and the sooner he realized it, the sooner things would get back to normal.

She was a little wobbly going down the steps but then she got the hang of things and started down the sidewalk at a good clip. She'd walked up and down this street a million times growing up, and the cracked, uneven sidewalk was as familiar as her own face. The place where the cement sank down just past the driveway, the buckled spot on the other side of the old oak tree, the handprints Lincoln and Jake dared her to make the year the city replaced the old sidewalk with new ones.

As she passed Mrs. Reece's house next door with its sunny yellow trim and mum-filled flower beds, Pooky barked at her from the front window, bouncing up and down like he was testing a trampoline. "Good afternoon, Pooky, you little darling," she sang out. As long as the dog was locked securely inside her neighbor's house, she would greet him like they were long-lost pals.

As she crossed the street to Jake's house, she could now hear hammering coming from the back yard. She walked around to the side and opened the wooden gate, letting out a "Hello" as she rounded the corner.

He was standing high on a ladder, replacing a board. A bandana was wrapped around his forehead, sunglasses covered his eyes, and he wasn't wearing a shirt.

It was quite a sight. She might've re-filed him back into the category of safe and unattainable, but still, it was quite a sight.

The smooth, sun darkened skin of his back flexing with each whack of the hammer. Impressively muscled arms, corded and bulging. A rivulet of sweat wending its way down his neck, past his shoulder blade, sliding down to the dimple at the small of his back. She watched patiently, knowing it would soon come to the end of its journey when it met up with the waistband of his jeans.

"Can I help you?"

Realizing the hammering had stopped, she was embarrassed to have been caught staring. He was silhouetted against the sky, but now that he'd twisted around on the ladder to face her, one thing was very clear. He wasn't Jake. Instead it was a man who seemed amazingly Jakelike. They were built the same. They both had black hair and once he removed his sunglasses she could see he had brown eyes. But this man, the man now scrambling down the ladder and ambling toward her, had a lightness about him that Jake had never possessed, not even as a young boy.

She didn't even pretend not to stare. "I'm sorry, I was looking for Jake."

He pretended deep disappointment. "Will I do instead?"

Marla Jean thought he would probably do very nicely for most things, but out loud she said, "I'm afraid not, Mr. . . . ?"

"Oh, excuse me, ma'am. I'm Theo Jacobson, Jake's younger brother." He held out his hand.

Shocked by the introduction, she took his hand and shook it. "Really? I didn't know Jake had a younger brother."

"I'm a well-kept secret." He winked, but Marla Jean wasn't sure he was kidding. After all, she'd known Jake most of her life. If he had a brother, wouldn't she know about it?

"So, is Jake inside?" She gestured toward the back door of the house.

"No, he went to town. Said he'd be at his office doing paperwork most of the afternoon. I'd be glad to tell him you came by, Ms. . . . ?"

"Oh, I'm sorry. I'm Marla Jean, Marla Jean Bandy from across the street, two doors down. I'll just try to catch Jake later."

Theo's face lit up with recognition. "You're Marla Jean? Lincoln's little sister?"

She smiled at his enthusiasm. "That's me. The one and only."

"Jake talks about your family all the time. I feel like I already know you."

"Uh oh. Should I be worried?" She didn't bat her eyelashes, but it was a close call.

He took a step toward her. "Maybe I can buy you dinner tonight, and we can discuss it?"

She stood her ground. "Wow, you move fast."

"Too fast?" His grin said he didn't think so.

"Not necessarily," she said merrily. "But I already have plans tonight." Her plans included her mother's meatloaf and working on a jigsaw puzzle with her dad, but she didn't want to appear too eager. Beside it would give her a chance to grill Lincoln for details about this Theo person first.

Jake's brother. She still couldn't quite take it all in.

"Well then, how about Friday night? A little dining, a lot of dancing. Take pity on the new guy in town."

She looked down at her walking boot. "I'm not too light on my feet these days."

"But you have to eat?" He looked hopeful.

She took a moment to consider him, smiling the whole time, enjoying herself. "Maybe I should take you to Lu Lu's."

"Lu Lu's?"

"Yeah, it's a bar with decent food and dancing. And if I can't manage, I don't think you'll have any trouble finding other dance partners. There's nothing the women around here love more than taking pity on the new guy in town."

He put his hand over his heart. "If you can't manage, Marla Jean, I won't care about dancing."

She started walking toward the gate. "You should save some of that charm for Friday night."

He caught up and pushed the gate open for her. With a big grin he asked, "Then it's a date? What time should I pick you up?"

"Let's say seven o'clock."

"Seven o'clock it is."

She spotted the beat up blue Jeep sitting in the driveway. If it had belonged to Jake, he would probably have named it after some woman, a practical, down-to-earth woman, more than likely. Thelma maybe, or Agnes. "By the way, Theo, do you name your cars?"

"No, I can't say that I do." Theo glanced at the Jeep and then back at her. "Is that a problem?"

She shook her head dismissively. "Not at all. In fact, I'm pleased as punch to hear it." Pushing off on her walking boot, she started down the driveway.

He looked puzzled and shouted after her. "Do you want a ride? I should have offered sooner."

"That's very gallant of you, Theo, but I need the exercise. I'll see you Friday night."

Chapter Eighteen

~

Marla Jean bit her bottom lip in concentration as she spread purple nail polish on the big toe of her right foot. A loud rapping on the front door caused her to jump and smear the color all over the cuticle. "Son of a sea biscuit," she snarled. It was only six o'clock, and Theo wasn't supposed to pick her up until seven. He better not be a whole hour early. She was still in sweats and had rollers in her hair.

Besides that, it hadn't been easy to situate herself so she could reach the toes sticking out of her walking boot. She'd finally taken the confounded thing off and didn't want to stop to get the door with her toes half done. "Mom," she bellowed with the grace of a fishwife, "somebody's at the front door."

Only silence followed her earsplitting call for help. She knew her father was out in the garage working on an old lawn mower. Dad gum it. There came another knock combined with an impatient ringing of the doorbell while she huffed and puffed to get herself up from the couch and hippity hopped her way across the living room floor.

"Hold your horses, I'm coming as fast as I can..." her words trailed off when she opened the door and found Jake standing on the front porch. As always he seemed to fill up the space with his broad shoulders and lazy smile. He was wearing soft-looking jeans, a deep blue shirt, and a light tan cowboy hat sat tipped back on his dark head of hair. Damn, he looked good.

From his casual manner no one would know they'd been at each other's throats the last time they spoke. No hint that she'd foolishly offered to let him have his way with her. Or that he'd said thanks, but no thanks. So, she sought to echo his devil-may-care pose, while wondering what the heck he wanted and why the heck he was there. He usually only showed up when he thought she needed rescuing from something.

"Hey, Marla Jean." He grinned and greeted her like they were long-lost buddies, best pals forever, and all that nonsense. That was good, she supposed. She would be glad to pretend nothing had ever happened. "I was in the neighborhood, and thought I'd stop by to give you the name of my real estate lady." He pulled a business card from his shirt pocket and handed it to her.

"Thanks, but you shouldn't have gone to any trouble."

"It was no trouble, and besides, I also wanted to give you this." From behind his back he pulled out a single cowboy boot and presented it to her with a self-satisfied smile. It was beige with green vines and daisies, orange and white ones, strewn across it.

She eyed it guardedly. "That's very thoughtful, but why

pray-tell are you giving me a boot?" She stood balanced on one foot with her hand braced on the doorframe.

"Because I owe you a boot." He held it out again, but she still didn't take it.

"You don't owe me a boot, but even if you did, what in tarnation am I going to do with just one?"

He shrugged like it wasn't his problem. "That's all you ruined when you kicked my tire. I don't think I'm responsible for the whole pair." Then he winked.

She blinked at him and then frowned. Why in the world was he winking at her? "You're a real funny guy, Jake. By the way, that boot doesn't even match the one I ruined."

"It's pretty close. Flowers and green winding viney things. No one will notice the difference."

She crossed her arms across her chest and decided to play along. "So, how did you manage to just buy one boot?"

"Hmm, well, that was a bit of a problem. They wouldn't sell me just the one, so I had to buy the pair."

"But you're just giving me this one."

"If you want to buy the other one, I'll give you a good deal." He smiled again, and she could have sworn he was flirting with her. But that didn't make a lick of sense. Not after the conversation they'd had in his office.

But she didn't have time to figure him out right now. She needed to finish getting ready for her date with his secret brother. "I don't mean to be rude, but I'm kind of busy right now, Jake."

His grin faded to a look of concern. "Hey, you shouldn't be standing up, and speaking of boots, why aren't you wearing that walking contraption?"

"I'm not wearing that walking contraption because you

interrupted me. As you can see, I was in the middle of painting my toenails."

He looked down at her bare feet. "That's an interesting shade of purple."

"Purple? I wouldn't dream of putting something so mundane on my toes. Don't you recognize Plum Rum Raisin Passion when you see it?" She started hopping back to the couch.

He followed, closing the door behind him. "Hey, hold up. Let me help you."

"I don't need any help. I'm getting around just fine these days." Marla Jean sat down and propped her injured foot back on the coffee table. She picked up the purple nail polish and shook the bottle. Then she unscrewed the top and started putting polish on her "this little piggy had roast beef" toe.

"So, I guess you have a hot date with Harry?"

"Not tonight. He's over at the high school watching film, getting ready for next week's play-off game."

"Oh yeah, the whole town's pumped up about the chance to beat Cedar Valley. Are you going?" Jake took his hat off and set it on the end table, then he made himself at home in a side chair, holding the cowboy boot in his lap.

"No, the game is up in Dallas, and Harry will be busy with the team the whole time." She'd tried to make it clear to Harry that she wasn't interested in anything serious, and she hoped he was beginning to take the hint.

Jake leaned forward in his chair. With great interest, as if she were performing a delicate operation, he watched as she painted her toenails. "I don't get it. Why do women like to paint themselves up so much?"

"For the same reason you like to remodel houses. We need a bit of caulk and Spackle to fill in all the cracks every once in a while. It gives us the illusion that we're bright and shiny and new."

"You don't need any remodeling. You've got good bones and a sturdy foundation."

"Well, if you aren't the silver-tongued devil?"

"You know what I mean, Marla Jean. You don't need make-up to look good."

"That's awfully kind, but maybe I enjoy putting on a little war paint now and then. It speaks to the inner hussy in me, so mind your own beeswax."

He held up his hands. "Hey, Spackle away. It's no skin off my nose. I was just trying to be nice."

"You forget I'm a single woman these days. Before I can even dream of stepping one foot out the door, I have to tart myself up, especially if I'm going to catch the eye of the eligible men in this town." She waggled her eyebrows at him.

"You don't seem to be having any trouble in that department." He didn't say it like he considered that a good thing. "Speaking from a man's perspective, I think most women look better without all that stuff on their face."

Marla Jean finished her toes and screwed the lid back on the polish. Keeping them propped up on the edge of the table to dry, she leaned back into the couch cushions, crossed her arms over her chest, and gave him an assessing look. "Just to satisfy my curiosity, name another woman you think looks better without make-up."

He gave her the fish eye. "Is this a trick question?"

"You started down this road, buddy. Just answer the question."

He looked up at the ceiling like he was pondering likely candidates. "Uh, Irene Cornwell, maybe?"

"Are you asking me or telling me?"

He nodded as if to confirm confidence in his choice. "I'd say she's a natural beauty."

Marla coughed. "Next thing you'll be telling me, you believe those boobies are original equipment, too."

He glared like he'd been insulted. "Not likely. We all have our area of expertise and the female anatomy happens to be mine."

His show of righteous indignation made her laugh. "Well, I hate to break it to you, big guy, but Irene wears more make-up in a month then I wear in a year. But I've got to hand it to her. She's a genius in applying it. The trick is to look like you're not wearing anything at all."

He scratched his chin like he wasn't buying it. "What about Mindy Shaffer?"

"Mindy owns stock in Maybelline."

"Leslie Gansert? Ruby Pitt?"

Marla pursed her lips and shook her head sadly.

"Well damn."

"Oh don't sound so disappointed. Your girlfriend Genna isn't exactly a stranger to cosmetics, and if you act surprised at that, I'm gonna pull up a stool and watch for your nose to start growing."

The mention of Genna seemed to annoy him. "Can we change the subject?" he asked.

She leaned forward to inspect her toes. "Fine with me. I met your brother Theo."

He froze. "You met Theo?"

"Yes, and wasn't that rude of you not to introduce us? You could have knocked me over with a feather when he said he was your younger brother, Jake. Who knew?" She'd never gotten a chance to ask Linc any questions about Jake's mysterious sibling.

Now looking completely out of sorts, Jake lunged to his feet and held out the boot. "So, do you want this or not?" He certainly wasn't flirting now.

Before she could answer, her mom walked into the room. "Jake? Is that you? Come here and give me a hug this instant."

His face lit up at the sight of Bitsy. After dropping the boot down on the coffee table with an indelicate thud, he walked over and wrapped her up in a big bear hug. Before letting her go, he twirled her around, making her giggle like a schoolgirl. "I swear you get younger and prettier every time I see you, Bitsy. When are you going to leave Milton and run off with me to Fiji?"

It was a standing joke between the two of them. When he was around eight, he'd seen some guy win a trip to Fiji on the Wheel of Fortune, and since then he was always promising to whisk her away.

She swatted his arm. "Oh, go on with you. You could charm the bark off that old oak tree out front. Have you had dinner yet? You should stay and eat. Linc and Dinah will be here any minute, and I want to hear how your mother's doing."

Taking advantage of the interruption, Marla Jean grabbed her walking boot and strapped it on her leg. Her mom would bend Jake's ear long enough for her to make an escape to her bedroom so she could finish getting ready for her date.

She made it to the edge of the hallway when her mother called out, "Marla Jean, did you offer Jake something to drink? Do you want something to drink, Jake?" He didn't get a chance to answer. "Where are your manners, young lady?"

Without slowing down she called back, "Sorry, Mom. I need to get changed." She could still hear her mother fussing over him when she closed her bedroom door.

Linc poured the last of the beer into Jake's mug. "The next pitcher is on me, but right now, I'm going to dance with my wife. Come on, Dinah, let's show 'em how it's done."

Dinah didn't need to be asked twice. She dragged her husband out onto the wooden dance floor while Willie Nelson sang about some woman who was always on his mind. Jake watched them go, trying to figure out exactly how he'd ended up spending his Friday night at Lu Lu's watching other people dance. By other people he meant Marla Jean and Theo. That's all he'd been doing since he arrived. Her white sweater drew his attention like a flag of surrender. Maybe he'd cut in later just to see if it was as soft as it looked.

Not that you could call what the two of them were doing dancing. Because of her walking boot, it could better be described as standing way too close and swaying to the music. They both seemed perfectly happy with the situation. And he couldn't come up with a single logical reason to object, but more and more his thoughts about Marla Jean defied anything resembling logic.

When he found himself in the boot store that afternoon looking at women's boots he hadn't allowed himself to examine the reasons too closely. He ended up spending way too much money for the silly-looking things, but he'd discovered he was willing to pay any amount of money to smooth things over with her. He couldn't stop seeing her face when she'd offered herself to him. Her body, that is. Certainly not her heart or soul. She'd looked fierce, and determined, and proud.

Everything in him had wanted to pick her up and push her against the nearest wall and kiss her until neither of them could see straight. After all, she was a grown woman and could make her own mistakes. That's what he'd told Linc. But then what? Nothing would be different, and he wasn't willing to be one of her mistakes.

He'd felt conflicted, and tempted, and furious all at the same time. Saying no had been the hardest thing he'd ever done. By comparison, not killing his father with his bare hands all those years ago had been a piece of cake. Okay, that was an exaggeration. And that was just for starters.

When he'd driven to her house, with the peace offering of a cowboy boot, it had been to make amends. Instead he found her getting all gussied up, wearing curlers in her hair, putting on toenail polish. There had been something intimate about watching her paint her toes. And then Bitsy had refused to take no for an answer, and before he knew what had happened he was sitting at the dinner table with the whole family, except for Marla Jean.

Linc and Dinah showed up, and Milton had come in all greasy from the garage. Jake had been corralled into helping Linc set the table, just like old times, and Dinah helped Bitsy bring the food to the table. By the time Milton was cleaned up and sitting down, everything was ready. But there was still no sign of Marla Jean. He'd seen neither hide nor hair of her since she'd run off to her bedroom. He found himself watching the hallway, listening for the sound of her door opening. The woman had him tied in knots, and he wasn't sure what to do about it.

He'd just helped himself to another pork chop and some mustard greens when the doorbell rang. That brought Marla Jean out of hiding lickety-split.

"Don't get up. I'll get it," she yelled as she waddled at a respectable pace past the dining room. Her hair was down from the curlers, riots of waves flying out behind her. He caught a glimpse of tight blue jeans and a soft-looking white sweater before she disappeared from sight.

When she reappeared she was leading Theo into the dining room. Thinking his brother must have come by looking for him, Jake laid his napkin on the table and pushed his chair back so he could stand up. "Hey, Theo, how'd you know where to find me?"

Theo looked at him and then back at Marla Jean and everything clicked into place for Jake even before Theo cleared it up for everyone else. "Hey, Jake, I didn't know you were here. I came to pick up Marla Jean."

Without a word, he sat back down, fighting the urge to protest. It wasn't any of his business what Marla Jean did. Wasn't that what he'd preached to Lincoln only a few days ago?

"We've got a date," Theo continued. "She was nice enough to offer to take me dancing at Lu Lu's."

Lincoln stood up and held out a hand to Theo. "It's been a long time, Theo. It's nice to see you again." The two men shook hands before Linc turned to his sister. "How are you going to dance with that thing on your leg, sis?"

Marla Jean ignored him and wrapped a hand around Theo's arm. "We should get going and let y'all finish eating." She looked anxious to be gone.

Milton stood up. "Aren't you going to introduce your young man to the rest of us, Marla Jean?"

"Sorry, Daddy. Theo, this is my father Milton, my mother Bitsy. You seem to know my brother Lincoln, and this is his wife Dinah. And of course, you know Jake. Everybody, this is Theo, Theo Jacobson. He's new in town."

Theo waved. "Nice to meet you all."

"Jacobson?" Bitsy's head swiveled back and forth from Theo to Jake before concluding, "You must be related to Jake. You look just like him."

Everyone started asking questions at once, and after the hubbub died down, Marla Jean dragged him out of there as fast as her orthopedic boot would let her.

As soon as the door closed on the departing couple, Lincoln asked, "So, how long has Theo been in town?"

"Just a few days. He's helping me finish my folks' house. He hasn't told me what he has planned after that." He didn't want to answer a lot of questions about Theo.

Lincoln looked thoughtful, but didn't ask any other questions. Neither did anyone else.

Dinah grabbed Lincoln's arm. "Let's go to Lu Lu's, Linc. I could use a night out on the town. Jake, you should come, too."

It hadn't been hard to persuade him to tag along. For some perverse reason, he'd convinced himself it would be a good idea to have a front row seat observing Marla Jean and Theo on a date. Now he wasn't so sure. But here he sat, surrounded by men and women drinking, dancing, and hooking up.

Except for him.

Not that a few women hadn't come around trying to interest him in a few sashays around the dance floor. Some like Irene Cornwell had been more persistent than others. But except to wonder how much make-up they had slapped on their faces, he couldn't seem to work up any enthusiasm.

He tipped his chair back on two legs, nursed his beer, and continued watching Marla Jean and Theo dance.

Chapter Nineteen

Get lost, Donny Joe."

Ignoring the suggestion Donny Joe pulled out a chair and sat down next to Jake. "Who's that dancing with Marla Jean? I thought it was you at first glance, and then I caught sight of you sitting over here all by your lonesome playing guard dog."

"I'm not playing guard dog. I'm here with Linc and Dinah." His eyes never left Marla Jean and Theo.

Donny Joe joined him in watching the couple for a few minutes. When Marla Jean threw back her head and laughed at something Theo said, Donny Joe was moved to remark, "That's one mighty fine-lookin' woman." Jake didn't respond, but Donny Joe was obviously feeling chatty. He pointed at Marla Jean with his chin, and asked, "So, who's the new competition?"

Jake took a sip of beer. "He's my brother."

Donny Joe's head swiveled around to gape. "You have a brother?"

"I just said I did, didn't I?"

Donny Joe poked the brim of his cowboy hat up with his thumb. "And he's going after your woman? If that don't beat all."

"She's not my woman, Donny Joe." Patience was a virtue, but he wasn't feeling all that virtuous at the moment.

"That's not what you insinuated when you pulled her out of my truck, now is it."

"That was different. I *was* playing guard dog that night."

"Whatever you say, old man." Donny Joe smirked and leaned back in his chair.

Jake fought the urge to knock him on his ass. He rose halfway out of his chair. "You want to take this outside?"

Donny Joe stood up, too. "Hell, no. I'm a lover not a fighter. Think they'll mind if I cut in?" With that he sauntered onto the dance floor with a troublemaking grin on his face.

Genna stopped by to see if he wanted to dance. He said sure, and led her around the floor a few times. She flirted like she always did, and he tried to respond. Tried to fall into the old familiar rhythm they'd had for years, but soon enough she got the message that he wasn't fit company, especially when she pointedly followed his gaze and found it trained on Marla Jean. He hardly noticed when she said, "Screw you, Abel Jacobson," and stomped off, leaving him alone on the dance floor.

From what he could tell, Marla Jean didn't seem to be suffering any ill effects from his rejection. And that was good. It wasn't like he wanted her to be all torn up just because she'd come right out and offered to have sex with him and he'd politely declined. Like she said, it was a straightforward offer of physical intimacy, not a marriage proposal. So, there was no reason to look for any emotional fallout. No reason at all.

He watched Donny Joe cut in, tapping Theo on the shoulder in the time-honored way. Theo gave a half bow and relinquished Marla Jean. She touched his arm as if to make sure he didn't mind, and then Donny Joe practically picked her up and whirled her away.

Damn it all. Jake sat there feeling like his best efforts with Marla Jean had missed the mark. Hadn't he'd tried to do the right thing for everyone concerned? But now he couldn't shake the feeling that despite the nature of her offer, and even if she was still hung up on Bradley, she'd honored him somehow—trusted him—and he'd thrown that trust back in her face. The idea didn't sit right with him. In fact, it made him feel lousy.

An idea flitted through his head. And the more he thought about it, the more he thought he might have a way of making things up to her. Linc walked back to the table carrying a new pitcher of beer, while Dinah accompanied him, balancing three fresh mugs.

They both looked happy and hot and invigorated. "We come bearing liquid refreshment." Linc barely set the pitcher down when Jake stood up, sloshing the beer onto the table. "Hey, watch it, buddy."

"Sorry, but I need to talk to Marla Jean." The three of them turned to look at her. She was still dancing with Donny Joe. Theo hovered nearby like he planned to move back in at any minute.

"What do you need to talk to Marla Jean about?" Linc demanded.

Dinah dragged him into his seat by his shirtsleeve. "That's none of our concern, Linc. Drink up, hon, 'cause they're about to play 'Cotton Eyed Joe,' and we aren't sitting it out this time."

Without giving Linc a chance to protest further, Jake ate up the dance floor with big strides, reaching the trio just as the song ended. Theo stepped back up trying to reclaim Marla Jean, but Donny Joe didn't seem ready to release her just yet.

"Marla Jean?" They all turned at his voice. Theo stood on one side of her, with a hand resting on her arm. Donny Joe held the other. Jake ignored both men, his eyes boring into hers. "I believe this is my dance."

For a split second Marla Jean looked uncertain, but she recovered and said smoothly, "I do believe you're right, Jake."

The strains of Johnny Lee singing about looking for love in all the wrong places poured from the jukebox as he stepped between the two men and then whisked her away. With his hand at the small of her back he guided her to a secluded corner. He'd been right about the white sweater she was wearing. It was soft, like the skin along the inside of a woman's thighs, and the warmth of her bled through the material, infusing his hand with hot memories of how it had felt to touch her. She moved gracefully to the music, even with the walking boot. Tilting her head back, she looked into his eyes. "Did you think I needed rescuing again?"

"You looked like you had a handle on the situation."

"So, you just had the sudden urge to dance? I'm pretty sure there's no shortage of willing women here tonight, Jake. You should take mercy on all the hearts you've broken, sitting alone at that table all night long."

He detected a heaping helping of sarcasm, but ignored it. "I needed to talk to you about something."

"If it's about your brother, and who I can and can't go out with—"

"It has nothing to do with the men you pick."

She didn't look like she believed him. "Go on then. I'm listening."

"It's about a house. You said you wanted one. Well, I have one I think you should consider."

"You do?" Her face lit up with interest. "Where is it?"

"It's out on Cowslip Lane—the old Brown place. I bought it a couple of years back. Never got around to fixing it up or selling it. I think it would suit you."

"The Brown place? Oh, my. When I was a teenager, Patsy Brown would have sleepovers there sometimes. She had the biggest bedroom with French doors that opened right onto a screened-in porch that held umpteen hammocks and all these wooden gliders. We'd fall asleep in the hammocks to the sound of crickets and wake up to the sound of birds singing."

He smiled at her enthusiasm. "And, Marla Jean, there's a converted chicken coop in the back. It gets good light. I was thinking it might make nice place for you to paint." Admitting he knew how important painting was to her bordered on letting things get too personal, and he was relieved she let it go without comment.

"Oh, Jake, I always loved that house, but it's huge and it must cost a fortune."

"It's not too big. And it does need work, so I'm willing to give you a good deal. You'd actually be doing me a favor by taking it off my hands."

"Oh, I don't know." She practically shimmered with anticipation. He could see her mind working as she mulled all the possibilities.

He swayed to the music, his thigh brushing against her leg. "We could go look at it."

"When? Not now?" she asked, though she looked ready to run out the door that instant.

It was tempting to sweep her away from this place and all these other people, put her in his truck, and drive out to the old house—all dark shadows and moonlight with her by his side. But he swiftly banished the fanciful idea. Besides, he'd kidnapped her from enough dates already, and Theo was beginning to look unhappy.

"How about tomorrow afternoon? I'll pick you up at four, and you can take your time looking around the place."

She threw her arms around his neck and hugged him, letting out an undignified squeal to punctuate her joy. "Oh, Jake, I can't thank you enough."

"No thanks are needed, Marla Jean. Now I better get you back to my little brother before he takes a poke at me for horning in on his date."

"Theo seems like a nice guy," she told him as if she needed to explain her newest conquest.

"He is a nice guy. You won't get an argument from me." They headed toward the edge of the dance floor where Theo stood ready and eager to reclaim his date. Jake handed her off to his younger brother and made a little bow. "Thank you for the dance, Marla Jean."

"Oh, it was my pleasure, Jake." She beamed at him like he'd restored her faith in Santa Claus, the tooth fairy, and light beer that didn't taste like dog piss. She grabbed Theo's arm, and said to Jake, "I'll see you tomorrow, and I can barely wait."

Theo looked back and forth between them, not hiding

his curiosity, but before he could ask any questions she said, "Can we sit this one out, Theo? I could use something to drink, and I should get off my foot for a while."

"Sure thing, Marla Jean. Later, big brother." With a wave in his direction they headed for a quiet table in a dark corner. Jake found himself standing on the dance floor while couples moved around him like water flowing around an unyielding boulder in the middle of a stream. He stuffed his hands in his pockets and moseyed back to the table where Dinah and Linc were hanging all over each other. Good God, how long did the newlywed phase last, anyway?

"I'm going to call it a night, guys."

Dinah stood up and gave him a hug and a kiss on the cheek. "Night, Jake."

Linc stood up, too, and offered his hand. If it hadn't been for a slight hesitation, Jake might have thought things were almost back to normal. "Night, buddy."

Jake took his friend's hand and gave it a firm shake. "I'm happy to play the third wheel for you two love birds anytime."

"Be careful going home," Linc advised him good-naturedly. Then he threw his arm around his wife and pulled her close to his side.

"Careful is my middle name," Jake confessed with a crooked grin. After a final glance in Marla Jean's direction, he walked out of Lu Lu's alone.

"I think he's dumped the whole job on me, but I'm glad to have the work." Theo was explaining what still needed to be done on the old Jacobson house. Marla Jean tried to concentrate on what he was saying, but her gaze followed

Jake while he said his good-byes and left the bar. She smiled at Theo, but part of her skipped and leaped and walked right out of the building beside Jake.

She'd been having a great time. Theo was funny, polite, charming, and awfully good-looking, and dancing with him had been the most fun she'd had in a month of Sundays. She still hadn't gotten the whole story about how he came to be Jake's brother, or where he'd been hiding all her life. Something about being a half brother and growing up in Derbyville, but he hadn't offered any more details, and she hadn't pressed him on the subject.

Even dancing with Donny Joe hadn't been a chore. Since she'd hurt her foot, his true nature, the nice guy he tried to hide for the sake of his reputation, had seeped out around the edges. She didn't understand the interest he'd been showing her. Given his history, it was hard to take him seriously, but he'd proven to be thoughtful and helpful more than once since her unfortunate run-in with the truck tire.

So why did Jake have to turn everything topsy-turvy by simply asking her to dance? It had been impossible not to notice the way he sat, brooding and alone the entire night. His cowboy hat, low on his head, shielding his eyes, his long jean-clad legs stuck out crossed at the ankles straight in front of him, claiming the space for his own, sending a message to all but the most reckless or the most fearless to steer clear.

Then out of the blue, he wanted to dance. Granted, it had been more of a standing out of the way and talking than a dance. But still, such a little thing, his hand on her waist sent sensations trampling through her like a runaway herd on a cattle drive. It wasn't fair. If she couldn't sleep with him, he was going to have to stop touching her. That was all there was to it.

Tomorrow when he took her to look at the house—the Brown house, of all places—she would be careful to stay out of reach. She suppressed another involuntary squeal and turned to concentrate on Theo. Only once or twice did she catch herself pondering the many ways he resembled his older brother.

Chapter Twenty

⁓

"Afternoon, Marla Jean." Jake jumped out of his truck and hurried to open the passenger door for her.

"Hey, Jake. Isn't it a marvelous day?" The bright smile on her face looked like it could only be removed with a chisel and a stick of dynamite.

He grinned, glancing up at the gray, cloudy sky. "I guess if you're partial to cold and miserable. It'll probably storm before the day is over."

"But who cares?" Throwing her arms in the air, she added, "I'm going to look at the Brown house."

When he had pulled up to the curb a few minutes before their agreed-upon time of four o'clock, he'd been pleased to see her sitting on her parents' front porch waiting for him. And then she'd blasted down the front steps and had been halfway across the yard before he could get out of the truck. For a woman with broken toes, she was awfully spry.

He got back in the truck and started the engine. Marla Jean bounced up and down on the bench seat beside him like a kid high on jelly beans. "All right mister, let's get this show on the road."

"Yes ma'am."

"I wonder if it's as wonderful as I remember."

He loved her enthusiasm, but he thought a little caution was in order. "Just remember it needs work."

It was only a ten-minute drive, but it took them to the outskirts of Everson. The neighborhoods fell away. The houses were set farther and farther apart, until the only evidence that anyone lived out there were the mailboxes at the end of long, winding driveways.

For the whole ten-minute drive he wondered why it mattered so much that she appreciate the house as much as he did. It wasn't as if he'd built the damn thing. But he'd always had a vision for what it could be, and since the idea of selling it to her had taken hold in his mind, he knew his vision wouldn't be complete without Marla Jean living there, making it her own. A simple idea had turned into a powerful, probably irrational need. He wanted her to have the Brown house the same way some other man might want to drown her in diamonds and pearls.

Feeling like his idiotic thoughts must be hanging in the air above his head he risked a glance in her direction. Her eyes were wide as fried eggs, and thankfully she seemed oblivious to his state of apprehension. She beamed and said, "I'm excited, in case you haven't noticed."

He smiled at her eagerness. "I've noticed. Hang on. Here we are," Jake said as he slowed down to make a turn. Large evergreen trees lined the drive, and Marla Jean's head swiveled this way and that as she tried to take it all in at once.

"Oh, it's exactly like I remember. Look at the trees, don't you love the trees? I love the trees."

He stepped on the brake and winked. "I can stop the truck if you want to get out and hug one."

She laughed and swatted his arm. "Maybe on the way home."

His uneasiness returned as they approached the house. He didn't want to disappoint her, and he still wasn't entirely sure what fueled his motives. As they pulled to a stop in front of the house, Jake leaned an arm on the steering wheel and turned to face her. "Despite the outward condition of the house, I can guarantee it's solidly built, not like the shoddy construction you get with some of the new houses they throw up in ten minutes nowadays."

"I'll take your word for it. You're the expert, after all." She opened the door and hopped down from the cab before he could help. By the time he got around the truck she was standing, staring dumbstruck with her mouth hanging open.

He shuffled his feet, unable to read her reaction. "Remember, I said it needed work." He looked at the peeling paint and a shutter that hung crookedly off the front window and could see how she'd be less than impressed. "When I bought it, I made sure the wiring and plumbing were up to code, but I haven't managed much of anything cosmetic yet."

She blinked and turned worshipful eyes toward Jake. "Oh my goodness, it's perfect. Simply perfect."

He shook his head and grinned. Everything in him relaxed. "I can see you're going to be a hard sell. Why don't we take the tour before you hire the movers?"

Since she was too busy gawking at the house to watch where she was going, he took her arm and led her across the leaf-covered yard and up the front steps. He noticed cracked stepping stones that would have to be reset and rips in the screening on the porch that would need to be replaced.

She stepped onto the wide wooden flooring of the porch and ran her fingers across the wire mesh that now separated them from the outside. "This porch floor used to be painted sky blue. If I buy this house, that's one of the first things I want to do."

He looked down at the faded porch flooring, and made a note to buy sky blue paint, then he unlocked the heavy carved wooden door and ushered her into the entryway. Once they were inside, he could barely keep up as she flitted from room to room.

In the living room she pointed to a corner flanked by two windows. "Patsy's dad used to sit there with a sour look on his face while he read his newspaper. He never said much, but we were all scared to death of him."

Swinging half doors separated the dining room from the kitchen. She pushed through them, laughing, making an entrance like a movie star. She found particular delight in the old-fashioned ironing board built into the wall, and the way it folded up and out of the way when it wasn't being used.

"Do you do much ironing?" he asked because of her enthusiasm.

She looked appalled. "You're kidding, right? I've been known to give things away rather than iron them. How about you? Do you iron your own clothes?"

"Do I iron? I can put a crease in a pair of pants that would make you weep."

She pushed the ironing board up and latched the door. "My my, what other domestic talents are you hiding, Jake?"

Before he could respond, she let out a little squeak. "Oh, the built-in breakfast nook. Isn't it wonderful?" A three-sided booth was nestled in the back corner of the kitchen with windows that looked out onto the back yard. "We would always eat breakfast here when I spent the night with Patsy, and her father would feed us a spoonful of honey."

"The same mean old father that didn't talk?"

"The same one. According to Patsy, he faithfully took a spoonful of honey every day, thought it was some health cure for what ails ya, but it didn't seem to sweeten his disposition any."

After she rhapsodized about the nook for a few minutes longer, she pulled him out of the kitchen. "Okay, I can't wait any longer. I have to see Patsy's old bedroom." He nearly lost his balance when she grabbed his arm and pulled him down the hall.

The bedroom was large and airy. Faded, peeling wallpaper covered the walls, but she didn't seem to notice as she flew to the French doors and opened them wide. With a look of awe and trepidation, she stepped out onto the porch and then turned back to him with a big smile. "Do you know how happy I am at this very moment?"

An odd emotion filled him as he stood watching her with his hands on his hips. He wasn't sure he could find his voice, but he asked, "Why don't you tell me?"

"I'm so happy, I think I could cry." She walked over and hugged him, a short, friendly hug.

His arms went around her for the briefest of touches. "That happy, huh?"

She pulled away from him, turning to gaze out the screen at the jungle of bare trees and neglected flower beds that made up the side yard. "I don't know if I can afford this, but I really, really want it." She glanced at him with a raised eyebrow. "I guess there's no point in offering to sleep with you so I can get a better price, huh?"

She was smiling when she said it, just an old joke between friends, but he felt a pang of regret for how badly he'd handled things. He tried to make a joke of it, too. "I don't think it will come down to that."

Feigning horror, she said, "Heaven forbid."

He felt it was important that she realize what she'd be getting into. "Listen, Marla Jean, I don't want to smash the rose-colored glasses you wear when you look at this place, but it needs work. Lots of it."

"Let me ask you something, Jake. Why did you buy this house?"

"That's what I do. I buy houses, fix them up, sell them, and start all over again."

"But why this one?"

"It's a great house. For about five minutes, I thought about keeping it for myself, but I decided it needed a family, or at least the possibility of a family, sometime in the future."

"And you're dead-set positive that a family's not in yours." It wasn't a question. It was a somber statement.

"How much do you know about Theo?" He couldn't guess how open Theo had been about their background.

"He was pretty close-mouthed. I think he enjoys being a man of mystery." She smiled.

He smiled in return, acknowledging Theo's sense of the dramatic. "You've probably figured out that Theo is my half brother."

She nodded. "I got that much. He said he grew up in Derbyville."

"You remember my father? He was a mean, controlling son of a bitch that made my mother's life hell."

"And yours, too, Jake."

"And mine, too. One weekend during my junior year while I was home for the weekend, I discovered he was a man with secrets."

"Secrets?"

"Part of the time when my mother thought he was on the road, he was spending time in Derbyville with another woman and their son. That son was Theo."

"Oh my God. You found out before he died? Did you confront him?"

"Let's just say if it wasn't for Lincoln, I would be in prison for murder. He pulled me off him before I could do more than break his nose."

"Lincoln was there?"

"Yeah, so now you know what I owe Lincoln. Anyway, I found out that day that the apple doesn't fall far from the tree. I could have killed him without a single regret."

"Jake, you are nothing like your father. You had good reason to be angry."

His expression darkened and some painful emotion played across his face before he shrugged and said with a lighter tone, "I appreciate the vote of confidence, Marla Jean, but let's get back to a more cheerful subject. You—buying this house."

"Okay, so why sell it to me? I'm as single as you are."

He wasn't sure if he could explain it. "I don't know. I can see you here. It fits you, somehow. I could never see myself filling up all these spaces. I would rattle around in this big old empty house and drive myself crazy. But you, you'll fill it with friends and family and all your artwork.

Even if no one ever lives here but you, you'll make it a home again."

She looked at him as if weighing his words for signs of insincerity. Finally she said, "I think that's the nicest thing you ever said to me."

"Hold that thought," he answered and bolted from the porch.

Marla Jean sighed as she watched Jake disappear. Hearing him talk about his father was chilling. She'd always known his father had been mean and low-down, and she'd always hated him on principle, as a show of loyalty to Jake. But she'd never imagined anything like the story he'd just shared. Jake was a good man, but it was clear he carried scars inflicted by that rotten old man. They held him back, keeping him from embracing the full life he deserved. If Stan Jacobson was alive today, she'd be tempted to kill him herself for what he'd done to his son.

If buying this house would help Jake, she was more than willing to do her part. Wandering back inside, she took another look at the bedroom, imagining her things arranged here and there. Her bed would fit on the east wall, and she would put her vanity in the nook by the closet. Oh, and having her own place to paint. That sounded like heaven. Other than in the class she was taking, she hadn't been able to pick up a brush since her parents had come home.

But Jake was wrong. She could see all the worn spots, see all the repairs that would have to be made, but she didn't care. She relished the idea. Moving into this house would be more than a new start. It would be a bold step, a giant leap, toward taking action, toward moving her sad excuse of a life forward again.

She'd taken out a loan to do some badly needed remodeling at the barber shop, and she was still paying that back, but Bradley owed her money for her half of their old house. She hadn't pushed him on it since she was living at her folks' place, but now she needed it. Having that conversation with her ex wasn't high on her list of things she wanted to do. He was such a tightwad, even when it wasn't his money to be tight with, but it was her money, and it would be enough for a down payment. A booming clap of thunder shook the house, and she jumped like a frog on a hotplate. She hated storms.

"Jake?" She walked back to the living room, wondering where the hell he'd gotten off to, when he came bounding back inside, raindrops glistening in his hair and dripping off the end of his nose. He was holding a cardboard tube in one hand and an adorable half-drowned puppy dog wrapped in a towel in the other.

She stared at him. "Should I ask if it's raining cats and dogs?"

He shoved the towel and the wet dog at her. "She was under the front steps. I couldn't leave her out there."

"Of course you couldn't. Hello, little doggie. Where did you come from, huh?" The puppy sat docilely while she used the towel to dry her fluffy dark fur. On closer inspection she could see that her fur was brown leaning toward black with a spot of white right above her nose. Another tuft of white fur ran down her chest and her white paws made her look like she was wearing baby booties. "Is she really a girl?"

"I haven't checked, but she batted her big eyes at me. What are you going to name her?"

"Name her? She's not my dog." One hand smoothed

the damp fur while the other scratched between her floppy ears. Big brown eyes stared at her adoringly.

"Well, we can put some signs up to see if anyone's lost a puppy, but my guess, this far out from town, is that somebody dumped her. I think she adopted this house as her new home."

"That would make her your dog then, Jake. You name her." The puppy barked and licked Marla Jean's chin. "Aren't you the sweetest thing?"

Jake pulled a blanket out from under his coat and spread it on the floor. He took off his wet jacket and laid it on a windowsill to dry. Then he kicked off his shoes and settled down on the blanket. "Come here, Marla Jean. I want to show you something." He took the top from the tube, and pulled out some papers. He unrolled the papers, spreading them out on the ground in front of him.

Marla Jean put the puppy down on the edge of the blanket and sat with her walking boot stretched out to one side. "What is all this?"

"Oh, just some plans I drew up when I first bought the house. I thought they would give you a better idea of what needs to be done."

Marla Jean leaned forward to get a better look, and the puppy pounced on the curled edges of the paper, attacking them ferociously. "So, you were going to tear out this back wall?" She pointed to the drawing.

"It's one possibility. This whole back section is an add-on, and I think some changes could be made while still maintaining the integrity of the original style. Let me show you what I had in mind." Bending his head close to hers he explained the way he'd planned to open up space and repurpose other rooms to make the house more livable. She watched his face light up as he talked, enjoying the way he got caught up in the project.

He was so close she could smell the barest hint of aftershave, or maybe it was soap. When his head bent over the plans, she discovered a smattering of gray hairs starting to distinguish his temples. A small crescent-shaped scar marred the top of his cheekbone, the scar he'd gotten when Linc threw a rock at him when he was twelve.

Her hand lifted to trace it, a downright foolish impulse, but she caught herself in time. Clasping her hands together in case some other reckless inclination attempted to undermine her common sense, she fought to keep her mind on the house plans instead of the man beside her.

"So," he was saying, "you can buy the house as is and not do a dad-blamed thing if you like. That will be up to you. But if you decide on some renovations, I'd like first crack at making a bid." He glanced up, and his eyes met hers.

Those deep, dark, brooding eyes of his. If she hadn't known better, she might have been dumb enough to mistake the look in his eye for desire. But she did know better. He couldn't have been clearer on the subject.

The bruise under his eye was almost gone. Only the barest trace of purple and green discoloration remained from where she'd hit him. The temptation to touch him flooded back stronger than before. She sat on her hands just to show them who was boss.

The little dog scampered into Jake's lap and settled down. Breaking the spell, he dropped his gaze and tentatively scratched the puppy's head. "Of course you'd be free to use somebody else to do the work, if you'd rather."

With a laugh that sounded unnatural to her own ears, she got to her feet. "Why would I do a silly thing like that?

But, let's not get ahead of ourselves. Why don't you write up a price, one with and without renovations, and if I don't faint dead away, I'll get back to you as soon as I know if I can swing it."

"That sounds like a plan. To be honest, you'd be doing me a favor by taking it off my hands. Financially, I can't afford to hold on to this place much longer."

"I can't believe you haven't had other offers."

"Oh, I've had offers. Bud Gailey is always after me wanting to buy the place. In fact, he just made another offer last week. But he'd come in and lower the ceilings and replace the screen porches with decks."

"Not the screen porches," she protested.

He shrugged. "I was all ready to grit my teeth and let him buy it, but then I thought of you. I'd much rather sell it to you. That would work out better for both of us."

She put her hand over her heart. "I promise not to lower a single ceiling."

Jake started rolling up the paper, while the dog scampered into the middle of everything.

Marla Jean scooped her up, rubbing her face against her fur. "You're a mess, aren't you puppy? Have you come up with a name for her yet?" She took a moment to examine her. "And you were right, she's a girl, but we can't keep calling her puppy dog."

Jake stood, stuffing the papers back in the tube. "I guess I'll have to name her, or she'll suffer the same fate as your poor cars. You're probably one of those people who would name her 'Doggie' and be done with it."

"Doggie is a good all-purpose name. But okay, let me think. What do dogs do? They bark and wag their tails. Waggy, maybe?"

"Waggy?" He laughed. "You really suck at this, don't you? I pity your future children."

She raised an eyebrow. "Okay, let's hear your brilliant ideas."

He took a minute to study the dog. "Well, you could always go with 'Boots' or 'Socks,' but they aren't too original."

Marla Jean rolled her eye. "I could have come up with those."

"But you didn't, did you? Hold on. Let me think."

"We can barely wait. Can we, puppy?" The puppy whined and nuzzled her neck.

"I've got it. How about Sadie? She looks like a Sadie to me."

Marla Jean held the pup up and looked at her face. Now that she was dry, her fluffy fur stood up at all angles. "Are you a Boots, or are you a Sadie?" The dog let out a little yip and Marla Jean was charmed. "I think so, too. Hello, Sadie. And your new daddy is going to take you home and feed you really soon, aren't you Jake?"

"Hold your horses, missy. I think her new mommy should take her home and feed her. It's obvious the two of you have already bonded."

"Can't. Dad's allergic."

He scoffed. "I never heard anything about Milton being allergic to dogs."

"Well, he is. The fur makes his nose run and his throat swell shut. You have to take her." She settled the puppy on Jake's shoulder.

"I think I'm being suckered," he protested even as he reached up a hand to hold the small dog in place. "But as long as you understand it's only going to be temporary. The minute you buy this place Sadie is moving in with you. I'm really not a dog person." Sadie licked his chin, and then settled onto his shoulder falling instantly to sleep.

Marla Jean thought Jake looked curiously content. She grinned and said, "Oh, I can see that. If you're nice we'll talk about joint custody."

Still carrying the snoozing puppy Jake walked over to the front window and looked out at the rain. The afternoon shower had turned into a full-blown thunderstorm. "Wow, it's really coming down out there. Maybe we should wait a while before we go and see if the rain lets up a little."

It had gotten really dark outside and the rain pounded on the roof. She walked over to stand beside him. A flash of lightning and a clap of thunder shook the house, making Marla Jean jump out of her skin. "That's a good idea. I'm not crazy about driving in heavy rain, and it looks bad out there." She rubbed her hands up and down her arms, trying to hide her nervousness.

Marla Jean couldn't contain herself at the next loud *boom*. "Yikes. Sorry. Ignore me."

Jake put the sleeping puppy down on the blanket and walked over to Marla Jean. He put a friendly arm around her shoulder. "Hey, you're really scared, aren't you?"

"I hate storms. It's silly, I know." She pulled the neck of her sweater up to her chin like she was trying to disappear inside it.

"It's not silly. I'm just surprised, that's all. You've always seemed so fearless. I'd have bet my last dollar you weren't scared of anything." This was a side of Marla Jean he'd never seen before. When they were kids she'd been too brave for her own good. Linc was always challenging her to stupid dares, and she never had the good sense to back down.

"I usually manage to put on a good front." A flash of lightning had her burrowing into his chest, and he hugged her good and tight until the rumble of thunder that followed faded away. "When I'm at home I hide under the covers."

"Why don't we move away from the window?" He guided her into the dining room. "We'll stay in here until the storm passes."

She let out a heavy sigh. "This is much better. I'll be okay, now." But she didn't let go of his arm as they sat down on the hardwood floor and leaned back against the wall. A panicky laugh escaped her throat. "Now that you know my shameful secret, you have to confess something, too. What are you afraid of, Jake? Ghosts? Clowns? There's got to be something."

He turned his head to look at her. The late-afternoon shadows fell across her face, washing her in shades of green and gray. "Hmm, I'm not sure I should admit anything. It might mess up my tough-guy image."

"Oh, come on. Tell me." A flash of lightning filled the room and she practically climbed onto his lap. She closed her eyes tightly and squeaked, "It'll keep me from envisioning my fiery death when lightning strikes the house and burns it to the ground."

He laughed. "A fiery death. That's it. I'm afraid of that, too."

He knew he needed to keep talking, to keep her distracted from all the flash and noise going on around them. But his body was busy responding to the way she was using him like a jungle gym. It was almost impossible to think while her arms wound themselves around his neck and her knee rested so close to his crotch. With her face buried in his neck every breath she took sent warm shivers of lust galloping right through him. He'd made such an effort to keep his distance, but it was only gallant to offer comfort under the circumstances. At least that's what he told himself when she snuggled closer, pressing her breasts against his side.

"That doesn't count." Her long hair tickled where it cascaded over his arms. "Quit stalling and tell me."

"Okay, but you can't laugh."

"I won't laugh. I promise."

"And you can't tell anyone."

"Cross my heart," she agreed.

He took a deep breath and paused. "Crickets," he said finally.

She raised her head to look at him. "Crickets? As in little-bitty, never-hurt-a-soul crickets?"

He made an icky face and shuddered. "Ugh. I can't stand them. As in creepy-crawly, oily-looking, disgusting bugs."

She laughed. She didn't just laugh; she rolled on the floor. "Sorry, oh Lord," she said between gasps, "but crickets? Big bad Jake afraid of crickets." That set her off again. At least she seemed to have forgotten about the storm raging outside.

"All right, have your fun. But remember a couple summers ago when we had that invasion? They swarmed everywhere. My parking lot was covered solid black with crickets. I'll never forget the crunching sound of my tires rolling over them. And when I had to get out of the truck they skittered and swarmed all over my boots and up my legs. It was awful. I still have nightmares about it."

The grin plastered on her face ruined any show of real sympathy. "Poor baby."

He warned her. "It's not that funny."

"It's pretty funny," she said, patting him on the cheek.

He caught her hand and pulled her close. "You think so?"

"I do." Her voice was less than a whisper.

A flash of heat flared between them, and his mouth crashed down on hers. He kissed her before he could drag out all the reasons he shouldn't do it. She was warm and willing, and he hauled her up against him without giving common sense a chance to intervene. She opened her mouth, and he savored the way she tasted on his tongue. He cupped her breast, loving the weight of her in his hand despite the rough barrier of her sweater. With a hand behind her head, he pushed her onto the hard floor, his lips molded to hers, keeping her beneath him as he found the button on her jeans. He touched the soft skin of her stomach, slipping his hand under her sweater, discovering her, inch by inch. She started on the buttons of his shirt, both of them working in a clumsy attempt to shed themselves of their clothing. Without warning a small, smelly bundle of fur jumped between them, whining and wagging her tail. Marla Jean sat up laughing, hugging the puppy to her chest. "Well, hello there. Looks like we've got company, Jake."

Startled, he sat up too. "I can see that. Hey, Sadie, did you wake up?" He scratched the puppy's head while trying to rein in the desire still thrumming through his blood.

Marla Jean nudged Jake with her elbow. "Thanks for, you know, keeping me distracted during the thunderstorm."

"Yeah, well—" He started buttoning his shirt.

He must have looked uncomfortable because she jumped in adding, "Look, I'm not going to start showing up on your doorstep for booty calls or anything. No need to blow things out of proportion, okay?"

"You're right." He laughed and tucked a strand of hair behind her ear. "I never claimed keeping my hands off you would be easy."

"If it was too easy, I'd be insulted. So, we're good?" she asked.

"We're good." He stood up, and then reached out a hand to pull her from the floor.

"And I still want to buy this house."

"And I still want to sell it to you."

She walked over to a small side window and looked outside. "The rain's stopped. Let's get out of here and go buy your puppy some food."

"Hold on now, Sadie's your puppy," he insisted as they headed out the door.

Chapter Twenty-one

Jake woke up with a dog curled up by his head. It took him a minute to remember why he had a dog at all, much less why it was sleeping on his bed. Then he remembered.

Marla Jean and poor abandoned Sadie. When he turned to look at the puppy, she opened her eyes and yawned. She was so small, he figured she'd been the runt of the litter, and someone decided they didn't want her. He might not be a dog person, but he didn't understand how anyone could dump a poor defenseless animal in the middle of nowhere and drive away. Heartless bastards.

He picked her up and moved her to the empty pillow next to his. "Hey flea bag, let's get this straight. You stay on your pillow, and I'll stay on mine." She stayed there for maybe two seconds before she stood up and walked back over to him. Walking in circles, she finally settled down, with her tail whacking him in the face. He sat up. It was time to get up, anyway.

Sadie seemed content to sleep, so he left her and headed for the shower. He turned on the hot water full blast and stood under the sharp needle-like spray until he felt at least half human again.

On the way home yesterday he'd left Marla Jean in the car with Sadie while he'd run into the grocery store long enough to grab the basic supplies. Some food for a start. Then he'd grabbed a couple of dog toys for good measure, since he didn't know the first thing about entertaining a canine. And he couldn't get over all the paraphernalia lining one whole aisle of the store. It was a good thing this arrangement was only temporary. He wasn't going to become one of those people who buys jogging outfits for his animal.

When he'd gotten home, Theo had been sprawled on the couch watching bowling on TV. The rain caused him to take off work early, so he'd let himself into the apartment. His face lit up like a kid with a sparkler when he'd spotted the puppy. "I didn't know you had a dog?"

Jake leaned over to set the puppy on the area rug, before continuing to the kitchen with his bag of supplies. When he walked back into the living room, Theo was on his hands and knees waggling a finger back in forth in front of Sadie, while she growled and prepared to attack. She bounced around before rolling over on her back. Theo scratched her tummy and she was in puppy heaven. Jake sat down in a chair watching them. "I don't have a dog. Theo, meet Sadie. She belongs to Marla Jean."

Theo sat up on his haunches. "Marla Jean? What are you doing with Marla Jean's dog?"

"I'm just helping out until she moves."

"She's moving? She didn't mention that last night."

Jake shrugged, like what she did or didn't mention to Theo on their date was of no importance to him. "She's trying to buy a house."

"Is that why you ran out of here so early? You were whistling in the kitchen this morning." The way he said it sounded like an accusation.

"Yeah, we had an appointment to look at the place she's considering."

"So, you're helping her in a professional capacity."

"And as an old friend capacity." He wasn't going to dwell on the way she looked sprawled under him on the dining room floor. He'd lost control, plain and simple. She'd asked what kinds of things scared him. Maybe being alone with her should be at the top of his list.

Theo got off the rug and sat back on the couch. Sadie followed and made a game of attacking his bare toes. "I like her, Jake."

He assumed he meant Marla Jean and not the dog. "She's a likeable sort," Jake agreed.

"So, what's with you and her, anyway?"

"What do you mean?"

"I get a weird vibe, like there's some kind of tension between the two of you. And hey man, if I'm stepping into your territory, just tell me, and I'll back off."

"Don't worry about it, Theo. We had a disagreement recently, but it's all behind us now. And Marla Jean is certainly not my territory. She'd probably take a swing at you just for suggesting such a thing." He'd certainly had trouble remembering what the boundaries were today, but essentially nothing had changed.

He'd steered the conversation in a different direction after that, and they'd spent the afternoon playing with the puppy, discussing the work schedule for the upcoming week and watching TV. Seeing that it was Saturday night and all, Theo had said he was going to run out to Lu Lu's for a while and tried to convince Jake to come with, but he begged off, saying he wanted to make sure Sadie took to her new environment without too much fuss. He hadn't asked Theo if he was meeting Marla Jean, not that it mattered one way or the other. After showing Sadie the newspaper he'd put down for bathroom purposes one more time, he'd gone to bed early, only to toss and turn, but determined not to notice what time his younger brother got home.

The next morning he finished his shower and just pulled on jeans and a T-shirt when the doorbell rang. Grabbing a towel to finish drying his hair, he walked out into the living room. Theo's blankets were folded neatly on the end of the sofa, but he was nowhere to be seen. The doorbell chimed again just as he pulled the door open to find his mother and Aunt Libby standing there smiling.

"Good morning, Jake. Can we come in? Your Aunt Libby has something she wants to talk to you about."

"Sure, come on in. Would you like coffee?"

They trailed in behind him, shrugging off their jackets and hanging them on the hall tree by the front door. Then they followed him into the kitchen.

"I never turn down a cup of coffee," his aunt said as she settled at the kitchen table.

His mother was rummaging in his refrigerator. "I'll take some, but only if you have some milk that's not a year past its expiration date." She straightened triumphantly with a carton of half-and-half. "This will do."

He poured the coffee, then sat down across from them. "What's this all about, ladies?"

Aunt Libby tittered nervously, "Well, Jake, it's about my wedding. We've decided we don't want to wait until Christmas."

"Okay." Jake waited, wondering how he could help.

"We've decided on the Saturday after Thanksgiving instead."

Jake's mom piped in. "They are going with a harvest-time theme. Isn't that lovely?"

"Great. I'll mark it on my calendar."

"Good, good, but there is something I wanted to ask you to do, as a favor to me." She fiddled with the handle of her cup and her voice sounded tentative.

"Sure, Aunt Libby, just name it." Maybe they were going to tell him that they'd have to skip the turkey dinner on Thursday with all the wedding preparations. Or maybe they wanted him to cook, instead. He could do that. He'd had a hankering to try deep frying a turkey for a while now, and this would be the perfect opportunity. He'd have to get one of those big buckets of peanut oil.

Aunt Libby got all serious, and he could swear she had tears welling up in her eyes. "Well, Jake, since you are in effect the man of the family, I was wondering if you might agree to give me away."

"Give you away?"

"Yes, walk me down the aisle."

"Oh." He shouldn't have been surprised. There really wasn't anyone else. He just assumed there wouldn't be any pomp and falderal, not at her age, and not with it being Bradley's second marriage and all. Evidently, he was wrong. She wanted him to give her away, give her away to Bradley, as if he approved, as if he gave their creepy sordid union his blessing.

His mother was making bulging, wide-eyed, young-man-don't-you-dare-embarrass-me-or-disappoint-your-aunt looks and kicking him under the table at the same time. He scooted his chair back out of the range of her pointy-toed shoes and gave her a bulgy-eyed look of his own. It wasn't as if he could kick her back. Mothers didn't fight fair.

Reaching across the table he took his aunt's hand. "Aunt Libby, I'd be honored to walk you down the aisle." What else could he say?

One of those tears slid down her cheek, and she rummaged in her purse for a hanky. "Thank you, Jake. I just know the day is going to be perfect now. Your mother will be my matron of honor, and I'll walk down the aisle on your arm to the man I love. I can't tell you what this means to me."

"What kind of tuxedo do you want him to wear?" Ellie asked in that gushy way she took on when she talked about the wedding. "They come in all colors these days."

"Oh land's sakes, Ellie, I've hardly had time to give it any thought. Bradley is wearing one of those cutaway coats with the long tails and the top hat. I guess that's what Jake needs to wear, too. Do they even come in anything but black?

Ellie looked thoughtful. "A soft tan would blend with the fall colors."

He tried to block out their gabbing. It was giving him a headache, and now it sounded like he'd have to wear a monkey suit on top of everything else. Bradley could stand in front of God and everyone in Everson wearing a goofy top hat if he wanted, but that didn't mean he intended to join him. Just let them try to make him.

His mother leaned across the table, waving a hand in front of his face. "Jake, yoo-hoo, Jake, what do you think?"

"Hell if I know. But I guess this means you don't want me to deep fry a turkey?"

Both women looked at him like he'd lost his mind. The

sound of yapping turned their attention to the kitchen door. Sadie stood in the doorframe, barking as if to tell Jake she hadn't liked waking up and finding herself alone one little bit. After she finished complaining, she made a beeline for him and tried to jump up his leg.

"Well now, who do we have here?" Libby asked.

Jake picked up the dog and settled her on his chest. "Ma, Aunt Libby, this is Sadie."

His mother looked elated and held out her arms. "Abel Jacobson, are you telling me I finally have a grand puppy? Let me see that baby this instant."

Jake handed her the dog, wondering why women had to be so danged silly. "No, you don't have a grand puppy. She belongs to Marla Jean." He glanced at his aunt, not wanting to make her uncomfortable, but Marla Jean was his friend and he wasn't going to tiptoe around it for anybody. Not even his aunt.

"Marla Jean," his mother repeated the name as if it held great significance. "Really? And what then might I ask is her dog doing here?"

With a straight face he said, "I decided to have a dog slumber party last night. Lassie, Snoopy, and Rin Tin Tin all left just before you got here."

Libby laughed, but his mother stopped cuddling the puppy long enough to scold him. "Nobody likes a smart aleck, young man."

He charmed her with a grin, and then explained, "I'm just keeping her temporarily. It's no big deal."

His mother started cooing like a pigeon. "This baby's starving, yes she is. Where's her food, Jake?"

He pointed in the direction of the pantry, but she didn't pay him any mind. "You need grandma to take care of you, don't you, sweetie pie?" Standing up, she carried the puppy to her food bowl, put her down, and started rummaging again, this time in the cabinets. Sadie was yipping and bouncing around her feet like she was promising a lifetime supply of doggie biscuits.

Libby leaned across the table and asked in a low voice, "How is Marla Jean doing, Jake?"

He frowned. He didn't want to discuss this with his aunt. He would support her any way he could, but he wasn't going to appease her guilt about breaking up a marriage. "She's getting on with things."

"I heard she broke her foot."

"Actually it was her toes." He wanted to add no thanks to Bradley, but he kept his big mouth shut.

"And I heard her folks are home for a visit."

"Yes, they came home to help her until she's back on her feet, so to speak."

"Jake, I know she's your friend, and I realize by asking you to give me away, I'm putting you in a bad position. I don't want to make you feel like you're choosing sides."

"There are no sides, Aunt Libby. It is what it is. Bradley and Marla Jean are divorced. Life goes on."

She was quiet for a moment. Ellie was still fussing with the dog. "Bradley and I love each other, but I'm not proud of the way we handled things. Sometimes I think I'll explode from sheer guilt."

Jake sighed. "I don't know what to tell you. I just know that Marla Jean is moving on. She's dating, looking to buy a house, getting on with things. As you can see, she's even got a dog. And if you didn't feel guilty, you wouldn't be the woman who helped raise me. I still love you, Aunt Libby. Don't ever doubt that."

She jumped up from the table and grabbed him in a hug so fast her chair nearly tipped over. "Thank you, Jake. You and Ellie mean the world to me. I don't want to ever lose you."

He patted her on the back. "You won't lose us, Libby. Speaking of houses, what do you plan to do with your house? Ma said you'd mentioned selling it."

"I thought about it, but now I think we'll keep it, maybe rent it out. I know your mother wants me to hang on to it so when Bradley dumps me, I'll have some security."

"Is that what she said?"

"Not exactly, but that's what she meant."

"Why are you two talking about me like I'm not in the room?" Ellie asked. "Speaking from experience, a woman is smart if she has something to fall back on when life doesn't turn out the way she plans."

"Well, the house on Crawford is safe for now. I hope that makes you happy, Ellie."

"It does. Uh oh. Jake, your dog just had an accident."

He turned and looked at the puddle on the floor. Scooping Sadie up, he walked out to the utility room and gently set her on the newspapers. "Good doggie, that's a good girl."

Then he walked back into the kitchen, grabbed some paper towels and a spray bottle of cleaner and mopped up the small wet spot on the floor. "I told you, Ma. She's not my dog."

"Why don't you just plunge a knife through my heart while you're at it? At this rate, I'm never going to be a grandma. Come on, Libby. Let's go shopping. The only thing that will make me feel better now is lunch at the tea room and a new dress."

Chapter Twenty-two

❧

I know Dad always leaves your sideburns a little longer, Mr. Taylor. If that's what you want, that's what we'll do." It felt great to be back at work, but in the short time her father had been home, he'd managed to roll back the cause of fashionable haircuts by at least forty years. If Ben Taylor had his way he'd be sporting mutton chops that ran the length of his face. On a young person they might be edgy or make a statement. On an old man like Ben Taylor, they made him look like he might be fixing to go out and found a country or establish a new religion. Next thing she knew everyone would come in demanding crew cuts and ducktails again.

At the moment Milton was sitting up front with Hoot and Dooley. They were in an important discussion, critiquing the new flooring she'd installed while he'd been away. "I can't believe Marla Jean put down a tile floor. Ceramic wouldn't have been my choice, but it looks good."

Hoot cackled. "It's not ceramic, Milt. It's linoleum."

"Linoleum?" He took off his glasses and leaned over to look closer. "That's linoleum?"

"Sure is," Dooley said. "It's got the grooves for the grout, just like tile and everything."

Mr. Taylor swiveled around, almost getting stuck in the ear by her scissors in the process. "Yeah, but it's got give to it, not so hard on your knee joints when you have to stand all day. Ain't that right, Marla Jean?"

"That's right, Mr. Taylor. Now be still unless you want to lose an ear. Come here, Dad, and tell us if I left his side-burns long enough."

Her dad walked over to the barber chair, but he was looking down at the floor the entire time. "If that don't beat all. Linoleum. I've been back how long, and all this time I thought it was tile." He walked around and gave Mr. Taylor a quick inspection. "Where'd you learn how to cut hair, girl?"

"Some old cowboy taught me."

"Ben, I think the student has surpassed the teacher. That's one mighty fine-looking haircut."

"Yeah, Milton, she does all right," Mr. Taylor agreed as he looked at himself in the mirror, then he caught her eye and winked. "It's good to see you back at work, Marla Jean."

"Thanks, Mr. Taylor." She brushed away any loose hairs and took off the plastic cape. "I'll see you in a couple of weeks, okay?"

"You bet." He put some money on the counter, and then stopped at the Parcheesi game to state his opinion on whether it would rain the rest of the week, or let up by the weekend, and then with a salute left the shop.

It was a slow day, almost lunch time, and they'd only

had four customers. Her father could have handled things without her help, but she needed to get back to work. If she played her cards right, he'd spend the day shooting the bull with Hoot and Dooley and they'd both be happy. She grabbed the broom and started sweeping when the bell over the door jingled again. She looked up to see Bradley standing in the doorway.

"Hey, Marla Jean."

Milton stood up. "Do you want me to take this one, girl?" Her father didn't have a very high opinion of Bradley since the divorce, and he didn't take any pains to hide it. She didn't think her father getting near Bradley with a pair of scissors was a smart move for anyone.

"That's okay, Daddy. I've got it. Why don't y'all go on over to the Rise-N-Shine? I'll join you in a minute."

The three men exchanged looks with each other, threw some warning glares in Bradley's direction and shuffled out the door.

Bradley looked annoyed, and not the least bit intimidated by their protective posturing.

"What do you need, Bradley? I don't think you stopped by for a haircut."

"No, I heard some interesting news, and I wanted to know if it's true."

Marla wondered what rumor was swirling around about her this time. She hadn't made a public spectacle of herself for a while now that she knew of. "I don't have a clue what you're talking about. You'll have to be more specific."

"I heard you were thinking of buying a house."

She frowned. "How would you have heard that?"

"Libby said Jake told her. So, it's true?"

"It's true that I'm considering it. Actually, it's good you

stopped by. I need to talk to you about the money you owe me for my half of our house."

He looked surprised. "Now is not the best time, Marla Jean. In case you've forgotten, I'm getting married and weddings aren't cheap. On top of that, things have been slow at the dealership."

"I'm sorry to hear that, but the money is mine. I haven't needed it before, but now I do."

He crossed his arms across his chest, looking mulish. "What if I say I don't have it?"

"Then I guess we'll have to go back to court. Half the house belongs to me, Bradley. You know that."

He tried a cajoling approach. "It's just the timing. Geez, Marla Jean. What's wrong with your parents' house? They won't be staying in Everson forever now that you're back on your feet."

"Are you really going to fight me on this?"

His chin jutted out an extra inch. "Take me to court. See if I care. By the time it gets sorted out, the wedding will be done and maybe business will have picked up again. For once don't be so selfish."

She picked up the nearest object from the counter and waved the rattail comb under his nose. "You know what, Bradley? There was a time when I would have felt bad about this. And you were counting on that, too. I would have said, don't worry. I can put off anything and everything if it's the least bit inconvenient for you. But not anymore. It's about time I started being selfish. In fact, I haven't been nearly selfish enough."

He batted the comb away. "For God's sake, get a hold of yourself."

"I don't want to get a hold of myself. I want to buy the

old Brown house, and that's what I'm going to do, even if that means you and Libby have to set up housekeeping in the Bookmobile. Make yourself a mattress out of those freaking Russian classics you're so fond of. It's not like you haven't already had lots of practice at that. I need my money." She wrestled with her frustration, anger seeping into her words. "And I need it now."

"The Brown house? Don't be silly. That place is way too big for you."

"Holding my money hostage does not entitle you to an opinion on the matter." Her voice went up a few decibels.

"When you get like this, there's no point in even trying to have a reasonable discussion." That was one of his favorite tactics when they'd been married. If he didn't like the direction the conversation was headed, he'd press the abort button claiming in that infuriating, level-headed, patronizing voice that he wouldn't discuss it further until she'd come to her senses. He put one hand on the door. "We can talk about this when you've calmed down."

"Okay," she said in her most level-headed, sensible voice. "But you better have my money in your hand next time I see you." The negotiations were over as far as she was concerned.

He shook his head sadly. "I knew the divorce made you bitter, and I'm sorry about that, but I didn't realize it made you vindictive, too. You'd love nothing better than to ruin our special day, wouldn't you? Well, I'm not going to let you do it."

"Ooh! You are the most self-absorbed man I've ever known in my life. I want to buy a house, and in your pea-sized excuse for a brain, it's just so I can ruin your wedding. You are un-frigging-believable."

"I guess you better contact your lawyer then. Blood from a turnip, though, Marla Jean, blood from a turnip."

"I'll show you blood, you bastard." She started at him with the pointed end of the plastic comb. He was lucky she hadn't picked up the scissors instead. She might be tempted to cut his heart out and feed it to the squirrels. "Get out of here, Bradley. Get out and take your no-good, rotten, cheating, lying, two-timing, unfaithful, fornicating pig-faced self out of my shop this instant."

He clasped and unclasped his fists like he wanted to put them through something, if not her face at least the nearest wall. His cheeks turned bright pink and mottled streaks of color flushed his neck and ears. His eyes turned to slits, and he was breathing hard through his mouth. Jerking the door open, he caused the bell to do a frantic jingle-jangle overhead. "Bitch," he finally yelled on his way out the door. He slammed it behind him, and the only sound in the shop was the dying tinkle of the bell and the echo of their angry words.

Bitch? That was all he could come up with?

She laughed, a sort of hysterical laugh, as she watched him stalk across the street. He always sounded so unnatural when he tried to cuss. Fussy and prissy like the very act of forming the words made him self-conscious. He even held his mouth funny.

That was small comfort to her now. She was going to nail the shit for brains, slimy bastard son of a bitch's hide to the nearest wall and use him for target practice if he tried to keep her from getting what was rightfully hers. She stomped out of the barber shop, barely taking the time to turn the open sign over to read "Closed."

Right now, she was furious, and exhilarated, and ravenous. It seemed like she hadn't eaten in about a year. Not where she'd actually tasted anything. All the things she'd wanted to say to Bradley when he first asked for the divorce, all the things she'd held firmly inside finally came spilling out and it felt great. It felt amazing, in fact. It felt like she'd been reborn.

During their marriage, she'd never had trouble speaking her mind, but something happened after he asked for the divorce. She'd shut down. Not physically. She had managed to get through each day by putting one foot in front of the other. But she'd never really confronted Bradley, never really dealt with the emotional damage he'd inflicted on her—as the woman he no longer desired, as the wife he cast off like a pair of pants he'd outgrown. So, this confrontation was a long time overdue.

But right now she had a hunger to feed. A clean, voracious appetite that sprang from somewhere deep inside her. Selfish. Hell, yeah. It felt good to be selfish. And the first person that got between her and the lunch counter was going to have their head lopped off and handed to them on a blue-plate platter special.

"There's not anything we can do without taking him to court, Marla Jean. I told you we should have insisted on selling the house at the time of the divorce. In these cases being nice usually comes back to bite you in the derriere."

Marla Jean closed her eyes while her lawyer went through her "I told you so" lecture. "I know, I know. I should have listened to you, Helen. I never expected Bradley to pull something like this. So how long are we talking about?"

"I don't know. A few months if we're lucky, but it could

be longer. The good news is that we will get the money eventually. I just don't know how long he'll be able to stall."

"Well, blast. I'm trying to buy a house and without that money as a down payment there's no way I can swing it."

"I'll go ahead and start the paperwork, but as I said, this could take a while."

"Thanks, Helen." Marla Jean flipped her phone closed and rubbed her temple. The week had gone from bad to worse.

After her fight with Bradley, and a carbo-loaded lunch, the furious rush to do battle for scorned women everywhere ebbed somewhat, leaving her drained but no less determined. She told her father that she needed to take care of some bank business and asked him to hold the fort at the barber shop until she returned.

Ollie Johnson at the bank had greeted her like a long-lost uncle, nodding his head as she explained that she was thinking of buying a house.

"It's a buyer's market," he agreed. Pulling her up her files on his computer he frowned when she explained that her money for the down payment was tied up in her divorce settlement for the time being. He grimly explained that without a down payment, what with the loan she'd taken out the year before to update the barber shop, he didn't think she'd qualify for much of a mortgage.

Adding the bad news from her lawyer on top of that, she tried to tell herself it wasn't the end of the world. Her parents would be going back to Padre Island after Thanksgiving, and she'd have the house to herself again. She knew she could stay there as long as she needed to, but she also knew that Jake needed to sell the Brown house.

He'd made it pretty clear that he needed to make a deal

soon. He might be willing to wait a few weeks for her to come up with the money, but it wasn't fair to ask him to wait forever. Not with Bud Gailey's offer on the table. None of this was Jake's fault, and she didn't want any special favors, either.

Weariness settled on her shoulders. Maybe she was getting way ahead of herself. Maybe buying a house was the last thing she needed to do right now.

That old notion of picking up stakes and moving on might be something to consider after all. But she had obligations. The barber shop naturally, but also the art classes she was going to be teaching soon. Signing up to take classes had been one of the only good ideas she'd had in a while. Her instructor had been so impressed with her work, he'd convinced her to apply for an opening in the continuing education department to teach some evening art classes. She'd been happily surprised when they hired her. It was something to look forward to.

Her dad left the shop early, telling her not to be late for supper. Her mother was making tacos. She closed up shop, climbed in her car, and headed toward, what at least for now, passed for home.

Chapter Twenty-three

～

Who'd like some good news?" Marla Jean's mother walked into the dining room wearing a big smile and carrying a tres leches cake.

Lincoln was still chewing on a taco, but he grabbed the last one from the platter as Dinah picked it up to carry it to the kitchen. Little shreds of lettuce and cheese covered the front of his shirt. "Tell me you're making chili and corn bread tomorrow night. That would be some good news."

"Don't talk with your mouth full, Lincoln." His mother set the cake down and beamed at her husband. "Do you want to tell them or should I?"

Milton pushed back from the table and patted his stomach. "Go ahead, Bitsy, tell them before you pop a seam."

"What is it, Mom?" Marla Jean asked. "Good news would be a welcome change."

"Your father and I have made a decision."

Dinah returned from the kitchen and sat back down beside Linc. They all turned expectant faces Bitsy's way.

"Let me guess," Lincoln said wiping his mouth with a napkin. "You and Dad are getting matching tattoos."

Ignoring her eldest, Bitsy sat down and folded her hands together in front of her chest as if to make a wish. "We've decided to move back home."

The room was quiet for about ten seconds before everyone started talking at once.

"I knew it," Lincoln declared.

"What about Padre Island?"

"What about the barber shop? Are you coming back to work full-time?"

Milton held up his hand. "One question at a time. We started realizing Thanksgiving is almost here, and we were both dreading the idea of leaving. The point of retirement is to be happy, right?" Everyone nodded. "And we couldn't think of a single good reason not to stay here if that's what makes us happy."

Marla Jean stood up and gave her mother a hug. "That's great, Mom."

Her mom returned her hug. "And since Marla Jean is buying the Brown house we won't be underfoot for too long."

Marla Jean put on a plucky face. She didn't want to put a damper on things by telling them that she'd probably be living with them for the foreseeable future. There would be plenty of time to deal with her living arrangement woes later.

"And we'll keep the RV. That way we can take off when the spirit strikes us for parts unknown. But Everson is home, and there's no getting around it."

"What about the barber shop, Daddy?"

"Girl, the shop is yours. I wouldn't mind putting in the

half day now and again, if it wouldn't cramp your style to have the old man around."

"Of course not, Daddy. Hoot and Dooley will be beside themselves." She would love having him around as well, but the simple truth was that the shop would always be his in spirit, if not in fact. And it was also true he'd second-guess every choice she made. He still hadn't recovered from the new linoleum, for heaven's sake.

Bitsy cleared her throat. "There is one more reason we're moving back home. Lincoln, Dinah, would you like to do the honors?"

Lincoln and Dinah smiled at each other with that private smile that shut everyone else out. Marla Jean wondered what everyone in the room seemed to already know that she didn't. Then it hit her. "Are you having a baby? When were you going to tell me?"

Dinah started nodding so fast that her head looked like it might fly off her neck. Lincoln preened and put his hand on her stomach. "We suspected for a while, but we saw the doctor this afternoon. We're due in June," he said in a voice filled with amazement. "Can you believe it? I'm going to be a father. And you're going to be an aunt, Marla Jean."

"I don't believe it. Holy cow." She scrambled across the room hugging them both. A baby. They were going to have a baby, and they'd be the best parents in the world, and Milton and Bitsy would spoil the kid rotten. And so would she. Aunt Marla Jean. She liked the way that sounded.

She'd wanted kids when she was married to Bradley, but he always wanted to wait. Considering how things turned out, she was glad. Honestly, she was. And the pang of wistfulness that surfaced for the barest moment was a natural reaction. She'd married so young, and Linc had stayed a bachelor for so long, she never expected him to have kids before she did. But picturing him with a child in his arms made her melt inside.

"And that's why we can't leave now," Bitsy said. "We don't want to miss a thing."

Dinah looked around the room at each of them with a tremulous smile. "I did a wonderful job picking my baby's family."

Then she started crying and Bitsy joined in. Marla Jean felt her eyes start to water and soon the three of them were crying and hugging like drunken sailors on leave.

"What is wrong with you three?" Lincoln demanded.

Milton threw an arm around his shoulder and said, "Hormones, son. Get used to it."

The house was quiet. Dinah and Lincoln had gone home an hour ago, and her mom and dad were fast asleep. These days they were always asleep by eight-thirty at the latest. Marla Jean sat out on the front porch wrapped in a blanket, pushing herself back and forth on the glider, feeling forlorn. Not that she wasn't thrilled with the news about the new baby. She was. Thrilled and tickled pink. She was also thrilled that her folks would be sticking around. Honestly, really, and truly, she was. If her chance of buying the Brown house didn't seem like an impossible dream now, she'd be jumping up and down for joy.

But still, she was giving herself permission, at least for tonight while no one was around, to feel sorry for herself, and forlorn was the best word to describe her mood. A nippy evening breeze whistled through the trees, and she pulled the blanket a little tighter.

Since the divorce she'd tried to carry on with things, one foot in front of the other, brave face to the world, but lately it felt like every step forward caused her to stumble two steps back.

On top of that, the whole town was abuzz about Bradley and Libby's impending nuptials. Thanksgiving was only a week and a half away, but apparently the holiday was being hijacked for the Bandy/Comstock wedding. She'd just heard from Lloyd Keener when he stopped by to get a haircut that the ceremony was going to be held in the town square, and they'd taken out a full-page spread in the *Everson Gazette* issuing a blanket invitation to the entire town. She would take a stab and guess the blanket invitation didn't include her. The inconvenient first wife.

Buying a house had seemed like such a good idea, a positive sign that she was refashioning her life to fit the independent person she wanted to be. But now it didn't look like that was going to happen. And as much as she loved her parents, she was too old to still be living under their roof.

Maybe she should rethink her goals. Instead of buying a house, maybe she should move out of Everson, think about getting an apartment over in Derbyville. It was only twenty miles away, but no one knew her, or cared about her one way or the other. And it would be convenient on the nights she taught her art classes.

Sometimes that sounded like heaven. She'd be close enough to commute to work, attend family dinners, and when the time came, close enough to spoil that baby once it arrived.

Yes, maybe downsizing was the way to go. She tried picturing herself in an apartment, but the only thing that came to mind was a sterile box with stark white walls, ugly all-purpose carpet, and avocado appliances.

But it would be her sterile box. And she could bring home a different man every night if she felt like it. No one would interfere. Not Lincoln, not Jake, not anybody. For some reason, that didn't make her feel any better. It just made her feel lonely. Everyone had somebody it seemed. Her parents were joined at the hip. Linc and Dinah had each other and now the new baby. And of course, last but not least, Bradley had Libby.

Across the street, two doors down the porch light flicked on, and she watched Jake and Theo walk outside and take a seat on the front porch. From a distance they looked alike, but Marla Jean recognized the unruly curls falling on Jake's forehead, could see the strong sturdy set of his shoulders. Lately, like a startled deer leaping into traffic, her heart would bound from her chest at the mere sight of him. Even from a distance. Damned inconvenient, adolescent thing for it to do. And she wasn't prepared to examine what it meant.

The sound of their laughter and the clink of their beer bottles carried to her on the night air. As she watched, Jake jumped up and scampered across the yard after Sadie. "Come back here, you overfed fleabag."

Humph. Even Jake had somebody now. Okay, so Sadie was a dog somebody and not a people somebody, but still. On top of that, Sadie would have been her dog somebody if Bradley wasn't being such an ass.

Standing up, she threw the blanket off and hobbled down the steps. She could see the dog stop and roll over in the grass as Jake approached. Then he bent to pick her up, petting her at the same time he scolded her. "If I've told you once, I've told you a hundred times, you have to stay on the porch."

Marla Jean grinned, and then yelled from her yard. "That's it, Jake. Let her know who's boss."

Jake straightened holding the dog. "Well lookie here, Sadie, if it isn't Marla Jean Bandy, your long-lost mother."

She crossed the street diagonally and walked over to where they stood. "So, how are the two of you faring?" The puppy wagged her tail as Marla Jean scratched her on the head.

"We're managing. Theo spoils her something awful though."

"That's good because the way things look now, she may be living with you permanently."

"What are you talking about?"

"You better see if Bud Gailey's still interested in the Brown house."

"And why would I do that?"

"I came down from the clouds and realized I can't afford a house right now. I'm thinking of finding an apartment instead. That's the most practical thing to do."

"But you love that house. I'm willing to work with you on getting the deal done."

That's exactly what she didn't want him to do, go to extra trouble just for her. "Forget it, Jake. I've looked at all my options."

"But you love that house," he repeated, sounding frustrated on her behalf.

She sighed and wrapped her arms around herself in a hug. "I do, but if these last few years have taught me anything, it's that you can't always get what you want. I'll live."

"But what about Sadie?"

She felt an unexpected tightness in her chest as the puppy let out a playful woof. "We'll see. Some apartments allow pets, don't they?"

"Where's this sudden apartment talk coming from, anyway?"

"My folks have decided to stay in Everson, and I'm happy about that, but not happy enough to keep living with them."

"Okay."

"And for the time being, an apartment is the more prudent choice, financially."

Jake stared at her like he wanted to ask more questions, but he nodded his head instead. "Okay. I guess you know best."

"Thanks, Jake. You don't know how much I appreciate everything."

"I didn't really do anything, but you're welcome."

Marla Jean wanted to change the subject. "Have you talked to Linc recently?"

"Not for a couple of days."

"Then I guess you haven't heard his big news. But I should probably let him tell you."

"Oh no you don't, missy. Spill."

She grinned. "Okay, I'm too excited to keep it to myself, anyway. Linc and Dinah are going to have a baby. They just found out today."

"A baby?" Jake's smile lit up the night, and then he shook his head in wonderment. "Linc, a father. Hell, I bet he's about ready to bust a gut."

"He's over the moon, he's so excited. Dinah, too."

"Who can blame them? I'll have to take Linc to lunch tomorrow to celebrate."

Theo walked down from the porch. "What are we celebrating?"

"Marla Jean's going to be an aunt."

Marla Jean smiled at Theo. "I plan to spoil her rotten, too."

"Her?" Theo asked.

She shrugged. "Or him. It's too soon to know."

"Well, that is good news. Would you like to join us for a beer?" He looked at her hopefully.

She glanced at Jake. He hadn't echoed Theo's invitation. In fact, he looked uncomfortable at the idea.

"Thanks, Theo, but I better call it a night. Tomorrow's a long day."

"What about Saturday night, then? You want to catch a movie?"

She couldn't think of any good reason to say no. Theo was amusing and uncomplicated. "Sure, that sounds like fun."

He smiled. "Great, I'll call you tomorrow."

"Sounds good." She allowed herself one more scratch between Sadie's ears and backed away from the brothers, who stood side by side. "You boys behave, okay?"

"Might as well if you're set on leaving," Theo said with a wink. "Night, Marla Jean."

Jake didn't say anything, just stood holding Sadie in his arms. As she crossed the street, she glanced over her shoulder to find him watching her with an odd expression on his face—an expression that matched her mood exactly. She'd say he looked forlorn.

As Marla Jean disappeared inside her house, Jake handed the puppy to his brother. "Take Sadie, will you?

I've got something to do." Without waiting for a reply, he climbed in his truck and backed out of the driveway. Once he got out of the neighborhood, he headed for the country roads that led out of town.

He didn't have anything he needed to do. He just needed to get away. He didn't want to sit and listen to Theo wax poetic about his pending date with Marla Jean. Okay, so Theo didn't wax poetic. But he didn't want to sit in the same room with him and witness the smug, self-satisfied attitude that would radiate from his pores because of his pending date with Marla Jean, either.

He pressed down on the accelerator, but he couldn't outrun the restless, sour feeling crawling around in his stomach. And it wasn't because Theo was taking Marla Jean to a movie. Not really.

It was more complicated than that.

The lights of the city faded away until dark silhouettes of tall trees lined the sides of the road. Slowing down, he turned down the driveway to the old Brown house. He pulled to a stop in front of it and sat with both hands on the steering wheel staring at the shadowed structure. Marla Jean wasn't going to live here, and that wasn't right.

Because she loved this house.

Okay, so he needed to stop saying that, but she did. If it was about money he'd let her pay whatever she could afford. But he knew she'd be too proud to accept that offer, so he'd bitten his tongue and kept the suggestion to himself.

Why the hell did it matter so much? It shouldn't, damn it. She was a grown woman, as she liked to remind him at every turn. And if she'd decided to live in an apartment instead, then so be it. The moon peeked through the trees, barely illuminating the lifeless house.

Whacking the steering wheel in frustration, he got out of the truck and stood looking up at the place. The sagging shutter on the front window drew his attention, so he went to the toolbox in the back of his truck for a hammer and a couple of nails. Holding the shutter even, he pounded the nails in place then stood back to examine his handiwork. It would have to do until he could do the repair properly.

The churning in his gut hadn't gone away. Maybe it was time he examined the source of that as well. That would mean being honest with himself, honest about his true feelings for Marla Jean.

Since he'd been a teenager he'd felt responsible for the people in his life. His mother, his aunt, even Theo. He was determined to be as different from his father as possible, and taking care of the people he cared about was the most obvious way to do that. It defined him, for better or worse, shaped him into the man he was today.

For a while he'd been able to convince himself that Marla Jean fell into the same category. Linc's little sister. An old friend—nothing more. And he'd wanted to believe he could tuck her safely away in this house, this shelter, and tuck his growing feelings for her away at the same time. He hadn't thought it out so clearly before this very minute, but he couldn't hide from the truth any longer.

He knew he wanted to protect her. But he'd always protected her. Nothing new. Nothing to get excited about.

He knew he wanted her. She'd grown into a beautiful woman, and he was . . . well, he was a man, for Pete's sake. Resisting had taken a heroic effort on his part. He mentally patted himself on the back, not that she seemed to appreciate what it had cost him.

It wasn't just about that, though. He really liked her. He

liked to talk to her, tease her, make her laugh. Hell, she made him laugh and that was something he needed a lot more of in his life.

And that's when it hit him. The unvarnished truth. He'd fallen in love.

Damn it all.

With Marla Jean. Things like this weren't supposed to happen to him. He'd lived his life in a way to insure they wouldn't, couldn't. But they had, and he did. Love her, that is. He sat down heavily on the porch steps like he'd taken a sledgehammer to the forehead.

What the hell was he supposed to do now? He didn't have a clue. Nothing had changed, yet everything was different. They were still the same people. And he was still all wrong for her. Love hadn't magically transformed him into the man she deserved. He rested his head against the screen door and looked up at the night sky like the distant stars might provide some kind of answer. After a while, he pushed himself up from the steps and walked to the back of his truck, hauled out the bucket of sky blue paint that rested like a promise in the bed of his pick-up and went to work.

Chapter Twenty-four

~

After putting in a full day at the barber shop Marla
Jean jumped in her car and drove to Derbyville. Instead
of going home to help her mother prepare the Thanksgiving sweet potato casserole and chop turkey giblets for
gravy, she pulled into the parking slot for number 215 and
climbed the stairs to her soon-to-be new apartment. She'd
signed the lease, but hadn't moved in yet. Passing her next-
door neighbor, a tall fellow with brown hair and an easy
manner, she smiled but didn't stop to introduce herself.

Using her new keys, she let herself inside and stood looking around at the empty space with its stark white walls.
She planned to take care of that little problem right away.
She'd come prepared with a change of old work clothes and
a kerchief to cover her hair. With a glance at the paint cans
and drop cloths piled in one corner she hurried to the bathroom to change. She could hardly wait to get started.

Once she'd decided to make the move from her parents' house, she hadn't seen any reason to delay. When
she announced her plan, her parents had been upset, feel-

ing like they'd pushed her out of the house with their decision to stay in Everson. It had taken some doing, but she'd finally convinced them she'd wanted her own place for a while. In the end they'd supported her decision.

Derbyville proved to have tons of apartment complexes to choose from. She'd spent the last week and a half looking at every one of them. This one, the Waterview Gardens, finally won her over.

The view of the water was sadly lacking, and the gardens seemed to have gone missing, as well, but her second-floor two-bedroom unit had a balcony with a view of a tiny park and a big window that flooded the small kitchen with lovely morning light. Best of all, for an exorbitant deposit, they allowed tenants to have pets and, thank the lord, paint color on the walls.

She came out of the bathroom buttoning one of her dad's old flannel shirts when a knock on the front door made her jump. She couldn't imagine who it could be. Maybe one of her new neighbors stopping by to say hello.

Peeping through the peephole, something she never bothered with in Everson, she was surprised and a little breathless to see who waited on the other side. She opened the door.

"Hey Jake. What in the world are you doing here?"

Jake stood holding a pot of ivy, his tall form filling the doorway. He was dressed in jeans, a white T-shirt, and that worn brown leather jacket that had sent her nerve endings into overdrive at the football game. When he tipped his cowboy hat up and grinned like the devil, rivers of awareness flooded her veins. "Nice to see you, too, Marla Jean."

"I didn't mean it like that. Come in. Come in. I wasn't

expecting anyone, that's all." His appearance made her feel rattled, so she tried to get the babbling under control. "How did you know where to find me?"

He handed her the plant, and his hand brushed hers. She could've been mistaken, but he seemed to make a point of lingering over the touch. "Lincoln gave me the address. What were you trying to do? Sneak out of town and leave us all behind?"

Fiddling with the yellow ribbon tied around the pot, she felt oddly moved that he'd sought her out, and on top of that, brought her a plant. It was certainly a step up from a single cowboy boot.

Walking into the kitchen she set the plant on the counter. "Of course not. Things have been crazy busy, and I wanted to get settled before I announced anything."

He followed her into the kitchen, capturing her with his probing gaze. "This was kind of sudden, wasn't it?" He seemed to have something on his mind.

"I told you I was thinking about getting an apartment."

"But here? In Derbyville? I never expected you'd leave Everson."

She slid past him and walked back to the living room, needing to escape the close quarters of the kitchen. He could unsettle her just by standing too near. "I haven't really left Everson. I'll be at the barber shop every day. But I decided a little distance was a good idea."

Again he followed her, closing the space between them. "Distance from what? The people who care about you?"

She met his gaze head on this time. "Sometimes all those people who care about me make it hard to breathe."

His voice grew gentle. "Is this about Bradley and Libby's wedding?"

She shook her head. "I wouldn't dream of giving them that much power over me, but I'll admit I won't be sorry to steer clear of the fuss this weekend."

"That wedding is turning into a circus." He sounded disgusted. "If I was in your shoes, I'd be tempted to run away, too."

She stuck her chin out. "I prefer to think I'm sashaying into a bright new future."

"Sashaying?" he asked with a grin.

She grinned back. "Sashaying, skipping, merrily row, row, rowing my boat—whatever you want to call it."

"I'm relieved to hear that." He smiled like he meant it.

"And I haven't told you the best part?"

"What's that?" He stuffed his hands in his back pockets and rocked back on his heels.

"I put down a pet deposit, so I can take Sadie off your hands as soon as I'm settled."

"Oh." He sounded surprised, and a little uncertain. "Well, that's good. I'll feel better picturing you here with Sadie instead of picturing you here all alone." He turned away from her, spotted the paint cans stacked along the wall, and then reached over and tugged the end of the kerchief on her head. "Were you about to paint? I know my way around a paint bucket if you'd like a hand."

She touched her scarf and looked down at her tattered jeans, realizing for the first time that she looked like someone who'd gone clothes shopping in the nearest dumpster. Oh well, he'd seen her in worse over the years, and the idea of having his help, having him here alone with her in this place had its appeal. Who was she kidding? It had a lot of appeal. "I'd be pretty silly to turn down help from an expert like you. But you aren't exactly dressed for it."

He held up a hand and headed for the door. "Never fear. I have work clothes in my truck. I'll be right back." And with a wink, he was gone.

Jake ran to his truck, rummaging around in the back for his work clothes. When he decided to show up on her doorstep with nothing but a lousy plant for an excuse, he hadn't examined his motives too closely. But helping her paint her apartment gave him a legitimate reason to stick around. She seemed determined to start a new chapter in her life, and he couldn't blame her. But he was also going to make damned sure she knew he'd be around if she needed anything. Maybe that wasn't the whole story, but it would do for now. He grabbed a roll of painter's tape and headed back upstairs.

She thought her skin might burst open like a ripe melon. If he brushed past her again, reached around her. If he placed his hands on her waist to scoot her out of his way. If he kept touching her, she was going to fly apart and flutter to the ground in a million confetti pieces. For two hours they'd painted, side by side, but he was faster, taller, knew what he was doing, so he worked around her, through her, surrounding her with his long arms and tall legs and the feel of his solid chest against her back. Fleeting touches, barely there and then gone. His sleeve against her arm. His breath against her hair. Nothing substantial. Nothing to make a federal case about. But her body didn't seem to agree.

Marla Jean ducked under his arm and put her paint roller in the tray. Except for one spot that Jake was finishing, the walls were now a lovely shade of baby poop yellow. That's what Jake called it. Marla Jean thought it looked more like soft mustard. Whatever it was, the five gallons had been a steal at the paint store. Somebody's mismixed color had been her gain. She looked around the extra bedroom, inhaling the smell of fresh paint, and smiled. "I like it, don't you?"

He finished covering the last bit of white. "I have to admit, it's growing on me."

"Just wait until it's filled with furniture. It's going to look terrific. And thanks for the help. It would have taken me all night if I'd done it alone."

"That's why you aren't supposed to sneak out of town without telling your friends. When do you plan to move the furniture in?" He put his roller down in a tray and started hammering the lid back on the paint bucket.

"I thought I'd wait until Friday. I'll be helping Mom with Thanksgiving tomorrow."

"If you need any help, let me know."

"Lincoln and Dinah said they'd help and Donny Joe and Theo already offered, too. I don't have that much to move, but you're more than welcome to pitch in if you'd like. I'm offering free beer and sandwiches."

He made a face. "I forgot about your faithful troop of followers. What happened to Harry?"

She scrunched her face up. "I hate to admit it, but you were right. Harry was way too serious. I finally convinced him I wasn't ready for anything exclusive, and unless he wanted to just be friends, he should look somewhere else."

His eyes seemed to search hers when he said, "Because you're not looking for serious, right?"

"Right." She met his gaze and nodded, wondering if that was the truth of the matter anymore.

"So, what about tonight?"

His deep voice washed over her like a warm bath. She could happily drown listening to him talk. "Tonight?" Her own voice sounded breathless.

"I don't know about you, but I'm starving. I could use something to eat. Why don't I follow you back to Everson, we'll get cleaned up, and I'll buy you dinner."

She quickly corralled her wayward thoughts. "Oh, I should buy you dinner, Jake. You're the one that got roped into spending your night painting," she insisted.

"Okay. You talked me into it."

"How about a cheeseburger? I could really use a big, juicy cheeseburger. Besides I need to have my turkey antidote."

"Your what?" he asked.

"My turkey antidote. I always like to squeeze in a cheeseburger before I'm subjected to the millions of turkey recipes I'll be eating for the next few weeks."

"You don't like turkey?"

"I love turkey, but by the time Mom makes turkey croquettes, turkey pot pie, curry turkey, turkey supreme, and turkey casserole delight, it's not so delightful anymore, and just the memory of that once and distant cheeseburger will carry me through until Christmas when it starts all over again."

"But now you can escape back to your own apartment and eat anything you want."

"Ha! You know my mother. If I don't show up to eat with them at least half the time, she'll sneak over here while I'm at work and leave leftovers in my refrigerator."

After they cleaned up the paint rollers, they headed back to Everson in their own cars, agreeing that he'd pick her up at her folks' house in thirty minutes. As soon as she got home she jumped in the shower and dried her hair in record time. Then she threw on a pink sweater and jeans and was waiting at the front door when he pulled up in Gertie.

She tried not to think too much about the excitement dancing around inside her chest as she climbed into his truck. She tried to think instead about the deep contentment that rolled through her when she was with Jake. Underneath the sexual yearning, under the lusty longing there lived an ease she didn't find with anyone else but him. Settling onto the truck's seat she reminded herself again. This wasn't a date. It wasn't anything but two friends eating hamburgers together. Still, the quivering in her stomach when she glanced his way made it feel like it might be more.

They decided on Scotty's drive-in, an old-fashioned hamburger stand with carhops on roller skates. Nina Lee, who'd worked there as long as Marla Jean could remember, skated up to Jake's side of the truck. "Hey there, Jake. Hey, Marla Jean. What'll it be?"

He looked at Marla Jean, who said, "I'll take a cheeseburger, cut the onions, and a diet cola."

He raised an eyebrow, but before she could explain the no onions he said, "That's right. You're allergic to onions, aren't you?" Turning back to Nina Lee he said, "Nina Lee, we'll take two cheeseburgers, cut the onions, and one diet and one regular cola. And two orders of fries."

"You got it, Jake." Even though she was old enough to be his grandma, she flipped him a flirtatious smile and skated away.

Once she was gone Jake tuned the radio to an oldie rock station and sat playing drums on the steering wheel to an old Rolling Stones song.

Marla Jean shifted in her seat, searching for something

to say, mesmerized by the sight of his wide wrists and strong forearms. Although they were separated by a good two feet, Jake as always seemed to take up more than his share of the available space. Finally she said inanely, "Nina Lee sure gets around on those roller skates."

He laughed. "She'll probably want to be buried with her skates on. I heard a rumor that she used to be a star in the roller derby in Dallas in her younger days."

Marla Jean's estimation of Nina Lee rose even higher. "Wow, I would have loved to have seen that."

"I don't know if it's true. You know how this town loves gossip."

"I do for a fact."

The conversation stalled. He kept time on the steering wheel while Mick Jagger sang about not getting any satisfaction. Marla Jean sympathized with Mick completely. Sitting so close to Jake wasn't helping. He was one of the many reasons she chose to move away to Derbyville. His complete lack of interest in her had bothered her more than she let on. But he'd shown up tonight offering a pot of ivy and his painting expertise, and she'd all but jumped at the chance to spend time with him. Probably not the smartest thing she'd ever done.

But it was time she faced it. She was crazy about him. Foolishly, stupidly, out-of-her-mind crazy about him. And that was the reason sitting in this truck with him was such a bad idea, because the more time she spent with Jake, the harder it became to deny her feelings. That old infatuation had flamed to life, maybe because he'd rebuffed her and it seemed safe to fantasize about someone she'd never have, or maybe she was simply destined to fall for men who in the end didn't want her.

But tonight, tonight something about him seemed different. He'd been quieter than usual, more intense. Several times during the evening she'd caught him watching her, like he had something important weighing on his mind.

It didn't take long for their food to arrive, and Marla Jean leaned across Jake to pay, brushing his sleeve in the process. Aware of how close together their heads were when she said, "Keep the change, Nina Lee."

"Thanks, honey. Here's some extra ketchup packets for your fries." She smiled at Marla and winked at Jake, then did a little spin before skating away.

Marla Jean settled back in her seat while Jake handed out the drinks and sandwiches, making a big production of arranging their food on the seat between them, making sure she had napkins and salt and pepper. Jake tapped his paper cup to hers. "Here's to new starts."

"New starts," she echoed merrily.

She hadn't realized how hungry she was, and inhaled her food like a farm hand after a full day's work. Marla Jean savored the last bite of her cheeseburger, eyeing Jake's fries, wondering if he was going to eat them, when he said in a serious voice, "Marla Jean, there's something I want to talk to you about."

She was still chewing, so she turned toward him attentively, raising her eyebrows to show she was listening.

He set his burger down on the yellow paper wrapper that identified it as cheese rather than a plain old hamburger, put his arm along the back of the seat, and wrinkled his brow. Clearing his throat he said, "Marla Jean, after giving it a lot of thought, I've decided, if you're still interested that is"—he paused then, a long, drawn-out pause—"I'd like to take you up on your offer."

Chapter Twenty-five

❦

Jake watched with alarm as Marla Jean's face turned red. When she started choking and sputtering like a car filled with bad gasoline, he started slapping her on the back. "Geez, Marla Jean, are you okay?"

She didn't answer, just shook her head and coughed some more. Grabbing her arm like his mother used to do when he was a kid, he jerked it straight up in the air and bounced her up and down like he was churning butter.

"Stop, please, I'm fine." Wrenching her arm away, she closed her eyes and coughed a few more times. "A piece of pickle went down the wrong pipe. That's all. Except for being embarrassed, I'm fine, perfectly fine." Her eyes were pink and watery and her voice sounded like a bullfrog had taken up residence in her throat.

She didn't look fine, so he figured he'd give her a few minutes to compose herself. He took a sip of his drink before continuing. "Maybe this wasn't such a good idea."

She cleared her throat and waved a hand in his direction. "No, please, go ahead with what you were saying. I'm all ears." The wary look she was giving him didn't fill him with confidence that she'd still be a willing participant.

Needing some resolve, he took a deep breath. "Well, as you know, and tell me if this makes you uncomfortable, the wedding is Saturday."

She looked confused but nodded and said, "Go on."

"And tomorrow is Thanksgiving, and Friday my mother has all sorts of errands set up for me to run."

"Okay." She frowned uncertainly.

He was momentarily distracted when she reached for one of his french fries, and started swirling it in a puddle of ketchup. Clearing his throat he continued. "I know I expressed my doubts about this."

"Doubts?" She scoffed. "You made it plain that even if hell froze over it would never happen."

"I know, and I thought about checking with your dad first, but it's a holiday and I hated to ask him." He pushed the rest of his fries toward her in case she wanted the rest.

"Wait a minute. Why on earth would you check with my dad?"

"Well, sheesh, I guess because he understands my tricky cowlick better than anyone, and I need a haircut before the wedding or my mother will disown me. That leaves Floyd, but he's closed for the holidays. So, I started thinking, hey, maybe I should take Marla Jean up on her offer."

"My offer—"

He kept talking right over her thinking to win her over with flattery. "After all most of the men in Everson trust you with their hair, so why shouldn't I? It's not like the whole town walks around looking like they got their head caught in the lawn mower, or anything. So, it's obvious you know what you're doing. But now with the move, I'm realizing you'll be tied up, and I guess it's out of line for me to ask you to do anything, even indirectly, for the wedding. But the main thing is I decided to trust you to cut my hair, even if you don't have time to do it now, though I hope you might." He spoke slowly trailing off at the end as he realized he'd been babbling on and on.

She sat looking at him like he'd just hatched from a snake egg. "You want a haircut. That's the offer you're taking me up on?"

He nodded and hurried on with his explanation. "You said if I ever changed my mind, the first haircut would be on the house, but of course I'll be happy to pay. I'll even pay extra under the circumstances." He trailed off again as she continued looking at him in that strange way.

All at once she started wadding up the wrappers from the food and shoving them into the sack. "Let's go."

"Let's go?" he asked.

"To the barber shop." She gave him an evil grin. "That's where I keep the special hair-cutting lawn mower, but I get my best results from the weed whacker."

"Are you sure? Right now?" he asked.

"Sure, I'm sure, and right now's perfect. I'd be happy to make you look all spiffy for Bradley and Libby's wedding. It will be my gift to the happy couple."

Taking the sack from her, he got out to throw it away in the nearby trash can. He got back inside and started the truck. "I want you to realize I'm putting all my trust in you, Marla Jean." He wanted to impress on her that for him this was a big decision.

"I know," she said with a wicked glint in her eye.

"With my cowlick," he added for emphasis as he pulled out of the parking lot and onto the road.

"I know," she repeated gleefully. Rubbing her hands together she said, "I can hardly wait. Step on it, Jake."

The moon hung like a bright yellow ball in the purple November sky, and a bracing wind swirled around her legs as Marla Jean unlocked the door to the barber shop. The bell over the door tinkled in the darkness as she ushered Jake inside. "Welcome to my lair."

His tall form was only a shadow in the unlit shop, and she brushed past him to turn on the lights. Outside, streetlights revealed an eerily deserted Main Street. Everyone was probably home baking and cooking, preparing for turkey day, but she closed the blinds just the same. The last thing she needed was for one of the many nose-poking, busybody citizens of Everson to see them inside the shop after hours. No telling what rumors they'd concoct with that tidbit of information.

Jake stood by the door, his cowboy hat in his hand. She walked over to her chair, patting it to indicate he should take a seat. "Come on. I won't bite, but I need to get a good look at your hair while it's dry."

He hung his hat on the hat rack and shrugged out of his leather jacket, hanging it up, as well. "I guess I better get comfortable."

"Absolutely, Jake. Relax, get comfortable, and surrender yourself to my care." This was going to be fun.

Although earlier, she'd been choking on more than a piece of pickle when he said he'd decided to accept her offer. She'd been choking on shock, astonishment, wonder, and a real case of "I can't believe I'm going to finally sleep with Jake"-itus. But of course she wasn't. Going to finally sleep with Jake, that is. And that sucked.

But if there was a silver lining, it was that she was finally going to get to cut his hair. Okay, maybe it was more like a tin foil lining when you stacked it up against sex.

But getting her hands on his thick, wavy head of hair had been a long-standing fantasy, even before she ever thought about following in her father's footsteps as a barber.

Many a day she'd bounced along on the rock-hard bench seat of the school bus, sat right behind Jake, her gaze glued to his gleaming, blue-black superman hair while he laughed and joked and horsed around with Lincoln. She'd stare at the back of his head, hoping he'd turn around, hoping he'd notice her, hoping he wouldn't.

She patted the chair again. "Have a seat right here, mister."

He approached slowly, circling her a bit as if she was a wild creature who might turn on him without warning. Easing around to the front of the chair, he sat, settling his feet on the shiny metal foot rest. "What the heck, it's only hair, right? It'll grow back."

She laughed. "But not in time for the wedding." When his eyebrows went up in alarm, she put a hand on his shoulder. "Just kidding—I want you to look your best. I promise. After all, my reputation's on the line."

He never took his eyes from her, but she could feel the tension seep out of his neck and shoulders as she started running her fingers through his hair. It was thick and soft just like she remembered from the few minutes he'd been on top of her in her bed the night she hurt her foot. It had a bit of a wave, and she could see that his tricky cowlick would be no problem in her hands. She took a comb and smoothed out the tangles, studying the way it fell naturally on his head. Grabbing a plastic cape and a towel, she fastened them around his shoulders and said, "Okay, let's get you shampooed."

"You're going to shampoo my hair?" He looked like she'd just announced she was going to take out his appendix. "Why do you have to shampoo my hair? Floyd doesn't shampoo my hair and neither does your father. I just sit down and they start snipping away."

"Good to know, but I'm not Floyd or my father. Are you going to let me do things my way or not?"

He looked like he wanted to argue, but stood up from the chair and said grudgingly, "Fine. We'll do it your way."

"Thank you." It was true. She didn't always shampoo. A lot of the old guys sat down, she'd take a little off the top and around their ears, and they were done. But some of her younger clients wanted more of a salon experience. They wanted a shampoo, cut, and blow dry. Some even insisted on color and styling products. Not that Jake needed anything like that, but now that she finally had him in her clutches, she wasn't going to miss a chance to wash his hair. Leading him to the back of the shop, she pointed to the shampoo bench. "Lie down and lean your head back."

He did as he was told, his body stretched out on the narrow vinyl-covered platform. She leaned over him, her breasts inches from his face, making sure his hair was over the basin before adjusting the water to a nice, warm temperature. His eyelids fell shut as she used the sprayer to wet his hair. Then pumping some shampoo into her hand, she massaged it into his hair and scalp, wallowing in the opportunity to study his face at close range.

The way his long, black lashes swept down to hide

those deep brown eyes, the faint scar on his cheekbone adding to his masculine perfection, the dark shadow of day long whiskers covering his stubborn jaw. For once she didn't have to resist the urge to touch him. Her fingers danced across his scalp, and down the base of his skull. He let out a little moan, and it vibrated right through her, dislodging all the longing that was trapped inside her like so much shrapnel. She straightened, reminding herself to remain professional.

"Oh, that feels good," he said with a sigh.

She smiled in satisfaction. "See? I told you to trust me."

The scent of rosemary and chamomile filled the air. He opened his eyes suddenly, looking up at her through her bent arms. "Hey, what kind of shampoo is that? I'm not going to smell like a girl, am I?"

"Rosemary isn't a girlie smell. This is a barber shop, remember? I only deal in manly products. If you'll stop talking and relax, it can be very soothing." She rinsed his hair once and then rubbed in another dollop of shampoo, creating more suds.

"Really? Name another flowery-smelling manly man who lets you wash his hair with this stuff." As he spoke, his warm breath whispered against her collarbone.

"Mitch Danvers, for one. And Sammy Lopez for another." Both were young men in their twenties, and both took great pride in looking their best. From what she could tell, all the young women in town seemed to appreciate their efforts.

He closed his eyes again. "Humph. You think those pipsqueaks are manly?"

"Sammy buys a bottle of this stuff every six weeks to use at home. It's rich in emollients. Very nourishing for the hair." She leaned closer, lifting his head to rinse the back of his hair.

He opened his eyes just so he could roll them at her, his face now only inches from her chest. "Well, if it's nourishing...Why didn't you say so in the first place?"

"Oh hush." She squirted a glob of conditioner in her hand and rubbed her palms together. "This conditioner has aloe, lemongrass, and thyme. I hope it meets with your nose's approval." She smoothed it through his hair, massaging again.

His eyes closed again, and he exhaled deeply. "It smells great. Let's just forget the haircut, okay? Just keep doing what you're doing for another hour or so."

She selfishly gave in to his request for a minute or two longer than necessary, letting her fingers play across his temples, over his ears and down the strong column of his neck before saying, "Okay, it's time to rinse now."

Using the sprayer, she turned his head this way and that until she was done and told him to sit up. Taking the towel from his shoulder, she wrapped it around his head turban-style and led him back to the barber chair.

Docile as a lamb, he followed her directions and sat while she towel-dried his hair and combed it. While looking in the mirror, she lifted strands of his hair and explained, "I'm not going to take much length off the top. I'm just going to shape up the back and the sideburns a bit. Does that sound okay?"

Jake nodded, feeling like all his bones had turned to sponge. Except one. He'd never been so turned on in his entire life. Luckily the big, black plastic cape she'd draped around him hid the evidence.

This afternoon, when Lincoln told him she planned to move to Derbyville, everything inside of him panicked. Derbyville wasn't that far away, and she'd still be at the barber shop most days, but damn it, he couldn't get a handle on what he wanted from her, what he could allow himself to want. Realizing he was in love with her only confused things.

Part of him thought not having her around so much was the perfect solution. A little distance, a chance to gain some perspective. But that only lasted as long as it took to get her new address from Lincoln and drive from Everson to Derbyville. Finding her alone in that empty apartment, helping her paint, finding every excuse to stand too close, brushing against her like a lovesick adolescent boy, had only fueled his growing need for her.

She was driving him out of his everlovin' mind.

So when he'd taken her up on her offer of a haircut, he'd been surrendering to a long-standing fantasy. When Marla Jean first started working for her dad, he always managed to avoid getting his hair cut if she was at the shop. Even back then he had to fight his attraction for her.

Back when she'd been Lincoln's little sister and strictly off limits. Later, when she'd been a married woman and absolutely off limits. And now, when she'd made it clear that her body wasn't off limits, but her heart most certainly was.

So, in a moment of weakness, he'd given in, allowed himself to indulge a little. He stretched out on that shampoo chair and allowed her to have her soapy way with him. Stupid flowery-smelling shampoo and that lemon conditioner that smelled like Marla Jean in a bottle. His head was swimming.

He watched her in the mirror now as she lifted a lock of

his hair, using her comb and scissors in tandem, her concentration on the task complete. He gripped the arms of the chair, resisting the urge to pull her into his lap and kiss her until they were both stupid with wanting each other. That's what he wanted. To stop thinking so much and just feel. To give Marla Jean what she wanted—to give her what she'd asked for when she'd approached him with that harebrained offer of meaningless sex. He'd always been good at keeping sex and emotions separate, hadn't he?

But giving in wasn't the responsible thing to do. It certainly wasn't the smart thing to do, so he held on to the arms of the chair like they'd save him. Save him from doing something reckless and dumb.

She made a few more cuts and thought she was finished. But wait. Almost. A snip here and there, watching a dark strand curl around her finger. Curl the way she wanted to curl up around his body and stay there for a day or two. It had taken years to get Jake into her chair. She wanted to enjoy every second. Her breath felt shallow, trapped inside her body. Being near him seemed to require additional oxygen, seemed to charge the atmosphere with thick strands of coppery need.

Ripping open the Velcro tab on the black plastic cape, she pulled it off, throwing it on the neighboring chair. With a soft brush she whisked away a few loose hairs on the back of his neck. Goose bumps traveled along his skin, and she watched fascinated feeling the same tingle travel up the inside of her arm.

She walked around the chair, dropping the brush on the counter, and turned to stand in front of him, examining him from a new angle. The haircut was done, finished, but she couldn't quite bring herself to stop touching him. She could feel his eyes on her, tracking her every move.

She played with one errant curl that fell on his forehead, refusing to be tamed. Leaning forward she pushed the stubborn curl up into his hairline, using all of her fingers, letting them travel across his scalp like a gentle rake. He grabbed her arm, stilling her hand and her eyes flew to meet his.

"Marla Jean." His voice was a low rumble when he whispered her name. It could have been a warning. It could have been a plea, but when he pulled her into his lap she didn't care. Was this what she wanted? It's what she'd asked for, wasn't it? Physical pleasure, the meeting of mutual needs. She wasn't going to stop now to ask if it was enough. Instead, she reached for him, pulling him down before words and regrets and consequences could cloud the moment.

He took control, arranging her until she straddled him, and then he was kissing her. And all she cared about were his hands moving across her skin, pulling her sweater over her head. Her hands pulling at his T-shirt until it was free from his jeans, dragging it up and off until he was uncovered and bare to her touch. His hands buried in her hair—her mouth skimming, licking, nipping at the muscles of his chest, lower to the hot flesh of his stomach before moving back to his mouth.

That glorious mouth.

And his hands finding the hook on her bra, freeing her breasts to his touch, his eyes devouring them with a hunger she longed to feed. His arms lifting her, moving her so her nipples became the willing victims of his lips and tongue and teeth, unearthing her weaknesses. Holding his head in her hands, urging him to never, ever stop.

Jake stood, taking her with him. She kicked off her shoes while he found the button and zipper on her jeans, skimming them, along with her panties, down her legs with a sweep of his hands. His eyes traveled the naked length of her, his gaze intent and smoky. His lips brushed hers, whispering her name once more, hot and dark across her cheek. "Marla Jean."

"Jake." She chased his mouth, needing the taste of him, and he answered with a heart-aching kiss that shuffled what was left of her senses.

Turning her to face the mirror, his shadowed gaze locked on the erotic image she made. Her riot of hair spilled out against his bare chest. With one hand he slowly traced a map around one breast, lazily, inch by inch, while the other hand skimmed across her flat stomach and down one thigh. "My God, you're beautiful."

Seeing herself in the mirror, she felt beautiful, with Jake's big, wide hands on her, with his eyes reflecting need and honest desire. His hand drifted down, moved between her legs, teasing, coaxing her to open to him. She spread her legs apart, giving him better access, gasping at the feel of Jake's fingers inside her, nearly weeping at the drenching desire his touch created. His other hand continued to caress her breasts, molding them, plucking at her nipples with his fingers. Her body arched, pressing her breasts against his hand, needing more, wanting everything, welcoming the building tension like a long-lost friend.

She bit her lip, and her eyes drifted closed.

A nibble on her neck got her attention before Jake's voice rumbled in her ear. "Open your eyes, Marla Jean. I want you to watch what I'm doing to you."

So she watched through heavy lids as he played her

like an instrument, strumming her until she hummed with pleasure. Pleasure that gripped her, picked her up, and carried her higher and higher. Her fingers dug into his jean-covered thighs for support, leaning against him while the whole world flew apart.

Jake took the weight of her, picking her up and carrying her to the shampoo bench in the back room. He laid her down gently and then straightened, taking off his jeans in a hurry, retrieving a condom from the pocket.

His penis sprang out proud and ready and he rolled the condom on before turning around to face her. "Is this what you want, Marla Jean? If you're not sure..."

"This is what I want, Jake. I'm sure. Now kiss me."

So he did. He kissed her, knowing his heart would almost certainly be broken before they were done with each other. But for now, he kissed her, placing his pitiful heart in her hands.

When she opened her legs, inviting him in, he pushed inside her body, certain he was making love for the first time in his life. With every thrust he fell more deeply. With every stroke he uncovered a new layer of need, need he saw echoed in Marla Jean's eyes. He kissed her again, seeking new ways to connect, new ways to reach her, wanting to hold on to the moment, make it go on and on. But her body tightened, pushing him closer to the edge, then stilled—a small quiet calm before exploding beneath him. Her sob of pleasure was his undoing. He let go, and mounting, tight-winding pressure slammed through his body while he roared his release.

Gathering her close, he buried his face in her hair, feeling, just feeling, not allowing himself to think.

Chapter Twenty-six

～

"That box goes in the kitchen, Theo. And Donny Joe, that one has art supplies. It goes in the extra bedroom."

"Yes, ma'am," Donny Joe said with a wink.

"Watch it, Lincoln. Don't you dare scratch the new paint on my walls." Marla Jean hauled boxes and directed traffic as the trail of friendly helpers unloaded her meager possessions from the rented moving van and dumped them in the appropriate spots. It wasn't much, but it was all hers.

Thanksgiving had been a day of cooking and eating and football, but later that night Marla Jean had finished packing her few belongings, so by early Friday morning when Theo, Donny Joe, Lincoln, and Dinah showed up at her parents' house, it had taken less than three hours to make the move to her new apartment. Bitsy contributed a big box of kitchen paraphernalia at the last minute as a kind of blessing on the move. She'd worried that their decision to move home had pushed Marla Jean away, but Marla Jean finally convinced her that it was something she needed to do whether they moved back to Everson or not.

She wanted to take her time unpacking things, especially in the kitchen, but having her friends around now was a blessing. They kept her engaged. They kept her from thinking too much. They kept her from thinking about Jake.

After they'd made love at the barber shop—okay, after they'd had sex, Jake had grown more and more distant. By the time he'd taken her home he was barely speaking. He'd walked her to the door and kissed her on the forehead, for God's sake.

She couldn't be surprised or even offended. He'd warned her that he thought anything between the two of them would be a gigantic mistake. But damn, how could anything that felt so world-rearranging be a mistake? Even now her body hummed with bursts of pleasure remembering the things he'd done to her. The ways he'd touched her. It appeared that the feelings were entirely one-sided.

But she couldn't regret it. She was the one who'd said she wasn't interested in anything serious. She was the one who'd told him she could handle casual, meaningless sex. She refused to regret it. Having sex with Jake could now be struck from her list of adventurous things to do. Checked off as part of becoming a woman who owned her choices. And didn't she sound so sophisticated and worldly? Check.

She deliberately chose to push any more thoughts of Jake from her mind and started unloading a box of books in the living room, carefully arranging them on the built in shelves. Dinah sat on the sofa, confined there by Linc who in overprotective father-to-be mode had allowed that she could only empty small boxes of odds and ends as long as they weighed no more than the average feather. Marla Jean thought it was sweet, but Dinah wanted to strangle him. "I'm pregnant, not an invalid," she complained as he stuck his head around the corner to check on her for the umpteenth time. As soon as he disappeared, she jumped up and grabbed Marla Jean's arm, pulling her down beside her on the couch. "Take a break and keep me company for a few minutes."

"I really shouldn't. I feel bad making the guys do all the work."

"Oh, pish, it's almost done. Sit. Talk to me."

"I have a better idea," Marla Jean said, "Come in the kitchen, and you can help me make sandwiches."

Dinah hopped off the sofa like she'd been released from a jail cell. "Great idea. Food. I'm starving."

Marla Jean waved her toward the kitchen table. "We can't have that. Have a seat and I'll get the sandwich stuff from the fridge."

"Turkey, I presume?"

"Bite your tongue. This is a no turkey zone, until Mom shows up with leftovers. I have ham and pastrami."

Dinah sat down at the kitchen table. "I like the color you painted the walls. It looks like rotten boiled egg yolk."

"Thanks, I think." Marla Jean grinned.

"You're welcome. It's a bold decorating choice. So," Dinah said drawing it out slowly, "speaking of bold, I understand from Theo that Jake helped you paint?"

"He did," she admitted. So much for not thinking about Jake. "He showed up just as I was getting started."

"I love a man with good timing."

"It was really nice of him to help," Marla Jean insisted casually.

"I thought he'd be here helping today, too," Dinah remarked not too slyly as she opened the loaf of bread and took out slices.

"I'm sure he has a million things to do since the wedding is tomorrow." Marla Jean pulled the sliced meat and cheese from the refrigerator. Then she grabbed mustard, mayonnaise, pickles, tomatoes, lettuce, and a stack of paper plates, and joined Dinah at the table.

Dinah looked concerned. "Oh, yeah. I forgot. How are you feeling about that? You haven't really said much."

She shrugged. "There's nothing to say. Life goes on."

"I know, but still, you and Bradley were married for a long time." Dinah picked up the slices of bread and started flipping them onto paper plates like she was dealing cards.

"That's true, and when I married him, I expected it to be for the rest of my life. Part of me is still surprised every day when I wake up and realize I'm divorced." Marla Jean grabbed a cutting board from a box on the counter, found a sharp knife in another, and started slicing tomatoes.

"So, do you still love him?" Dinah sounded surprised, like the idea hadn't occurred to her.

Marla Jean finished slicing the tomato with a few enthusiastic whacks of the knife. "Who, Bradley? Lately I want to wring his neck every time I see him. Part of me still loves him...We practically grew up together. Maybe I just love the boy he used to be. But I'm not in love with him, and I don't want to talk about Bradley anymore. Please."

Dinah squirted mustard on half the bread and mayonnaise on the other half. "Okay, so we won't. You know what I think? I think we should go out and celebrate tonight. Your big move, the new baby. I'd say we deserve a night of dancing at Lu Lu's, don't you?"

Marla Jean's first reaction was to say no, but then she realized if she stayed home she'd just brood, not about Bradley's pending marriage, but about Jake and what she'd say to appear carefree and lighthearted the next time she saw him. "That sounds like a great idea, Dinah. I'm going to go get the guys and tell them it's time to eat."

"Please, Mr. Jacobson, be still." Mr. Smythe—it rhymed with tithe—made the request in his clipped English accent. He trained watery blue eyes on his latest victim while the jowls of his cheeks quivered with disapproval. "You're fidgeting. And if you fidget, this suit will not fit properly."

"Sorry, Mr. Smythe," Jake said as he fidgeted again. "But I think it looks fine."

"This is your aunt's special day, and you want to look your best. Two minutes longer, sir. That's all I require."

"Fine. If it will make Aunt Libby happy." Standing still for Smythe wasn't the only thing making him fidget. Trying not to think about the night he'd spent with Marla Jean was about to make him jump out of his skin. Once again he'd proved himself to be a selfish bastard, thinking with his dick, and damn the consequences for Marla Jean. He'd given into temptation, and even now all he wanted to do was drive over to her new place, throw out the crowd of admirers helping her move and take her against one of those butt-ugly yellow walls. He stifled a groan at the idea and closed his eyes.

"Mr. Jacobson, I must insist you stop moving."

He took a deep breath and let out a lusty sigh. "Sorry, Mr. Smythe."

Ellie and Aunt Libby sat outside the curtain at the tailor's shop, waiting to make sure he passed their final inspection. The wedding was a day away, and just to make his mother happy, he'd shopped for new dress shoes and some new socks before meeting the two of them for lunch. When they discovered he hadn't been to Mr. Smythe's for his final fitting, they freaked out, dragging him almost literally to the shop by the scruff of his neck. As a favor, Mr. Smythe had agreed to a rush job.

It was a suit for Pete's sake, a suit with a long, goofy-looking tail. And despite his protests, they were insisting he wear that silly top hat, too. Oh well, no one would be looking at him, anyhow. His Aunt Libby's voice drifted to him while he stood letting Mr. Smythe pin the hem of his trousers.

She was saying to his mother, "I've decided to stay at my old house until the wedding."

He did a mental eye-roll when his mother said, "Oh, I think that's so romantic. A little time apart will build anticipation for the big day."

"It is turning into a big day, isn't it?" He thought his aunt sounded worried, but he supposed pre-wedding jitters were normal.

He could practically see his mother tut-tutting. "Now Libby, your wedding is supposed to be a big day."

"Yes, but it can be a big day, without being a big production. It's costing a fortune. I would have been happy with a small, quiet ceremony. Bradley wouldn't hear of it though."

"I know, Libby, and we've been over this a million times. You just have to relax and enjoy it all."

"I was starting to, but then the other day I heard Bradley on the phone talking to his lawyer. It had something to do with money he owed Marla Jean. Something about their house. I just assumed all of that had been resolved when the divorce was finalized."

That got Jake's attention.

"Did you ask him about it?" his mother asked.

"I did, and he insisted it wasn't important. But whatever it was, he wasn't happy with Marla Jean. That's for sure."

Jake stepped down from the platform, pulling Mr. Smythe off balance as he walked over and pulled back the curtain. "What did Bradley say, Aunt Libby? Exactly."

Libby looked startled at Jake's appearance. "I didn't realize you were listening, Jake, but it's really none of your concern."

His mother stood up from the wicker sofa. "Watch your tone, young man."

"I'm sorry, but if it's about Marla Jean, I'm making it my concern. She was all ready to buy the old Brown house, and then out of the blue, she decides to get an apartment instead. I'm beginning to think Bradley and this money he owes her had something to do with that decision."

Mr. Smythe trailed after him with his measuring tape draped around his neck. "Mr. Jacobson, please, I'm not finished."

Jake started taking off the suit jacket. "Well, I'm finished. If you won't go talk to him, Aunt Libby, then I will." Without retrieving his own clothes, he threw the jacket at Mr. Smythe and slammed out of the shop.

His aunt followed him out to the sidewalk, reaching out a trembling hand to stop him. "Please, Jake, wait. I'm sure you're overreacting." But she didn't look or sound so sure. Her brows knotted in worry, and she started to pace. "I'm sure it's nothing."

Jake wasn't buying it. "If he's the wonderful man you say he is, then he'd want to do everything in his power to make sure the woman he *dumped* is getting a fair shake."

His aunt jumped when he yelled the word "dumped" but he was tired of pulling his punches. His mother appeared carrying his clothes and grabbed his arm. "Stop it, Jake. You're making a scene, and you're upsetting your aunt." She pasted a bright smile on her face and waved at Bertie Harcourt, who'd stopped sweeping the sidewalk in front of the Rise-N-Shine to watch them.

"Good. It's about time Aunt Libby realized she has some responsibility in this situation. It's not enough to blame it on falling in love—and damn the consequences."

He saw the color drain from his aunt's face, but he was on a roll.

"And I'm not overreacting. You and Bradley, the two that cheated, for God's sake, get to keep everything you had before. He keeps their house, and you keep yours. Isn't life grand? Except for Marla Jean. What does she get? She gets to go live in a crappy apartment with baby poop walls. That's what."

His aunt was blinking now to keep the tears from falling, and he felt a pang of remorse. Her voice was shaky when she said, "I intend to talk to him, Jake."

In a softer tone he said, "You do that, Aunt Libby. Otherwise, I don't think I can be part of this wedding."

His mother tried again. "Jake, you apologize at once."

"If I'm wrong, I'll apologize. Until then, I stand by what I said, and the wedding will have to go on without me."

Mr. Smythe came out of the shop and marched over to

where they stood. "I hate to interrupt this family discussion. But if you would be so kind, Mr. Jacobson. I must insist that you take off your trousers."

From across the street Bertie Harcourt yelled out, "I'll vote for that."

"Give me those," Jake growled. Grabbing his clothes from his mother, he stalked back inside Mr. Smythe's shop to change.

Jake sat on his sofa with his head thrown back and his eyes closed. Sadie slept, curled in his lap. He'd upset his aunt. He'd upset his mother. And now he was expected to spend the evening at Bradley Bandy's bachelor party. And that upset him.

After he calmed down, he'd promised his mother he wouldn't rock the boat until Aunt Libby had a chance to talk to Bradley, so he wouldn't. In fact, at this point, he was past caring. Marriage was for chumps. Falling in love was for chumps, too.

Jake opened his eyes and looked up when Theo walked in the front door whistling. "What the hell are you so happy about?"

"No reason. Life is good, big brother."

Jake scowled in reply and closed his eyes again.

Theo sat down and propped his booted feet on the coffee table. "I take it you don't agree."

Jake sat up, rubbing his hands over his face. Sadie woofed when he idly scratched her on the nose. "I just had an argument with my mother and my aunt."

Theo moved some scattered newspaper and sat down on the sofa. "Ah, pre-wedding stress. I'm sorry to hear that, but you'll be glad to know we just finished getting

Marla Jean moved in to her apartment. Except for a few unpacked boxes, she's all settled."

"Oh, that's right," Jake said derisively. "You and Donny Joe and half the other single men in town." Sadie seemed to sense his agitation. She jumped from Jake's lap over to Theo on the couch and resettled in his lap instead.

"Actually, except for me and Donny Joe, it was just Lincoln and Dinah." He looked annoyed. "What's your problem, Jake? From what I can tell she's excited about having her own place. And we're all going to Lu Lu's to celebrate later tonight. If you can find a better mood, you might think about joining us."

Jake didn't want to find a better mood, and watching Theo celebrate with Marla Jean sure the hell wouldn't improve it. "I'm going to Bradley's bachelor party."

"I thought you'd decided to skip it."

"Well, I changed my mind. Brad and I have a few things to discuss." He was going to make sure Aunt Libby had talked to Bradley like she said she would.

Theo shook his head and petted Sadie, who now slept soundly in his lap. "I guess you know what you're doing. Speaking of discussions. I'd like to talk to you about something else, Jake."

He sounded serious, so Jake shook off his irritation with the world long enough to focus on his younger brother. "Sure, what is it, Theo?"

"After we finish the job on your folks' house, I'll be moving on."

"What? I thought we made a good team."

"We do, and I'm not saying I'd mind if you keep a spot open for me in the future, but I got a call from a buddy up in Alaska. He runs a wilderness tour company and wants me to come work for him. And you know me. I could never resist the call of a new adventure."

"What about Marla Jean?"

Theo shrugged. "What about her?"

Jake felt like a hypocrite for asking now. He hadn't once considered Theo's feelings while they'd been making love. "I thought you liked her."

"I do, but you know how it goes. I'm not interested in banging my head against a brick wall, not even one as pretty as Marla Jean. Not that she hasn't been straight with me from the start. We're friends. End of story."

"I'm sorry," Jake said. He wasn't, but it didn't seem like the right time to say so. Jealousy made a man feel low down and mean. And every time Theo had walked out the door to go on another date with Marla Jean, he'd felt low-down and mean. He could admit that now.

"That's all right. Let's just say I won't be breaking her heart when I leave."

"Well, damn, Theo, I've just gotten used to having you around. This is the first time in years we've spent this much time together."

"Yeah, and in all this time you've managed to avoid talking about our father."

"What's there to say? As far as I'm concerned the man was a bastard who shortchanged everyone in his life."

"I never saw that side of him while he was alive. He wasn't around much, but when he was, he was a good father."

"I know we see him differently. I guess I've just never seen the point of rehashing all this."

"The point is there are things I think you need to understand."

"Like what?" Jake didn't think Theo could tell him anything he didn't already know.

Theo closed his eyes and took a deep breath. "Well, let's start with when he died. I saw what it did to my mother—finding out he had a wife and another son. It almost destroyed her, Jake. I hated him for that. I hated his guts for a long, long time."

That surprised Jake. Theo always acted like his father had treated him like a prince growing up, and he wasn't interested in having his illusions tarnished by cold, hard reality. Jake had tried to honor those wishes the best he could. "I never realized you felt that way."

"Well, Jake, I guess that proves you don't know everything, doesn't it?"

Chapter Twenty-seven

I guess there's a hell of a lot I don't know," Jake admitted tiredly.

"Damn straight," Theo said with a grunt.

"Okay. Let's have it," Jake said settling back into the cushions of the couch.

"Hold on. I'm getting there." Theo took a deep breath and looked Jake straight in the eye. "I remember the day when you showed up on our doorstep out of the blue. You'd just graduated from college and moved back to Everson and said if we ever needed anything, all we had to do was call. My mother didn't want anything to do with you—I think you looked too much like our dad, and you were living proof that their whole life together had been nothing but lies."

Jake nodded. "I understood. My mom felt the same way. She wanted to act like neither of you existed. But I couldn't do that. You were my little brother, and if you needed anything I wanted to be there. My mother finally came to accept that. But for your mom's sake I tried to stay on the sidelines."

"But still, you showed up for every one of my high school baseball games, even though I rode the bench half the time. When Janie Benton dumped me for Cal Price, I got stupid drunk, and you came and dragged my ass over to your apartment until I sobered up. You helped me keep that junk heap of a car running until it died."

"That old Buick was on its last legs when you got it."

"And then you loaned me the money for a down payment on a better car when I got that job at the Piggly Wiggly and had to have a reliable ride to get back and forth to work."

"You paid back every nickel."

"The day I graduated from high school, after my mother's face, yours was the next one I looked for in the crowd, and you didn't let me down. There you were, standing in the back. Just like always."

"You're my brother, Theo. That's what families do."

"No, that's what you do, Jake. You look out for the people you care about. And the crazy thing—the thing I've never understood—was why you cared about me. I had to be a constant reminder of how much our father hurt everyone around him."

"You were just a kid. How could I blame you for his sins?"

"So, why do you keep blaming yourself? You weren't much more than a kid yourself when he died."

"I don't know what you're talking about."

"Sure you do. Why do you act like 'love' and 'commitment' are dirty words? Don't you ever want to settle down and have a family? If you aren't careful you'll end up alone with no one but Sadie to keep you company."

"How many times do I have to say it? Sadie is Marla

Jean's dog. And hey, I don't see you making plans to rent out the chapel any time soon."

"Because I haven't met the right woman yet."

Jake didn't say anything for a long time, and then he asked in a quiet voice, like he wasn't sure he wanted to hear the answer, "What the hell makes you think I've met the right woman?"

"Don't treat me like I'm an ignoramus, Jake. Anyone with eyes can see how crazy you are about Marla Jean. And when we were out together? She spent half the time talking about you. But you are too stubborn and pigheaded to allow for the idea that you've got a real shot at having something special with her. I'm telling you, brother, you better wake up before it's too late. She's already moved to another town. It won't be long before the men in Derbyville will be vying for her attention, too."

Jake rubbed a hand across his face and confessed in a dull voice, "There are a few things you don't know, either, Theo."

"Like what?"

"I actually found out about you and your mother before Dad died."

"What are you talking about?" Theo nudged Sadie off his lap and stood up. "How?"

"During my junior year, I was home from college for the weekend. Lincoln and I rode over to Derbyville to check out some party we'd heard about. We were driving down Central Avenue when I saw Dad coming out of the drug store big as you please, with his arm around your mother. First I thought he was just cheating, but when we followed them and saw the house with the name Jacobson on the mailbox, I realized it was something much worse."

"Damn. What did you do?"

"I wanted to go knock on the door and drag him out of there by his balls. Then I planned to beat the holy crap out of him."

"Why didn't you?"

"Linc stopped me. We could see a bicycle in the yard. He said if there was a kid in the house it would be better to confront him after he left."

Theo started pacing. "I don't believe this. So what happened?"

"We sat in front of the house all night. The next morning he left early. Your mother walked him to the door and kissed him good-bye just like they were a normal family."

"We thought we were normal until he died," Theo reminded him.

"So, he got on the road toward Everson, and I kept him in sight. When he got out away from town where there wasn't any traffic, I caught up and honked my horn and motioned for him to pull over. He had no idea that I'd seen anything, so he stopped. When he opened his door I just started whaling on him. I was shouting, calling him a liar and a cheater and a bastard and every foul name I could think of. Linc finally pulled me off of him, or I swear I would have killed him that morning."

"I don't believe that, Jake."

"Well, I do. I wanted him dead, but all I managed was to break his nose and crack a few ribs."

Theo's eyes widened. "I remember that. He said he'd had a car accident."

"I told him I'd seen him in Derbyville. I told him I'd seen him shacked up with that other woman at that other house."

"What did he say?"

"He didn't even try to deny it. He said I was old enough to understand that his marriage to my mother hadn't been good for a long time. God knows, they fought all the time."

"Did you ask him why he didn't just get a divorce?"

Jake laughed. "Oh sure, and he said divorces were expensive and messy, and he didn't want to hurt my mother. Dad could rationalize anything if it meant he got to do what he wanted. He'd managed to enjoy his happy family in Derbyville for years, and no one had ever been the wiser."

Theo shook his head. "My mother told me later she could never understand why he refused to marry her. He'd always laugh and say a piece of paper didn't mean anything even though he obviously loved her. And he was a good father to me when he was around. But she honestly didn't know he was married. And when he died it all blew up in her face."

"Dad did a number on us all," Jake agreed.

"I still can't believe you never told me any of this. Go on. What happened next?"

"I told him the game was up, and he just sat right down in the middle of the road and started crying, saying he'd never meant to hurt anyone, but that he'd fallen in love. With your mother. Like love somehow made it all right. I kicked him in the ribs hard, and he didn't even flinch. Linc had to pull me away again because all I could think about was how much this was going to destroy my mom.

"Dad promised to come clean with my mother. And I said after he told her he was going to give her everything she asked for in the divorce, and if he didn't I would tear his heart out of his chest and feed it to the dogs at the junk yard. He was still just sitting in the road bawling like a baby when we left."

"Jesus, Jake."

"He didn't come home that night. He called Mom and said he'd been delayed for another week, but he'd see her that weekend. She promised to make meat loaf—his favorite. He died of a heart attack in your mother's bed two days later."

Theo looked stunned and sat back down. Sadie whined and climbed back into his lap. "And you never told anyone you already knew about us?"

"Except for explaining things to my mother I didn't see the point. Things were hard enough on her without airing our family's dirty laundry for the whole town to hear. So, I guess you can see why I don't hold love and marriage in very high regard."

Theo sat quietly, like he needed time to process what he'd just heard, but then he shook his head and said, "I don't know, Jake. Our dad turned out to be a jerk. So what? You knew that even before you caught him cheating. And if I'd been in your shoes I'd have wanted to kill him too."

"But you—" Jake tried to interrupt but Theo kept talking.

"You aren't anything like him, and you never will be. And you don't have to keep paying for his crimes."

"Maybe I do. Maybe if I hadn't confronted him, you'd still have a father. You loved him, and I took that away."

"That's a load of crap. He had a bad heart, Jake. And on his best day he wasn't half the man you are. But because of him, you don't think you deserve a woman like Marla

Jean, or any other kind of real happiness. But I'm going to tell you a secret, Jake. She'd be damn lucky to get you. Any woman would be, and I'll beat the crap out of anyone who says different. I'd even be willing to beat some sense into you, too, if I thought it would do any good."

"You should learn some respect for your elders." Jake scowled at his brother, who sat smiling serenely while petting Sadie like he didn't have a care in the world. "And give me my dog."

Theo grinned. "You mean Marla Jean's dog?"

Jake narrowed his eyes.

Theo stood up. "Here you go, Jake. I hope the two of you will be very happy. Now, I'm gonna go get all spruced up. Then I'm gonna go dance the legs off every pretty girl I can find. Maybe a few ugly ones, too." Theo winked at his big brother and sauntered out of the room like he'd just won France in a poker game.

Chapter Twenty-eight

"Poor thing."

From the moment Marla Jean and her friends walked into Lu Lu's she heard the whispers, saw the sidelong glances, felt the weight of pity that emanated from the people she'd known most of her life. She should have been used to it by now. Ever since the divorce and especially with the impending wedding she'd heard enough "poor thing" whispers to last her a lifetime. Just one more reason the move to Derbyville had been a brilliant plan on her part.

Holding her head high she headed toward the bar. As thanks for their help she'd insisted over Theo and Donny Joe's protests that the first pitcher was on her. Linc tagged along, wanting to get something non-alcoholic for Dinah. "Do you think they have milk?" he asked.

"You're going to have to lighten up, Lincoln, or you are going to drive Dinah crazy."

"What? I'm just trying to take care of her. Everyone's always telling me I need to be more sensitive."

"Sensitive and overbearing are not the same thing, but I give you points for trying. It's very sweet." She reached over and patted his arm.

As they pushed through the Friday night crowd, it seemed the buzz of whispers got louder and the smiles more forced the closer they got to the bar. And then she understood. The gossipy concern wasn't only directed at her this time. It also included the woman sitting alone at the end of the bar.

Jake's Aunt Libby. Bradley's intended. Her nemesis.

Miss Comstock perched crookedly on a bar stool with a drink in one hand and her head lolling on the palm of the other. Her normally neatly coiffed hairdo stuck out at odd angles from her head. Her red nose and streaked eye makeup made it plain to see she'd been crying.

Marla Jean was shocked and a bit alarmed. What was she doing here, and all alone? This was the night before the wedding. Libby should be somewhere with her middle-aged girlfriends putting dollar bills in male strippers' G-strings, not sitting all alone at Lu Lu's, looking for all the world like her life had ended.

Folks were happy enough to whisper about the poor woman, but no one stepped up to find out what was wrong. They were all content to keep their distance. Marla Jean sighed. She was tired of tiptoeing around the drama that was her life these days. "I know I'll regret this, Linc. But I'm going to go talk to her."

While Marla Jean had been gawking at Libby, Linc had ordered drinks for the table and now balanced them on a tray. "I don't see how it's your problem, sis."

She blew out a weary gust of air. "You're probably right, but I'm not gonna have a lick of fun tonight if I don't find out what the Sam Hill's going on. Go on back to the table. I'll be there in a bit."

Without giving herself time to question her sanity, she marched over and sat down on the barstool next to Libby. "Hey, Miss Comstock. What's going on?"

Libby raised her head and fixed one bleary eye on Marla Jean. In a loud voice she said, "Well, well, well. If it isn't Marla Jean Bandy. I hope you're happy now, missy."

Marla Jean wasn't surprised that somehow this—whatever it was—was going to end up being her doing, but she asked anyway. "Why should I be happy?"

"The wedding." Libby waved her hand around like she was shooing flies. "I'm calling it off. And I think that calls for a drink, don't you? Let me buy you a drink."

"You're calling it off?" That was the last thing she'd expected to hear. Surely, there wasn't trouble in paradise already. "Why would you do that?"

Libby stood up. Leaning over the wooden bar she yelled in a very un-librarian-like voice at the bartender. "Mike, can we get some drinks down here? I'll take another margarita on the rocks. And one for my good friend, Marla Jean, too."

When she sat back down nearly missing the stool completely, Marla Jean caught her by the arm and steered her back onto her seat, then she tried sending Mike a she's-had-enough signal, but he obviously didn't get the message.

With a glance in their direction he yelled back, "Coming right up, Missus Comstock."

"Thank you, Mike. Mike is so nice. Don't you think he's nice? I knew his sister, Norma Lockhart. She used to teach home economics. Did you ever have her in school, Marla Jean?" Libby twirled in her direction and demanded in a dead-serious voice, "Did you?"

"Yes, as I recall she taught me how to make gathered skirts and macaroni and cheese." Marla Jean tried to get her back on topic. "Libby, tell me what happened with the wedding? Did Bradley do something? He can be thought-less sometimes, but it was most likely pre-wedding jit-ters. I can't believe it could be anything that serious." She wasn't sure why she was defending Bradley, but she really did believe he loved Libby.

"Bradley doesn't even know yet—I didn't want to ruin his bachelor party. But I can't marry him."

"You've decided not to marry him, and you're worried about ruining his bachelor party? That's crazy."

"It's not crazy. I've come to realize that he hasn't let go of you or his old life completely. I know about the money he owes you for the house, and if he really cared about our new life together he'd just give you the money so we could move on with a clean slate. I tried to talk to him about it, but he wouldn't even discuss it." She was sniffing, and a tear ran down her cheek.

Marla tried to feel sympathetic, but the whole idea was ridiculous. "Oh please. The only reason he wouldn't give me the money is because he's a selfish bastard—sorry— and all he does care about is his new life with you."

Miss Comstock wailed, "You see? We've both been so selfish. Only thinking about what will make us happy." Her nose was running, her black eye makeup ran down her cheeks, and she made loud sobbing noises.

Marla Jean could feel people watching them, so she patted her on the back and said, "That's normal when you decide to get married. It's easy to get caught up in all the plans." Hoping to calm her down she added, "He just wants to give you the perfect wedding."

She rolled her eyes and seemed to lose her balance momentarily. Righting herself she declared, "Pooh on that. Who needs a perfect wedding? All this fuss feels like putting a paper frill on a pork chop. When you take off all the frou-frou and take a bite, it's still just a pork chop."

"I can't argue with that." Who knew Miss Comstock was such a philosopher? And Bradley had turned out to be a bit of a pig, after all.

Libby pounded on the bar with her fist and demanded stridently, "Mike, where's my drink?" In a sweet voice she added, "And can I have one of those paper umbrellas this time?"

Mike set a margarita in front of each of them, then reached under the counter and produced two paper umbrellas. "Here you go, ladies."

Libby picked up a purple one and opened it, twirling it between two fingers. "I simply love these cute little umbrellas. They remind me of the first drink Brad ever bought me." She got all misty-eyed again.

"Charming," Marla Jean muttered with a forced smile. "Why? Did it have an umbrella, too?" She really didn't want to hear any sordid details from one of Bradley and Libby's illicit assignations, but if she could get her talking instead of carrying on at the top of her lungs it would be an improvement.

Libby sniffed loudly. "No, but we'd been walking in the park, discussing Chekov's use of weather to create mood and atmosphere, when we got caught in a rainstorm. I was soaking wet, and I must have looked a sight, but Brad held my hand and told me I looked like a puppy he'd had as a boy. Sweetie was her name."

"I remember Sweetie." A nervous poodle with bad breath, but it didn't seem like the time to mention it.

"And he said if he called me Sweetie, people would get the wrong idea. I laughed, but then he kissed me right there in broad daylight. Then we stopped at Bertie's and had pie and coffee and that was the first drink he bought me. So, no, it didn't have an umbrella." Libby looked all dreamy-eyed at the memory.

Indignation, familiar and white hot, flared inside Marla Jean at the thought of the two of them prancing around town like two giddy lovesick adolescents. But just as suddenly the feeling faded, and was replaced by the dawning realization that she honestly didn't give a rat's ass anymore. They could spend their honeymoon naked as jay birds in the gazebo in the town square for all she cared. Hell, she'd sell tickets. And after that dreamy-eyed reminiscence she didn't believe for one minute that Miss Comstock would seriously call off the wedding. No way. No how.

Out of the corner of her eye she saw Mike making come-over-here gestures in her direction. "That's a darling story, but could you excuse me just a moment, Miss Comstock—"

"Please call me Libby."

"Okay, Libby. Hold that thought," she said brightly. Scooting down to Mike she asked quietly, "How much has she had to drink?"

"Two. I swear she's only had two drinks. The rest have been strictly lime juice and ice cubes, but she's a real lightweight."

"You should call Bradley, maybe. Get him to come pick her up," Marla Jean suggested.

Libby lurched off the stool, crashed into Marla Jean's side, knocking Marla Jean's untouched margarita over in the process. "Whoops! Sorry, sorry. What are you two whispering about over here?"

Marla Jean jumped back but not before she got splashed with the sticky liquid.

"Not a thing, Missus Comstock," Mike said while throwing a clean towel in Marla Jean's direction and mopping up the mess on the bar with another.

"Oh, come on, Mikey. I heard you say somethin' about Brad. Don't try to kid me. Is it a secret? I can keep a secret, too." She put her finger to her lips and loudly shushed everyone around them. "Shh—we're telling secrets."

"Speaking of Brad, would you like me to give him a call?" Mike asked. "He's probably stopping by with his bachelor party sometime, anyway."

Libby looked alarmed, grabbed her purse, and slapped some money on the bar. "No way. Absolutely not. He's the last person I want to see. I'll be going now." She made a show of straightening her skirt and patting her mussed hair before stumbling off toward the front door.

Marla Jean stopped scrubbing at the wet, sticky fabric that had once been her I-look-hot-tonight top and watched her go. It wasn't her concern. Let someone else take care of it. She was the last person on earth who should have to give up her night on the town because Bradley and Libby had had a fight that Bradley didn't even know about yet. She took a step toward her group's table. Linc and Dinah were smooching. Theo was dancing with Cindy Connors. She noticed absent-mindedly that they made a cute couple, and Donny Joe was nowhere to be seen. She risked a glance back at Miss Comstock, who'd almost reached the front door, but was weaving and tottering like a spinning top on its last go 'round.

Mike continued to wipe the bar, but remarked worriedly, "I better call a cab."

"Don't bother. I'll take care of it." Calling Everson's one and only cab to take a soused Libby Comstock home from Lu Lu's was the same as putting a screaming headline in the local newspaper. Bo Birdwell couldn't be discreet if he was promised his own fishing hole and a lifetime supply of stink bait. Marla Jean threw the soaked bar towel at Mike and cursed a blue streak as she hurried after Libby. "Damn it all to hell and poop-faced son of a dodo bird."

The older woman was in no condition to drive, and hell, it wasn't her responsibility, but she was going to make sure Bradley's future wife got home without killing herself. It was no more than any civilized person would do. On top of that she was Jake's aunt, and he loved her. She'd do it for Jake.

Libby made it to the parking lot and fumbled in her purse for her keys. Catching up to her, Marla Jean reached over and plucked them out of her hand. "You better let me drive you home, Miss Comstock."

"Aren't you sweet, but I can't possibly go home." She started off across the parking lot, and Marla Jean realized with a start she was headed for the Bookmobile. Miss Comstock had driven the Bookmobile to Lu Lu's? Well, crap. That was probably against every municipal regulation in Everson. Some old law about not allowing city vehicles on any property that served alcohol.

The woman could lose her lending license or whatever the hell was required to operate the read-a-book-and-wreck-a-home mobile. Just because she was having cold feet about marrying Bradley, and all because of a momentary lapse in judgment. After all her years of service to the community, that didn't seem fair.

She herded Libby into the passenger seat of the vehicle and hurried around to the driver's side. The Bookmobile was really just an oversized step van with special shelves installed in the back to hold the books. She figured it would be easy enough to maneuver, until she noted with her umpteenth curse of the evening that the dang thing was a blankety-blank stick shift.

"Well crud. I haven't driven one of these since high school. Bradley tried to teach me." Back when he was still trying to impress her, he tried to teach her to drive a stick. It turned out he loved his Mustang more than he loved her, so the lessons weren't long in duration. A nervous giggle escaped her throat. "I hope I remember what to do. You might have to remind me."

But Libby didn't offer any advice; instead she lolled against her door, with her eyes closed tight, while breathing heavily through her open mouth. Just great, the woman had picked a splendid time for a nap. Marla Jean sent up a prayer to the god of manual transmissions, pushed in the clutch and started the engine. Scrunching up her face in concentration she moved the shifter to first gear. So far, so good. After a few jerky starts, she gave herself a mental thumbs-up as the van headed for the exit in the farthest corner of Lu Lu's parking lot. The far corner where she was less likely to be seen escaping with her ex-husband's suddenly reluctant fiancée in tow.

The van lurched onto the road heading toward Libby's house on Crawford Road, and the herky-jerky motion roused Libby from her slumber. She sat up and asked in a voice as thick as oatmeal, "Where are we going? What's going on?"

"Hey, Miss Comstock, we really shouldn't be driving the Bookmobile around town, so I thought I'd take you home." Marla Jean sped up and winced at the awful grinding noise the gears made when she tried to shift from second to third.

Libby sat up in alarm. "For Heaven's sakes, Marla Jean, try being a little more careful with Marion." Sounding wide awake now, she'd reverted to her prim and proper librarian self.

"With who?" Marla Jean had enough on her plate trying to remember which foot needed to step on what and when it needed to step on it. She didn't have time for guessing games.

Libby patted the dash in front of her. "Marion—you know after the librarian in *The Music Man*. Bradley would always sing a few bars when he first started getting books from me." Without warning she bellowed in an off-tune voice. "Ma-a-a-arion—Madam libra-a-a-arian."

Marla Jean grimaced. So much for prim and proper. "That must have been irritating. Bradley can't carry a tune in a bucket, and oh Lordy, let me guess. You name your cars, just like Jake."

"Well, more likely Jake gets it from me and his mother, but of course you're right. We can take Marion and drop her at my house, and I'll pick up my other car."

"Great." Marla Jean was just glad she'd agreed to ditch the Bookmobile, and once they did, she'd convince her to stay home for the night. One thing at a time.

"Marla Jean, you must think I'm awful. I want you to know I'm normally not so irresponsible."

Suddenly the whole conversation hit Marla Jean as absurd. "I don't know why you care what I think. You certainly didn't when you started seeing my husband." The words flew out of her mouth before she could stop them. She'd never been one to mince words, but at the time of the divorce she'd morphed into a timid rabbit. Afraid saying the wrong thing would blow up what was left of her shattered world. For a while she'd turned into someone she didn't recognize.

So telling Bradley off had been long overdue, but one glance at Libby's wilted expression and she backed down. It seemed utterly unimportant now. "I'm sorry, Libby. That was uncalled for."

Libby shook her head fiercely. "No, you have every right to be outraged. I've never apologized to you, for my part in breaking up your marriage. There. I've said it out loud. I'm not proud of it. In fact, I'm ashamed, and when Jake told me that we'd practically forced you out of town, and I found out Brad still owed you money for your house, and you couldn't buy a house when we all have houses to spare, well, it was too much. I realized I couldn't marry him. I can't stand up in front of everyone in town tomorrow and pretend that love justifies everything we've done. You poor thing." She let out a sudden sob.

Marla Jean's back went up at the well-meaning words. They made her out to be so sad and pathetic, and as usual it amounted to nothing more than pity. Dismal, wretched, mealy-mouthed pity. She'd had all the pity she intended to take from every living soul in this town, including Miss Libby Comstock. It was time to take the bull by the horns.

"Look, you still love him, right?" Marla Jean spared a glance at the distraught woman beside her before returning her attention to her driving. She was getting the hang of it now—feeling a little more confident by the minute.

Libby looked stricken. "Of course I love him. But I shouldn't. It's wrong and nothing good can come of it," she wailed.

Marla Jean rolled her eyes. Could the woman be any more melodramatic? Before she could think of a suitable response, the light at the intersection of Mitchell and Park Row decided to test her newfound shifting abilities by turning red just as she approached. Libby cried more quietly now, which was good. She didn't need any distractions while she stepped on the brakes and attempted to downshift. The light turned green and as soon as she stepped on the accelerator the Bookmobile died. "Rats."

Libby stopped whimpering long enough to say, "You really must keep the clutch engaged, dear."

"I know, Miss Comstock." She tried again but the traffic light was on a slight hill and after a series of jolts the car shuddered, died, and rolled backward.

Libby sniffed. "Let the clutch out as you step on the accelerator. It's quite simple, really."

Through gritted teeth, Marla Jean muttered, "I'm trying, Miss Comstock," and floundered for the delicate balance of easing up on the clutch and giving it some gas. But then—miracle of miracles—they were moving. "I think I've got it this time," she yelped as they rolled out into the intersection.

But getting back to their woman-to-woman talk, Marla Jean continued, "Before you make any drastic decisions there's something you should know about me and Bradley."

Libby stopped crying and focused sharply. "What about you and Brad?"

"I'll always love him—"

The honking of horns and the blare of headlights came out of nowhere as a car barreled through the intersection right in front of them. Startled and panicked, she wrenched the steering wheel to the right and took both feet off the pedals and hit the brakes. Marla Jean's head slammed into the side window and bounced off, leaving her dazed.

When the car stopped they were nose down in a shallow ditch. Books including a dog-eared copy of *Dr. Zhivago* rained down from the shelves, despite the safety straps designed to hold them in place, and landed like flat cannonballs on their heads and shoulders. Marla Jean threw up her hands in an effort to protect herself until the barrage stopped.

The driver's side of the Bookmobile flew open and a female voice said excitedly, "Miss Comstock, don't worry. I'm here to rescue you."

Marla Jean turned her bleary eyes toward the voice and found Genna Stanley standing outside the door. Genna's voice changed from concern to outrage in a matter of seconds. "And Marla Jean, are you plum crazy? What in the world are you doing taking off in the Bookmobile with Miss Comstock?"

"Oh jeez, Miss Comstock?" Marla Jean unbuckled her seat belt with shaky hands and scrambled over to check on Libby. She listed sideways in the passenger seat, held in place only by the seat belt. Her head slumped forward and her eyes were closed. Blood ran from a gash on her face. "Miss Comstock, oh gracious, Libby, are you okay? Can you hear me?"

Genna leaned into the open door and upon spotting the unresponsive woman screamed loud enough to wake hibernating bears in far-off caves, "Oh my God, Marla Jean, you've done it now. You've killed Miss Comstock."

Chapter Twenty-nine

⟋⟍

Jake didn't want to drink cheap booze and smoke expensive cigars while watching half-naked women gyrate on a poorly lit stage. He didn't want to, but that's what he'd been doing for the last two-and-a-half hours. The fact that he didn't want to might have concerned him under normal circumstances. After all, he appreciated a half-naked woman as much as the next guy, but between last night with Marla Jean, today's talk with Theo, and Aunt Libby's wedding tomorrow he had too much on his mind. His attention wandered while the blonde wearing not much more than a dragon tattoo and a smile shook her charms in his face. He smiled to be polite, handed her a ten-dollar bill for her valiant efforts, and then picked up his drink and moved to a table at the back of the room.

Some of the guys at Bradley's dealership arranged this little bachelor wing-ding to celebrate his last night of freedom, and Jake had to give Bandy some credit. He actually seemed a little embarrassed by it all. Jake watched an extremely limber redhead do a backbend and pick up a twenty-dollar bill with her teeth. Bradley barely seemed to notice. That's when Jake started thinking he really might love his Aunt Libby after all.

Libby's future husband had done nothing but talk about her all night long. He'd even tried to call her a couple of times, but had only reached her voice mail. "I guess she's out with your mother and her own friends," he said sheepishly. "I'd really like to hear her voice right now. I can't believe we're really getting married tomorrow. I tell you, Jake, I can't wait." And he'd smiled from the inside, like a guy who'd found the key to making himself whole.

None of that changed Jake's long held opinion of the guy, and it certainly didn't excuse the crappy way he'd treated Marla Jean. But then again, who was he to talk? He had made love to Marla Jean for all the wrong reasons, hadn't he? Selfish, self-centered, self-indulgent reasons, and now because he felt guilty, he was going to attempt to lessen that guilt by sticking his nose into something that was really none of his business. Aunt Libby told him to back off. It was her life, her business, and she'd said she would handle it.

So for now he sat at his table and watched Bradley's buddies buy tequila shots and make toasts to Libby's many virtues. He tilted his chair back against the wall, stretched his long legs out in front of him, and settled in for a long night. He couldn't wait for this entire weekend to be over and done with. Then maybe life would get back to normal.

Normal.

A memory of Marla Jean sitting beside him in his truck, laughing and stealing his french fries, barged into his head, and he knew for dang certain he didn't have a clue what normal meant anymore.

• • •

"Come clean, Marla Jean. Have you been drinking?"

"No, I told you that already, Sheriff Watson." Marla Jean squeezed her eyes shut and hoped when she opened them she'd only see one of him.

After Genna quit screaming at the sight of Libby collapsed in the passenger seat, she'd called 911 and the sheriff and an ambulance had arrived shortly after. Libby lay on a stretcher surrounded by the EMTs while Sheriff Watson grilled Marla Jean like a common criminal. Genna was giving her version of things to Officer George Mendoza on the other side of the intersection. Her arms waved around dramatically, and she pointed at Marla Jean in an accusatory manner.

Marla Jean's head couldn't hurt more if someone decided to use it for batting practice, and the double vision thing wasn't helping her mood, either. She tried to refocus on what the Sheriff was saying.

"I know what you told me, young lady, but you smell like a brewery, and by your own admission, you just left Lu Lu's." Sheriff Watson fingered his bushy Tom Selleck mustache while he studied her. He'd been a *Magnum P.I.* fan back in the day, and off duty sported nothing but Hawaiian shirts. Thankfully, he skipped the short shorts and stuck with blue jeans. Marla Jean always thought he looked uncomfortable in his khaki uniform, and even now fidgeted and pulled at his too-tight shirt. Somberly, he added, "And you failed the field sobriety test."

Walking a straight line had proven to be too much for her, and she'd poked herself in the cheek when he'd asked her to hold her arms out to her side and then point to her nose. "But I wasn't drinking. You can ask Mike."

"I'll do that. I intend to do a thorough investigation. But right now we're looking at failure to maintain control of your vehicle, suspicion of driving while under the influence, and possible kidnapping."

"Kidnapping?" she yelped and regretted it when pain exploded inside her brain. She grabbed her head in both hands. "Come on, Sheriff Watson, you know me better than that." For years she'd cut his hair and trimmed his mustache every two weeks whether it needed it or not.

"Listen, Marla Jean, everyone knows you haven't been yourself lately, and it's conceivable you, being heartbroken and all, couldn't face the idea of Bradley and Miss Comstock tying the knot tomorrow. Until we get this sorted out, I have no choice but to take you in."

"Take me in? To jail?" She couldn't believe it. "You're kidding, right? And I'm *not* heartbroken," she insisted as he herded her toward the squad car. Apparently, he wasn't kidding. She noticed Libby struggling to sit up. "Can I at least check on Miss Comstock first?"

"I'm sure Miss Comstock is getting all the medical attention she needs. Watch your head." He put his big paw of a hand on her head and guided her into the back seat of his car.

Marla Jean settled into the seat as a wave of nausea washed over her. "Sheriff Watson, I think I'm about to be sick."

"Nice try, Marla Jean." He started to close the back door. "If I had a nickel for every suspect that's pulled that one on me, I'd be rich enough to retire."

His words seem to come from very far away. Clamminess gripped her entire body and her eyes and mouth watered with that awful precursor of things to come.

Before he could close the car door all the way, she leaned over and threw up all over his shiny black boots.

"Jake, Libby's been in an accident. Come on, she's being taken to the hospital." Bradley rushed across the bar, his eyes wild with fear.

"Is she all right?" Before Bradley could answer, Jake's phone rang. It was his mother. "Mom, are you okay? What happened? I just heard Aunt Libby was in an accident."

"I'm fine. I wasn't with Libby, she begged off her party at the last minute, but Deputy Mendoza just called and told me she was taken in an ambulance to Everson Memorial. I'm on my way there now."

"Bradley and I will meet you there. Be careful, Mom, and don't worry. Everything will be okay."

Jake insisted on driving and Bradley offered no objection. He could barely sit still during the five-minute drive to the hospital. "Why wasn't she with your mother? I thought they had a big party planned for her tonight. I should have known something was wrong when she didn't answer her phone. Jake, she's got to be okay."

"Hang on, Bradley. Here we are." Jake drove up to the emergency entrance, and Bradley jumped out of the truck while it was still rolling. He parked in the first spot he found and then sprinted back to the entrance. Bradley was practically wringing his hands as he implored the nurse behind the desk, "Libby Comstock. She was just brought in by ambulance."

Everson was a small town, but Jake didn't recognize the woman who looked through her records at a snail-like pace. For God's sake, how many women had been brought in to this rinky-dink hospital in the last hour? Jake was seconds from jumping over the desk and finding the information himself when she said pleasantly, "Here it is. She's been admitted overnight for observation. Room 229. But I'm afraid visiting hours are over."

They headed for the elevators, ignoring the woman's protest. Taking the elevator to the second floor, they bolted down the hall. Aunt Libby's room was easy to find. Sheriff Watson stood outside talking to Jake's mother. She looked distraught, and Jake's heart sank to his toes. The news must be bad. Jake felt Bradley wobble beside him and caught him by the elbow.

"Mom? Tell us. How is she?"

Jake's mother turned at the sound of his voice and rushed forward. "Oh, Jake, Bradley, I'm so glad you're both here. Libby is going to be okay."

Bradley barreled toward the door. "I want to see her."

Ellie stopped him. "I'm not sure she wants to see you."

"What are you talking about? Of course she wants to see me."

"Bradley, she says she's calling off the wedding."

His face paled like he'd been struck a physical blow. "The hell she is." He pulled open the door and stopped halfway inside. "Marla Jean? What are you doing here? And where in the hell is Libby?"

Chapter Thirty

Marla Jean whirled around, blindly grabbing for the flapping edges of her gown, and scooted backward toward the bed over by the window. Libby was in the bed closest to the door, so Bradley's attention immediately switched to his fiancée as soon as he spotted her.

"Oh Libby, sugar, what happened?" Panic laced his question.

Bradley was joined by Ellie and Sheriff Watson, and Jake. They all crowded into the room, talking over each other, asking questions. It was all too much. Marla Jean climbed back into her bed and pulled the covers over her head. Her skull felt feel like a melon cleaved open with a machete, and all she wanted to do was sleep. Nobody would let her. Every time she'd drift off a nurse would come and ask her to count backward or name the President of the United States. That was bad enough, and now this. All these people yammering on and on.

She heard Jake's voice. "Are you all right, Aunt Libby?"

"I'm fine, Jake." Through the layers of linen she heard Libby from the next bed. The scratchy sheet tickled her nose, but she didn't care. "What is everyone doing in my room? Ellie, I told you I didn't want to talk to Bradley tonight."

"Well, that's too bad, Libby." Bradley's voice came through loud and clear and full of hurt and indignation. "First, I hear you've been in an accident, and before I can recover from the shock of that, before I can even find out if you're okay, you announce that our wedding is off and that you're not going to talk about it. I don't think so, Libby. I don't think you can stab me through the heart like that and not tell me why."

Almost at once the distinct sound of sobbing commenced. Oh wonderful. Libby was turning on the water works again. Not that she blamed her. Calling off a wedding was a big deal. She'd give her that. It wasn't a decision one came to lightly. But she'd been in Libby's company going on four hours now, and she'd been bawling for roughly three and a half of them.

She closed her eyes, waiting impatiently for the ensuing fireworks that would surely follow Brad's bold pronouncement. Jake would tell Bradley to leave his aunt alone. Bradley would yell some more. Sheriff Watson would tell them all to settle down, or he'd haul everyone down to the station. Maybe then she'd get some rest.

Instead, she felt a hand grab the edge of the sheet and pull it back from her face. The hand belonged to Jake. "Marla Jean, good God, are you okay? What in the world are you doing here?"

"It's a long story," she muttered. It seemed she was capable of being embarrassed and happy to see someone at the same time. Her heart swelled at the sight of him, and for now his gaze was filled with worry and concern. He probably wouldn't feel the same once he found out she'd run his aunt's Bookmobile into a ditch. "It was a stupid accident, but I'm fine. Hit my head, so they want to watch me for a bit. I hope Libby is okay." Before she could say more a new voice interrupted the proceedings.

"Sheriff Watson, can I get a comment about this evening's foiled kidnapping attempt of Libby Comstock?" Alarmed, Marla Jean glanced over to see who the new voice belonged to. Snoopy Boggs, a reporter for the *Everson Daily*, was standing in the doorway holding a notepad in one hand and a camera in the other. She pulled the sheet back up over her face. Great. A nice write-up in the paper was all she needed.

"Kidnapping?" Bradley jumped from the bed. "What's he talking about, Sheriff?"

"Now Bradley, wait a minute—" Libby interjected, trying to get his attention, but he'd honed in on the newest development and wasn't listening.

"There wasn't any kidnapping, Snoopy." The Sherriff growled his disapproval at the intrusion. "And you don't need to be barging into hospital rooms looking for stories. Go on, now. Get out of here."

Before the reporter could even think about leaving Genna Stanley pushed him aside and rushed into the room. "Oh Lordy, Miss Comstock, are you okay? I was a witness. I saw the whole thing."

Marla Jean stuck her nose out from the sheet and rolled her eyes. Genna was starting to get on her last nerve. She watched as she hurried over to Jake and grabbed his arm. "Oh, Jake, honey. I'm still shaking. I'd just pulled into the parking lot at Lu Lu's when I saw your aunt and Marla Jean get into the Bookmobile. Marla Jean was driving and that seemed peculiar, so I followed them. It's a good thing I did, too."

She did a half turn toward the door and flashed a smile for the reporter who was busy snapping photos. With disgust Marla Jean noticed that Genna had some-how found time to freshen her bright pink lipstick and fluff up her blonde hairdo before making an appearance at the hospital. Meanwhile she'd caught a glimpse of her-self in the bathroom mirror earlier and knew her own curly hair stood out at odd angles from her head and the black smears of mascara under her eyes were the only bits of makeup left on her face. Perfect for her pending mug shot.

Genna, finding an interested audience, launched into storytelling mode. "Marla Jean was driving like a crazy person, starting and stopping then rolling backward for no good reason. I could tell something was wrong. And sure enough not two minutes down the road she drove off into that ditch. I saw it all and called 911." She sounded like she expected a medal.

"Excuse me." A deep bass voice cut through the buzz of conversation that filled the room. "Pardon me. Can I get through here?" Judge "Pinkie" Pinkerton pushed his way through the crowd at the door. The judge was a short man of florid complexion who favored pink suspend-ers and tall women. Besides presiding over the munici-pal court he performed civil marriages when there was a need. "I was told this was Libby Comstock's room." Spotting her in bed he made his way to her side. "There you are, Libby. I got your message. Now what's this about calling off the wedding? Are you injured? Do we need to postpone?"

Sheriff Watson cleared his throat. "I think we need to clear out and let these people have their privacy. Come on, everyone, let's go."

The sheriff started herding everyone out of the room, including a protesting Ellie.

"Remember, you don't have to do anything you don't want to do, Libby," her sister called out as he nudged her out the door.

The door closed on the chattering group, leaving Marla Jean stranded in the room with the judge, her ex, and his emotional wreck of an intended.

Libby sniffled. "Judge Pinkerton, I hate to do this at the last minute. I know how much work has gone into the arrangements, but I can't go through with the ceremony. I'm sorry."

"Don't listen to her, Judge. She's just shaken up from the accident, and she's got a case of the pre-wedding jitters. That's all. We still want you to perform the honors tomorrow just the way we planned."

"I'm not marrying you, Bradley." Libby sounded stubborn now.

"Libby, please." Bradley sounded pitiful.

Judge Pinkerton spoke up. "Now Bradley, why don't we listen to what Libby has to say?"

"Okay, I'm sorry. I'm listening, honey."

They were talking quietly now, and Marla Jean could hear Libby explaining things to Bradley and the judge. But it was still the absolute last place on earth she wanted to be. She used the blanket like a shawl, swung her legs over the side of the bed, and tried to stand. The room swam around her, and when her stomach lurched in a dangerous way she sat back down. Before she could try again, the door swung open and Jake came striding back into the room. Marla Jean caught her breath at the sight of him. He seemed so intent, so purposeful, and he headed straight for her.

He smiled and asked with a wink, "You wanna get out of here?"

"Are you offering to spring me?" She launched herself from the bed, hoping not to fall, but he caught her, lifted her into his arms, and started for the door. She laughed and then winced when it made her head hurt. She closed her eyes and hung on to Jake for dear life.

Before they could get out the door Bradley stopped them. "What's going on, Jake?"

She opened her eyes in time to see Jake glare at Bradley. "Marla Jean doesn't need to be stuck in here while the two of you work out your problems," he said.

Bradley had the decency to look embarrassed. "You're right. Marla Jean, Libby told me some of what happened. She said she wasn't in any condition to drive and you tried to help. I appreciate it."

Libby sat up in her bed, her lip trembling. "I'm awfully sorry, Marla Jean. This whole thing was my fault."

"Don't be sorry," Marla Jean said. "And don't start crying again. Please. Just marry the man and put him out of his misery. Not that you care, but you both have my blessing. I'll even walk Bradley down the aisle and give him away to you personally if it helps, Libby." The room was spinning again, so she laid her head on his shoulder. "Can we go now, Jake?"

He shifted her in his arms so he could grab the door handle. "We're already gone."

Sheriff Watson stood right outside the room, but thankfully the rest of the crowd seemed to have disappeared. The sheriff told Jake his mom had gone to find coffee. If he thought it was odd for Jake to be lugging her around like a sack of potatoes he didn't mention it, but he blocked their path as they came out the door. "I need to have a quick word with Marla Jean."

Jake immediately objected. "Can't it wait, Sheriff? Marla Jean needs to lie down."

"Hold onto your britches, son. This will only take a minute. I'm closing the book on this one, Marla Jean. I checked with Mike, and he said you weren't drinking. Libby's account backs up your story as well. As for the damage to the Bookmobile, I'll leave that up to the insurance companies since no one else was involved."

"So that's it?" She sagged with relief.

"That's it. Take care of yourself."

"I'll try, Sheriff. Come see me next time you need your ears lowered."

"You bet, but stay out of trouble until then." With a little wave the lawman sauntered off toward the elevators.

"It's about time someone around here showed with some sense," Jake snorted. He headed toward the small waiting room at the end of the hall. "Let me get you situated, and then I'll go find a nurse. And by the way, I called Linc. Your family should be here soon." The worry in his voice washed over her like a soothing balm.

She wasn't able to resist wrapping herself in his quiet strength. "Thank you, Jake."

"You're welcome." The words were a whisper against

her hair. He put her down on the sofa in the waiting room at the end of the hall. "I'll be right back."

She reached out a hand to stop him. "Sit with me for a minute, please?"

He sat down beside her so she could lean against his shoulder.

"Do you know why Libby wasn't going to marry Bradley? It was so silly. It was because he wouldn't give me the money he owes me for the house. Can you imagine?"

"Maybe that's reason enough. Maybe it shows he's not the kind of man she thought he was."

"Except the only reason he wouldn't give me the money right now was because he wanted to lavish her with this ridiculously overpriced wedding so everyone in town would see how much he loves her. I'll get my money eventually, but he's putting his new life with your aunt first. For Bradley, that's actually a step in the right direction." She felt woozy, and closed her eyes.

In a quiet voice he said, "I would have loaned you the down payment money for the house. Hell, I would have given it to you."

"Thanks, Jake, but I don't want any special favors. It's time for me to stand on my own for a change."

He picked up her hand and held it gently, "Marla Jean, maybe we should talk about what happened at the barber shop."

Her heart skipped a beat at his suggestion. She'd wondered when they would have this conversation. The one where he said it had been a big mistake. The one where he said it wouldn't happen again. The one where he said he was so, so sorry.

And she didn't want to hear any of it.

Especially his apology. Not now. Not while her head hurt so badly she wanted to bawl. Not tonight of all nights. She was too bruised and battered, and that conversation demanded she be operating at full strength.

So she stopped him, cut him off before he could start.

"Don't be silly. There's nothing to talk about." Her voice sounded thin as morning mist when she needed to sound breezy and assured. She took a half breath and pushed on. "No strings. No worries. Remember? That's what I promised, and I meant it. And everything's working out perfectly for me. I'm thrilled with my new apartment. And my new life in Derbyville is about to begin."

Before he could respond the elevator doors opened, and her entire family poured out, surrounding her with cries of comfort and concern.

"Jake called us and told us what happened. Linc's been beside himself since you disappeared from Lu Lu's," Dinah said fretfully.

Linc leaned down and gave her a hug and then punched her softly in the arm. "You all right, sis?"

"I'm fine, Linc. I'm sorry I worried you."

Her dad squatted at her feet. "How's my baby girl?"

"I'm okay, really, Dad."

Jake stood up and offered his place on the sofa to her mother so she could fuss over her properly. "Why in the world are you out here in the hallway? Where is that doctor? I'm going to have a word or two to say when I get a hold of him."

"What in tarnation are you doing out of your room, young lady?" Nurse Bloomfield came storming into the waiting room and advanced on the group with a frown on her face. "I came up from emergency to check on you, and this is what I find? You're out here having a party instead of resting?"

"My room was a little too crowded," Marla Jean said meekly.

"Humph. We'll see about that." She gave everyone a disgusted once over and marched off toward the nurses' station.

Half an hour later, Marla Jean was installed in her own private room, happily leaving Libby and Bradley to hash out their marital future alone. Linc had taken Dinah home. Bitsy was crocheting in the chair next to her, and Milton was napping on the extra bed.

Jake stuck his head in the door. "Looks like you're settled in for the night."

"Gosh, I hope so. Don't you want to ask me what year it is or if I can name the President of the United States?"

"And give you a chance to show off? Not a chance. I'm going to make sure my mother gets home, and since it looks like everyone's in good hands now, I guess I'll call it a night, too."

"I'm in the best hands possible." Marla Jean smiled over at her mother, who reached out to pat her on the knee. "But thanks for everything, Jake. I was ready to jump out a window when you showed up."

"You're welcome. I'm glad I could help." He shuffled his feet like he had more on his mind but finally just said, "Well, good night then."

"Good night, Jake. Hey, what's the word on the wedding?"

He looked as if he didn't know if he was delivering good news or bad. "It's back on."

Marla Jean nodded. "Well, you better get on home then and get some rest. You have a big day tomorrow."

"Looks like it. I'll check on you tomorrow then?"

"We'll see. Weddings tend to be crazy chaotic, so if not tomorrow, we'll talk soon."

His eyes met hers and held. "Count on it. Good night, everyone."

Marla Jean watched the door shut behind him. "Good night, Jake," she said, though it felt more like good-bye.

Chapter Thirty-one

As it turned out, Marla Jean didn't give Bradley away, after all. She'd gotten a nice note from Libby thanking her for all her help, but Marla Jean decided the happy couple deserved the gift of her absence from the wedding festivities. But that didn't mean she didn't hear every juicy detail. Hoot and Dooley had plenty to say, and every customer who came in to the barber shop couldn't wait to add their two cents describing the extravaganza.

And she hadn't spoken to Jake the next day, either. She heard all about how handsome he looked in his suit. Hoot seemed to think she'd be particularly interested. She heard how Libby cried through the entire ceremony. Now there was a surprise. And how Bradley wrote his own vows and delivered them without missing a beat. She heard the wedding cake was pumpkin, courtesy of Cal's giant pumpkin, and it was shaped like the Bookmobile with little marzipan books scattered all around. And everyone that came in to the shop had to give Dooley a hard time. It seems he drank too much punch, and when he danced the jitterbug with his wife, he fell down and took half a dozen couples with him, knocking them over like bowling pins. Hoot wouldn't let him hear the end of that for a good long while. She heard Genna Stanley caught the bouquet, and Donny Joe caught the garter. And she heard the two of them danced together until the wee hours of the night. There probably weren't many details that some kind soul didn't see fit to share with her. And that was all right. She'd also heard through the grapevine that Bradley and Libby had returned safely from their honeymoon in Russia, and they appeared blissfully happy.

Good for them.

The *Everson Daily* ran a small story about the accident that destroyed the Bookmobile, complete with pictures of photogenic Genna alongside images of crying Libby and of Marla Jean sticking her nose out from under a hospital bed sheet long enough to glare at the camera. Genna hinted to anyone who would listen that she'd heroically saved Libby from being kidnapped before the wedding and strings had been pulled to get the charges dropped. Marla Jean didn't have the energy to bother disputing it. Her friends knew the truth, and they were the only ones who mattered.

She'd settled into her apartment in Derbyville, although a few boxes still remained unpacked. Despite the yellow paint, the place was a little cold and sterile, but between teaching art classes and working she didn't spend much time there, so what did it matter?

The barber shop still took up her days, though she'd worked out a schedule that had Milton working some half days and gave her some flexibility in her work week. Having her dad back at the shop had turned out to be a real blessing.

Because she was teaching evening art classes at the community college she had a legitimate excuse for not eating dinner at her parents' house every night of the week. Bitsy worried about her being alone, but the truth was, for the first time in her life, she allowed herself that choice. Choosing to be alone felt powerful and luxurious and a little bit decadent.

Teaching had proven to be an unexpected pleasure. She hadn't been certain that loving to paint would translate into loving to teach it. But when she was working with someone who shared her passion, she felt herself blooming, opening up in ways she never could have predicted. All in all, she was content with her life.

And it wasn't as if she sat home alone all the time. She'd gone on a couple of dates. A fellow teacher from the college took her to dinner one night after class, and she'd had coffee a few times with her next-door neighbor. Both were nice guys, but it was painfully clear that neither of them was Jake.

When she was alone, she'd allow herself to think about Jake, relive the night she'd spent in his arms, and wonder if she'd ever feel that way about any other man. She still saw him in town occasionally, and somehow managed a friendly façade that hid anything deeper. They even had lunch together once in a while, but he usually seemed preoccupied and distant. Nothing was ever again mentioned about the night at the barber shop. Not a word. Not since he'd broached the subject at the hospital and she'd cut him off like the coward she was. It was as if it never happened. That should have made it easier to accept that Jake was a closed chapter, but it didn't. If she was smart she wouldn't dwell on the one night she'd had with him, and she certainly wouldn't dream of what might have been. But then, whoever said she was smart?

One day Theo stopped by the barber shop right at closing time. Said he was on his way out of town to start his Alaska adventure, and wanted to say his good-byes. Instead of his usual carefree manner, he took her hand and with an earnest expression asked if she'd do him a favor while he was gone.

"Of course, Theo. Just name it." She studied his face, so like his brother's, and realized how much she'd come to value Theo's friendship in the short time she'd known him. If she was going to miss having him around, she could only imagine how hard it would be for Jake.

As if he read her mind he said, "It's about Jake. This may sound strange, but if you could promise to maybe watch out for him while I'm gone."

"Me? I don't know—"

"Listen, Marla Jean, my brother is big on taking care of everyone else and their grandma, too, but when it comes to admitting he could actually use a little help himself on occasion, he's got those big thick walls built up, and from what I can see, you are the only person he lets wiggle inside sometimes."

"I think you misunderstood, Theo. We've known each other a long time, that's all."

"Whatever. He's different with you. Better. More easy-going. So just promise you'll check up on him once in a while. Okay?"

She'd opened her mouth and said the right words. "I promise, Theo." He'd hugged her, said he'd send her a postcard and with a jingle-jangle of the overhead bells disappeared out the shop door.

But she hadn't done it. She hadn't watched out for Jake. He would've laughed at the very idea. And she couldn't quite admit how dangerous the suggestion was to her peace of mind.

But one night while she was having dinner at her parents' house, her mother mentioned over peach cobbler that Jake had sold his folks' old house to a young couple with two small children. A boy and a girl, and a boxer that barked all night long, her father added.

Finally, after all these years and all the work he'd put into it with Theo, he'd sold the house. It felt like some kind of cord to the past had been permanently severed. His childhood home sold to strangers. No more off chance of running into Jake in the old neighborhood. No more glancing up to see his old truck parked across the street, two houses down.

Was he happy that the last tie to his father was gone? Or sad? Maybe she'd ask him next time she saw him. She usually tried to avoid heavy subjects that might evoke anything uncomfortable or scary like feelings. But then again, she had promised Theo.

Christmas was only a couple of weeks away, and since she had Mondays off, she'd promised her mother they'd have a girls' day—shop, do lunch, shop, have tea and pie at Bertie's, treat themselves to a pedicure, and then maybe shop some more.

She showed up early, noticing that her dad put the Christmas lights up over the weekend. Garlands of greenery draped the porch rails, and a wreath of fresh pine decorated the front door. The whole family would gather on the weekend to decorate the tree, but Marla Jean hadn't done anything to get into the holiday spirit.

Maybe she should pick up a small tree for her apartment and put some lights around her front window. That might be fun.

She entered the house, greeted by the welcoming scent of cinnamon and bacon. It smelled like her entire childhood. A mild current of longing for things past rippled through her, but she blamed it on the upcoming holidays and the fact that this would be her first Christmas in her new apartment.

"Is that you, Marla Jean?" her mother called from the back of the house.

"It's me, Mom."

"I'll be ready in a minute. Oh, there's a letter for you on the front hutch. It looks official."

"Thanks." She picked it up and turned it over, not immediately recognizing the return address. Opening the envelope she realized it contained a check. It was from Bradley's lawyer in the full amount he owed her for their house. She hadn't expected to get the money without a messy fight and inconvenient court dates. Maybe Libby was already proving to be a good influence on her ex.

Her mom walked in adjusting her earring. "What was in the letter, if I'm not being too nosy."

Marla Jean flapped the check around in the air. "It's my house money." She did a little jig. "Bradley sent a check for my half of the house. Hot dang, Christmas just came early."

"Well then, I say lunch is on you, kiddo. Does this mean you're going to look into buying the Brown house again?"

Marla Jean stopped in her tracks. "The Brown house? I don't even think it's for sale anymore." That was a chapter she'd closed along with any idea of having a relationship with Jake. "I know he had another interested buyer at the same time."

"Well, that's a shame." Bitsy slipped on her coat, grabbed her purse, and pulled Marla Jean out the door. "Let's go. I have a long list, and I don't want to miss the sales while you dawdle around here daydreaming."

Marla Jean followed her out the door. "Hey, I was here early. I don't think I'm the one dawdling."

Her mom dug in her purse and pulled out a giant ring of keys. Jangling them at her daughter she said, "Watch your manners, missy."

"Yes, ma'am," she said contritely. The Christmas wreath on the front door bounced as she pulled it closed behind her.

Marla Jean stuck her fork into her lemon meringue pie and twirled it this way and that, destroying its pie-like shape without ever taking a bite. She sat in a booth, staring out the diner's front window, all her attention focused on Jake's Home Remodeling Service across the way. Lucinda was parked out front, so she knew he was in his office. The big fat check in her purse was the perfect excuse to get up, walk across the street, and ask Jake about the old Brown house. Just to satisfy her curiosity. Not that she wasn't perfectly happy in her new apartment. But it couldn't hurt to ask, could it? Who was she kidding? She was curious about the house, but if she was honest, what she really wanted was a good excuse to go see Jake.

While she was at it, she could talk to him about Sadie. Somehow, the time had never seemed right to take her to the new apartment. The puppy seemed so happy with Jake. But she'd put down the pet deposit, for Pete's sake, and she couldn't expect him to keep her forever.

Another good reason to go see Jake.

Her mother was in the middle of a spirited discussion with Bertie about the pros and cons of including leeks in her potato soup recipe. They'd moved onto the merits of split peas, so she figured Bitsy would hardly notice if she stepped out for a minute. She could zip over to Jake's and be back in plenty of time to go have their toes done at Durinda's Sweet Feet Spa before they hit the outlet mall on the highway.

She took a fortifying bite of pie for courage, stood up before she could change her mind, and declared, "I'll be right back, Mom."

"It's not for sale." Jake hardly looked up from the paper he was scribbling on when she walked in the door. If he was happy to see her, he was doing a mighty fine job disguising his glee.

She sat down in front of his desk. "Oh, so I guess you sold it to Bud Gailey after all? That's what I figured, but I thought it couldn't hurt to check." Disappointment welled up inside her chest. She'd tried not to get her hopes up, but once the Brown house became a whisper of a possibility again, she'd been a goner all over again.

He put down his pen and looked straight at her. "I didn't sell it to Bud."

"Oh, well then, someone else made an offer?" She didn't even want to imagine who was living in her house now.

"Actually, after I sold my folks' house, the need to

unload it wasn't so pressing. My lease was up on my apartment, so I decided to keep it for myself."

"You did? But I thought you said it was too much house for you. That it needed a family, and all that." Maybe he'd changed his mind about wanting a family. The very idea of him living in her house with some woman now or anytime in the future had her clenching her fists and grinding her teeth.

"I'm actually living out there now. Sadie's having a grand time exploring." She noticed he didn't address his change of heart about the house.

"Gosh, Jake, that's great." She didn't mean it. Not for a minute. Jake and Sadie living in her house, while she was all alone in a cracker box of an apartment in Derbyville. What was wrong with this picture? "I guess you've got all sorts of plans for it. Oh, of course you do. You showed them to me, didn't you? Well, I'll rest easy knowing it's in good hands." She was babbling, but she felt herself getting unexpectedly weepy. She was acting like an idiot, working herself all up over something that was never hers to begin with. And she wasn't just talking about the dumb old house.

He didn't seem to notice her distress. In fact, his whole body lit up with eagerness as he started talking about the house. "I'm just getting started, but you'll have to come out and see what I'm doing to the place when you get a chance, Marla Jean. Your approval would mean a lot to me."

His big brown eyes met hers, and she felt her insides melting like butter cream icing spread on a cake fresh from the oven. The afternoon sun streamed in through the front window, playing across the planes of his face, gilding each strand of his dark hair with golden light. Why did he have to look so freaking perfect? Why did he have to look like a man who needed to be hugged? Where had that idea come from? She was used to having lust-filled thoughts about him, but this was more of an "isn't he adorable, and grand, and wonderful" kind of feeling. Her heart couldn't afford to keep entertaining those kinds of thoughts about Jake. Especially if he had plans to move some other woman into her house.

She tried to listen as he rambled on, looking more animated and alive then she could ever remember. You'd think he was the one with childhood memories of the place tattooed onto his heart.

She swallowed hard and nodded. When she spoke her voice was brittle and wobbly. "I'd love to come see it, but I'm sure it will be wonderful. Really, wonderful, Jake."

"Are you okay, Marla Jean?" His tone changed to one of concern.

She found a smile. "Oh, sure. I've just been thinking about Sadie, lately. You're probably ready for me to take her off your hands."

He stood up, looking genuinely troubled. "Oh. Of course. I thought I'd let you settle into your apartment before I mentioned it. But I guess you are settled now, right? It's been almost a month." Now he was the one babbling.

"I appreciate it, but yeah, I'm as settled as I'll ever be."

"Well then," he said. "Come by tomorrow night, and I'll make dinner."

"Oh, you don't need to go to any trouble."

"It's no trouble. I haven't started tearing up the kitchen yet. And I'm a pretty good cook." He crossed his arms over his chest.

"All right. It's a date. Well, not a date." She shrugged, thinking she should stop talking altogether.

"Great. I'll have Sadie's stuff all gathered up and ready to go. So, say, seven?"

"Seven it is."

Chapter Thirty-two

~

Jake juggled the bags of groceries while he unlocked the front door. Sadie met him in the entry, her tail wagging madly while she bounced around his ankles, barking, telling him about her day.

He laughed at her antics even as he nearly tripped over the dog, and made his way to the kitchen. "Sadie, you're gonna cause me to break my neck." He put the bags on the counter and scooped the dog into his arms. "Guess who's coming to dinner? Your mom. We've got to get this place spiffed up, and you've got to be on your best behavior, okay?"

She yipped her agreement.

"You don't want to go live in Marla Jean's old cramped apartment, do you? That wouldn't be any fun. We need to convince her you belong right here." Convince her that she belonged here, too. Sadie licked his chin and blinked at him with big brown eyes. He stroked her tiny head, suddenly feeling choked up, trying not to think how empty the house would be if she left.

After he put up the groceries, he walked to the back of the house and looked around at the room he was remodeling. The talk he'd had with Theo before he left town had given him a lot to think about while he was tearing down walls and putting up new ones. He realized that despite everything some part of him still loved his dad, and he'd been so mad when he died that he'd never mourned his passing. He finally allowed himself to grieve the way a son should when he buries his father. As a result he'd started letting go of the anger and hurt he'd carried around all those years. It had given him a whole new outlook on what really mattered.

Like the way he felt about Marla Jean.

About how hard he'd fallen for her, and how that wasn't going to change just because she'd moved off to Derbyville. And about how he wanted a chance to make a life with her if she'd ever consider having him. But she'd made it clear that she didn't want to talk about what happened at the barber shop. So, he wasn't going to push her. Not yet.

But he'd gotten this crazy notion that he could move into the Brown house, fix it up, and once it was finished, once it was perfect, he'd present it to her like a jewel, like a pledge. She'd see that he loved her and just maybe, she'd be willing to give him that chance.

Once the idea had taken hold he couldn't let it go. So for weeks now, he'd been working on the renovations day and night. But then she'd jumped the gun. She'd barged into his office yesterday, and before he realized what he was doing, he'd invited her to dinner. As soon as she walked out of his office, he panicked. He was an idiot. It was too soon. The house wasn't ready. He wasn't ready. And now

Marla Jean was coming over tonight, and he only had a torn-up, half-finished house to try and win her heart.

Not wanting to seem too eager, Marla Jean waited until five minutes after seven before getting out of her car and walking up the front pathway to Jake's house. She opened the screen door and caught her breath as she stepped up onto the sky blue painted porch. From the moment she'd stepped out of her car she'd been blown away by the work he'd already done on the house. The yard was manicured, the house was freshly painted, and the shutters no longer tilted crazily at the windows.

And now this. The porch, sky blue, just as it had been when she was a child.

Before she could ring the doorbell the carved wooden front door opened. Jake stood in the entryway, dressed casually, in jeans and a T-shirt, but just the sight of him made her heart flutter like a sheet hung out to dry on an old-fashioned clothesline. Someday her pulse would stop racing at the sight of him, but apparently today wouldn't be the day.

"Hey, Marla Jean, come on in." He smiled a casual, good buddy smile and waved her inside.

She braced herself to face the emotional toll of spending an evening in his presence. Brightly she said, "Jake, the place looks wonderful. And the porch, you remembered."

"I remembered." He helped her with her coat and purse, hanging them on an old arts and crafts hall tree.

The sound of tiny claws clattering across the wooden floor got her attention and Marla Jean turned just as Sadie scampered into the entryway. "Hey, Sadie, you've gotten so big since the last time I saw you." She reached for the puppy and hauled her up into her arms. "What are you feeding her, Jake?"

Jake smiled at the two of them. "She's very particular. She'll only eat grizzly bear and frog legs. You'll have your work cut out for you with this one."

"He doesn't spoil you or anything, does he?" Sadie settled a paw on each of her shoulders, panting happily.

"You'll notice I haven't done much to the front part of the house yet," Jake said as he pulled her into the living room. The spacious room seemed to dwarf the furniture from his old apartment scattered here and there. "I've got some major rebuilding planned for the back of the house first, and in the meantime I'm making do."

"I can't wait to see what you have planned."

"Why don't we eat first, and then I'll give you a tour of the house." Jake took Sadie from her arms, settling the puppy in her doggie bed where she turned in two and a half circles, then lay down with her head on her front paws and went to sleep.

"Sounds perfect. I could eat a horse."

"A healthy appetite has always been one of your many charms, Marla Jean. I made enough to feed an army." He took her elbow, guiding her toward the dining room.

The mere touch of his hand set off quivers of desire trampling through her body, but she schooled her expression to hide the traitorous reaction. Back in the safety of her apartment she'd vowed to remain unmoved and unaffected in his presence. She'd been here five minutes, and she could already wash that promise down the drain.

A massive walnut table with ten heavy carved chairs filled the room. A hutch set against a wall, though the shelves were mostly bare. "Aunt Libby insisted on giving me this table. Since she moved into Brad's house she didn't have any use for it, and my mother gave me the hutch. Said it was taking up room in her storage shed."

"Nice. You'll have to take up entertaining." What a dumb thing to say. She didn't want to encourage him to bring other women here.

He seemed embarrassed. "It's not really my style, but I think they're convinced if they load me up with enough furniture it will domesticate me. And it made them happy."

"You're such a pushover. And here I thought you were dead set on anything resembling domestication."

He didn't answer, but guided her to a chair and pulled it out for her. He'd already set the table with placemats and dinnerware. In honor of the season a potted poinsettia sat in the middle of the table surrounded by dozens of flickering candles. "You sit, and I'll be right back."

She watched him disappear through the swinging doors, amazed by the cozy atmosphere he'd created. He seemed so comfortable here, as if he'd already turned it into a home. In minutes he was back with two bowls of beef stew. He set them down, and slipped back into the kitchen, returning with a basket of hot cornbread and a butter dish. "It's not fancy, but I thought it might hit the spot since the temperature dropped twenty degrees since yesterday."

She took a bite of stew and moaned her approval. "Man, this is good. Since I moved I haven't done much cooking. I tend to live on crackers and cheese."

"I figured you still ate at your parents' house most nights."

"I try to limit myself to one or two meals a week. Otherwise, what's the point of moving away? Speaking of which, how do you feel about selling your old house? I saw the new owners when I took Mom home last night."

"I can honestly say it's been a relief. I've never been one to dig around in my head, analyzing my feelings, but I was holding on to a lot of garbage about my old man. Before he left Theo made me see what a dead end my life was headed down, and when I realized I loved—" He broke off suddenly like he'd nearly said too much. "Anyway, it was all tied up in that house, and when I let it go, I was able to let him go, too."

Reaching over, she touched his forearm. "Good for you, Jake." She asked if he'd heard from Theo lately. He asked about the classes she was teaching. They covered all the latest gossip, and any other topic they could safely discuss.

After they finished eating they stacked the dishes in the sink, and she nodded when he asked, "Are you ready for the tour?" He took her down the hallway toward the bedroom first. "As I said before, I haven't done much to the front of the house yet, as far as renovations. But I did paint the bedroom, and I did some work on the side porch."

She walked into Patsy's old room, noticing the old wallpaper was gone, and the walls were painted a soft sage green. A big four-poster bed filled one wall, but her attention was drawn immediately toward the screened porch. She opened the French doors and stepped outside. "Hammocks? And wooden gliders?" Again just like she remembered. It was as if he was stealing her dream and recreating it for himself. Letting her see it, but not share in it.

He came out behind her, standing too close.

"I can't tell you how much time I spend out here. This is my favorite spot in the whole house. But, come on. Let me show you what I'm doing in back."

In a daze she followed him down the back hallway, looking this way and that as he pointed out the rooms where he'd started tearing down walls, the back bathroom he'd torn out so it could be updated. Then he grabbed a flashlight and took her outside down the back steps and across the yard. He flashed the light on the old structure that didn't look so old anymore. "The chicken coop, remember?"

She remembered. He'd said it would make a good place to paint. He apparently didn't care if everything he showed her broke her heart into a million pieces. Unlocking the door, he pushed it open so she could enter. "I realized it would make a great workshop." He flipped on the light and she saw workbenches lining one wall, a table saw at one end of the room, and a peg boards holding every kind of tool imaginable.

Wandering around, she examined the assortment of drills and clamps and power tools she couldn't name. "Wow, now this is what I call a workshop." She noticed a door on the far wall. "What's in here?" She turned the knob and pushed open the door.

"Oh don't bother with that, Marla Jean. It's nothing."

His warning came too late, as she found the light switch. What she found inside that room made no sense to her. A large wooden easel dominated the middle of the room. Blank canvases were stacked against each other, leaning here and there against the walls. Jars holding paint brushes sat on a worktable beside rows of unopened tubes of paint. A big picture window was covered in a shade that when lifted would let in the perfect amount of morning sun.

"What in the world?" She turned back to him, searching his face for an explanation.

"I'm sorry, Marla Jean. It's not what it looks like." He seemed uncomfortable.

"What does it look like?" She was confused.

He sighed. "Well, I guess it is what it looks like. It's an art studio, for you."

"For me?" Wandering inside she picked up a paintbrush. "I don't understand."

"I know, it's crazy. You have your new life and your new apartment. You've moved on, and I understand that. But even before I came to terms with how I felt about my father, I finally came to terms with how I feel about you."

"I know how you feel about me, Jake. I've always known."

"Have you?"

"Of course. We're friends, good friends I hope."

"Just friends? I'd say things are different since the night you cut my hair."

"You mean the night we had sex. I know you feel guilty because I managed to seduce you. And now you think you owe me something, but you don't."

"You didn't seduce me. I took advantage."

"Oh for heaven's sakes." She rolled her eyes. "I was a willing participant. And what does that have to do with the fact that there's an art studio in your workshop?"

He seemed embarrassed and began a rambling explanation. "At first I started fixing little things you'd mentioned, like painting the porch blue, and then I bought the hammocks. One thing led to another—you know, so they'd be ready in case you managed to buy the house, and when that fell through and you actually moved away, I couldn't seem to give the place up to anyone else, because I couldn't see anyone else living here but you." He sat down on a stool, looking defeated. "So I kept it."

A flare of hope flickered inside her bound-up heart, but she wasn't about to jump to any cockamamie conclusions. She walked over until she was standing right in front of him. "Jake, I'm going to ask straight out. Is this just you taking care of me the way you take care of everyone in your life, or is this something different?"

He gazed into her eyes. "You're going to make me say the words, aren't you? Isn't it obvious?"

"Nothing about this is obvious, so yes. I need the words. Something simple and uncomplicated I can't misunderstand."

"Okay. How about I love you? Not like a friend. I love you like the woman I want to spend my life with."

"You do?" She was stunned. "You love me?" Talk about universes flipping upside down.

"And I know that's not what you want to hear. I know you have your new life in Derbyville—"

"How do you know what I want to hear?"

"Well, you made it clear you were looking for good times and meaningless sex."

"I don't think I said 'meaningless.'" She moved closer and put her arms around his neck. She placed a whisper of a kiss at the corner of his mouth.

At her touch his voice grew dark and husky. "I'm pretty sure you said meaningless. And you said you weren't ready for serious, and you needed time to sort out your life after your divorce." His hands settled on her waist.

"Sometimes I talk too much." She moved in until her blouse brushed against his T-shirt before placing another kiss on the side of his neck. "Let's go back to the important part where you love me and want to spend your life with me."

"Why is that important?" She could read the flare of hope in his eyes.

"Because I love you, too, Jake."

When he kissed her it wasn't gentle. It was a greedy, grasping kiss that rode over her with raw passion. His words belied what his body was telling her. "I'm not trying to rush you into anything. I thought maybe we could try dating first." He held her close until they were touching thigh to thigh.

Her fingers made feathery trails through his hair. "Dating would be nice."

"We can take things slow, if you like. How long's the lease on your apartment?" His big wide hands were tracing shivery patterns up and down her back.

"Six months." She kissed the other side of his mouth. "Only five months to go."

"I'm not sure I can wait that long, but I'll try. In the meantime, I have this fantasy of you and me in one of those hammocks."

She grabbed the flashlight and pulled him out of the workshop. "I'll show you my fantasy, if you'll show me yours."

Marla Jean stood just inside the entrance of Lu Lu's, slowly scanning the joint. An hour earlier she wiggled into her tight red dress, tugged on her favorite cowboy boots, and headed out on that hot summer Saturday night to the local watering hole. It had been five long months since the first time Jake had told her he loved her. He'd been serious about taking it slow, about not pushing her into anything too quickly. But as of next week her lease would be up on her apartment, and she was ready. Ready to spend her days and nights with the man she loved. She was sure of exactly what she wanted, and now, by God, she, Marla Jean Bandy, was going to get it.

The smell of stale beer and the sound of country music poured out of Lu Lu's as she pulled the door open and walked inside. She spotted her prey seated at the bar talking to the bartender. Linc and Dinah sat listening on one side of him and Irene Cornwell and Genna Stanley were on the other. Marla Jean didn't take the direct route but circled around the edge of the dance floor, keeping her target in sight.

"Hey, Marla Jean, how about a dance?" She glanced up at the tall man who'd stepped into her path.

Grinning she said, "Sorry, Donny Joe, my dance card's full."

He nodded toward the bar and winked. "Go get 'em, tiger."

"Thanks, Donny. I think I will."

As she made her way through the crowd the place got quiet. People parted until a path opened up leading straight to the bar and the man seated there. Jake sat with his back to her, and just as she approached, Linc let out a whoop, and then leaned over and slapped him on the back. Before she had time to wonder what that was all about, Irene Cornwell made the mistake of putting her hand on his arm.

"Take your hands off him, Irene." Marla Jean's voice

was friendly enough, if a rattlesnake could be considered friendly. Without taking her eyes from Jake, Marla Jean pulled a ball-peen hammer from her bag and bounced it against her palm. "And I've gotta warn you, I don't fight fair when it comes to the man I love." Irene held up both hands and beat a hasty retreat.

Jake spun around with a big smile on his face. "Hey, Marla Jean. It's about time you got here. Let's dance."

"I didn't come here to dance." She sighed as he swept her onto the dance floor. Her arms went around his neck, and he pulled her closer than might be considered polite in public.

"So, what did you come here to do besides cause a riot in that dress?"

"I told my landlord I wasn't renewing my lease. I thought you might like to know."

"Hallelujah, woman."

She squealed when he picked her up and spun her around before setting her back on her feet. Snuggling back into his arms, she murmured, "I thought you'd like that. So tell me, mister. When I came in it looked like you were entertaining everyone at the bar. What's going on?"

"I wasn't entertaining anyone. I was showing them something important." He winked and his grin lit up the room.

She pretended to scold him. "I thought we agreed you didn't show any of your important parts to anyone but me these days." Being in his arms had her softening like a snow cone on a warm day.

He laughed. "I like it when you're possessive, and the hammer's a nice touch."

"You said it was for keeping bozos at bay. You didn't

say the bozos couldn't be women." She fingered the soft dark curls at the back of his neck.

He stopped dancing. "I have something that will do the job better than that old hammer. Why don't we make a trade?" Reaching into his shirt pocket he pulled out a ring and went down on one knee smack dab in the middle of the dance floor. "Will you marry me, Marla Jean?"

Her heart hitched in her chest, and her tight red dress hitched up to an indecent length as she sank down beside him. She reached for him, and the hammer clattered to the floor, forgotten. He waited for her answer, his beautiful face awash with masculine grace and hope. Was there a word bigger than "yes"? A word that really said all she felt for him?

A crowd gathered around, bombarding them with hoots and catcalls.

"Come on, Marla Jean, you know you want to," Donny Joe yelled.

"Say yes, Marla Jean," Dinah hollered.

Jake leaned in, his voice hot and smoky. "Come live in that old house with me and let's have lots of puppy dogs and babies."

At his words, images of a future filled with laughter and love and the family she'd always wanted flooded her head. She nodded, giving him her private answer, giving him everything that was in her heart. For the benefit of the crowd she followed with a loud "hell, yes" that had them clapping and carrying on like drunks at a church social. Jake slipped the diamond ring on her finger and then picked her up and started carrying her toward the front door.

"Kiss her, Jake," someone shouted from across the room.

"I don't plan to stop there," Jake called back without pausing as he shouldered his way out into the parking lot.

Marla Jean bounced along in Jake's arms grinning like a loon until he dumped her onto the front seat of his pick-up truck. "Kiss me, Jake," she insisted.

"Hold your horses, woman." He tucked her inside and shut the door, and then ran around to the driver's side.

He got behind the wheel and turned to pull her into his arms. "Now then. Where were we?"

"You were about to kiss me."

"Oh yeah." He wrapped her in his arms and looked deep into her eyes. "I love you, Marla Jean." And then he kissed her like he had every right, like she was all he'd ever wanted.

"I love you, too," she murmured against his lips, like he was all she'd ever need. His hand slid halfway up her skirt, and she nipped at his lip and moaned, "Take me home, Jake."

He leaned his forehead against hers and with great reluctance nudged her to the passenger side of the truck. "Okay, but you stay over there, and try not to be a distraction." He started the truck, and pulled out of the parking lot, his big hand settled possessively on her thigh.

She held up her left hand, studying the ring he'd placed on her finger, watching it twinkle in the moonlight. "Hey, you know all those babies we're going to have? Well, I've been thinking about names. Maybe Lotus Petal for a girl, or Jiminy for a boy."

He hit the brakes. "Now hold on, Marla Jean..." He launched into a lecture about the importance of picking exactly the right name for their future children. How they couldn't go off half-cocked and saddle them with some God-awful moniker that would scar them for life.

She closed her eyes and listened, a contented smile on her face.

Who said you couldn't find love at Lu Lu's on a Saturday night?

Nothing can faze a
no-nonsense city girl …
except maybe a smooth-talking
country boy.

Please turn this page
for a preview of

Crazy Little Thing Called Love

Available in April 2013

Chapter One

You can't take time off now. It's out of the question."
Diego Barrett, head chef at *Finale's*, made his decree and
turned back to the stove as if everything was settled.

Etta swiped at a lone tear and sniffed. It was hard to
believe she'd ever thought she was in love with this guy.
"Diego, I'm not asking for your permission. My grandmother died, and I'm going to Texas to take care of the
arrangements."

He never looked her way as he banged around the restaurant kitchen, lifting lids, stirring a pot here, tasting a
sauce there. "What about your sister? She lives in Texas.
Why can't she handle things?" He stomped over to the
table that held menu plans and supply lists. "And how
the hell am I supposed to get anyone to cover for you on
such short notice? The Mann party is coming in tomorrow night, and they could make or break our reputation.
Remember, Etta? The Mann party. The big opportunity
we've been working our asses off for?"

"If you could stop ranting long enough to listen I'll tell

you. Mimi will cover for me tomorrow, and everything will be fine. But I'll be gone at least a week. Adjust the schedule accordingly."

"For God's sake, why can't you wait a day or two? Why do you have to leave right now? I need you here."

"The question you should be asking is, 'Are you okay, Etta? Is there anything I can do to help?' "

Sounding like a spoiled child, he tried guilt. "You know what kind of pressure I'm under. Thank you for adding to it."

She took off her apron and started gathering her things. "And thank you for your support, Diego."

"How's this for support?" He sat down at the table, his tone overwrought. "If you leave me now, don't bother to come back."

Without a second thought, she picked up a vat of cold soup, a lovely vichyssoise, and dumped it in his lap. "Oops. There goes the soup of the day."

His howl of outrage and the pungent smell of leeks followed her out the door.

Donny Joe Ledbetter hated funerals.

He huddled in his thin black suit coat as an uncommonly bitter wind whipped through Everson Memorial Gardens and battered the mourners who'd gathered graveside to pay their respects to the dearly departed Hazel Green. Miz Hazel, as she was known by one and all, had lived a colorful life and had died too soon at the frisky age of sixty-eight.

Amen and bless her soul.

She would be missed by the good folks in Everson, including Donny Joe. She'd been his next-door neighbor, a grandmother figure of sorts, a neverending source of unsolicited advice—some good, some bad. And of late, his business partner.

He didn't treat her passing lightly, so when he was asked to be a pallbearer, he agreed without hesitation. He had a real affection for the old girl. He let his gaze travel over Etta Green, Miz Hazel's granddaughter. Too bad he couldn't say he felt the same about her.

She had steamed back into Everson a few days ago to take care of the funeral arrangements for her grandmother, but grief could only go so far in excusing her surly attitude. She'd bulldozed everyone in her path, and out of the respect people had for Miz Hazel she'd gotten away with it. Now she perched on one of the spindly chairs set up for the family in front of the casket, her fireplug of a body vibrating with defiance and anger.

What a piece of work.

She wore a long-sleeved black dress that covered her from chin to ankle. Her fists were clenched tightly in her lap as if it were all she could do not to shake them at the heavens for taking her beloved Grammy away too soon. Her pointy, high-heeled black pumps tapped out a nervous rhythm on the dry winter grass, suggesting she might kick the shins of the first person who dared express any hint of sympathy. Donny Joe planned to keep his distance.

By contrast her older sister Belle had arrived just in time for the service. Ah, Belle. They'd had a short-lived flirtation one summer a long time ago, and he hadn't seen or thought about her since. She'd grown into an attractive and, from all appearances, even-tempered woman. Sitting demurely, ankles crossed, she wore a simple gray dress set off by a wide-brimmed black hat. A veil covered her face giving her the air of an Italian film actress. She sobbed quietly behind the filmy material while her daughter Daphne stared straight ahead. She looked to be maybe eight or nine years old, but she didn't squirm or wiggle around like most young kids he knew. In fact she showed no emotion of any kind.

Donny wished he could be as stoic. Miz Hazel's death hit him harder than he'd expected. Despite her untimely demise she'd lived a good life, and the gathered crowd was a testament to how many people she'd touched. Shivering in the cold of the cemetery, surrounded by grave markers of Everson's deceased, made him wonder about his own life. Who would shed a tear if he was to meet his maker tomorrow? Would anybody really give a damn if he lived or died? It gave a man pause.

Brother East, the Baptist preacher, asked everyone to bow their heads in prayer. Then after a chorus of murmured "Amens," he instructed the pallbearers to say their final farewells by placing their boutonnieres on top of the half-lowered glossy white casket. Donny Joe removed the pearl-tipped pin holding the pink rosebud onto his lapel and trailed along in line with the others. Each man said a quick good-bye to Miz Hazel and laid their rose beside the giant funeral spray that adorned the box holding her remains. Donny Joe could feel his eyes start to water and blamed it on the stinging wind. When it was his turn, he stopped and took a moment with his thoughts.

"Good-bye, Miz Hazel," he said in a choked voice. "I'm going to miss you." He glanced up and his gaze locked unwillingly with Etta Green. She lifted an eyebrow as if doubting his sincerity and maybe his manhood, too. What the hell was her problem?

Rattled, he broke eye contact and stepped forward, boutonniere in hand.

His foot caught on a half-buried tree root from the stately old oak that would stand sentry over Miz Hazel's final resting place. He stumbled, arms flailing, and then he fell. Fellow pallbearer Mitchell Crowley made a grab for him, catching only a handful of his suit coat as he landed squarely on top of the funeral spray and the casket underneath. Half the crowd gasped, and the other half laughed like things were just starting to get interesting.

For a stunned moment he lay there, his breath sawing in and out of his chest, feeling the polished wood and crushed blossoms pressed against his cheek, clutching the ornate edging that outlined the lid of the coffin to steady himself. The overwhelming floral smell filled his nose, and he could feel the tickle of a sneeze building. "A-a-achoo."

"Bless you, Donny Joe," someone yelled from the buzzing crowd.

That got him moving. A shower of roses, carnations, daisies, and lilies of every color and hue scattered like a potpourri of rats deserting a sinking ship while he scrambled on hands and knees to get up. Phone cameras appeared throughout the crowd, capturing the moment for posterity.

Mitchell finally got a grip on one arm and helped haul him to his feet. "Get a hold of yourself, buddy. We're all going to miss her, but she's in a better place now."

"Sorry. Geez, I'm really sorry." Donny straightened up, rearranging his coat and brushing off his pants. The crowd mumbled and tittered—probably discussing how much he'd had to drink.

Undoubtedly dismayed by his oafish performance, Miz Hazel's granddaughters now stood, and he put out a hand in their direction, an apology of sorts. Belle Green lifted her veil, revealing her pretty tear-streaked face. Then she smiled and winked before letting the gauzy material fall back into place. Etta Green clinched her knotty little fists and skewered him with a glare hot enough to permanently singe all the hair from his body. Young Daphne stayed in her chair, stuck her thumb in her mouth, and started to suck.

Etta hated lawyers.

She sat stick straight on the edge of a big leather wing chair in front of Mr. Corbin Starling's scarred walnut desk, impatiently waiting for him to commence with the reading of her grandmother's will. Not that she actually hated Mr. Starling. He seemed nice enough, but she'd never had anything good come from dealing with those in the legal profession, so the sooner they could get this over with, the sooner she could be on her way back to Chicago.

Her sister Belle lounged carelessly in the chair to her left, relentlessly texting and checking her phone for messages. Their appointment had been for ten a.m. They had arrived ten minutes early. It was now five after, and her grandmother's lawyer, after greeting them and asking if they wanted coffee or tea, left them to their own devices while he rifled through papers on his desk. Etta looked at her watch, and her foot started to tap.

Mr. Starling seemed to notice her impatience and glanced up. "I apologize for the delay. We're just waiting for Mr. Ledbetter to arrive, and then we can get started."

Etta's foot stilled. "Mr. Ledbetter? As in Donny Joe Ledbetter?" The idiot who'd made a spectacle of himself at the funeral? Good Gawd.

"Yes, there are provisions that concern him."

Belle leaned forward in her chair, giving Mr. Starling a generous view of her generous bosom. His eyes widened in appreciation of the gesture. Etta stifled a flash of irritation. Her sister's idea of proper attire for a visit to see the family lawyer was a ruffled, low-cut red silk blouse and a pair of tight blue jeans. "I understand Donny Joe and Grammy Hazel got real close before she died," Belle informed them.

Etta turned to look at her sister. "They did? How do you know that?"

"I had a real nice conversation with Donny Joe after the service yesterday afternoon. And Grammy was always going on about how much help he was to her around the house."

Etta's foot started tapping again. Donny Joe Ledbetter was her grandmother's next-door neighbor. She had vivid memories of him from the summers she and Belle had spent at her grandmother's house. Flirtatious, smooth talking, and too cute for his own good. That was Donny Joe, then and now. From what she'd heard he ran some kind of swimming pool business these days. Now that she thought about it, she did remember her grandmother mentioning him a lot during their frequent phone calls of late, but she realized with a sharp pang of regret, she hadn't paid much attention to the details.

Etta's first instinct was to suspect he'd taken advantage of her grandmother's trusting nature. But on the other hand, so what if he'd schmoozed his way into the old lady's affection and she'd left him some small token of her appreciation in her last will and testament?

Fine and dandy. What did she care?

But he could at least have the decency to show up on time so they could get this whole ordeal settled and be done with it. Her business in Everson, Texas, was almost finished. Now that Grammy Hazel was gone, she couldn't think of a good reason to stay any longer than necessary. Despite her assurances to Diego that he'd be fine without her, she couldn't help worrying.

Finally, there was a knock on the office doorframe, and Donny Joe stuck his head around the corner. "Sorry I'm late, Corbin."

Mr. Starling stood up and waved him into the room. "Come on in, Donny Joe. We're ready to get started."

Donny doffed his cowboy hat and hung it on the coat rack by the door. "I had an emergency at the Senior Center. The pool wasn't heating properly, and if 'Splashing With the Oldies' doesn't go on as scheduled there's hell to pay. But I apologize."

"Hey, Donny Joe," Belle looked up from her phone and gifted him with one of her dazzling smiles.

"Belle." He returned her smile with a dazzling one of his own, and then with the slightest nod in her direction acknowledged Etta's presence as well. "Morning, Etta."

He pulled a wooden chair up next to her, and sat with legs splayed wide, taking up more than his share of space in the room. Donny Joe was all lanky swagger, and Etta found herself bristling for no particular reason. Turning slightly in her chair, she angled her body so he was out of her line of sight, but a faint whiff of his cologne still wafted her way.

Mr. Starling cleared his throat and began addressing them somberly, so she focused on his words. "This is a sad occasion for us all. Hazel was a great friend to me and my family. We will miss her dearly, and you girls have my deepest condolences." He put both hands on his desk and sighed. "This is the will drawn up by your grandmother three and a half years ago on her sixty-fifth birthday." He opened the file on his desk and began reading,

I, Hazel Faye Green, being of sound mind and body do hereby bequeath the following:

- My string of pearls and matching earrings, the family recipe box, and my complete set of Nancy Drew Mysteries I leave to my great granddaughter, Daphne Jonquil Green.
- My enamel turtle pin, my Joni Mitchell albums, and my Volkswagen bus I leave to my cousin, Beulah Cross.
- My house, its contents, and the surrounding five acres I leave to my granddaughters Etta Place Green and Belle Starr Green. I trust they will do all they can to keep the house since it has been in our family for over one hundred years.

Signed,
Hazel Faye Green

Etta slumped back in her chair fighting new tears. The provisions in the will were basically what she'd expected, but hearing the words read out loud made the pain of Grammy's death rise up and threaten to choke her all over again.

Grammy's house. Growing up, it had always been a safe haven, a place to escape the neverending circus of her parents' chaotic marriage. She loved the nooks and crannies, the tall ceilings, the wooden floors. It wrapped around her, comforting her like one of Grammy's crocheted afghans. Built by her great-great-grandfather and passed down to each new generation, the house still stood tall and strong, despite the human frailties of those who'd occupied it through the years. She was momentarily stirred by the connection with those who'd come before her. And now it belonged to both her and Belle.

But she would never seriously considered living in it. She had a life to get back to in Chicago.

Probably. Oh, of course she did.

Surely Diego hadn't been serious when he'd fired her. Just because he'd told her if she left not to come back. Just because she'd dumped a vat of cold potato soup in his lap on her way out the door. She could be volatile, and so could he. That's why they made such a good team. It wasn't the first time one of them had used food to emphasize a point, and it wouldn't be the last. They shared a passion for their work and a passion to make *Finale's* one of the best restaurants in Chicago. Unfortunately, he held a controlling interest, and that put her at a disadvantage.

But she couldn't worry about any of that until things were settled here. As far as Cousin Beulah was concerned she could continue to live in the house if that's what she wanted. Maybe rent out a room if she needed help around the place.

Or maybe Belle would consider moving back to Everson. It would provide a stable home for eight-year-old Daphne. Everson would be a great town to raise a child.

And a stable home was something her niece hadn't known from the day she'd been born. They certainly had a lot to discuss. She glanced at Donny Joe. Why was he here again? The will hadn't said a word about him. She looked at Mr. Starling expectantly.

"You said there were provisions that concerned Donny Joe, Mr. Starling. I don't understand."

Mr. Starling cleared his throat again and picked up another file. This one was two inches thick. He opened it carefully and sighed. "As I said, your grandmother's will was written over three years ago. Since then circumstances have changed."

"In what way?" Belle asked glancing up from her phone.

"Over the last few years your grandmother has struggled some to make ends meet and to put it simply, the house is no longer hers alone to bequeath."

Etta scooted forward to the edge of her chair again. "What do you mean? Of course it's hers. And she would have told me if she was having problems."

"Well, why don't you explain, Donny Joe?"

She turned her head slowly taking in the tall man sitting beside her.

He wasn't smiling anymore, and he seemed all business now. "Your grandmother approached me about turning her house into a money-making venture to offset some of her expenses. A Bed and Breakfast to be exact. You may have noticed some of the renovations that have already taken place."

Actually she had noticed and thought her grandmother had gone off on one of her many remodeling kicks. She was always repainting the walls and changing the drapes.

"A Bed and Breakfast? Was this her idea or yours, Mr. Ledbetter? I assume you have some financial interest in this project? That must be the reason you're here this morning." Her tone suggested she was speaking to the lowest form of dirt—a dirty, low-down, sleazy, cheating scumbag who'd taken advantage of her sweet grandmother's trust.

Mr. Starling stood up. "Ms. Green, let me assure you that this was your grandmother's idea, but yes, at this point Donny Joe has made a substantial investment that can't be recovered if the work isn't completed. Your grandmother's greatest fear was that she'd lose the family home altogether, and now with her untimely death everything is up in the air unless you two are willing to follow through with her wishes."

Etta glanced at Belle, who seemed bored by the whole proceeding, then turned back to the two men. "So," she asked tightly, "what's the bottom line here? Where does that leave us?"

"It means Donny Joe is already part owner of your grandmother's house. If you and your sister don't honor the existing contracts and open the Bed and Breakfast as scheduled, he will own it all."

THE DISH

Where authors give you the inside scoop!

♥ ♥ ♥ ♥ ♥ ♥ ♥ ♥ ♥ ♥ ♥ ♥ ♥ ♥

From the desk of Cynthia Garner

Dear Reader,

You've now met several characters from my Warriors of the Rift series, and in SECRET OF THE WOLF you get to know Dante MacMillan and Victoria Joseph. Dante's a man with a lot of people depending on him, from his colleagues to his sister, who's just getting over chemotherapy treatments and an unexpected divorce—as well as three lovely four-legged friends named Big Ben, Studmuffin, and Sugardaddy.

Some of the real events that happened in the Phoenix area while I was writing this book included a huge dust storm called a haboob. The first one that blew through the area shut down Sky Harbor Airport. The monster was around 5,000 feet high when it slammed into Phoenix, but radar indicated it had reached heights of 10,000 feet prior to hitting the city. It was caused by the winds that come with our monsoon season, but instead of a rain storm the Phoenix area got a dust storm.

I think I'd rather have monsters in the form of werewolves and vampires, thank you very much. A 10,000-foot-high wall of dust is too apocalyptic for me. (Come to think of it, I may actually prefer a zombie apocalypse over a haboob. The one we had was very reminiscent of that one scene in *The Mummy*. Of course, if Brendan Fraser came along for the ride...)

While Dante and Tori didn't have to put up with monster dust storms, they did have to work with other monsters while they focused on a special project during their off-duty hours that brought them close in more ways than one.

As with *Kiss of the Vampire*, I have extras up on my website: a character interview with Tori, some pictures of Scottsdale where the story takes place, and a character tree showing the Council of Preternaturals and their hierarchy.

Look for the next installment, *Heart of the Demon*, coming soon! Finn Evnissyen may not be all he seems to be.

Happy Reading!

Cynthia Garner

cynthiagarnerbooks@gmail.com

http://cynthiagarnerbooks.com

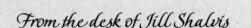

From the desk of Jill Shalvis

Dear Reader,

A few years ago, my family went camping. We brought our boat, and on the first day there, we launched it on the lake for the duration of our stay. My husband gave me my choice of driving the truck and trailer to the campsite or driving the boat across the lake to the dock. It was windy, and I'm a boat wuss, so I picked the truck. Halfway around the lake, I got the trailer stuck on a weird hairpin turn and had to be rescued by a forest ranger. He was big and tough and armed and overworked, and undoubtedly underpaid as well, but the man helped me out of a jam so my husband wouldn't kill me. Ever since then, I've wanted to write a forest ranger into one of my books as a hero.

Enter Matt Bowers. Big and tough and armed and overworked and underpaid. Like my real-life hero, he also stopped and helped a damsel in distress. Of course, Matt gets a lot more in the bargain than my poor beleaguered forest ranger ever got. Matt Bowers gets waitress Amy Michaels, beautiful, tough, jaded...and in desperate need of rescuing. She just doesn't know it yet.

Hope you enjoy watching these two warily circle each other on their path to true love. Like me, neither of them takes the easy way. I mean, what's the fun in that?

Our family had a great summer at that lake, and it's a great summer for me this year too with not one, but three Lucky Harbor novels. So if you enjoy AT LAST, don't miss sexy Special Ops soldier Ty Garrison in *Lucky in Love* and handsome doctor Josh Scott in *Forever and a Day*, coming in August.

Happy Reading—all summer long!

Jill Shalvis

http://www.jillshalvis.com

http://www.facebook.com/jillshalvis

♥ ♥ ♥ ♥ ♥ ♥ ♥ ♥ ♥ ♥ ♥ ♥ ♥ ♥ ♥ ♥

From the desk of Molly Cannon

Dear Reader,

There used to be a bar way out in the country where my husband and I would go with a bunch of our friends to dance on Saturday nights. We'd drive for miles and miles down these dark, unlit roads, and then in the distance we'd see the glow against the night sky from the pole lights in the parking lot. We'd pull in, the gravel crunching under our tires, and the place would be packed. After we found a place to park, we'd scramble out of our cars and head inside. The sound of country music and the smell of beer would hit us like a wave when we walked in the door. And the building—it was gigantic, a big, barn-like place—but we'd find a table and settle in for a night of two-stepping, drinking beer, and hanging out with our friends.

As I danced, I couldn't help but do a little people watching. The women would all be dressed to the nines in their dancing outfits, trying to catch someone's eye. The men would be on the prowl but doing their best to play it cool. I'd keep my eye on the blonde woman in the yellow dress: She'd come with one guy, but she danced with another one all night long. Or the tall, stern-looking cowboy at the bar who never took his eyes off the short, dark-haired girl in the pink shirt for a single second. She huddled up with a group of girlfriends, so I wondered if he'd ever work up the courage to ask her for a dance. There might be a couple arguing in one corner, and a couple kissing in another. It was always quite a show: love, lust, broken hearts, maybe some cheating, and a lot of hanky-panky—all played out to the quick-quick, slow-slow beat of a country song. That dance hall is gone now, and the countryside has been swallowed up by neighborhoods and paved roads with streetlights, but I haven't forgotten the nights I spent there.

So it's no accident that the first scene of my book AIN'T MISBEHAVING takes place in a parking lot. Not just any parking lot, but the parking lot outside of Lu Lu's, the local watering hole in Everson, Texas. When Marla Jean Bandy decides it's time to quit spending nights home alone after her divorce, when she decides it's time to bust out and have some fun, Lu Lu's is just the kind of place I thought she needed. Decked out in a tight red dress and her best cowboy boots, she's ready to get back out there and have a good time...until Jake Jacobsen, a childhood crush, shows up and tries to run interference. Marla Jean is about to find out that a parking lot on a Saturday night can be full of delicious possibilities.

I hope you enjoy AIN'T MISBEHAVING and have fun getting to know Marla Jean, Jake, and all the meddlesome, well-meaning folks in Everson, Texas.

Happy Reading!

Molly Cannon

www.mollycannon.com

Facebook.com

Twitter @cannonmolly

VISIT US ONLINE AT

WWW.HACHETTEBOOKGROUP.COM

FEATURES:

**OPENBOOK BROWSE AND
SEARCH EXCERPTS**

•

AUDIOBOOK EXCERPTS AND PODCASTS

•

AUTHOR ARTICLES AND INTERVIEWS

•

**BESTSELLER AND PUBLISHING
GROUP NEWS**

•

SIGN UP FOR E-NEWSLETTERS

•

**AUTHOR APPEARANCES AND TOUR
INFORMATION**

•

SOCIAL MEDIA FEEDS AND WIDGETS

•

DOWNLOAD FREE APPS

BOOKMARK HACHETTE BOOK GROUP
@ WWW.HACHETTEBOOKGROUP.COM